the HEALING QUILT

Also by Lauraine Snelling in Large Print:

An Untamed Land
A New Day Rising
A Land to Call Home
The Reapers' Song
Hawaiian Sunrise

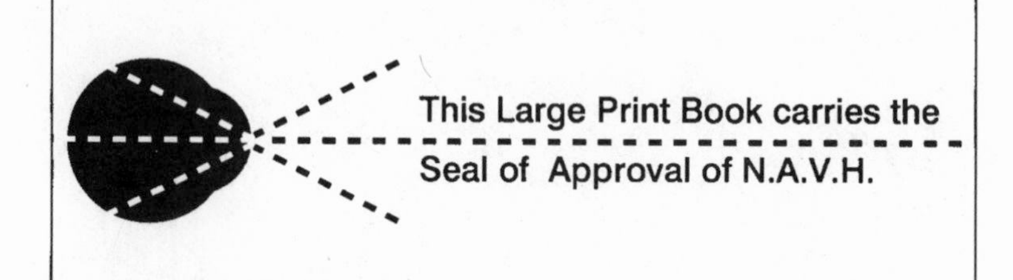

the HEALING QUILT

LAURAINE SNELLING

Thorndike Press • Waterville, Maine

Published in 2003 by arrangement with WaterBrook Press, a division of Random House, Inc.

Thorndike Press® Large Print Christian Fiction Series.

The text of this Large Print edition is unabridged. Other aspects of the book may vary from the original edition.

Set in 16 pt. Plantin by Liana M. Walker.

Printed in the United States on permanent paper.

Library of Congress Cataloging-in-Publication Data

Snelling, Lauraine.
The healing quilt : a novel / Lauraine Snelling.
p. cm.
ISBN 0-7862-4955-2 (lg. print : hc : alk. paper)
1. Cancer — Diagnosis — Fiction. 2. Female friendship — Fiction. 3. Quiltmakers — Fiction. 4. Quilting — Fiction. 5. Large type books. I. Title.
PS3569.N39 H43 2003
813′.54—dc21 2002043084

To my daughter Marie,
who is already experiencing the wonders of heaven
and is waiting for us to join her.

To God be the glory.

ACKNOWLEDGMENTS

No book comes into being by itself, and this one more than most is the product of feedback from multiple sources. This odyssey of an idea started with Lisa Tawn Bergren asking me whether someday I would write my daughter's story when I'd healed enough from the grief. Others had mentioned it earlier, but hey, she was an editor. I said I would when God made it clear the time was right.

Years passed, and she'd ask whenever she saw me. When God said "now," we began the process, and what a lengthy one this turned out to be. Thanks to Lisa at WaterBrook Press, David Horton at Bethany, and other editorial readers, the ideas began to take shape. I have wonderful friends who brainstormed with me, including members of the Round Robins. A writing week with Chelley Kitzmiller and Woodeene Koenig-Bricker saw me through three revisions of the first chapter. Kathleen Wright read the manuscript and offered comments. My agent, Deidre Knight, went back and forth persistently with the two publishing companies.

After the contract was signed, there were more readers and more suggestions. Lisa left WaterBook, and Erin Healy took over. I threw my hands up and wrote an entirely new first chapter, my seventh version. I wrote the complete rough draft with more brainstorming from many of the friends I just mentioned, turned it in, and Erin, who had a far better overview of this book than I did, made ten pages of suggestions.

I make jokes about this being a patchwork book by a blind seamstress. Quilting books helped me. Sue and Claudia, who teach quilting, gave advice. I have no idea how many people prayed, but I know there were many and I thank every one of you.

This patchwork is stitched together with prayer and lots of love and tears. My assistant, Cecile, has cheered and encouraged and spent extra hours typing in changes and keeping my timeline straight, not easy with four strong characters, each wanting to take over the story. Husband Wayne has learned more about cooking and is always a patient sounding board, knowing that even vacation trips, like to Hawaii, are working time for his wife (who got behind again). While in Hawaii, I met Lailani and

Charlotte, who introduced me to Bosom Buddies and Healing Touch, organizations that offer help to those with breast cancer. The Internet, too, has many resources for those seeking help.

So, *The Healing Quilt*, far different than its beginning, is finished. May it bring glory to God, hope and help to those who need it, and my prayer always that readers will laugh a little or a lot, cry some, and be sad when the book is finished.

ONE

The calendar never lies.

Kit Cooper stared at the hummingbird forever sipping from a pink and purple fuchsia blossom that topped the black-bound, numbered squares on the calendar. As it always did, her gaze slipped to the middle week of June.

The worst week of her life, the worst day, the fifteenth.

Two years ago today Amber died. Kit sucked in a deep breath and turned back to the silent kitchen. Surely she'd grieved enough, cried enough. Some said today should be a day for rejoicing. After all, that's what Amber was doing. At least that's what the Bible said people did in heaven, spent their time praising God and singing heavenly songs.

Kit blinked hard and rolled her eyes to stare at the ceiling, a trick she'd learned that helped ward off the tears. *I will not cry again. It's bad enough I woke up with a soaked pillow, thought I was past that.* Her gaze caught an errant cobweb, so she went to the closet to fetch a broom. Opening the pantry door, she saw that the bag filled with plastic grocery sacks had fallen down, so she reached to hang that back up and discovered that the hook had fallen out of the wall. Bending over to search for the hook, she bumped the broom and clawed her way up the handle.

Heavy air smothered her, air that held tears, shed and unshed, air so thick and black it clogged her throat, burned her eyes, and set her ears to ringing. She raked long fingers through shoulder-length hair, now pepper sprinkled with salt, pulling it back away from her face and fumbling in her jeans pocket for a rubber band that wasn't there.

"Dear God, not again. I cannot do this anymore." She leaned against the wall, between the mop and the vacuum, her tears gushing forth like a newly broken fire hydrant. "I . . . I thought I was beyond this." She hiccuped and coughed. "God, I'm so alone."

She stepped out of the closet, snagged a dishtowel off the oven handle to mop her face, then pulled a tissue out of the box and blew her nose. While she so often felt the tears would never stop, at least she'd learned one thing.

They did. But they left her feeling ravaged and raw, as if she'd been mauled by a pit bull or a cougar. While she lived, so did the pain.

Missy, Amber's basset hound, whined at Kit's feet, then lifted her muzzle in a tenor howl, her sad brown eyes a reflection of Kit's, sadder than any hound's eyes should ever be.

Kit crossed long legs and sank down beside the dog, wrapping her arms around the warm neck and resting her wet cheek on the boney head. "Ah, Missy, do you still miss her, or have you forgotten how much she loved you?" Kit stroked the dog's long, soft, black-and-tan ears.

Back when she was fighting the cancer and the pain was terrible enough to make her cry, Amber used to say that Missy's ears were the perfect tear mop. Amber had not only a high pain threshold but a will strong enough to conquer most of life's hard knocks. Except for cancer.

Amber hated crying.

"She wouldn't want us sitting here, all maudlin and tear-soaked either, would she, girl?" Missy twisted and planted her two front paws in Kit's lap. She stared into Kit's eyes as if either seeking or giving reassurance, then whined, a tiny sound, more whimper, more comforting.

Kit pushed herself to her feet, returned to the pantry for a puppy treat, as Amber had called the dog biscuits, and arched one through the air toward Missy, whose tail now wagged, as she jumped and neatly caught it.

"Ah, dog, if only all of life could be cured by a rock-hard, bone-shaped cracker."

The ringing of the doorbell made Kit wipe her eyes, give Missy one more pat, and, dog at her knee, make her sniffing way to the front door.

"Yes?"

The boy looking up at her wore his Mariners baseball cap with the bill to one side, sported freckles across nose and cheeks, and a grin made all the more charming by one missing front tooth.

"You got any kids to play with?" He stuck his hands in the front pockets of hand-me-down jeans, the hems frayed to strings.

"No, I'm sorry, my children are all grown."

"Oh." The sparkle in his blue eyes dimmed. He started to turn away, then stopped and looked over his shoulder.

"You got any grandkids?"

Do I look that old? Kit shook her head, wishing she had something to offer him. "I have a dog that needs someone to throw the ball." She motioned toward Missy, whose tail had upped the wagging speed to tattoo.

"What's his name?"

"Her name is Missy."

"She's kinda funny lookin', ain't she?"

"Not really, she's a basset hound."

He peered in the doorway. "Can she run? Shortest legs I ever seen."

"Would your parents mind if you came in our backyard?"

"Nah, Dad's at work."

"Who's taking care of you?" *Surely this boy isn't a latchkey kid, not as young as he looks.*

He shrugged. "My sister. She's bossy." He reached a tentative hand to pat Missy and received a drooly kiss for his effort.

"She likes you." *What's the best way to handle this?*

The boy knelt and Missy made quick work of cleaning his face. He giggled, laid his cheek against her ear, both arms around the dog's neck.

"What's your name?"

"Thomas." Missy wriggled from nose to

tail, her nails clicking on the tile of the entryway.

"Where do you live, Thomas?"

"Over there." He pointed to a house three doors down on the opposite side of the street.

She'd seen a U-Haul rental truck in the drive a few days earlier and meant to bake something and take it over but just hadn't gotten around to it yet. Like she hadn't gotten around to lots of things lately.

"How about if Missy and I walk you home and ask your sister if it is all right for you to play in our backyard."

"She won't care none."

"Just the same, I'll get Missy's leash." She reached inside the coat closet and lifted the blue nylon leash from the hook. Once she'd snapped it to Missy's collar, she closed the door behind her and smiled at Thomas. "How old are you?"

"Seven."

"Second grade?"

"When school starts. You think I could hold the leash?"

"Watch how I do it and then you may." She folded most of the leash in her right hand and, as Missy took her place at Kit's left knee, held the leash in her left hand at a heel position. "Missy knows to walk on the left side like this."

"Did you teach her that?"

"Ah, no, my daughter Amber did. Missy was her dog." Together they stepped off the porch and down the three wide wood steps to the brick walk, which led to the maple-lined street named after the trees.

"So how come Amber let Missy live with you?" He looked up, questions in his blue eyes.

Oh, Lord, how do I answer all these questions? I don't do questions anymore. "How do you like your new house?"

"Okay." Thomas hung back a trifle as they started up the three concrete steps to his yard. Overgrown junipers formed a spiky green mat on either side of the steps. Missy's nose twitched, and she turned her head to catch a whiff of whatever lived in the evergreens.

"Do you have a dog?"

Thomas shook his head, his chin drawing closer to his chest. All Kit could see was the button on the top of his blue hat. *Why doesn't he want to go home? What's going on here?* When she started toward the front door, he motioned her to take the concrete walk around to the back.

"You wait here, okay?" His eyes beseeched her to agree.

"Of course." Kit sat on one of the green plastic lawn chairs, Missy plopping down at her feet.

Thomas crossed the silvered redwood deck and opened the sliding glass door.

Kit leaned back in the chair, letting the slanting sun bathe her face in golden warmth. Strange how comforting the sun felt, not like the gloom in her house that felt cold and . . .

Trying to prevent the intense introspection that always brought on tears, she opened her eyes to study the backyard. Like many of the others in Jefferson City, Washington, situated halfway between Tacoma and Mount Rainier, or "out in the boonies" as her son Ryan used to say, the permanently white-crowned mountain sat like a sentinel on the southeastern horizon. Towering Douglas fir trees flanked the peak, looking like deep green, near-to-black velvet from this distance.

June in Jefferson City held the sparkle of the finest diamond.

Except for the fifteenth.

It's only another day, she reminded herself. *The same twenty-four hours as any other day. Even if you cry all day, which you aren't doing, it will still turn into the sixteenth at midnight and the worst will be over.*

"Please, God, let it be over."

Missy raised her head from the ground and bumped against Kit's knee.

"Yes, I know, you'd rather walk than lie here. Let's give the kid a minute, and then perhaps he'll play ball with you." At the word "ball," the dog's ears rose and her tail brushed the grass. Her head swiveled to see the deck as a teenage girl followed Thomas outside. Straight hair, badly in need of a trim, swung from a center part, partially obscuring her thin face. She tucked one side behind her ear.

"Thomas said you live a couple of houses up on the other side of the street. If you don't mind him playing with your dog, he can go."

Kit stood. "Is that all? Don't you even want to know my name?"

"Uh, yeah, I guess." Fingers hooked the hair back again. "He better be home in an hour or so."

"No, I don't." Thomas stopped his forward motion toward the dog.

She glared down at him. "Yes, you do." Each word came out clipped and hissed. "Or you can stay home."

"Aw'right."

"I'm Kit Cooper and I'll make sure he comes home on time. He'll be doing *me* a favor, besides Missy. If she doesn't get more exercise, she'll get fat." *Why are you talking so much? You can see she's already tuned you out, just as if she's turned on a radio to blast other sound to infinity.*

"Can I hold the leash?" Thomas looked up, his blue eyes pleading.

"Sure you can." Kit handed him the loop and watched as he carefully mimicked what she had done, then turned and walked down back around the house. Missy waited until Kit said, "Heel," then, tail in the air, picked up her broad feet and skipped in rhythm alongside the boy. Kit shot another look to the deck and saw that the sister had disappeared inside. Kit shrugged and followed her new friend back out to the street.

"Now, you walk good, Missy, you hear?" Thomas ordered. "Don't you go chasing no cats or nothing."

Kit let them into the backyard, showed Thomas Missy's box of toys, and went on in the house, only to stop and watch out the window. If she closed her eyes, she could pretend it was Ryan out there with Skip, the basset they'd had before Missy. Ryan throwing the ball, Ryan tumbling in the grass with a dog, him laughing, the dog barking in the bass tones of a hound.

Amber coming around the corner to join the fun. Amber and Ryan playing keep-away from the short-legged dog that could still jump to catch the ball and then, ears flying, keep it away from them. The phone's ringing broke into her reverie.

"Hi, Mom."

"Speak of the angels, I was just thinking about you. I have a little boy playing out in the yard with Missy."

"Where did you find him?"

"He showed up at my door asking if I had kids. His family moved into the Snyder place. So how are you?"

"Not good, how about you?" His voice clogged for part of a moment.

"Cried some earlier. Thomas's coming by helped."

"Mom, sometimes I miss her so much I . . ."

Want to hit something? Scream? Curse? "I know." *Oh, how I know.* Ryan, two years younger than Amber, thought his big sister could do no wrong. She had been the person he loved most to tease in this world, one who gave as good as she got. Now Ryan was in college at Washington State University in Pullman, the last one to leave the nest. His sigh matched her own.

"What's Dad doing?"

"I . . . ah, he hasn't called yet today, still on that last consulting job."

"When's he comin' home?"

Oh, please stop asking questions I can't answer. "Not sure." *That's right. Not sure, not even sure where he is.*

"So nobody's with you?" His voice went up a couple of notes on the last word.

"No, I have Missy and now Thomas."

"You know what I mean."

She could hear music in the background. Ryan always needed music on when he studied. Amber liked everything quiet. That used to be one of their bones of contention.

"I thought Jennifer would come home, or Dad."

Me, too, but no such luck.

"Jennifer didn't dare ask for time off right after starting a new job like that." Jennifer had graduated from college in mid-May and started her new accounting position the first of June. "So how is everything else?"

"Cool. Thanks for letting me stay on for summer school. You rattling around that big house?"

If you only knew. Kit could feel tears burning at the back of her nose and eyes. "Yeah, well, maybe I'll take in boarders."

She listened. "Hang on, someone's at the door." Laying the receiver down, she headed for the front door and found a young woman hiding behind an arrangement of mixed flowers in vivid pinks, reds, and whites with yellow mums in a milk glass bowl.

"Flowers for Kit Cooper."

"Thank you." Kit reached for the vase and inhaled the spicy aroma of carnations.

"Make sure you add water."

"Thanks, I will." She closed the door with her foot and crossed to set the arrangement on the coffee table. Taking the card from the pronged plastic holder, she headed back to the phone, opening the card as she went.

"Jennifer sent me flowers," she told Ryan. "And in a milk glass bowl. You know how much I love milk glass."

"Good old Jen. What kind?"

"Carnations, mums, and some others." Kit read the card aloud. "Dear Mom and Dad, just to tell you how much I love you and how I wish I could make this day easier for you." Kit's voice broke halfway through, and she had to gulp to finish. "All my love, Jennifer."

"That's Jen. You think she likes Dallas?"

Kit finished wiping her eyes with a

tissue. She'd learned to keep boxes of tissues handy at all times, including a pull-out packet in her pocket.

"Mom?"

"Yes, I'm all right, Ryan."

"I should have come home." That was her Ryan, the tender-hearted one.

"No, I'll get through this. If I was too bad, I'd go out to Teza's and have a cup of tea." Her aunt Teza had bandaged many of her owies in life, many more than her own mother had. Teza had stood by when Kit's mother died of cancer and then when Amber followed in her grandmother's footsteps.

Aunt Teza could fix anything.

Except a daughter dying.

"I better get going, talk to you later."

"Thank you, dear." She sniffed again and sighed. "I love you, son. Take care of yourself." Her nose was so plugged she had to breathe through her mouth. She knew he was crying too. Hanging up the phone, she leaned her forehead against the refrigerator, trying to drive the memories out of her mind. Amber lying in the hospital, fighting to live, Amber weeping when all her hair fell out, Amber telling a joke and laughing so hard she would forget the punch line or at least not be able to get it out around the giggles.

God, why? You didn't need her near as much as I do. And now Mark isn't here either. Bring him home this evening, please.

The tears calmed enough that she could hear a small boy's laughter and the barking dog. She glanced at the clock. *About time to send him home so his sister wouldn't get angry with him.*

She checked the freezer. No Popsicles or ice-cream bars. She knew the cookie jar was empty. Were there no snacks here a small boy would enjoy?

She checked the pantry. *Same song second verse, a little bit louder and a little bit worse.* One of the old songs she'd taught the kids when they were little. She could hear them all singing on the car rides to anywhere over an hour.

She found a bag of chips on the shelf, poured some into a Baggie, and clamped the big bag closed again. Like a Greek bearing gifts, she wandered out to the backyard and called. "Thomas, time to go home."

"Aw, so soon?" He flopped back on the grass. Missy planted her ponderous paws on his chest and stared down into his face.

"Sorry. I have a treat for you. And one for Missy, too. You can give it to her." Kit sat down on the steps.

"Get off, dog." He pushed her off and Missy leaped back at him.

"Missy, puppy treats." At the familiar call, the dog charged across the grass, leaving a giggling boy behind to get on his feet and stagger after her, straightening his hat so the bill hung to the right. Grass greened the front of a T-shirt that had never met Tide and could use a few stitches here and there. Kit thought about the sewing machine sitting at the ready in her sewing room. She could sew that up in a minute, but then what would Thomas's mother think? Nosy neighbor? Interfering old woman?

Missy reached up to rest her front paws on Kit's thigh and looked into her face, tail wagging expectantly.

Kit handed the snack to Thomas. "Here, you give her this."

"Hey, Missy." The puppy treat was gone with a gulp. "She didn't even chew it."

"I know. She never does with those small ones."

Thomas scuffed the toe of his tennis shoe on the stairs before looking at her from under lashes long enough to make every girl in the neighborhood envious. "Can I come back?"

"Of course you may, perhaps tomorrow." She handed him the bag of chips. "Thanks for giving Missy her exercise. She'll sleep well tonight."

He held the bag aloft. "Thanks for the chips."

She watched him trudge out the gate. "Watch out for cars on the street."

The look he threw over his shoulder told quite clearly what he thought of that advice.

Yeah, well, once a mother, always a mother.

The ringing phone brought her to her feet. "Come on, dog, dinnertime." She caught the phone just as the answering machine clicked in.

"Just a minute till that runs out." One of these days she would need to learn how to shut the stupid thing off, but like other technological beasts, it, too, would most likely best her. She'd ask Ryan to fix it when he came home. Or Mark.

"There now. Hello again."

"Kit?"

Who else did you think it would be? And if you're calling, you aren't on your way home. So much for God answering my prayers today. Not that I plan on praying anymore anyway.

That last bit had just slipped out.

"Yes." A silence stretched.

"Uh, thought I'd better let you know that I'll be moving on to another job."

"Will you be coming home first?" There, she'd asked the question that should have been answered weeks ago. Or was it months now?

"Uh, no. Their time frame is too tight. Uh . . ."

Kit waited. Her mouth dried as the moments melted away. Where had the words gone? Why had they fled like phantoms flitting away in the dusk?

"Uh, I just wanted to touch base with you. I better get going."

Where are you, Mark, who are you? Why won't you even talk to me? "Take good care of yourself." The trite phrase squeezed by the sandstone boulder lodged in her throat. She listened for the click and the pause that turned to buzzing on the line. The receiver clattered into the base, and she fled to the sink. Water. Like a Sahara sojourner, she needed a drink of water. Taking a glass out of the cupboard, she ran it full and drained it just as fast. She set it on the tile counter, precisely and with a nearly imperceptible sound. Her jaw felt as though it locked with the same chink. She stared at the faucet. *Water. The flowers. Where was he?* She strode to the coffee table and picked up the arrangement, cradling the milk glass bowl in both hands. *God, where is he? I can't even call him, since he never gives me the number and his cell phone always transfers to voice mail. What is the matter with him?* She heard the sound of glass shattering against tile and saw flowers scatter across the counter and sink, one red carnation like blood on the floor. The water dripped off the cabinet and crept toward her living room carpet. Kit watched it, making no move to wipe it up.

TWO

The calendar never lies.

"Half a year gone and I still haven't made a decision."

Elaine Giovanni left off glaring at the calendar and moved over to the gilt-framed mirror in the hall. She frowned at the reflection and pushed her freshly tinted strawberry blond hair off her forehead. Pressing her palms against the sides of her face, she pulled backward, tightening the skin around her eyes, forehead, and jaw. She relaxed it somewhat to a more acceptable image and stared, all the while her mind teeming with all the reasons, both yea and nay, she'd been considering a face lift since January.

She'd look more like herself. The surgeon's scalpel might slip. She'd feel younger. The cost was beyond reasonable, not that they couldn't afford it. George might find her more appealing. She might look like a wax doll. Should she do dermabrasion? Only if she could hide out for weeks until her skin healed. Perhaps a spa where it could all be done at once and she'd be pampered as well. Her thoughts circled round and round like a carousel with a permanently imbedded microchip that made it run forever.

Why can't I make a decision? This isn't like me.

She glanced at her watch and saw that the mailman had surely come by now. Perhaps her order from Sharper Image had arrived. Leaving the front door open behind her, Elaine ambled down the Italian-tiled steps and out to the mailbox, checking along the way to see if the gardener had edged the front lawn properly this time.

"Mrs. Giovanni!"

The call made Elaine cringe. Only one voice in the entire world could sound like that. Had she been watching and waiting for Elaine to come out the door? *Why me? Why today*? She spun on her heel and faced her adversary.

"That fire was all your fault!"

Elaine clamped both hands on her hips, stretching her five foot, two inches as tall as they would go. Right now she wished she were a six-foot, three-hundred-pound linebacker. Perhaps then the fool who lived next door would pay more attention. But one had to have a brain in that case, and that was one thing she seriously doubted her neighbor owned. Mrs. Smyth-with-a-y had not displayed any kind of cerebral acumen in all the years they'd shared the fence line.

"If you kept those fir trees cut back, there wouldn't have been a fire." Mrs. Smyth snorted and panted like the English bulldog at her feet.

"Mrs. Smyth, we've been over this a thousand times. You know my trees had nothing to do with the fire. The power line broke in the wind." Elaine stepped closer to the shared property line. "The reason *you* had a fire in *your* backyard is obvious. *You* have oil spots on the concrete and greasy rags lying around to catch fire."

"Your trees broke the power line."

Elaine kept her voice in a lower register but cut each word with surgical steel. "I realize it's difficult for you to understand, but I will say this again. The power company admitted the lines broke due to high winds and old lines."

"The fire *your* trees caused burned up Bootsie's house. *You* could have killed my Bootsie too!"

"And then we would not have had dog turds in our yard," Elaine muttered. Bootsie had never slept in the doghouse in his entire slobbering life. "The power company . . ."

"Your trees started the fire." Mrs. Smyth, now red of face and screeching voice, turned toward her house. "You can expect to receive a notice from my lawyer any day now!" The woman who closely resembled the mostly white bulldog now waddling toward Elaine paused only long enough to slap her thigh. "Come, Bootsie," she commanded. Bootsie growled low in his throat and glared his hatred for Elaine before snuffling and snorting his way after his owner.

"Why do I even bother talking to her?" Elaine raised her hands shoulder high, then let them drop to her sides. She consciously unclenched her jaw and ran slender fingers through hair that always fell back into perfect sleek lines. *That woman is a menace. All these years, dug up daffodils, dog poop, motorcycles. Her kids were worse than the dog. Why I've put up with such misery, I'll never know.* The slam of Mrs. Smyth's door set her in motion. "Forgive and forget," Elaine could hear her mother's usual advice. "Love your neighbor," she'd said. *Right, I'll show that old bag next door forgive and forget.*

Back in the silence of her white-on-white

house, Elaine paced from one end of the arched glass solarium to the other, running the fourteen-carat gold chain at her neck around her fingers. Call George? Waste of time. Her husband always had more important things to do than worry about her problems. For some reason his patients were more important.

Of course, now if I murder her that will gain his attention. Elaine shook her head at the thought. No way would she ever beat a murder rap, even if every homeowner in the country sat on the jury.

Call Frederick. No, this had not escalated to calling in an attorney . . . yet.

Call the president of the homeowners association? "Fat lot of good that will do." She'd complained to him about the grease spots, the unkempt yard, the blinding porch lights more than once. The homeowners board of directors had about as much teeth as a sixteen-year-old Chihuahua.

Speaking of which, she leaned over and picked up the quivering little Chihuahua at her feet. "Doodlebug, what do you think I should do?"

Having cleaned Elaine's chin, ears and neck, the fawn-and-white-spotted dog yipped his answer, then placed a slender paw on her collarbone and laid his head on it. His sigh said it all. Forget your worries and come let's cuddle.

Elaine eased down into a rattan chair with hibiscus flowered cushions and straightened the crease of her cream silk pants. Ankles crossed, she caressed her dog's head, staring out over the evergreen clad hills undulating toward the Cascade Mountains.

"I could send her a mail bomb. Even your ears are too tender, Doodlebug, for the names I want to call her. Strychnine in chocolates. Now, that's worth considering."

She set the dog on the floor much to his displeasure and rose to pace again. A glass of Chardonnay. She glanced at the black-and-gold clock. No, the day was too young. "Chocolate, that's the answer. And" — she looked down at the dog — "if you quit whining, I'll share." Doodlebug's oversized ears stood at attention. Chocolate, he understood that word for sure.

She returned to the sunroom with shortbread dipped in chocolate. They had a good thing going — Doodlebug got the buttery end, and she the chocolate, since it was bad for dogs.

Other women's husbands dealt with

matters like fires and power lines, but George? She shook her head and fed her eager companion bits of the buttery shortbread. "Why can't I depend on my man, Bug? Why?"

THREE

The calendar never lies.

Especially not in this case. Beth Donnelly tried to focus on the desk calendar, but seeing through tears was like looking out a window beaten by a Northwest rainstorm. Only dim outlines were visible in either case. Regular as moon and sunrise, ever since her twelfth birthday, her period showed up on the twenty-eighth day of her cycle. Except for those two months in her sixteenth year. And the five short months she'd carried their long awaited son.

"Lord, is it too much to ask for a baby? You give everyone else babies." She amended her monologue. "Well, most people, even those who don't want them or have too many or don't take care of the ones they do have." She crossed to the window that overlooked her neighbor's yard, where two small children who had dim acquaintances with a bathtub and less with soap played with nary a hint of supervision.

Beth clutched her elbows with chilled

hands. If they were hers they would be loved and cuddled, sang to and read to, dressed in overalls and T-shirts, or shorts for the boy and sunsuits for the little girl. Oh, such fun she would have sewing for them. But another month had passed, and all she had to show for it was a new box of tampons. Twenty-nine and still no children. Garth's birthday was tomorrow, and how she'd prayed to be able to give him good news.

Tears again. "I hate crying." She dashed the drops from her eyes, turned back to the sink, and ran water in the teakettle. A cup of tea, that's what she needed. Peppermint, since it was supposed to calm one's stomach. And the first day of a period she always needed calming, along with a Midol or two to kill the cramps. *Even a friend to drink it with is apparently too much to ask.* Or else the Lord ignored that prayer, too. Her Bible lay open on the table. "Ask and it will be given you; seek and you will find, knock and the door will be opened for you." She didn't need to read the words. They'd been drilled into her heart when she was a little girl in Sunday school.

"Well, I've been asking all right, I've sought, I've knocked, I've just about pounded the door down and still nothing."

She waited for the water to steam and poured it into the mug sitting ready.

"Honey, wake up." Garth gently shook his wife. "Beth." He wrapped his arm around her quivering body and pulled her into his warmth. "You're having a nightmare again."

She burrowed close, clinging to his arm, blinking away the horror of someone snatching her baby from her arms. "I can't stand this anymore." She hiccuped on a sob. "Garth, we wanted our baby, and he's gone."

Gone wasn't quite the truth. Their baby had not made it full term. The doctor said it died in utero. He said things like that happened.

Beth could still hear his gentle voice. *You'll have other children, Beth. I know that doesn't make up for this one, but time will heal the wound.*

She'd gone to the funeral, using the tranquilizers he'd prescribed.

Beth wiped her eyes on the pillowcase and reached for a tissue to blow her nose.

"God will give us another child when he feels the time is right."

Her husband's words tickled the hair on her neck. He meant to comfort, she knew that, but for her there could be no comfort. *Oh, Garth . . . if . . . if only I could tell you.*

But she said no more. His even breathing told her he'd slipped back into sleep.

Beth slid out from under his arm and headed for the bathroom, where she could cry in secret. Perhaps a shower would help.

She let the hot water beat down on her back and shoulders and rinse the tension away.

The baby would have made all the difference. "God," she whispered into the steam. "You know how much I want a baby. I would be a good mother, and you know Garth would be the best daddy anywhere. We both love little kids. Couldn't you trust me, please?"

She pulled a clean nightgown out of the drawer and, after slipping it over her head, slid back under the covers.

Garth slept on. She glanced at the clock. She could get another two hours sleep before the alarm went off. If the nightmares didn't return.

Sometime later Garth sat down beside her on the bed. "Honey, why don't you stay in bed? I can catch breakfast at McDonald's."

Beth brushed strands of mahogany hair from her eyes. "I . . . I'm sorry. I didn't hear you get up." She pushed back the covers to rise, but he was in the way.

"No, with circles like that under your eyes, someone will think I've been beating you." His smile said he was kidding.

Oh, Garth, you are such a fine man. You deserve so much better. But instead of saying the words, she reached up to stroke his freshly shaven cheek. She sniffed, a smile tugging at the corner of her mouth. "You smell good."

"Thanks." He took her hand and kissed her palm, curling her fingers over and kissing them. He leaned over to nuzzle her neck. "If you like, I could leave a bit late." He nibbled the lobe of her ear.

Beth loved the curl of heat in her middle, the way he kissed her. She clasped her arms around his neck and pulled him closer.

The ringing of the telephone made him lift his head and glare at the intrusive instrument. "If that's someone selling something . . ."

Beth giggled as he reached for the receiver. He winked at her. "Just stay the way you are," he mouthed. "Hello, Pastor Garth here."

He sat straighter. "Sorry, John, let me go to the other phone."

Beth watched him leave the room without looking back. As soon as she heard his voice on the phone, she hung it up and rolled over again, one hand tucked beneath her chin.

She studied the gray clouds scudding past the bedroom window. So many gray days here in western Washington. Would she ever get used to the gray? She, an Arizona girl who thrived on sunshine, loved the green of Washington state, until the rains came and came. She could hear Garth's voice but not the words.

Feeling the urge, she tossed back the covers and headed for the bathroom. If she hurried she could get her teeth brushed, apply a spritz of scent that he loved, and be back in bed for him.

One look at her swollen eyes and rat's nest hair killed her desire.

She went back to bed and curled up under the covers. Although she tried to hold them back, the tears escaped, drenching her neck and the pillow.

Worthless, you can't do anything right. The silent words added to the freshet.

"Sorry, honey, I have to leave." He crossed the room and leaned over her to drop a kiss on her forehead. "Sleep for a while and perhaps you'll feel better."

She nodded, holding in a sniff until he turned away. "God bless." When she heard the door close, she pulled the covers up over her shoulders. Why not stay in bed? There was no one who needed her, no one who would call or drop by. Even though the women of the congregation greeted her warmly on Sundays, she'd not been invited to much. When she'd mentioned the lack of social get-togethers, Garth had reassured her that they were giving her time to settle in. He hadn't needed to suggest she should make the first move. She'd declined an invitation to a baby shower without telling him. Baby showers were just too hard for her to handle.

Her conscience screamed it at her every chance it got. After all, when she agreed to be a pastor's wife, she knew the expectations that would be placed on her.

With one more glance at the gray outdoors, Beth pulled the covers over her head and drifted back into oblivion.

The ringing phone pulled her back to reality. She swallowed to clear her throat as she reached for the receiver. "Good morning, Donnelly residence." She knew she'd failed again. She sounded as if she just woke up.

"Ms. Donnelly, how are you today?" a cheery male voice asked.

"Fine. Who is this?" She knew before she asked. A telemarketer. She pushed herself up on the pillows, glancing at the clock at the same time. Well, at least most of another morning had passed. She politely declined a credit card offer and hung up. Staggering into the kitchen, pushing the hair out of her eyes, she dove for the coffeepot, the red eye winking at her. By now the coffee would be pure sludge, but the extra caffeine was probably just what she needed.

She took her full mug to the table and sank into a chair, resting her elbows on the open paper. A headline caught her eye. "High Incidences of Breast Cancer in County." Beth continued to read:

> "Recent studies have shown that women in Jefferson County have a higher rate of breast cancer than other regions of the nation. Not only is the rate of diagnosis higher, but more cases are terminal, according to studies done by the University of Washington.
>
> "Our studies raise serious questions

for the residents of Jefferson County," said Dr. Adam Ramirez, head of the oncology unit. "While high voltage power lines transverse the county, various studies show that this may be a contributing factor, but there is no solid proof at this time."

When asked about cancer clusters, Dr. Ramirez refused to comment.

Further investigation is promised by Dr. Jason Heath, head of the State Health Commission. "We promise to get to the bottom of this," said Kyle Winthrop, elected representative assigned to the commission. "As far as I understand it, women must be encouraged to seek annual mammograms to detect this culprit in the early stages when treatment is more effective."

Breast cancer strikes one in eight women, mostly over the age of forty. The first line of defense is regular self-examination and yearly mammograms for those over the age of forty or who have a history of breast cancer in their family.

When caught in time, this cancer is amenable to treatment and should no longer cast a death sentence on the patients. The American Cancer Society has materials available by contacting the local chapter.

After finishing the article Beth was grateful she'd had her mammogram before they moved. After all, with her family history of breast cancer, she was taking no chances.

Beth sipped her cream-laced coffee and thought about the article. Why would this area have a higher rate than any other? And what was being done about it?

FOUR

The calendar never lies.

"Oh, my gosh, her mammogram is today." Kit charged up the stairs and down the hall to change her clothes. If she really hustled, they could still make it, though why Teza couldn't take herself to her appointment was beyond Kit's comprehension. Teza got herself to everything else.

She needed clean pants. Mud from kneeling to weed the iris bed caked her jeans. She stopped with that and grabbed the phone to dial Teza's number. Four rings and the answering machine clicked in. Phone clamped to her shoulder, Kit waited through the message and slipped her feet into a pair of sandals. "Teza, I'm on my way. In case you've forgotten, your mammogram is today. Please be ready and we can still make it."

Kit grabbed a blue shirt off a hanger and stuffed her arms in, buttoning it as she descended the stairs. She paused long enough at the mirror to pull her hair back into a club at the base of her neck, smoothing errant strands several times before digging a coated rubber band out of her pocket and wrapping it three times around the club, pulling her hair carefully through each time. She'd apply lipstick as she drove, normal modus operandi. She loved the sound of words like modus operandi, and while she usually saw it in the murder mysteries she read, it certainly applied today.

She wheeled into the pink hawthorn-lined lane to the Bit of Heaven Farm. The lane ran past the house and yard on the left and back to the red hip-roofed barn that now housed the fruit stand. The sight of Teza still out in the strawberry patch made Kit beep the horn.

Stubborn didn't begin to describe Aunt Teza.

Kit sucked in a deep breath, counted to ten, and reminded her fingernails that they weren't to be doing imprint surgery on her palms. Keeping a smile of sorts on a mouth that wanted to scream, she started again and counted to twenty, nodded, and deliberately released each finger. When her last pinkie hung limp, she started again.

"But I made that appointment for you

today since you said that was the only time you had."

"I'm sorry, dear, but something came up."

"Something came up — like weeds or too many ripe strawberries?"

"Oh no. Vinnie Lambert needed to go visit her mother in the hospital, and her car wouldn't start." Aunt Teza looked up from the row of strawberries that were indeed in need of picking. The patch spread around their feet in dense rows of deep green leaves hiding their fruit from those who would snatch them away, be they birds or humans. The sweet fragrance of strawberries and rich dirt warmed by a welcome June sun rose as palpable as the frustration coloring Kit's rejoinder.

She leaned over and began picking, knowing she and Teza always were able to talk more freely when their hands were busy. "And?"

"And so I took her in. Her mother doesn't have long to live, you know." Teza sat back on her heels, the knees of her jeans wearing traces of the mulch she spread between the rows. "It about breaks your heart, watching someone you love die bit by bit like that, even though you know that one day you will be back together again." She shook her head and returned to picking. Teza's fingers had a will of their own, sorting through the dark green leaves in search of succulent fruit while she glanced up from under the wide brim of her straw hat. "You'd have done the same."

Kit knew she'd been nailed again. There was really no sense arguing. She never won. "Don't you ever listen to your messages?"

"I haven't been back up to the house." Berries continued to fill Teza's crate at a speed to be revered by most other berry pickers.

"That's why I called to remind you last night, too. You know you are supposed to have a mammogram every year." Kit plopped a handful of berries in Teza's narrow wooden box, built to fit between the rows. A sturdy wooden handle enabled Teza to move it along easily. The fragrance of sun-warmed strawberries reminded her she was inhaling summer.

"I know that, but my year isn't over — yet." Teza moved the box forward and continued brushing the leaves from side to side to find the ripe red berries among the green. Strawberries could hide better than small children. "Besides, with only one breast, I should only have to go in every other year."

"Teza!" Leave it to her aunt to come up with that. "How much more do you have to go?"

"On the berries or my year?" Teza stopped to pop a perfect berry into her mouth, closing her eyes as the flavor exploded over her tongue.

Kit groaned and followed suit. Some berries pleaded to be eaten immediately. The season had been perfect for strawberries, just enough moisture and plenty of sun. She was convinced that nowhere else in the world would strawberries grow with more flavor than in the Pacific Northwest. As with other plants, the soil had a lot to do with it, but unlike large growers who planted varieties that could be shipped without so much loss, Teza insisted on planting the more flavorful Ogallala.

"Do you think there are strawberries in heaven?" Teza pushed her crate forward. "You know how Amber always loved strawberries."

Kit swallowed the tears that hit the backs of her eyes and blinked to keep them inside. *No fair, Teza, I've been doing fine up to today, up until now.* Why after all this time, do I fight the tears? *God, shouldn't I be over* them by now? "I . . ." She swallowed again and willed her throat to unclog so she could speak normally. "I don't know." What she did know was that it was a rhetorical question.

Or was it like so many other things in her life for which there were no answers?

"She'd come out here to help me weed, and we'd have a contest to see who found the first ripe strawberry. In August our hunt was for the first ripe peach, and in the fall — ah, how she loved apples. I never trusted her to tell me when they were ripe. Amber loved them green."

"Just like Ryan and Mark. You always said they'd get a stomachache from too many green apples, but they never did."

"Speaking of which . . ." Teza stood at the end of the row and handed Kit the crate mounded halfway up the handles with berries. "Make him strawberry shortcake for dinner and he'll love you forever."

Apparently Teza didn't realize Mark hadn't been home lately either. Good. Kit had decided to keep this as her secret. "You sure you don't need these?" Kit ate the biggest one before it could roll off its perch, ignoring the clutch in her stomach.

"No, there's plenty more where those came from. Make Mark some freezer jam."

She kneaded her middle back with strong knuckles. "By the way, remind him he promised to build me some more of those planters, would you? I need to get the flowers out of the greenhouse before they take it over." Teza lifted her face to the sky, her straw hat falling over her shoulders, dangling by the rawhide string. "I sold every planter he made last year. People went nuts over them."

Kit let her aunt talk on. Who knew when Mark would be home? Even more, where in thunder was he? Six months he'd been gone, a record. Surely she was worrying unduly. Surely he was just busy. Surely she knew better.

The two women headed for the house, walking shoulder to shoulder, looking more like sisters than aunt and niece. Both with shoulder-length hair worn pulled back in a rubber band, Teza's more salt and Kit's still pepper. Tall at five nine, Teza had long legs that still looked good in jeans and a stride that covered the ground with unconscious grace. They'd inherited their strong facial bones from a Sioux warrior generations earlier and their wide smiles from a Norwegian grandmother. Teza's gray eyes could be turbulent like a storm-tossed sea or, more usually, quiet and gentle as a garden pond. Kit inherited her father's hazel eyes with flecks of green, the only one of her siblings to do so. Hands with long fingers and nails clipped short were equally adept with needle as trowel — they both had the quilts to prove it — and both were imbued with a sensitivity that brought comfort to whomever they touched.

As if strung by the same puppeteer, they stopped at the Calypso rosebush near the garden gate and leaned to sniff its spicy fragrance. Kit brushed an aphid off the stem. "If you're leaving these for the birds, those Bushtits better get busy."

"I know. I hate to use the systemic, but I might have to." Teza pulled the clippers out of her back pocket and snipped two stems, the floribunda habit of many blossoms on a stalk giving a full bouquet with one or two stalks. "I'll put these in water, and you can take them home too. I can't keep ahead of this one, need to pick from it every day it seems."

"Are you bragging or complaining?" Kit teased. She started to sniff the flowers and pulled back to let a honeybee escape. "One of these days I'm going to take a cutting from this one. Looks like a sunset gone berserk." She set the berries in her car keeping cool under the shade of a maple tree and followed Teza up the steps to the back door of the two-story farmhouse. A pillared porch skirted the house on three sides, with hanging baskets of rioting fuchsias already dropping blossoms on the wide board topping the railing.

While all the Aarsgards inherited greens thumbs, Teza had ten of them.

Kit sniffed as strawberry scent intensified by cooking wafted out the open door. "You have preserves cooking?" She followed Teza into the sunny kitchen.

"Yep, in that new copper kettle you gave me for Christmas. Makes the best jam I've ever tasted." Teza filled a glass pitcher with water and stuck the rose stems in it up to the blossoms. "Sold the first batch almost before I got it bottled. Folks drove up for berries and smelled that aroma . . . Why, some of them waited until I poured it in the jars. All I do is put whole berries and sugar in the kettle and remember to stir it once in a while." While she talked, she set the red enamel tea kettle to heating and reached for the tea boxes above the stove. "You want licorice or Red Zinger?"

Kit knew there was no chance of leaving before sharing a cup of tea, so she retrieved the bone China cups from the glass-fronted cupboard. "Zinger, I guess."

"There are ginger cookies in the cookie jar. Made 'em fresh just this morning." Teza took the lid off the copper kettle and stirred the contents with a long-handled wooden spoon. "Recipe book says this makes great apple butter too. I can't wait to try the blueberries."

"How about I pour while you get your calendar?" Kit took a matching China plate over to the apple cookie jar on the blue-and-white-tiled counter. "In case you haven't figured it out, there is no way you are getting out of that mammogram. I lost mother and Amber to cancer, and I won't lose you, too."

"Yes, ma'am." Teza had the grace to look sheepish. "But I know you would have taken Vinnie in too."

Kit sighed and shook her head. So, let Teza have the last word. Kit would reschedule the appointment and hogtie her aunt to get her there if need be. *'Bout time you did your own, too,* reminded her inner critic, *only not the same day as Teza's.*

FIVE

Following church on Sunday, which she'd attended alone again, Elaine idly flipped through the Sunday paper without much hope of discovering something of interest. Doodlebug lay curled in her lap, but every time he yawned, his pink tongue curling out and in, he slipped around on the silk of her lounging outfit. She'd changed from her white silk suit into something more comfortable as soon as she walked in the door.

After reading the society column, where she wasn't mentioned for a change, she read the *Parade* section. The health columnist made another diatribe against unnecessary surgeries, face-lifts at the top of his list of horrors. But then, men could age gracefully while women had to fight tooth and toenail to stay young enough to hold their place. Just think of all the lovely young beauties coming up, each seeking a wealthy husband, who would be future trophy wives for those who could afford them.

And George could. But did he dabble?

The question plagued her more nights than she cared to count. Especially nights when the phone had rung and he'd flung on clothes for an emergency surgery, the price of being the best general surgeon in a hundred-mile radius.

She stroked Doodlebug's sleek head with one hand and turned the pages of *Parade* with the other. A recipe for barbecued turkey breast caught her attention. That might be a tasty alternative. George insisted on low-cholesterol meals, said his heart had to stay strong. She ripped out the recipe, the sound loud in the stillness.

Until the roar of a motorcycle, pipes rattling, came down the street.

"So much for peace and quiet. Those hooligans ought to be locked up." Motorcycles were prohibited by the homeowners covenants. Another restriction they'd not bothered to enforce.

"Why me, Bug? Why does every decision in running this house have to rest on my shoulders?" At the shift in her legs, he slid off to the seat of the leather couch, scrambling to get a footing. He glared up at her, sniffed, and went to curl up in a corner of the white leather cushion.

"I'm going now." Juanita Hernandez, her dark hair pulled back in a bun, made the announcement from the dining room. "I set the table. All you have to do is heat the turkey piccata and the salad is ready for dressing."

"Thank you, Juanita." Elaine picked up the torn-out recipe. "Here is something that looks good for our file." Juanita, full-time cook, housekeeper, and sometime confidant, crossed to take the paper.

"Hmm, does look good. You want for tomorrow?"

"No, I have a dinner meeting tomorrow night, and George has that meeting with the hospital board. He won't come home before that, and the meeting will run late. He'll most likely eat at the hospital." Elaine turned to look over the couch back. "If you'd like to take tomorrow off, you're welcome to do so."

"You sure? Termite man come in the morning."

"That's all right. I'll be here."

"Good, then I stay at my sister's. Be home in evening." Widowed Juanita lived in a small apartment over the garage, but her family lived about twenty miles away in another small town. While not a recent immigrant, she'd never lost her Hispanic accent. Elaine had helped her get her citizenship papers as soon as she qualified, so she no longer had a green card. George had been adamant about that process, back in the days when he paid attention to what was going on at home, before he became head of the surgical unit of the hospital.

"Why don't you take the rest of the cake with you. The children might enjoy that."

"*Gracias.* I bring back fresh strawberries from the farm."

"Only if you let me pay for them. Your sister needs every penny she can get from her produce."

"We see."

Elaine shook her head, the motion setting her hair to swinging and falling back into perfect order, as if she had not moved. "Sometimes I don't know what to do with you."

"You give much, people want to give back. You have everything, make it hard to give back. You need accept good as you give."

"You've been listening to too many of Father Spencer's sermons."

Juanita chuckled. *"No hablo inglés."*

Elaine laughed in return and laid her hand on *Parade*. A thought struck. She stood and looked fully at her helper. "See all these lines?" She pointed to the edges of her eyes and down her cheeks. "Do you think I need a face-lift?"

"Do you need a new hole in your head?"

"That's not exactly what I meant." What she wanted to ask was, *Do you think George is having an affair?* but she kept her hands on her face and her gaze on the woman across the room.

"You mean this?" Concern drew lines on Juanita's broad forehead and deepened the slashes from nose to chin.

"Yes, I do." *I'm not taking a poll for the media for Pete's sake.* She could almost hear the thoughts grinding through Juanita's mind.

"You are beautiful now. Why mess it up?"

"Thank you, but in American society, all women want to look younger."

Juanita shook her head and a torrent of Spanish burst forth.

Elaine held up both hands in a stop motion. "Too fast, I can't follow you."

Juanita waved her hands, her whole body screaming the negative. "No can translate, but no, no you do that."

"All right, I get the message." While Elaine had learned some Spanish, rapid fire and unusual words did her in.

"You no do, you talk with Doctor

Giovanni first." Both face and tone pleaded for Elaine's agreement.

Fat chance I'll ask him. In the first place he won't listen, and if he does, he'll throw a holy fit. Now, if you'd gone into plastic surgery, dear George, and set up practice in a real city, we'd be affluent, such a satisfying word, not just well off. Of course they weren't poor by any means, but income was relative after all.

"Thank you for your opinion."

"You ask what Juanita think, you get what Juanita think." Like throwing a light switch, the humble servant returned. "You need anything else?"

"Would I dare ask?"

A smile crinkled Juanita's dark eyes. "You can try." She flapped a good-bye wave and headed back for the kitchen. "*Adios.*"

"*Adios.*" Elaine returned to the couch, pushing a black-and-gold pillow up behind her. The pattern of lions and elephants of the African Veldt always pleased her. So far the pillow fabric was the closest she'd come to the safari to Africa that George had promised her back in the days when he'd vowed to make her dreams come true. Before the hospital took over his life.

She pulled the pillow out and laid it in

her lap, tracing the elephant with a wine red enameled fingernail. It was one of the many pillows she'd sewn. She had even made the intricate tassels of gold, tan, and black thread, weaving around the top of them with shiny black rayon. While the sewing had started as a way to pass some of the long evenings with George gone and Ramsey off to school, she'd donated many pillows to charity events, and they always went for good money. More than one friend had suggested she go into the pillow or home-decor business, but giving them away pleased her more. If she ever needed to earn her own living, that was what she would do.

Doodlebug jumped up onto the sofa and then onto the pillow, sitting in the middle as if she'd made it especially for him. After all, he was royalty too, at least in his mind.

"Bug, you're impossible."

He cocked his head, one fawn ear perked, the tip flopped over. She cupped her hands around his head and kissed the end of his tan-and-white nose. Petting him until he lay down, she picked up the paper again, skimming each page until a letter to the editor caught her eye.

"I am writing in response to the article last week about the increased incidence of breast cancer in our county. Another thing I think should be taken into consideration: The mammogram unit at the hospital is older than Methuselah. And if the increased radioactivity due to the high-tension power lines that cut our fair county right in half is the real culprit, how about moving them? Just sign me a concerned citizen."

Elaine read the letter through again, wishing she had seen the original article. When had it run? She dumped Doodlebug to the floor, set the paper on the glass-topped coffee table held up by two carved Indian elephants and their howdahs, and headed for the utility room where the papers were stacked in the bin for recycling.

She found the article a third of the way down the pile, put the others back, and laid the paper open on the top of the washing machine.

Fourth page, the one for local events, a third of the way down. "High Incidence of Breast Cancer in County." Only two or three inches long, the article cried out for more research. She tucked a lock of hair behind one ear and, after washing her hands of the newsprint ink, took the section out to the kitchen. She poured herself a cup of coffee from the coffee maker and brought it to the table in the bay window where she sat to sip and think.

Would they print something like this if it weren't true? And if it were true, what was being done about it? Where had the "concerned citizen" gotten his or her information? Was the mammogram unit really at fault? She surreptitiously felt for lumps in her left breast with her right hand. She'd had a mammogram down at the hospital six months before, and the radiologist said she was all clear. Could there be cancer growing in either of her breasts that had not been detected? The thought made her slightly nauseous.

Perhaps the meeting of the hospital guild tomorrow afternoon would be covering something more crucial than the annual Summer Frolic.

SIX

"Honey, I really think it is time you get involved with something. This staying home all the time is . . . is . . ." Garth looked into Beth's eyes and stuttered to a stop. He crossed the room and took her in his arms. "Oh, Beth, I love you so, and this is scaring me half to bits." He ran a hand down her back. "You've lost so much weight a breeze could blow you away."

Beth burrowed into his embrace. If only he would hold her like this all the time, maybe the monsters would go away. But she knew they wouldn't, monsters like guilt and fear and . . . and . . . They took to the sky on wings and covered the sun. And now she was always so cold, even though here it was nearly July. Of course, Washington wasn't Arizona, but she should be warm. Things were piling up; three months in Jefferson City, and she'd still not finished unpacking.

Not that she much cared about the boxes stacked in the spare bedrooms. After all, it didn't look as though they'd need a room for a baby anytime soon.

She pulled back to look her husband in the face. "I'm sorry, Garth. Here you come home for lunch, and I haven't even cleaned up the kitchen from breakfast. You must think I'm a real loser."

"No." He shook his head, leaning his forehead against hers. "I've prayed and prayed for you, but now I think maybe you need to see a doctor. Depression is nothing to fool around with, you know."

"No!" She tried to step out of the cage of his arms. "No! I don't need a doctor. He'll just put me on pills or something, and you know how I hate taking medications of any kind. You're right though about getting out." *I'll promise you anything if you won't make me see a doctor. They ask too many questions . . .*

"You could work in the backyard. They say planting is good for the soul and body."

She made a face. "You know how I am about plants. I don't make them grow. I kill them." She raised her hand, fingers spread wide. "Do you see any green thumb there?"

He took her hand and, cupping it, placed a kiss on her palm, then folded her fingers in to hold the heat in place. "I didn't marry you for your green thumb."

"Good thing, because —" The phone rang and cut off her comment.

Garth crossed the room and picked up the receiver. "Pastor Garth."

She watched as a smile stretched his lips, freeing the dimple in his right cheek. He motioned her with his free hand. "Yes, of course, she's right here. Thank you for calling." He handed Beth the phone, ignoring the questions flashing across her face.

"Hello?" She knew she needed to put some vitality into her voice, but knowing and doing were two different things.

"Beth — if I may call you that. Or would you rather I said, 'Mrs. Donnelly'?"

"No, of course not, Beth is fine." She paused, her eyebrows doing the wiggly questioning of her husband, who had assumed his most innocent expression. "Did you set this up?" she mouthed.

He shook his head adamantly.

"This is Harriet Spooner. I've met you at church and I have to apologize for not calling you sooner, but I thought perhaps you needed time to settle in, and anyway, I don't know what your interests are, but I was wondering if you would like to attend a WECARE meeting with me this evening, and I would come by and pick you up and a couple of others go from our church and I do hope you can fit this into your busy schedule."

"Uh . . ." Beth caught herself nodding and racing to catch up to the running monologue. WECARE, whatever that is, must have something to do with community outreach. After all, what could go wrong with a group by that kind of name? "Sure, I guess I could fit it in." She gave Garth a rolled-eye look and almost smiled at his answering shrug. "Good, I'll see you then. Thank you for thinking of me." There, good company manners, the stock in trade of all pastors' wives. She hung up the phone and sucked in a deep breath, blowing out her cheeks on the exhale.

"She's a talker, that's for sure." She felt behind her for the chair. "You need to be sitting down for that one."

"She does have a tendency to run her words together, but from what I've seen and heard, she has a heart as big as Mount Rainier."

"You know anything about a group called WECARE?"

"Nope, not a thing."

"She said she'd been waiting so I could get settled in first."

"See, I told you. I've found the people

here very friendly, and I know you will too." He took her hand, pulling her to her feet. "Come on, wife, I'm starved. Surely there is something good that goes along with that wonderful aroma."

"I did start a pot of chili." *At least I got something done today.* She glanced down at her jeans. *Besides getting dressed, that is.*

After Garth left, she cleaned up the kitchen, then scrubbed the guest bathroom, hanging fresh towels and even digging into one of the boxes for the soap dish and acrylic tropical fish to set on the top of the toilet tank. She leaned a wicker shelf unit against the wall. Perhaps Garth would put that up when he came home. After dusting and vacuuming the living room, she treated herself to a relaxing bubble bath, something she'd been wanting to do for a while. Until now she'd not had the energy to turn on the water. "Lord, how disappointed Garth must be with me. And how disappointed you must be." She leaned back against the inflated neck rest. "I am such a failure." She moved the rose scented bubbles around with a languid hand. "I really need a friend or two here." She thought back to their former parishes. Getting to know church members should be easy by now. After all, though everyone looked to the pastor's wife to be open and friendly, too often they feared she might come in and take over. "Well, that's not me, for sure. Little miss mousey, hiding in her corner. Must drive Garth nuts, but he never says much." She watched the soap bubbles amble down her raised arm.

With the water cooling, she washed and rinsed, then watched the water gurgle down the drain. If only her problems would disappear as easily. She dressed in a red-and-white striped cotton sweater and her standard denim skirt with the buttons up the front. Not too casual and not too dressy, since she had no idea what this WECARE meeting was all about.

Staring in the mirror to brush her hair, she paused in midstroke. Surely this couldn't have anything to do with abortion. The pro-life movement was Garth's major political platform. Surely he didn't set this up.

Later, when she heard him enter the kitchen, she turned from the stove and pointed a spatula in his general direction.

"You didn't set this up, did you?"

"Set what up?" His look of total confusion reassured her. Garth never lied. He never even stretched the truth the tiniest bit when telling a story.

"This WECARE thing?"

He crossed the room, shaking his head. "My little worrier." He kissed her cheek and raised the lid on the frying pan. "Fried chicken, I thought that's what I smelled. Ah, I think I've died and gone to heaven." He clutched both clasped hands to his chest.

"And if you will hang that shelf thingy over the toilet in the bathroom, I will mash the potatoes."

"Slave driver." But he went off whistling to get his hammer.

She stared at his back. *You are so good to me, and I have let you down so far you'll never know.* She closed her eyes, the weight of her agony pulling her down into a puddle of sludge in front of the stove. Or at least it felt that way. *Stop it! Stop it right now!* The command seemed to echo all around her. Her eyes flew open and she stared around the kitchen. Shades of her big sister, Melanie, sounded right in the room, bossy as ever and right, as usual.

Back then, that tone had meant trouble for their teasing baby brother, but today, she, Beth, was on the receiving end. Why haven't I called her? Another one of those questions with no answers.

Beth drained the potatoes and dug the old-fashioned, wood-handled masher out of the drawer.

"Honey, you better come check this so I don't get it in the wrong place."

"Coming." Garth had a tendency to hang everything according to his eye level, and, at over six feet, that was higher than most, Beth's in particular. She stopped in the bathroom door and nodded. "Good, that's just right."

"Is it centered? Look close."

She came on into the room to stand in front of the stool. "Looks good to me."

"You're sure?"

"Garth."

"I know but I've moved too many pictures and shelves and . . ."

"Nail it in." She caught the twinkle in his eyes and donned her most pious expression. "I do hope you located the studs first." So many times she didn't get things hung just where she wanted because the studs were in the wrong place, and Garth had a flaming battle with molly screws.

"Mashed potatoes, right."

"On the table by the time you're done."

They'd just finished eating when the

doorbell rang. Garth raised an eyebrow, and Beth flapped her hand at him as she went to the front door.

"Hi, come on in." Beth stepped back to indicate invitation.

"Why, thank you, dear, sorry. I think I'm a mite early but I stopped by the grocery store and allowed plenty of time, but this time I got right through and so since I didn't have enough time to go home again and really I didn't see any need to do that and I hope I'm not intruding, you know I would never want to do that, so if you are ready we could just go on and be one of the first ones there but that's all right because I could help hand out papers or something like that and if you'd like you could help with that too."

Before she could take a deep breath and be off again, Beth placed a hand on the woman's arm. "Perhaps you would like a cup of coffee. Garth and I were just about to bring ours into the living room."

"Why, how lovely but you're sure I'm not putting you out or anything? I would most hate to do that what with we haven't gotten to know each other at all well yet . . ."

At the briefest of brief pauses, Beth indicated a chair. "I'll be right back. Do you take it black or . . ."

"Black is fine." Mrs. Spooner sat where indicated.

Beth kept from grinning at her husband's discomfiture and proceeded to pour three cups of coffee. If only she had baked some cookies or something. She always used to have cookies in both the cookie jar and the freezer. Garth did love his cookies. Another place she'd let him down.

But Beth refused to allow the thoughts to bring on the gray. She nodded to the silver tray holding three hand-thrown mugs she'd received from a friend as a going-away and housewarming present.

"I take it you want me to carry that?" Garth looked from the tray to the door to the living room as if she'd asked him to go shopping with her at Victoria's Secret. She rolled her eyes and nodded toward the door.

He winked at her, and backing through the swinging door, turned with a smile. "Why, Mrs. Spooner, how good to see you."

"Oh, you must call me Harriet. When I hear Mrs. Spooner, I look around for my mother-in-law, bless her soul."

"Well, then, Harriet it is." Garth set the

tray down on the milk-painted coffee table that Beth had refinished so professionally at their last house. She'd found the beat-up old table with turned legs put out for the trash in front of a house and had gone up to the door to ask if she could have it. When the owner said, "help yourself," she'd rushed home and had her neighbor and friend bring their truck to haul it home.

When Beth picked up her coffee and sat down, she trailed a hand over the table, suddenly wishing she had the energy to find another piece to do. To think she hadn't even set her sewing machine up, and here she had a room to call her own. Until they had children, if they had children . . . *no, don't go there. You sit right here and be pleasant to Mrs. Spooner and go to the meeting, and perhaps you will find a new friend in the process. After all, that's how you met Shawna, at a meeting. Yeah right, another person I haven't called.* Shawna had been her best friend back in Arizona, where they'd lived before Jefferson City. She sipped her coffee and listened to the decidedly one-sided conversation between Garth and their guest.

"I hate to drink and run here, but . . ."

"Oh, Pastor Garth, you are such a comedian. You remind me of Harold, my late husband, bless his soul, he . . ."

Garth broke in before she picked up speed again. "I hope you two have a good time." He turned and dropped a kiss on his wife's forehead. "Have fun," he whispered, his eyes twinkling. "I shouldn't be late."

He answered her question before she could ask it.

"Such a fine young man. Our church is certainly blessed to have found him. Why, the things I could tell you about some of our former pastors, we have about run the gamut. I remember the time . . ."

Beth set her coffee cup down on the tray with a bit of a clang to get Mrs. Spooner's attention. Calling her "Harriet" just didn't seem at all possible. "Can I get you anything else?"

"No, no thank you, not at all." A glance at her watch and the flagpole woman rose, brushing imaginary crumbs off her brown polyester knit pants. Crumbs that might have been there, had there been cookies.

"We must be on our way, the traffic, you know, my car is right out front and I . . ."

If only I could drive myself. Beth smiled around the thought and took her purse from the table under the hall mirror. She turned in time to see Mrs. Spooner picking up the tray to carry to the kitchen.

"I'll get that later."

"No, no, can't be an imposition, not after that lovely coffee. You must have ground the beans yourself — it tasted so fresh and good." The words trailed behind her, like everything else, unable to keep up.

By the time they reached the meeting hall, Beth knew most of the history of the Jefferson Community Church, who had married whom, the two divorces and who was at fault, a baby or two born a bit premature, the trials of earlier pastors, the wonders of the former pastor and how, due to health, he'd been forced into early retirement.

Beth felt like clapping her hands over her ears, but no matter how she tried to change the subject, doing so was like stopping a roller coaster in free fall — with one hand. They arrived at the meeting just as it was due to start, and Mrs. Spooner hustled her down the aisle to the front row.

"So we can see better," she insisted.

A four-foot banner hung behind the table, and the speaker's podium proclaimed the name of the group, WECARE, in green capital letters.

"What does WECARE stand for?" Beth

whispered, but Mrs. Spooner just made a shushing motion as the leader stepped up to the microphone.

"Welcome. Welcome. Glad to see you all here." His voice matched his shape, round and fully packed. His megawatt smile flashed around the room.

Beth couldn't resist smiling back. Talk about contagious energy.

"Before we introduce our speaker for the evening, let me just get a show of hands. Did your tilth improve with our new methods, which are really ancient methods being brought back?"

Beth glanced over her shoulder to see indeed a raise of hands, including her hostess. Tilth? What is tilth? And what kind of meeting is this?

"Your compost bin, have you aerated it properly?"

Someone from the back announced, "It gets more air than I do," causing laughter to ripple around the room.

"Good, good. However, Arthur, maybe you should go back to manually turning yours, gives you more wind thataway."

Another ripple of laughter.

"How many of you took Lesley's barrel-and-crank pattern home and built that model?"

"Yes, even egg shells decompose fast with that method."

By now Beth was getting whiplash from turning to see who responded.

"Good, good." Mr. Moderator rubbed his hands together in what looked like glee. "I can see we will make a difference here in Jefferson City and our entire county. Now I'd like to introduce our expert for this evening, and then we will have a Q and A session following, so keep your questions for the end, and if he can't solve your problems, perhaps some of our master gardeners here will have answers for you."

Gardeners? I thought . . . Beth sucked in a deep breath. Her houseplants grew up in a silk flower factory. With her minimal interest in digging in the dirt, she shuddered to think what the evening might contain. Shame she didn't bring that quilt square along that she'd started piecing so long ago. At least then her entire evening wouldn't have been wasted. If she could have found it, of course.

But if you'd stayed home, you most likely would have assumed the fetal position either in front of the television or in bed, now, wouldn't you?

Admitting to the accusing voice, she

made herself sit a bit straighter in the chair.

"Isn't he just the most darling man?" Mrs. Spooner's slight overbite and pink nose made Beth think of a rabbit, a rabbit's head on a lean race-horsy body, that was her hostess all right.

Beth turned her attention back to the front to catch the last of the speaker's credentials.

"And here he is, the foremost advocate of God's original recyclers, red worms, one of the earthworm family, scientifically known as *megadrili*."

A tall man, weathered of face and hands and with the lanky build one often associated with cowboys, took his place behind a bank of boxes lined up on the table. "Good evening, friends. Thank you for inviting me to speak on my favorite subject." He clicked a pointer on and turned to a slide that filled the screen off to the side. At the same moment, someone dimmed the house lights.

Beth lasted about the first three minutes of the slide presentation on buying, growing, caring for, and sharing red squiggly worms.

The song from her childhood that meandered and wiggled through Beth's mind had something to do with nobody loves me, everybody hates me, think I'll go eat worms and die, including all the various worm descriptions. None matched the can of red wrigglers that was passed around for everyone to look at and touch if so desired.

Beth desired to touch the nest of moving threads in the can about as much as a nest of garden snakes, or perhaps rattlers. She'd never seen either, but the thought alone made her shudder.

When at the end of the interminably long meeting they passed out baggies of red worms, she started to refuse hers, but when Mrs. Spooner announced that surely she didn't want to miss out on such an opportunity, she took the bag with only a slight shiver.

"Here, you may have these." She passed the bag to Mrs. Spooner as soon as they got outside the door.

"No, no, you keep them."

"Harriet, how are you?" A tall woman with a smile warm enough to melt snow turned around to greet them.

"Good, good, I saw that you put that composting idea to use."

"Anything to make things easier, but I have learned to just bury much of the garden and house refuse between the rows and let the earth itself do the work." She smiled at Beth.

"Teza, meet our new pastor's wife, Beth Donnelly. Teza Dennison has a wonderful little farm outside of town where most of those who don't grow their own can go and get fruit and vegetables."

Beth shifted her worm sack to her left hand and stuck out her right. "I'm pleased to meet you."

"Ah, you love gardening too?"

Beth slightly tightened her mouth and sucked in her bottom lip. "I . . . uh . . ."

Harriet stepped in. "I invited Beth so she could get to know some new people, and so I'm really glad you came by and I think we better go now, so we will see you later."

"Good."

Was that a wink in Teza's eye? Beth smiled too. "I hope we have a chance to meet again."

"Oh, we will. Jefferson City isn't so large people lose sight of each other like big cities. Come out to the farm. My strawberries are wonderful."

"And they are," Harriet added as someone else spoke to Teza.

"My, that was a good meeting, wasn't it?

Did you get the handouts as we left?"

"Uh, no."

"That's all right. I picked up a set for you, too. I thought maybe you weren't feeling too well, the way you looked there at the end."

"Why, uh, thank you." *If only you knew.*

"And I'll just spread these little fellers among the rosebushes out front of your house along with some alfalfa leaves I brushed up from the barn floor out to my son's farm. Roses do love alfalfa sweepings. Banana peels, too. You just dig them in around the roots."

"Oh, really?" Beth nearly collapsed against the car seat. She stared at the paper that had appeared in her hand. "What did you say that WECARE stands for?"

"Why, it means 'Where Everyone Composts And Recycles Enthusiastically.' I thought you knew that." She glanced toward her passenger. "I get the feeling you aren't much into things of the soil."

"Oh. Oh no, I enjoyed the meeting tonight and I learned a great deal, but you see, Ga— Pastor Garth is the one with the green thumb. I . . . I wouldn't want to take away one of his pleasures, so I leave the gardening to him."

"Oh."

"But I'm really glad you invited me."

"What do you like to do then?"

"I sew and quilt, and I've discovered I like refinishing furniture."

"Inside stuff, eh?"

Beth did not need the accusations. *Someone has to keep the house and make a home for the pastor too, you know.* "I love arranging the flowers Garth grows," she said instead. *When he can find the time to grow any.*

"Well, if he wants any help with his composting, he can come to me." Harriet reached over to pat her arm. "In the winter I like to sew, too, along with start all my annuals from seed, of course."

After this evening's entertainment, Beth now knew what composting was, but she also knew for a solid fact that Garth had never evinced the slightest interest in building a compost heap — bin, barrel, or whatever.

"You know God is the original recycler. He never wastes anything. He calls us to be good stewards of this earth he gave us, and recycling everything we can is one way to do it. Even to those newspapers I saw stacked up by your kitchen door. I use all mine for mulch."

Thank you, God, we're home again. Beth

smiled as warmly as possible. "Good night, and thanks again." She got out of the car and saw Harriet do the same, then bend down to the flowerbed.

"You are most welcome. You go on in, and I'll just give your roses here in front the treats that we have for them. Roses respond well to loving conversation, too, you know. Why, you must come over one day and see my rose bed. Tell Pastor I'll bring goodies for the staff meeting in the morning. 'Night." Mrs. Spooner climbed back into her car, the roses sufficiently fed with worms and alfalfa leavings, reversed, and was out on the street before Beth made it halfway to the front door.

I'm sure Garth will be delighted to see you in the morning. She chuckled to herself as she let herself in the front door. Since the garage light was still on, she knew Garth wasn't yet home, so she left the empty Baggie on the hall table where he would see it first thing. Catching a glimpse of herself in the mirror, she paused. The ghost of the last weeks seemed to have disappeared. Her cheeks had some color, her hair curled softly on her shoulders as it used to, and the woman in the mirror stood straight like the former Beth. Had getting out to one meeting where she'd been more repulsed than invigorated worked magic after all? Or was the other Beth lurking in the bedroom, ready to come out and grab her?

SEVEN

"It wasn't so bad after all, was it?"

Teza lifted one shoulder in the way she had of disparaging something that was said. "Just took time away from the important things, that's all." She slid from the car and bent back down to look in again. "You've got *your* mammogram scheduled for Monday. See how much *you* like it." She shut the door and stepped back, waving Kit out of the yard and down the lane to the road.

"Always has to have the last word. Always." Kit watched her aunt through the rearview mirror. And no, she was not looking forward to it either, but duty called. Besides she had to live up to her own word. "Oh, chicken feathers." She thumped the heel of one hand on the steering wheel. "I forgot to ask her about the picnic." The Fourth of July celebration was only four days away, and Jefferson City went all out to have an old-fashioned celebration, not only patriotic but reminiscent of the early years of the city, now well over a hundred years old. People dressed in period clothing, mostly turn-of-the-twentieth-century, and rode in antique cars, horses and buggies, and big-wheeled cycles. The parade could be counted on to bring in entrants from all over Jefferson County and those surrounding it. As far as local folks were concerned, the Fourth of July parade equaled the Daffodil parade in Tacoma in the spring or the Rose Parade in Pasadena, California, at the New Year.

This would be the first year in a long time that she had no offspring taking part in the parade in some fashion. Ryan had played tuba in the high-school band, Amber belonged to a clown group from the time she was twelve, and Jennifer had been a member of the high-school drill team. For years Kit helped with uniforms and grease paint, always assisting whichever group she was mothering at the moment, then driving farther down the parade route and joining the cheering section before helping again at the end.

"Another milestone." She took in a deep breath to calm the tension zinging out to her fingertips and buzzing the backs of her eyes. Back in the early days, before his job took him on the road so much, Mark had helped build floats or booths or whatever needed a man — or anyone for that matter — who was good with a hammer. Glue gun had been her specialty, so the both of them were in high demand. *Ah, Mark, where are you? How are you? Are you thinking about the hometown parade? You could come home, you know.* Like a shooting star, hope flared and died when she saw the still-empty driveway. Missy met her at the door, demanding attention. After pats and ear rubs, she fled out the door into the backyard.

Kit set to making the pies she had promised for their church women's booth, storing three rhubarb and two apple in the freezer and baking crusts for both chocolate and lemon meringue. She'd bake the frozen ones the morning of the festival, since she didn't need to be at the parade at sunrise or thereabouts.

Three days later Kit rearranged her clothes after suffering through her yearly mammogram. Her chest still stung from being smashed between the two cold plates. She turned as the technician nurse reappeared and hung the films on the viewer.

"So, Marcy, how am I doing?"

"Clear as far as I can see. Doctor will have to read them to be sure." The woman with dark hair, cut cap-style, smiled over her shoulder. "You have been doing self-exams, right?"

"Yes, I do. Thank goodness, I'm done with this for another year." Kit finished buttoning the front of her white cotton camp shirt. "You know, I've got some questions if you have a minute."

"Sure do." Marcy snapped off the viewer and removed the films, sliding them into a folder in one smooth motion. "Now, how can I help you?" She perched on a wheeled stool and faced the tall casual woman who leaned against the wall.

Kit searched her mind for the right way to bring up a subject growing more painful by the day and more confusing. *Just jump in. Why do anything other than normal?* The voice in her mind sounded exasperated.

"Why . . . ?" She rolled her lower lip, rubbing it with the tip of her tongue. "Now, Marcy, please don't take this personally, okay?"

"Me? Take something personally? Come on, Kit, think who you're talking to." Marcy's eyes crinkled at the corners.

"You're right. You know Annie Nelson has advanced-stage breast cancer?" The nurse nodded. "But yet she had her yearly mammogram less than six months ago. And she was always faithful about that, especially after the previous mastectomy."

Kit felt a flicker of anger somewhere in her middle. "Her mammogram came back clear." No way should Annie have had cancer. Or at least not to such a degree. Kit thought about her neighbor several doors down, a young woman with two school-age children and a husband who looked as though he'd been given a terminal sentence himself with the news. They were talking radical mastectomy again with certainty now that the cancer had metastasized.

"I know." Marcy glared at the hulking machine that took up most of the room. "That's the reason right there. This machine is so old, Noah might have had it on the ark. It just doesn't pick up the minute clusters of cells that the newer, state-of-the-art machines do. And . . ." She paused as if considering how to continue. "Now mind, if you ever tell anyone I said this, I'll deny it till I die. These old machines use so much radiation that they can be harmful." She stared down at her clasped hands. "I'm sorry."

"So why didn't someone tell us this before? Why do we have to learn about it in the newspaper? Why don't we have one of the new ones? It's not like we're close to a major teaching hospital or anything. We count on Jefferson Memorial Hospital to take care of us in this town." Kit paced to the window and stared out. "So why is there no new machine here when we've had so many breast cancer reports? I've even heard the word *cluster* bandied about." She stopped pacing to look directly at the nurse. "You read the articles in the paper."

"Of course." Marcy stood, taking a step back, and ducked her chin. "Same old, same old. Money or lack thereof. And something most people don't know, Medicare and other insurances have cut back on what they pay for mammograms and the radiologist to read them, so our department has become a serious drain on the operating budget."

"But it's so important!"

"Hey, don't shoot the messenger. I'm just telling you what I know."

"Sorry." Kit resumed her pacing. "Then why the new look? That hospital refurbishing cost thousands of dollars."

"More than you know. While the start-up money was donated, they went way over budget, and now all the departments must cut back to pay the bills."

Kit shook her head. "This doesn't make any sense whatsoever. Who was the nitwit that authorized all that?" Her mind leaped onto a treadmill and upped the speed to the max.

"Why, Jefferson City's own golden boy." Sarcasm dripped from Marcy's tone. "None other than our new head of the hospital board, Winston Henry Jefferson IV. Now that he has returned home, he is using his money and clout to get things done the way he wants."

"And paint, new carpets, and the other things are visible."

"Right on, honey." Marcy rubbed her scalp, setting her short hair on end. "Makes me so mad I could sizzle. But what can you do? He offered money to start the refurbishing, and it's not like it wasn't long overdue."

"Be that as it may, we women need a new machine here." Kit snatched an idea off the racing treadmill. "We can earn the money ourselves. For a change the women of this town can get behind one venture and show those" — she tiptoed around the word she thought — "jerks what we can do."

"You mean those male chauvinist porcine jerks?" Marcy raised an eyebrow.

"Those very ones. Surely there will be a way to get a . . ." She paused with a wrinkle on her forehead. "What are the new machines called?"

"Mammogram machines."

"Well, one of those right here in Jefferson City." She stuck out her hand. "Thanks, friend."

The two women shook hands.

"You got any ideas?" Marcy walked her down the mauve and light gray hall.

"Well, I know we're going to need lots of cooperation. You know anything about grant writing?"

"Nope, sorry. But I read about some other town that kicked off a fund drive by auctioning a specially made quilt."

"Hmm. Really? How could that make enough money to make a difference?"

"It would be a start, could garner some publicity, get the ball rolling. You know who is good at that kind of thing is Elaine Giovanni. Plus she creates knock-out pillows. You can see them in the gift shop." Marcy stopped at the door of the gift shop. "I gotta get my chocolate fix and head on back. Let me know what you come up with." She stopped and looked over her shoulder. "Kit, if I were you, I would drag Aunt Teza up to Seattle and have her tested again, just a precautionary measure."

"Really?" The two women exchanged a long look. "Okay, I will." Kit waved and headed out to her car. She hadn't felt this energized since — she stopped and caught her breath. Since before Amber died.

The thought released the burning throat, and before she could catch herself, the incipient tears started again. She fumbled with her keys, a veil of moisture blurring the keyhole. Once in the safety of the car, she let the tears flow, as if she had any control over them. When the storm passed as she'd learned it would, she started the car. Before pulling out of the parking lot, she blew her nose and wiped her eyes, then pulled out a fresh tissue to clean her glasses. "Lord, one more thing here. How do I get Teza to Seattle? Or even Olympia if the mobile unit comes there? More to look into." She shook off the unease and concentrated on her driving. As she exited the parking lot, the gleaming new entrance to Jefferson Memorial Hospital caught her attention.

All that money spent on looks when women were suffering for the lack of an up-to-date mammogram unit. The slow burn she'd banked flared orange and yellow spires.

"Who, what, how?" She watched an elderly couple enter the hospital through the new automatic door. A car honked behind her. *Ah, take it easy.* She glared up into the rearview mirror before pulling out into the main drive, then the street.

What do you know about raising that kind of money? How much would we need? Where do I start? Who will help? The questions chased one another in circles in her mind.

Another car honked at her at the stoplight. Kit thought about using an obscene gesture in return but, appalled by her own thought, gunned her car through the intersection instead. "What's with all these speed bums today? Take a Valium or something." Times like this she understood the meaning of road rage.

Knowing that an empty house awaited her, she drove on south of town to Teza's small farm tucked into a jewel of a valley. Raspberries hid beneath green leaves on prickly canes, their aroma more pungent than strawberries, and the cherry tree limbs sported clusters of black Bings and cream and pink descendants of the old Royal Annes. As Kit turned into the driveway, Teza turned from filling more baskets at her fruit stand and arranging them enticingly. For a change there were no customers choosing fruit and chatting with her.

"Teapot's on, or will be in a minute. Can you use some of these cherries? I know how you love them."

Kit leaned on the roof of her car, inhaling summer. "Sure, but not too many. I'm not canning when there is no one home to eat them but me."

Teza placed the basket on the front seat of Kit's car and linked her arm through her niece's. "You've been crying."

"Does it still show?" Kit shook her head. "My eyes get red if I even sneeze." She squeezed her aunt's arm against her side. "Here you are worrying about me when it should be the other way around."

"No need to worry, that's God's job. He said he'll take care of us, and I trust that he will." Teza pushed open the door, and a billowing cloud of raspberry and sugar fragrance enveloped them.

"Raspberry preserves." Much safer to change the subject. Kit refused to agree or even comment on the God-care thing. They'd been over this ground before. "Are you using the copper kettle?"

"Sure am." Teza nodded toward the industrial size gas range that reigned over the other appliances in the enlarged country kitchen. "Should have two dozen pints ready to sell by tomorrow."

"Wonderful. What are you bringing to the Fourth of July celebration?"

"I was hoping for cherry pies, but the pie cherries aren't ready yet. So raspberry shortcake I guess. Keeping the whipping cream cold would be a problem."

"Not if you used the store-bought kind."

The look Teza gave her made Kit shrug. "Just a thought."

Teza picked up the whistling teakettle and poured the water into the teapot. "You want apple spice or licorice? I'm out of Red Zinger."

"Apple spice." Kit reached for the teacups and saucers and carried them to the table. Teza insisted that tea tasted better in bone China. Mugs were for coffee and hot chocolate.

Sitting down at the round oak table with a red-and-white-checked tablecloth, Kit watched her aunt. If they were to do a fund-raiser and use the quilt idea, Teza would be the automatic woman to ask to head up the quilt project. She knew more about quilting than anyone in Jefferson

City or County. But perhaps it was too soon to ask; after all, it was just an idea at the moment.

Teza poured the steaming tea from the teapot and into their cups. "You seem pensive."

Kit sighed. "I know. On the way out here I was thinking back to other parades and celebrations. This is the first time I'm not right in there, making sure everyone is in place and properly clothed. No Cooper kids are in the parade, at least not from this Cooper family."

"Time marches on." Teza took her chair.

"Bad pun."

"You have to admit I tried."

"You're trying all right." *In more ways than one, but I sure couldn't do without you.* They both chuckled and sipped their tea.

Inhaling the steam, Kit thought back to Marcy's warning. Take Teza to Seattle. How in the world would she get Teza to take a day off and do that? With no concrete reason?

EIGHT

I hate eating alone.

"Will there be anything else?" Juanita stopped at the door to the kitchen.

Elaine looked up from her coffee cup. "No, I don't think so, thanks."

"You have meeting this morning?"

"Yes, and George said he would be home for dinner, so let's have something nice." *As if there is any chance he will live up to his word.*

"Pork chops baked in applesauce?"

"That sounds good. I'll be at the hospital library for a while before the meeting, so don't worry about lunch." Elaine paused and scrutinized Juanita. "I have a question."

Juanita nodded. "Okay."

"Did you have a mammogram like I told you to?"

Juanita's broad brow creased in confusion. *"No comprendo."*

"Pictures of your breasts." Elaine squeezed her own between her flat hands to signify the procedure. "At the hospital."

"Big machine? Smash flat?" At Elaine's nod, Juanita smiled. "*Sí.* They say I am good and healthy."

"Good." *At least I hope it is good. If our machine is not picking up cancer cells early enough, we are all in danger.* She kept her hands from searching for lumps in her own breasts through a sheer act of her will. With no history of breast cancer in her family and with always doing manual examinations both lying flat and in the shower with soapy hands, she felt fairly safe. That was one good thing to say about George. He'd insisted she set up and follow her own schedule. "Is there any breast cancer in your family?"

Juanita shrugged. "Don't know. My family in Guadalajara no have such machines. My sisters here, I tell them go and get squeezed, like you tell me."

"Did they?"

Juanita shrugged. "I ask them."

"Good." Elaine smiled her dismissal and picked up her pen to continue her list for the day. At her feet, Doodlebug sat staring at her, waiting for his bite of toast. When it was not forthcoming, he put his paws up on her leg, his big eyes pleading.

"Sorry, Bug, my mind was elsewhere." She slipped him a tiny morsel of buttered toast, and when he chewed that and asked for more, she shook her head. "You know better." Brushing the crumbs off her robe, she stood and scooped him up for a hug. "Good dog. You go see Juanita." Setting him down, she watched as he picked up a stuffed toy and scampered off to the kitchen. If only all the other pieces of her life obeyed as well as the little dog.

When she left the house an hour later, she was armed for her research, including a handheld digital recorder to take notes. When finished she could snap it into the cradle, and her notes would appear on the computer screen. She also had the notes from her online research the night before, a list of topics she needed to look up, and a small tape recorder that fit right in her pocket. When she went before the hospital board, she would be well prepared.

Since clouds hid the mountains and grayed the sky, she shrugged into a natural-toned linen blazer over matching pants and a silk tee with a hint of gold. Staring in the mirror, she inserted gold hoop earrings and hung a gold chain with a diamond to nestle just above the swell of her bosom. Gold bangles on her right wrist and a gold watch on her left finished the ensemble. She straightened the jacket and smoothed her eyebrows. A summer power suit, that's what she wore with every intention of influencing the board toward at least partially funding the new mammogram unit.

Swinging down the hall of the hospital a short time later, briefcase in hand, she nearly groaned when she saw Winston Henry Jefferson IV coming toward her. Definitely not the man she wanted to see at the moment, but she donned her most charming smile and extended her hand. After all, shaking hands was only polite, in spite of her aversion to anyone with a limp handshake. And his really was, even though nicely manicured.

"Good morning, Mr. Jefferson."

"Ah, Mrs. Giovanni, please call me Winston. What a pleasure to see you."

"Thank you. And how is your family?"

They continued to exchange pleasantries until Elaine glanced at her watch. "I need to get some work done before our coming meeting, so please excuse me."

"Is everything all right for the booth on the Fourth?"

"Of course. The guild members so appreciate your donating the tent. Your generosity will make it much nicer for our ladies, either rain or shine."

"Thank you. How do you like our new look?" He swept his arm in an arc to include the new carpets, paint, and artwork loaned by a local gallery.

"Very nice." *I can't stand here and chit-chat. My time is running out.* She eyed his square-cut chin and smiling blue eyes. If only his handshake had the same forcefulness. "I'll see you later, then." She smiled but stepped out with purpose, forcing him to take a step back to get out of her way.

"Is there anything I can help you with?"

"No thank you." She tossed the words over her shoulder and kept on walking. Did he not realize the primitive state of their diagnostic equipment? Or . . . The alternative did not bear thinking about. Was the need for new diagnostic equipment dismissed because it was only used for women? She could feel his curious gaze drilling a hole between her shoulder blades, but she refused to turn and acknowledge the feeling.

Once settled at a table in the library, she called up the available resources on the computer and began searching for articles that had not been accessible from her home computer on current and cutting-edge breast cancer research. She also sought information on the latest diagnostic equipment.

By the time she had to stop for the luncheon meeting, she had added considerably to her fund of knowledge.

One thing was for certain: the new mammogram units did not come cheap. Another: she needed far more time than she'd spent so far on the research.

Elaine sat staring at the circles and curves forming and reforming on the computer screen, seeing them but not seeing them. *What is the best way to handle this? Whom do I talk to first?*

When she clicked on her digital recorder, she laid out a plan that formed as she spoke. Look out, "Call me Winston" and all you board members. She kissed the little recorder and tucked it into her left jacket pocket to record other ideas as fast as they came.

She stopped by the ladies room to freshen up, then joined the others filing into the boardroom where the hospital kitchen staff had set up a buffet like no hospital patient ever saw.

"Where have you been? I tried to call you." George Giovanni appeared at her side, brushing back hair gone more gray than black and worn straight back to cover a balding spot centered on the crown of his head.

"Good morning to you too, dear." Elaine smiled in spite of his disgruntlement. "What was so important that it couldn't wait until now?"

"I wanted you to bring some folders I left on my desk."

"Sorry, I was already here. Do you need them before the meeting?"

"I sent Phyllis over for them." Phyllis Nesbit was his secretary of twenty years and had been his gopher longer than that.

"Please, folks, let's get our food and take our places so we can begin." Winston banged a gavel on the long cherry wood table, another of his new acquisitions in the remodeling frenzy.

Elaine looked around for George to see him beckoning her to take a place in front of him in the line.

"Hey, no cutting in," teased one of the other members.

"I'll leave some of the shrimp for you," Elaine shot back and they all laughed, seeing the number of large pink prawns already shelled and waiting for them in a cut-glass bowl of ice centered with red cocktail sauce.

By the time they were all served and

seated, the noise level had risen to deafening proportions. Winston had to use the gavel again to gain their attention.

When the din settled he cleared his throat and began with a greeting, thanking them all for coming out on such a nice day.

The minutes were read, and old business dispensed with, sending a recommendation for hiring a new landscaper back to committee. The budget was never mentioned, and Elaine suspected the postponement could be blamed on a shortfall. She listened as the process was repeated with another item and waited for her turn as head of the auxiliary to make a report. Today it seemed that much of the business had been conducted beforehand and the meeting was just a formality.

"Mrs. Giovanni, would you like to share with us what the ladies have decided?"

She steeled her jaw against the condescending way he said "ladies" and rose. "The women of the auxiliary have agreed to a sprucing up of the gift store, but instead of tapping hospital finances, we will do the painting and refurbishing ourselves, using our labor and proceeds from our various charities."

A smattering of applause greeted her announcement.

She smiled and nodded her thanks, then continued. "The two new neonatal isolets have been ordered and will be delivered within the month. That completes our current projects."

"The hospital and the mothers of our community thank you."

"You are most welcome." She wanted to remind him of the hospital's reneged promise to pay half but kept it to herself.

She paused long enough for him to ask if there was anything else. Ending her inner debate, she opened a file folder in front of her and pulled out the article from the *Jefferson Star.*

"I would like this matter brought to the attention of the board."

His "well, um . . ." did nothing to stop her.

"I believe it more than a shame, actually a crime against the women of our county, to learn of the lack of adequate diagnostic equipment here at our own hospital through an article in the local paper. But thank God for a reporter who dug out these appalling statistics." She picked up a sheaf of papers. "I've made copies for all of you so that we will all be singing from the same page," she said, quoting a line Jefferson had used in nearly every meeting of the board. She passed papers in both directions and glanced around the table, unable to catch anyone's eye. Being that they were all men, she was not surprised. She laid her copy of the article on the table.

"Now I know I could start a really provocative discussion here if I happened to mention that if new diagnostic equipment were needed for prostate problems, we'd have it in a flash. Since I hesitate to use such inflammatory practices, however . . ."

Someone groaned and a dry chuckle or two broke the silence.

"I shall just say that we will get to the bottom of this, knowing that you gentlemen want the best for our female patients as well as the male. Therefore, I move that we form a committee to look into these allegations and determine what we can do in the near future to rectify the situation." She tapped a two-inch thick file. "I have here an abundance of research materials for those committee members to read. Since this is a project rather near and dear to my heart" — again snorts and chuckles, albeit with slightly guilty expressions — "I volunteer to head up this committee and ask for volunteers."

When no hands went up, she cocked her

head and let an eyebrow raise. "What, no takers?"

"You know there is no money in the budget for new equipment." The hiss came from her right.

"We're not asking for money but a research committee." *When we need the money, I know where it will come from.* But keeping her expression bland, she continued to look around the table.

"Now then, surely one or two of you could volunteer so this is all done decently and in order." Jefferson paused. "Although I believe there is a motion on the floor. Is there a second?" He waited.

"I second and I'll volunteer to assist in the research," the owner of the larger pharmacy in town added.

Elaine knew the man's wife had found a lump herself and recovered quickly from a lumpectomy. She was one of the lucky ones.

"Any discussion?" Jefferson waited, but the fingers on his right hand took up a drill of their own on the edge of the desk. "No, then — Yes, what is it, Harold?"

"This doesn't commit us to any financial outlay does it?" an older man from the end of the table asked.

"No, none. Anything else? Good, then

all in favor say aye. Any opposed?"

Elaine glanced around the table, virtually daring any to disagree.

"The motion passes. If there is anyone else who would like to serve on this committee, please talk with Mrs. Giovanni after the meeting."

"Thank you." Elaine took her seat and clicked off the small tape recorder she had in her jacket pocket. She sat through the remainder of the meeting, enjoying her lunch and refusing to meet the glowering looks Jefferson sent her way. *Too bad, sonny, you've taken on the wrong group of people. When women get stirred up, look out. And you can bet your manicure, we'll be stirred up. Really stirred up.*

At one point she stopped, as did the others, at the wail of one ambulance followed by another.

A call came over the PA system. "Dr. Giovanni, to OR 2, stat."

Elaine turned in time to see her husband push back his chair and stride from the room without a backward glance.

Might as well not cook the pork chops, Elaine thought. *If it is a bad one, he could be tied up a long time.*

NINE

"Beth, I have a favor to ask."

"Of course, what is it?" Beth looked up from stitching on the quilt block stretched on a hoop in her lap, her smile warm and open.

Garth pulled up a chair and sat facing her. "First of all, I want you to know how proud I am of the effort you are making to overcome the depression." He laid a hand on her knee. "Do you know how long it has been since I saw you quilting like this?"

Too long, I know. "Thank you." She wove her needle into the fabric and clasped her hands over his. "What is it you need?"

"I know you don't like to help with the pro-life booth, but we really need another warm body at the festival tomorrow. Two people have backed out, or else I wouldn't ask."

Although she tried to focus on her husband's face, Beth could feel herself withdrawing. "Garth, you know I've told you I cannot do that."

"I know, but I don't know why, and it isn't as if you would be calling on an abortion clinic or something. Just handing out leaflets. I know you believe in our cause."

"Of course, that's not the issue here." She leaned back in her chair, seeking to put as much space between them as possible, clamping her arms over her chest, locking her elbows with her shaking hands. *I can't do this, Garth, can't you understand? I can't.* All the while her thoughts raged, she kept shaking her head.

"Beth, I'm just asking you to smile and hand out leaflets. Why are you making such a big deal out of it?" Garth rose to his feet and started pacing. "This makes no sense to me." He turned and glared at her. "None at all."

"You agreed you would never ask me to do this. You agreed, Garth, and now you are going back on your word." She bit her lip until she tasted the salt of blood, all the while willing, commanding herself not to cry. In spite of her every effort, the tears leaked out. She stood, laid her quilting hoop down in the chair, and headed down the hall to the bathroom where she could lock the door.

Stripping off her clothes, she turned on the shower and stepped under the pounding water, keeping it as hot as she could stand. Anything to drive out the dark, the dirt, the despair. She heard Garth knock on the door and call her name, but she raised her face to the water, unable to answer.

God, all these years I thought I was all right, but now . . . What's happening? I can't keep going this way. Is there no relief? She slumped against the wall, sobbing until the water ran cold. Shivering, she stepped out onto the mat. With one towel wrapped around her head and another knotted over her chest, she opened the door and crept to their bedroom. The silence in the house roared in her ears.

Until this evening she'd been looking forward to the celebration, finally feeling somewhat better, and now — now how could she even attend?

And Garth was angry with her. Of course he was; why wouldn't he be? He'd put up with so much, and now she had let him down again. She pulled her robe off the hook in the closet and shrugged into it, then dried her hair with the towel. After pulling the brush through her still-damp curls, she looked out the window to see if Garth was working in the garden. Digging in the earth seemed to calm him just as placing perfect stitches in a quilt soothed her. Or maybe it just gave her too much time to think.

So what's the big deal about handing out leaflets? Just act as if you're handing out information on composting. Come on, you're a big girl. Surely Garth isn't asking anything more than you can handle. Go out there and tell him you'll do it. The thoughts bombarded her like small birds dive-bombing a marauding crow.

A cup of hot tea, that will help. She made her way to the kitchen and, after pouring water into the teakettle, set it to boil. Since the back door was open, she could hear children shrieking in play in the backyard next door. She braced her arms on the edge of the counter, locking her elbows to hold herself up.

I'll do it. I can't. I'll do it. I can't. The words sped through her mind like a cyclone. With the shriek of a trapped animal, she clamped her hands over her ears and burst into sobs. Slowly she slid to the floor, cowering against the cabinet. "I can't, I can't, I can't." Her head pounded in tempo with the words.

"Beth, darling, Beth." Garth jerked the shrieking and spluttering teakettle off the burner and knelt to gather her into his arms. "You don't have to help me, Beth. I'm so sorry. I just thought . . . ." He stroked her hair back and cupped her face in his hands. "Please, Bethy, don't cry anymore. Please. Please."

She could hear his voice as if he stood at the other end of a football field. She could feel his hands, gentle on her face and shoulders, but it was as if he burned her with every touch.

"Can I make you a cup of tea?"

She shook her head. "I just want to go to bed. My head, I have such a headache." Her stomach roiled and she staggered to her feet, ricocheting off the walls as she headed again for the bathroom, barely making it in time to heave her dinner into the commode. When she felt Garth's strong arms lock around her middle, she leaned into his strength, having none of her own. He ran water in the sink and dipped a washcloth to wipe her face, then half led, half carried her into the bedroom. Pulling back the covers, he laid her on the sheet.

"Can I get you some aspirin or something?" He knelt by the bedside.

"Please, my prescription in the medicine cabinet." She forced the request past her raw and burning throat. "And pull the drapes." The whisper sounded like a scream to ears sensitized by the throbbing pain in her head.

Garth brought her the pills and a glass of water, helping to brace her so she could drink. When she lay back down, eyes closed, he pulled the drapes and started to leave. "I'll be out in the backyard if you need me."

Nodding took more effort than she could summon. She pulled the burgundy star-burst quilt her grandmother had made for their wedding up around her shoulders, curling into its comfort.

"Beth, Beth — wake up, you were screaming again." Garth shook her, dragging her back from the precipice.

She turned into his chest and clung as though he were the only stability on earth. When she could speak without choking, she sucked in a deep breath and let herself go limp on the exhale.

"Thank you."

He rubbed her back, making murmuring noises and kissing away her tears. "Was it a bad dream?"

"I . . . I don't remember, but I must have been terrified. My heart is still pounding." She laid her head on his shoulder and her arm across his chest, burrowing as close as she could. "You are nice and warm. It was cold, so cold."

"You're safe, honey, but I think you need to get help. I can count every rib and vertebra. How much weight have you lost?"

"I don't know." *Because I'm afraid to get on the scale. Like I'm afraid of most everything. I didn't used to be so afraid.*

"Are you reading your Bible every day?"

"Most of the time." *Sure, it says "be not afraid," and I'm a cowering idiot. I'm not strong in the Lord. He is casting me out.*

"Did you read the list of verses I gave you?" He stroked her hair with one hand.

"Yes." *But all they made me do was cry. Garth, God, whoever is listening, I am so tired of crying, of this land of gray nothing where I wander.* She drifted off to sleep, clinging like a limpet to a rock to withstand the pounding surf.

When she awoke the following morning, she could hear the marching bands tuning up in the school yard one block over. She had planned to go to the parade and even to help Garth and the others at the church booth selling raspberry sundaes and soft drinks. She could hardly focus on setting the dial for the burner to make her cup of tea. Tea and toast, the only things that sounded like they would stay down. *The drums, please, Lord, turn off the drums.* She wasn't sure which were coming from the band and which were in her head.

Finally huddled in her chair, toast and tea on a plate on her lap, she forced herself to stay awake long enough to eat and drink, then crawled back to bed.

Garth, you would be better off with a wife who could help you like she should, not with this miserable failure you are married to. One who can't even give you a baby, because . . . because . . .

Tears leaked from her eyes and ran into her ears, but she had no strength to blot them away — or to stop them.

"Beth, Beth, where are you?"

She heard his voice, but by the time she'd roused enough to answer, he was coming in the door. "You're still in bed. Didn't you read my note?"

"No." She sat up and used both hands to push her hair back from her face. "What note?"

"The one on the kitchen table. Didn't you even go to the kitchen?"

"I . . . I think so. Yes, I had tea and toast for breakfast. I . . . I just didn't see a note."

She cringed back against her pillows at the look of censure that darkened his face. Not that she could see well in the dimness. "What time is it?"

"Seven. I asked you to meet me for dinner at six and we'd walk around until the fireworks started. I think everyone in Jefferson City and the surrounding county is there."

She finished his sentence, *but for you*. "I'm sorry."

"We can still get some barbecue and watch the fireworks."

Even the thought of barbecue beef and ribs made her throw back the covers and head for the bathroom. Dry heaves made her dizzy.

"Do you think you have the flu or something?"

"Maybe." But she knew the difference. "You go on. I'll just stay in bed until this passes." She crept back into the waiting bed like a mole heading for the safety of his earthen burrow.

"I hate to leave you like this."

"Don't worry. If it is the flu I wouldn't want anyone else to catch it." She turned over on her side to face the wall. She heard him cross the floor and felt his hand on her shoulder. His kiss tickled the hair around her ear. A few moments later she heard him leave, and she sighed with relief.

Sometime later, she woke to hear something crying. She sat up, at first thinking it was a baby crying, but listening intensely, she realized it was a kitten or cat.

She lay back down. At least the headache was gone. And while she felt like a space cadet in weightlessness drill, at least her stomach had settled back down where it belonged.

The cat continued to cry.

What if it is hurt? The thought propelled her out of bed, into her robe and slippers, and clear to the kitchen. It sounded like it came from the back door. She flicked on the back porch light and looked out to see a half-grown, orange-and-white tiger cat. At least she thought it might be orange and white, though the dirty, matted fur made her wonder.

Softly she opened the door, then the screen door and hunched down. The cat darted to the edge of the porch, staring back over its shoulder.

"Are you hungry, kitty? If I get you some milk, would you like that?" The cat mewed but kept its distance.

Beth closed the screen door. After getting a saucer from the cupboard, she poured milk into it and returned to the door to set it out on the porch.

The cat waited until she closed the door before creeping over to sniff and then lap the milk, taking care to keep a wary eye on her.

"You poor thing," Beth crooned. "Whatever happened to you? Did you get lost?"

Pointed ears flicked back and forth at the sound of her voice, but the cat didn't move, other than his twitching tail and furiously lapping tongue, until the saucer was empty.

"Tuna, I bet you would like some tuna." Beth retrieved a can of tuna from the cupboard and opened it with the can opener from the drawer. She debated pouring off the spring water but instead opened the door and dumped the entire can onto the saucer. "There, now, how do you like that?"

The cat had slunk halfway across the porch and still waited until she closed the door before sniffing the offering and settling down to eat.

"You've had a hard time, huh, kitty? Look, you won't even trust me when I bring food. Where is your home? Did someone dump you?" She heard Garth's car in the driveway, the garage door open and close. When he entered the house, he stopped behind her.

"What is it?"

"See the kitten?"

Garth peered over her shoulder. "That mangy cat? It's been hanging around for the last couple of days. I shooed it away."

"Oh." *How could you ignore something so pitiful?* "I fed it."

"Oh great, now it'll never go back where it belongs."

"What if someone dumped it and it no longer belongs anywhere? You'd let it starve?"

"Well, no, uh . . . Beth, when our Sophie died, you said no more cats. Remember?"

She nodded and her hands crept back to cup her elbows, rolling her shoulders forward. "But we can't let it starve."

"I'll call the Humane Society."

"No!" The word exploded out her mouth.

"But you said . . ."

"I think I've changed my mind." *If I have any mind left to change.* "Poor pathetic kitty." She turned to look into her husband's face. "You think it would sleep in a box if we put a towel in one and set it up by the wall?"

"It's an ugly cat."

"You might look kind of ugly too if you were half-grown, starved, and filthy dirty. Looks like another cat or a dog has beaten up on him too."

Garth sighed and dropped a kiss on her ear. "I'll get a box."

After they'd cut one side of the box down, puffed up an old towel and laid it in the bottom, he held the door open while she stepped outside and set the box against the wall. The cat leaped down the steps but didn't run beyond the circle of light from the porch.

"You sleep here, and as soon as you feel brave enough, you can come into the house, okay?" Beth shut the screen door behind her and watched for a bit as the cat crept back up the steps and returned to the dish to sniff for any remnants of tuna. He sniffed the box and slunk back off the porch.

Beth leaned back against Garth's chest. "Just like some people, afraid to take a gift that's offered."

Garth yawned. "I have the men's Bible Study at 6:30 in the morning, so let's get to bed. He's survived on his own this far, so what's another night?"

"How do you know it's a he?"

"I don't. Never tried to get close enough

to find out. But if it's been brawling, you can bet it's a male." Garth stopped in the bathroom to brush his teeth.

Beth stood at the bedroom window, looking out at the streetlight. Bugs and moths fluttered around the light, a bat swooped through, winnowing the population. If only she could stay in the light, perhaps the nightmares wouldn't attack.

TEN

"Thomas. I'll ask him if he wants to go to the parade."

"Woof." Missy sat at her side, tail brushing the carpet.

"Sorry, girl, I used the *g* word, didn't I?" Kit stooped to pat Missy's head and rub her ears. "Not now, but I'll come home later." Missy leaned into her ministering fingers, adoring gaze announcing full appreciation. Kit rose. "All right, backyard, you, while I load the pies in the car." She let the dog out, checking to see that the gate to the six-foot cedar fence was locked. Missy had been known to nose it open and go visiting down the street.

Kit opened the door to the garage and then raised the back of the van. She had left the rear seat out ever since she took Ryan to college, the better to have hauling space. When did she ever drive six people anywhere anymore anyway?

She carried low-cut boxes filled with pies out to the car and slid them in. When done she dusted off her hands and stood back to close the hatchback.

"If I hit someone now, we'll have a mess of pies all right. Should put up a 'drive safe, pies on board' sign in the window." She chuckled to herself as she slammed the door closed.

After calling Missy back in the house, she grabbed her purse and a collapsible lawn chair and stepped up into the van. The vehicle, in spite of being loaded with all the pies, seemed far too big for a lone woman, especially on a holiday. She stuck the key in the ignition and sighed at the same time. A week since she'd heard from Mark.

But who was counting?

She swung into the driveway at Thomas's house and waited a moment before getting out. Perhaps it was too early in the day. What if they slept in, since it was a holiday? She debated with herself but continued up the steps to the front door and rang the bell. When no one answered, instead of ringing again, she turned away, mentally scolding herself for not thinking of this earlier so she could have made arrangements. She was halfway down the steps when the door opened.

"Hey, Mrs. Cooper." Thomas stepped outside.

"Hey, yourself. I came by to see if you wanted to go to the parade with me, unless your parents are taking you . . ."

"Nah, no time."

"You want to come?"

He nodded and headed back inside. "I'll go ask, don't go without me."

"I won't." Kit stared at the lawn that had missed out on at least two mowings and flowerbeds badly in need of weeding. Obviously no one in this family liked yard work. *Maybe Thomas would like to garden with me. After all, that's how Mark and I taught our children, working side by side together.*

"I can go." Thomas crammed his Mariner's hat on his head as he shut the door.

Kit noted the dirty T-shirt. "You might want to change your shirt first." Once a mother, always a mother, and one seemed to be lacking here.

"Oh." He stared down at the ketchup stain. Hat askew, he looked up at her. "Really, I gotta?"

At her nod, he ran back in the house. He left the door open, and she could hear him clattering down the hall. If someone was sleeping, they wouldn't be for long. But no one yelled "Be quiet!" and Thomas returned, still sticking one arm in the sleeve. He pulled his shirt down and looked up for her approval.

Wrinkled but clean. One out of two ain't bad. "Okay, let's go." *Strange,* she thought. *I'd never have let my kids be gone for the day with someone I didn't know.*

"What smells so good?" Thomas latched his seat belt without being asked.

"Pies. I have to drop them off at the booth before we go to the parade."

"What kind?"

"Oh, apple, rhubarb, chocolate, and lemon meringue."

"No cherry?"

"Sorry. Perhaps someone else will bring cherry."

"What are the pies for?"

"We sell pieces of pie to earn money for our church."

"Oh. How's Missy?"

"She needs someone to play with her again, any time you want to come over."

"I came two days ago but you weren't home."

"Sorry, I'll be home tomorrow."

"Good. Where we gonna watch the parade?" He stared out the window.

"I thought a couple of blocks from the park. That's where the parade ends." She signaled a right-hand turn and glanced over at her young friend. "I see you like baseball. Are you playing this summer?"

"Nah, got here too late. The teams were already full."

"Does your dad like baseball?"

He nodded and turned back to the window. Obviously that wasn't a topic he wanted to discuss.

"Who's your favorite player?"

"Who's yours?"

"Bret Boone."

"You watch the games?" His look bubbled with amazement.

"Sometimes, when I have time."

"Baseball is for guys."

"Since when? You ever looked around the stands to see how many women go?"

His shrug said he didn't believe her in spite of any evidence she might produce. "Softball is for girls."

What a sexist, and at his age! But she remembered Ryan talking about girls with the same tone, back in the days before his hormones kicked in.

"What position do you play?"

"Catcher — sometimes, or out in the field."

"When my son, Ryan, comes home from college, perhaps he'll pitch to you."

"When's he coming home?"

"August for a couple of weeks." She parked the car as close to the booth as she could and got out. "You want to help me carry these pies?"

"What if I drop one?"

"I'll have to break your arm."

He hooted at that, like she'd hoped he would, and bailed out of the car to join her as she opened the hatch. "Wow, what a lotta pies. You baked 'em all?"

"Yep. You take that one there." She pointed to a rhubarb, then picked up one of the boxes and led the way to the back of the booth where bakery racks stood at the ready, along with a woman playing traffic director. Six trips later the job was done.

"I see you've got a new helper there." Sue Gunderson, Kit's longtime friend, smiled down at Thomas.

"My new neighbor. This is Thomas and Mrs. Gunderson to you."

"Everyone calls me Granny G, so if you'd like to, you may." Set off by a tan earned while working in her garden, Sue's blue eyes were lit with the sun's warmth. Her short silver hair fell straight from a center part.

Thomas nodded. "Did you bake all the rest of these pies?" His eyes looked about as big as some of the pastries themselves.

"No, 'fraid not. All the church ladies bake. Have to have homemade pies, nothing store-bought allowed. Your mom like to bake pies?" Sue pushed the rack back in place.

Thomas shrugged and turned away. "Is that the parade coming?"

"Sure enough, we better hustle on up there." *Interesting. He never answers direct questions about his parents.* Kit promised herself this was something worth looking into.

"Here." She handed Thomas a gallon-sized plastic bag when they got to a place to set up her chair.

"What for?"

"To put your candy in?"

His look of confusion made her realize he'd never been to a small-town parade before.

"The clowns and people in the parade throw candy. I thought you'd like to get some. You might need more than your pockets to hold it all."

"Man oh man." His chuckle made her own smile widen. A little boy's grin could do that to the most hardhearted, and Kit knew she was a softy.

By the time the Rotary Club members

came after the last horses with pooper-scoopers, Kit's hands tingled from clapping, and she desperately needed a drink of water, which she'd forgotten to bring. Thomas had a wad of bubble gum in his cheek and a bag half full of candy. Kit folded up her chair.

"Well, what do you think of parades now?"

"Cool." He blew a big bubble but sucked it back in just before it popped.

"How many pieces is that?"

He held up three fingers. The kid was a pro.

"Do you have a time you need to be home?"

"Nah." He blew a small bubble and popped it, sucking the gum back in with a grin.

Good grief, now what? He'll get bored and it's time for my shift at the booth. I could trust my kids to stay within the park. They always went off to play with their friends, but . . .

"Are you thirsty?" Kit asked as they approached the pie laden tables.

He nodded.

"Good, there's bottled water in the van. Please put this chair in the rear and help yourself." She handed him the keys. "Just click this."

"I know." He trotted off, the folded chair banging on his leg.

"How'd you two meet?" Sue set the sectioned pie cutter in place on a rhubarb pie and pushed down.

"He showed up on my doorstep, asking if I had any kids to play with him."

"He's a cutie. Kelly, my granddaughter, will be here shortly and needs some company."

"Thanks, Sue." Kit looked over the array of slices of pie on small paper plates on the table. "You think we made too many?"

"You always say that, and you know we have to beat off those who want to buy a whole pie until the end of the day."

"I guess." Kit tied her white apron on and stepped up to the table. "What kind would you like?" she asked a hungry-looking young man. When she turned around a few minutes later, she saw Sue's granddaughter and Thomas, followed by one of the older kids, heading for the swings.

"I told them no farther than the swings without getting more permission." Sue handed another customer a piece of pie. "You want whipped cream on that?" At the nod, she picked up a can of whipping cream, shook it, and squirted a mound in the middle of the pumpkin wedge.

By the end of two hours, Kit was more than glad to pass on her apron.

"They're over at the ball field. I gave them money for sodas," Sue answered Kit's unspoken question. "That Thomas sure has good manners. Please and thank you and even a ma'am. They come from the South or something?"

"Got me. I've just met his teenage sister, and she was none too friendly. Thomas enjoys playing with dogs, though. I let him wear Missy out or vice versa."

"He's got energy, you gotta admit that."

"Yeah, and an unending supply of questions." Kit turned at a hollered greeting and waved back. "Think I'll go check the ball field. You want to come?"

The two friends strolled down the wide aisle between stalls of every kind: foods, crafts, politics, and games with people everywhere, laughing and teasing with the barkers. Children ran through the gathering, winners laughed, and losers groaned. A long line waited to pitch and dunk the high-school principal, who heckled the crowd and badgered the hecklers. Red, white, and blue bunting decorated all the booths and looped from post to post along with the recently strung white lights, all set for the evening. One of the local politicians behind the podium on the bandstand promised everything but his jacket.

"You tell 'em, sonny," yelled a grizzled man leaning on his cane in one of the back row seats.

Two teenage girls shrieked when doused by squirt guns from two boys of about matching age.

Kit and Sue laughed and continued their stroll. "I wouldn't be that age again for all the milk in Wisconsin."

"Me, either." Sue side-stepped a toddler, bent on catching a fat dachshund who waddled on his leash behind a woman who was oblivious to the goings-on.

"What did you think about that article in the paper about breast cancer here in Jefferson County?" Kit brought up the subject that had been niggling in the back of her mind.

"I was appalled, had no idea things were so bad. Why?"

"Well, I have an idea. You still doing any quilting?"

"Some. Haven't had as much time since Janey and Kelly moved back home."

"Where's Janey today?"

"At work. Nurses don't get holidays off, you know."

"So you have Kelly all summer?"

"You got it. Never thought I'd be in this predicament, but what can you do? I'd much rather it was me taking care of her than some stranger. And Janey helps a lot around the house and such, not like some other families I've heard in the same situation."

"I'm thinking some of us ought to get together and start a fund-raiser to get us a new mammogram unit. You know, the machine that . . ." Kit made squeezing flat motions with her hands.

"Thing like that must cost a pretty penny."

"I'm sure. Marcy gave me the idea of using a handmade quilt to auction for seed money. You be interested in helping on something like that?"

"Sure. Just let me know when."

"Good, I'll keep you posted." They stopped behind the backstop and looked out at the field.

"Mrs. C!" A shout from the outfield and a waving arm told her where Thomas was playing.

Sue turned to look at her. "Mrs. C?"

"Guess so."

"Grandma!" Kelly played next to Thomas.

The batter hit a high arching fly. Thomas took a couple of steps forward, and the ball fell right into his mitt. Kit couldn't tell if it was shock or awe that stretched his face, but she led the cheers for him. "Thataway Thomas! What a catch!" When his team came up to bat, she gave him a high-five and went to find a place on the bleachers where several other women had congregated. Thanks to Sue, the quilt became an instant topic of conversation. By the time the game ended, four more ladies were interested in helping, one who said she couldn't stitch a straight seam but could bake cookies and make lunches for those who could.

Kit quickly realized she had too few answers for too many of the women's questions. "I'll have a meeting at my house on Tuesday . . ." She thought a moment. Tuesday was the day she'd promised to take Teza to the traveling mammogram unit in Olympia. "Make it Wednesday morning, say ten. I'll put the coffeepot on."

After the game they walked on back to the booths, Thomas beside her and Kelly beside him. "I imagine you're both starved by now."

"I am. Mom gave me money for a hot dog." Kelly dug in the pocket of her shorts. "See." She held up a five-dollar bill. "I can spend it however I want."

"Hot dog okay with you?" Kit asked.

Thomas nodded.

"Or two?"

His grin broadened. "With mustard and relish."

"How about I buy the dogs and you dress your own?" At his nod, she added, "And then we call your folks to make sure it's all right for you to stay through the fireworks tonight."

"All right!" He and Kelly swapped cheers and raced ahead to the hot dog stand, run by the local Kiwanis.

Kit watched the two kids fix their hot dogs and giggle when the mustard bottle squirted half on the white paper covering the table, missing most of their sandwiches. So many years since hers had been that age, and yet it seemed like only last week.

"I hear you've decided to go ahead with the quilt idea," Marcy said some time later as they stood in line for barbecued chicken at the Saint Ignatius Catholic Church food booth. The men of Saint Ignatius were famous in five counties for their grilled chicken and the ladies for their potato salad.

"My, but news travels fast in this town." Kit shook her head. "I just mentioned it this morning, and here we're having a planning meeting at my house on Wednesday. Want to come?"

"No thanks, but I'll buy tickets or come bid at the auction. You know, you might invite Elaine Giovanni to join the group. She'd be good help on lots of levels. And once the quilt is finished, I think there's a blank wall at the hospital that would be a real good place to display it."

"That would be kind of like carrying coals to Newcastle, wouldn't it?"

"Perhaps, but those bars at Newcastle might need rattling."

"Might that young man over there be one of the bars you're meaning?" Kit's eyebrows rose as she nodded over at a group of people eating their chicken and sipping from foaming glasses of golden liquid.

"I thought beer was supposed to be kept in the Beer Garden." Kit glanced back at Marcy.

"It is. But then some people don't feel

the same rules apply to them as to the rest of us peons."

"Hi, Kit, what's this I hear about a quilting project?" Harriet Spooner stopped in the chicken line behind them.

"Good to see you, Harriet. The quilt is to earn money for a new mammogram unit for the hospital. You interested in helping?"

"I was thinking that I'd come if you wanted more sewers and invite our new pastor's wife. She said she loves to quilt. It'd be a good chance for her to meet more of us, and I know how these things go, there are never enough hands and you know I'd rather garden in the summertime, but this sounds like something we should all take part in and . . ."

When she took a breath, Kit broke in. "I'm really glad you thought of her. Teza mentioned meeting her at the WECARE meeting, didn't she? The meeting's at my house at ten o'clock on Wednesday."

"Good, I'll be there. Your roses are always so beautiful, and by the way, the chicken is even better this year than last. Dessert, that's what I need. Choices, choices."

"Thanks, Harriet." Kit watched the woman stride off toward the Jefferson

Community Church booth. "My word, can she talk! Whew!"

Marcy whispered, "Amen to that. But so good-hearted."

"Mrs. C, can I have a corn dog with Kelly?" Thomas, blue ribbon pinned to his chest for winning the sack race, skidded to a stop in front of her.

"Wouldn't you rather have chicken? You ate a hot dog for lunch."

"No thanks."

"Your grandma said yes?" Kit asked Kelly, who nodded emphatically. "Then fine with me, but make sure you find our blanket before dark. Your grandma and I are sharing. We'll light sparklers before the fireworks begin."

"Okay." The two ran off.

"Cute kids."

"Thomas is my neighbor."

Marcy leaned closer. "Did you hear, Annie's reached stage four? It's all through her lungs. They just closed her up yesterday and sent her home."

Kit shut her eyes, clasping her middle where she was sure she'd been sucker-punched. *Dear God, no!*

ELEVEN

Elaine tied the tails of her red-and-white-striped blouse together at the waist and straightened the collar. The shirt, buttoned halfway up, showed off a red tank that topped navy pants. She rolled the cuffs on the long-sleeve blouse and slipped her feet into navy slides. The sun promised a nice day, and the weatherman said seventies, a perfect Fourth of July. She hooked American flag earrings into her ears and stepped back from the mirror to assess the outfit. "Can't get more patriotic than this."

"Are you going to the park today?" she asked Juanita as she sat down at the table for breakfast.

The housekeeper nodded. "*Sí,* my whole family. We all American citizens now."

Elaine smiled back. She knew Juanita's sister and her husband had passed their tests and been sworn in as citizens only days earlier. Juanita had helped them, as she had helped Juanita.

"My *madre,* she not like to study, to speak new language." Juanita picked up the pot and filled Elaine's coffee cup. "I bring fruit."

"One egg, over easy, and toast are all I want." Elaine glanced over at George's place. The paper was refolded as neatly as if never opened and lay by the plate. She reached over and flipped it open to read the headlines. Three people had died in a truck crash the other day, two more critically injured. The local VFW would have their entourage of veterans marching in the parade. One lone survivor of World War I would be pushed in his wheelchair. The Mariners won against the Yankees. When Juanita placed her food before her, Elaine smiled her thanks and ate without paying attention to the meal, except for giving Doodlebug his bit of toast. She finished with the Dear Abby column and closed the paper, folding it again, all in the same order just in case George found time to read more in the evening. He liked his paper in order and without wrinkles, definitely without articles or recipes cut out. She'd learned that early in her marriage, at times thinking she might order her own paper, like the *Seattle Post Intelligencer*, so she could do with it as she pleased.

After brushing her teeth, she gathered up the sacks of decorator pillows she'd sewn to sell at the hospital guild booth and checked to make sure she had her car keys before going out to the garage.

"Have a good time today," she called just before closing the door. Juanita's distant *"adios"* came down the hall. Elaine set the sacks in the trunk, opened the garage door with the remote, and backed out her silver BMW, all the while humming a tune under her breath.

A snuffling, snorting dog doing his business on her side lawn made her hit the brakes. Bootsie finished by digging his rear feet into the sod, scattering grass and dead clippings over his offering.

"Get home, you stupid mutt, before I call the pound on you." She slammed the car into park and bailed out to storm across the driveway, heading for the dog with murder in her eyes.

Bootsie, slobber drooling from his jaws, barked at her, his front legs jumping off the ground with the force of his effort.

"If only I had a stick, a shovel, anything, I'd . . ." When her feet hit the grass, Bootsie huffed once more and turned to wobble home, fat rolling on his haunches.

"Don't you frighten my Bootsie!" Mrs. Smyth yelled from her brick front steps.

"Then keep him home to use your own

yard. Look at this, a pile big enough for a horse! You just better have this picked up before it turns the grass yellow." Elaine could feel herself shaking with rage. *Frighten Bootsie; I'd rather kill him.* She glared at the retreating duo and stomped her way back to the car. All dressed up and dog poop to scoop up. Hardly! If they had another yellow spot on the lawn, she'd send Mrs. Smyth the gardener's bill . . .

She turned left on Main only to meet the roadblocks set up for the parade one block down. She thumped the steering wheel. Such a peaceful beginning to the day and now this. "I swear that woman sends her dog to our yard deliberately. Deliberately!" She turned off and circled town to get to the park. *Stupid not to have remembered the parade. Perhaps if I hadn't had to chase off the dog I would have remembered — and not been late.* She glanced at her watch again. Ten minutes late. Inexcusable.

Two women were already setting up the tables, chatting while they worked, when she arrived.

"Good morning, sorry I'm late." Elaine set her bags down and helped spread table drapes. "I think we should make a U so that more people can come in to shop, with the cash register here, out of the way."

She pointed to the right.

"Sounds good to me," said Joan, head of the booth committee. "A different look will be nice." Both women nodded.

Well now, isn't that amazing? No "we've always done it this way" jazz. Together they shifted the eight-foot tables around into the new formation.

"I brought these closet accessories. Thought we could use them to hang things down the poles," Joan said, holding up a line of hooks.

Elaine gave her a wide smile. "Wonderful. Now, why didn't we think of these things before?" By the time the others from the hospital guild arrived, the three women had emptied the plastic bins and arranged all the hand-made items on the tables or hung them from the poles.

"Don't we have power yet?" Elaine asked as she shoved the last crate back under the tablecloth.

"No, but I'll go find out why not. I forgot to ask Sherman when he came by earlier."

"I'll take care of it." As Elaine strode off, she caught a glimpse of Joan's face, frozen as if she'd been reprimanded.

I did it again. When will I learn? What is it about Joan that makes me do that? Elaine castigated herself clear to the booth set up as office. Sherman, ops manager for the festival, turned to greet her.

"What do you need?"

"Power for the cash register and credit card machine. We had that written on the application."

"Sorry." Sherman, looking similar in body build to his namesake, reached under the table for a power cord. "You take this back with you and get set up, and I'll string line from the closest hookup. You ladies need anything else over there?"

"Customers when we open." Elaine took the orange cord, coiled in a figure eight.

"You know the hospital guild always outsells the other vendors, except for food."

"Good thing. Someone's got to pay for the extra, but necessary, things."

"Yeah, like new carpets, fancy furniture . . ."

Elaine drew herself up straight. "Sherman, none of those things came out of our money, and if you don't like them, let the boy wonder know. He thinks pretty is as pretty does, as if sick people came to a hospital to admire the decor." Icicles dripped from her words.

"Ah, guess I put my foot in my mouth there." He took a step back. "Need anything else, give me a holler." He turned to answer someone else's question, giving her a wave at the same time.

Elaine had perfected the stomp-'em-into-the-ground walk while smiling and answering greetings as she went.

"What happened?" Joan took the offered cord.

Elaine inhaled deeply and let it out. "If I hear one more snide remark about the money spent on redecorating the hospital, I swear I'll . . ."

"And I'll help you. People think our money went into *that*." The three women clustered together.

"After all the work we do."

"And the good we've done."

"You can make sure there will be pictures of the isolettes in the newspaper with our board on hand to do the donating." Elaine looked to each of them. "We've always stayed in the background, but now might be the time to do some real PR. Maybe I'll take Yvonne Parrish out to lunch." Yvonne Parrish wrote the Jefferson City society news and an "about town" column.

"Time to call in a few marks." The three shared a chuckle at her sinister tone.

"Hey, your power's over here," Sherman

called, holding up the end.

"No, actually, our power is right here." Elaine tapped the others' shoulders. Handing the pronged end to Joan, she began to play out the cord.

Later in the day, after wandering around the festival, Elaine returned to the booth to do another stint. Joan stopped to talk with her.

"Did you hear about the quilt project?"

"What quilt?"

"One to help earn money for a new mammogram unit?"

"Really? Where'd you hear that?"

Joan shrugged. "I think Kit Cooper is heading it up, or at least coordinating the planning stages. She's going to have a meeting at her house Wednesday morning at ten."

"Hmm." Elaine thought a moment. "Well, there's more than enough work to go around. We'll take whatever help we can get." She gave Joan a brief synopsis of the board meeting. "Those men have no interest in a mammogram unit, so we'll do it ourselves."

"Thataway."

"Right! Someone has to get the ball rolling."

Three other women had joined the discussion.

"You think that stuff about the power lines is for real or just scare tactics?" Two shoppers joined in.

"It's for real," Elaine said, nodding and raising one hand, manicured forefinger straight like a candle. "I looked up the research. Getting the power lines moved is a long-term problem. In the meantime, I say we buy the women of this town a new mammogram unit."

"I hear you're inciting the women to violence." George had come to escort her to the Saint Ignatius barbecue booth.

"Not violence, teamwork." She turned to look at her husband. "How'd you hear?"

"Over at the raspberry shortcake booth." He gestured in the general direction. "Some women were talking about it."

"Thanks to that newspaper article, there's lots of questions. You can count on the hospital board getting a few."

"Great. My wife, the Pied Piper of Jefferson."

"At least I'm leading the children to life and not to death."

"True, but you've got to remember to count the cost. There's always a cost."

TWELVE

"The van's been canceled — again?"

Shaking her head, Kit punched the answering machine's rewind button with more force than necessary. Surely she'd not heard right. While she waited for the click that signaled ready, she took coffee filters and a bag of vanilla coffee beans, medium roast, from the grocery sack and set them in the cupboard. After stuffing the plastic bag into the red calico tube hanging from the pantry door, she punched the machine again.

"We're sorry to inform you that, due to circumstances beyond our control, the mobile mammogram unit will not be making its scheduled stop in Olympia. We will be sending a mailing for you to reschedule when we know the next available location in your area. Thank you for using Mammograms Plus." Click.

Kit eyed the machine. Sometimes the thought of maiming the messenger held certain appeal, especially when technology played a role in bearing bad tidings. Although she made jokes of being technologically disadvantaged, answering machines and voice mail rated high on her hit list.

"Now I have to call Teza and cancel, which will please her mightily. And getting her to agree to go to Seattle . . ." She looked down at Missy, who watched her with hopeful eyes. "I know, you're hungry and need to go out." The hound wagged her tail and glued her nose to her mistress's calf as Kit led the way through the kitchen to the back door. When the door opened, Missy swung her head from the door to her dish and back to Kit. "I get it, food first. You are something else, and to think some people consider animals dumb. You sure have me well trained." All the while she talked, she poured dry dog food and a glucosamine tablet into the dog's dish, then added water and stuck the hard bowl in the microwave for thirty seconds. She popped open the oven door and set Missy's dish on the floor.

Missy looked up with adoring, soulful eyes and sniffed once before digging in. The wagging tail added thanks.

"I know, you're welcome."

Kit poured herself a glass of iced tea from the pitcher in the refrigerator and sat down at the kitchen table to read her mail.

A card with no return address but a postmark of Denver, Colorado, caught her attention. Recognizing the handwriting immediately, she slit the envelope with her letter opener and smiled at the sad-looking Charlie Brown on the front. The lettering said, "I'm sorry." Inside, "For not writing more often."

She cocked her head. "Well, that's a switch. No phone call, but a card and one that lets me know his general whereabouts." She read the brief handwritten message that said absolutely nothing and slid the card back in the envelope. "So I guess that shows he thinks of me from time to time." Staring out the window, she tapped the edge of the envelope on the table. She was suddenly aware of the sound of Missy eating. Crunch, tap, tap, crunch, tap, tap and a big sigh. Her own. *Ah, Mark, what is happening to us — or is there even an us anymore?* Sometimes Kit wanted to scream at him. But now, a sadness so heavy she could hardly breathe smothered her. Standing would take too much lifting. Her arms weren't strong enough to bench-press the world of hurt his leaving caused. She thought back to that day, six months ago.

"I can't stay here anymore. Too many memories, too many tears. I just can't." Mark had his suitcase packed and sitting by the backdoor, ready to be loaded into his car. His gold-flecked eyes, usually so warm and charming, looked gray like the rest of his face. He'd lost weight since the funeral, and black hollows under his eyes showed lack of sleep.

Many times she awakened in the middle of the night to find his side of the bed empty. Sometimes she found him in Amber's room, sometimes in his chair in the family room, no lights on, staring into space or the past. The past before the cancer returned.

They'd lived through the first attack and round of radiation, chemotherapy, vomiting, hair loss, mouth sores so bad Amber could barely talk, and tears shed over an unfair life. In those five years, Amber had continued to play basketball, volleyball, and summer softball. She graduated from high school. They believed God had healed her, since she'd done far better than the doctors predicted. The bone had grown back faster than normal and more fully than early estimations. While Mark had helped when he could, his business travel often kept him away during hospital overnights and outpatient care.

Kit remembered his hasty departures any time the nurses had to find a vein in Amber's arm. Mark and needles were not compatible. But he had held basins and helped distract their daughter while she fought off the nausea. Together they'd kept their family life as normal as possible, enjoying their times together, looking forward to the future.

Until Amber died.

"Woof!" Missy nudged her knee, and the look on her face clearly questioned why she was being ignored. Kit, wiping her eyes with her fingertips, leaned down and cupped the dog's ears with both hands. "Do you still miss her, girl? Sometimes I think I could die from the hurting. Or maybe I just wish I would. Living is much harder, and with Mark gone . . ." She shook her head, dropping her chin to her chest. Missy lifted both broad front feet to Kit's thigh and whimpered, her pointed nose and sad eyes seeking and giving reassurance. At least petting the dog helped Kit focus on something besides the hole in her heart.

Okay, Cooper, straighten up and fly right, she ordered herself. You have no time for a pity party now or anytime. Besides, you've done enough of them.

Someone knocked on the back door. Kit sniffed, wiped her eyes again, and stood, sucking in a breath of composure at the same time. Seeing no one through the lace sheer, she opened the door to see Thomas sitting on the deck chair.

"Hey, Thomas."

Missy charged out, catching Kit's calves and nearly knocking her over. Her woofs of delight and flapping ears stretched a grin from ear to ear on her guest. "I think she likes you."

Thomas fell to his knees, hugging the dog and laughing at her slurpy kisses. When he looked up at Kit again, he studied her for a moment.

"You're sad. Why?"

Leave it to Thomas. She sniffed and wished for a tissue, but rather than going back for one, she sat down in the other chair.

Thomas didn't take his gaze off her, all the while petting Missy but obviously waiting for an answer.

What to tell him? *The honest truth, that's what you tell people. But then I might cry again, and this child doesn't need to see me wallowing in self-pity.* "I got a card in the mail, and it brought up sad memories, that's all."

Missy knocked Thomas's Mariners cap off his head. He snatched it before Missy could run off with it and returned to studying Kit.

"What memories?"

"Of my daughter."

"I forgot. What's her name again?"

"Amber."

"Where does she live now?"

"In heaven." Kit rolled her lips and eyes to keep the tears at bay.

"My grandma's in heaven. She watches out for me." Sitting on the deck floor, he crossed his legs and took up scratching Missy's belly, still gazing at Kit.

Go away, child, this hurts too bad.

"Amber watches out for you. That's what angels do."

"Who told you that?"

"My dad."

"Your dad is pretty smart."

"Yeah, I know." Thomas grinned at Missy's wriggling to keep him rubbing her tummy, then glanced up at Kit from the corner of his eye. "How long since Amber got to be an angel?"

Got to be. Interesting. "Two years."

"You miss her, huh."

It was more a statement than a question,

as if he understood all about death and life and missing ones you love. "More than I can say." Tears flowed unchecked, dripping off her chin.

"I bet she loved Missy a whole lot."

"She did." *She loved life a whole lot.* "You want a Popsicle?"

"Do you?"

"Yeah, I think so. You can give Missy a treat. That's one of the things Amber loved to do, only most of the time she just shared what she was eating."

"Does Missy like Popsicles?"

"Most likely, but I'll bring her a puppy treat."

"Can I get the ball?"

Missy scrambled to her feet at the *b* word, again making Thomas laugh.

"Does she know 'ball'?" His eyes grew round when Missy Tigger-bounced around the deck.

"I call it 'the *b* word' if I don't plan on throwing it for half an hour. I don't think she's ever given up before I did."

"I can throw it."

"I know." Kit opened the door and crossed to the refrigerator while he fetched the red nylon ball from the toy box. "Put it in your pocket for a bit, or you'll never get to eat your Popsicle.

What color do you want?"

"Purple."

"We have red, green, and yellow."

"Green."

She took out banana for herself and smacked it on the edge of the counter to separate the two sections. "You want yours divided too?"

"Okay." He nodded and shoved the ball in his jeans pocket. "Thank you," he said, taking one half and watching her return the other to the freezer.

"You can have that when you're done with the first."

He nodded again and nibbled on the end of his Popsicle.

Someone sure taught you good manners. I wonder why you never mention your mother. Kit pulled a couple of tissues from the box on the counter, dug out the puppy treats, and followed her guest back outside. After blowing her nose, she could smell the spicy scent of the Sunset rose floating by. A robin dug in the soil of the dahlia bed, where worms were plentiful and easy to find. Hummingbirds clicked and chased each other from the two feeders she had hung, one from the eaves, the other on a shepherd's crook, a cast-iron hook attached to the edge of the silvered cedar deck. While Kit loved mornings, too, evenings like this were her favorite time of day.

She leaned back in the chair and watched as Missy caught her treats in midair. The dog danced on snowshoe feet, waiting for Thomas to throw the ball, ready to dart off at his first motion. When he hesitated, Missy bowled him over. Getting run into by Missy was like being hit by a low-slung Rottweiler, solid and below the knees.

Kit ate her Popsicle, enjoying the evening, the flowers, and mostly the joy shooting out of boy and dog like the sparklers they'd lit at the park on the Fourth. She ignored the voice that said she should be weeding the garden or working on Ryan's quilt or . . . Her inner mother could always find more to do and scold for wasting time. She even ignored the ringing phone, letting the answering machine pick it up instead. She'd call back later, after dark.

Flushed with running, and smelling pure boy, Thomas skidded to a stop in front of her. "Can I get your other Popsicle, too?"

"Yes, that would be very nice of you." She watched him tell Missy to wait while he went inside, and the dog did just that, staring at the door as if he might not come back if she took her gaze away. But he did.

"Thanks." She took the proffered treat and ambled down the two steps to the lawn, deadheading the early marigolds she'd started from seed and pulling a weed or two from the well-mulched flower bed. When she noticed that the streetlights had come on, she turned to call Thomas.

"Time for you to go home. How about if Missy and I walk with you?" The look he gave her made her smile and add, "I haven't walked yet today and I need to."

Sure, then, that she wasn't treating him like a little kid, he nodded. "Come on. Missy, want to go for a walk?" Missy responded with more Tigger-bouncing and woofs of sheer joy. Missy didn't enjoy walking as much as sorting through all the scents she would pick up on the way. Bassets always walked nose to the ground, and that didn't mean a stroll either. She pulled Thomas ahead at a half trot, his laughter floating back to make Kit smile. If this was what grandparenting felt like, she would look forward to babies in the family that would grow into interesting boys and girls.

"Tell her to heel and make her mind. You know how to do that."

His giggle told her he had no intention of stopping the fun as Missy dragged him from one side of the sidewalk to the other, up to and around a tree in one yard, and under the bushes in the next, then back to the fire hydrant by the curb.

Kit let them walk past his house, glancing up to see if anyone was watching out for him. The drapes were pulled on the front window, and no one had turned on the front light. In fact, she didn't see light in any of the windows. The next block passed in a spray of giggles and Missy's *basso profundo* discovery of a dog behind a fence. The yapping terrier quieted when the two sniffed noses through the slight gap between fence boards.

"Come on, Missy." Thomas jerked on the leash, bringing Missy back to the sidewalk just as Kit caught up with them.

"Thomas, is no one home at your house?"

"My sister's there. She's probably watching TV in the family room."

Who will make your dinner? When will your father get home? "Won't she be worried when you aren't home yet?"

"Nah, she said to be home by dark, and it's not all dark yet."

"I see." *But without the streetlights, not*

much longer. "We'll turn back now so she won't worry."

"She don't worry."

"Oh." *What to say, what to think?* When they reached Thomas's house, he handed her the leash, knelt down to give Missy one more hug, accepted one more slurpy kiss, then headed up the stairs. "Thank you."

"You are most welcome. Thank you for playing with Missy." Kit walked on past her own house and around three more blocks. Missy might be about worn out, but she wasn't. Later, after she ate her dinner of leftovers, baked a lemon pound cake to serve at the meeting in the morning, flipped through her quilting book to find some patterns to offer as samples, put the dog out, let the dog in, threw a load of clothes in the washer, sorted through the remainder of the mail, locked the doors, and did her evening ablutions, she glanced at the clock and groaned.

"Oh, nuts, I didn't call Teza. Too late now." Of course she'd already let Teza know about the meeting, but sometimes her aunt needed a reminder or she'd get busy out in the garden and forget. "Like I forgot to call her."

Kit scribbled a note on the pad by the bed, eyed her Bible, and turned off the light. When had she stopped reading her Bible every night? Was it after Amber died or after Mark left? Dates seemed to run together, blurred by all the tears she'd shed. She stared heavenward. "You could have changed all this, kept if from happening. You were the only one who could have, but you sat on your hands and did nothing. Why?" It promised to be another long night of unending questions and no answers.

THIRTEEN

"I must have pulled a muscle yesterday." Teza rubbed the sore area just to the front of her shoulder. "I'll put some liniment on it tonight." She finished dressing and glanced out the window. Gray. The weatherman had said no rain, and sun by afternoon, so she'd have time to pick cherries. If it rained now, they'd split for sure, and then she'd have to make preserves of all of them.

Once downstairs, she fixed her first cup of tea and took it to the wicker chair in the bay window where she read her morning devotions whenever it was too chilly to be outside in her rocking chair on the wrap-around porch. She read two chapters on her way through reading the Bible from cover to cover again. Then, leaving the Bible open on her lap, she folded her hands, took in a deep breath, exhaled, and recited, "The Lord is in his holy temple; let all the earth be silent before him. Be still and know that I am God." Breathing deeply she imagined Jesus in a meadow and saw herself sitting at his feet. He laid his hand on her head, and she began to praise and thank him for her home, for her small farm that not only kept her busy but provided a steady income through much of the year, for her friends, for air to breathe, for Christ himself and God who loved her, for Kit, for friends, for customers who also became friends, for her flowers, for hands that loved to garden and sew and all the other things she loved doing. From her praises she segued into her prayer list, which she took from within the pages of her Bible and read aloud. After each petition she paused to listen, something she had resolved she would do more often. "Be still and know that I am God." Chattering to God and then hanging up she'd decided was rude.

"And, Father, please take care of Mark while he is away on this business trip. Please bring him home safely and continue to work healing in his soul and spirit. Lord, I know your plan is for that marriage to grow stronger with all they've been through with Amber." She waited and the words *trust me, you and Kit must both trust me* filled her mind. She nodded, keeping her eyes closed and listening with both inner and outer ears and mind. *Trust me.* She'd been hearing a lot of that lately.

Tipping her head back against the high, curved chair, she waited again. "And about Kit, she is carrying such anger at you. I remember when Karl died, I went through the same grieving, but I know it is worse for someone losing a daughter. Teach me how to help her, how to help them before that root of bitterness digs in so deep we need major excavation to dig it out. Lord, you who can do far beyond what we know or think, I thank you for the answers you have already put into action so we can see them when we need them. You said, 'Before you call I will answer.' Thank you and praise you. In Jesus' precious name I pray, amen." She kept her eyes closed for a bit longer, enjoying the sense of peace that hovered in the room and her heart, bringing a golden light in spite of the gray outside.

By the time she opened her eyes the tea had grown cold, but she felt as warm as if she had been sitting in the sunshine. "Thank you, Father." She stood and stretched both arms over her head and then bent forward until her fingers touched the braided rag rug under her feet. "Not bad for a nearly seventy-year-old woman."

She glanced at the chalkboard where she

kept her to-do list for the day. So much to get done before that meeting at Kit's. She poured herself a bowl of Raisin Bran, added milk, and took the bowl and spoon to stand at the window so she could look out at her orchard. Bing cherries hung nearly black and heavy on the branches under the netting that kept the birds at bay. A wonderful crop this year; she would have to put out the you-pick sign when she came back from town. She'd never get them all picked without help. She set her watch to remind her to come in at 9:30 and headed to the fruit shed for buckets. There was something about picking fruit that brought her even closer to God, not that all her gardening didn't do much the same, but the Bible mentioned good fruit so often — She stopped her forward motion as though she'd hit an invisible wall. *Bear much fruit, bear much fruit* . . . The ideas tiptoed in, then ran like a dead heat. A quilt with appliquéd fruit on the squares and the fruits of the spirit embroidered above them, verses that fit embroidered all around in the border. Plain blocks of white or another color quilted in stylized fruit designs. She could see the colors, rich and vibrant. The design could be done for a full-sized quilt or a wall hanging, or even a cross-stitch. On the blackboard in the fruit shed, she jotted down her ideas, picked up her buckets, and danced her way out to the orchards, singing, "Oh, Lord, thank you, thank you. What an idea, thank you, I praise you." Her fingers itched to get started on the quilt, but she set them to picking instead. When her wrist alarm sounded, she set the filled buckets on the flat-bedded wooden wheelbarrow Mark had made for her years earlier, during the days when Karl was so ill, and trundled her produce up to the barn.

On the drive to town she let her mind roam free with the quilt idea, seeing it done and hanging in the fruit shed along with the other farm-related handicrafts she sold there. She thought of her stash of fabrics at home, trying to think if she had enough fruit prints for the border trim. "Of course, I shall have to do the lining in a fruit patterned fabric." She thumped on the steering wheel. "Oh, I wish I could get started on it." She waved at a person who honked behind her when her mind skipped watching traffic lights and played on with the quilt. "That old child's coloring book, I bet that's where I've seen fruit the way I want." Wondering where she had it packed away, she parked her truck in front of Kit's house and ambled up the walk, sniffing the roses as she went.

"You know what?" she asked when Kit met her at the front door. "I haven't saved rose petals for potpourri yet. How about saving some of yours for me?"

"Hello to you too." Kit stepped back. "Come on in — or should we meet out here on the porch? The sun looks to be coming out soon."

"The porch, of course." Teza hugged her niece. "But don't let my preferences choose for the group."

"You're glowing. You must have some good news."

"Here, sit down." Teza pointed toward the cedar glider. "I have the most stupendous quilt design idea ever, and I think it could be made into other products as well."

"You need paper and a pencil?"

"No." Teza patted the seat beside her. "Just sit." As soon as Kit took her place, Teza described her idea of the fruit quilt. "Maybe I should call it 'Good Fruit.' We can talk about that, but each square could also be a potholder or —"

"An apron bib or the design on a tea towel," Kit picked up. "When we get the first one done, we can digitize it and use machine embroidery. You could make up kits for any of the products made, why, I bet you'd need to hire seamstresses to keep up with the demand." Kit took her aunt's hands in hers. "What a bombshell idea!"

"Interesting, because I'd had my morning devotions, and I've been asking God to help me listen better. I had my breakfast, and on the way out to the barn, that song about the fruit of the spirit — you know the one — started running through my head, and all of a sudden I saw this glorious quilt, in full color, all finished. I've never had an idea come to me like that." She thought a brief moment. "Place mats and napkins could come of it, too."

Kit leaned forward to give Teza a hug. "I have no idea how you will do all this along with the farming." She shook her head, but her eyes were dancing. "But I know you enough to know you will."

"I think the cherries did it. Oh, I brought you some. I don't think I've had a better year for Bings, so pray for no rain or I'll have a ton of jam."

"The pie cherries aren't ripe yet, are they?"

"No, but the Royal Annes are lovely too. And I still have some raspberries. The ever-bearing strawberries are coming on for another picking. I sure do miss Ryan. He was always such a help, he and Amber both. Well, when I think of it, all three of the kids were. Jenny just didn't like messing around with garden and farm like the other two."

"Hey, you two look like you've got all the problems solved," Sue Gunderson called as she strolled up the walk. A basket over her arm said she'd brought more than ideas to kick around.

"Teza's got a wonderful idea for a new quilt" — Kit spread her hands apart — "and a whole bunch of ideas to go along with it. Wait until you hear."

"I thought we were coming to discuss a cancer quilt." Sue set her basket down and wiped her forehead. "I do hope we're meeting out here. These hot flashes about do me in. They say exercise helps mitigate them, but just now walking in from the car and the thing blindsided me."

"This too shall pass?" Teza raised her eyebrows and tipped her head slightly to the side, her smile bringing forth one in return.

"I know. There's no sense griping about it, but I have to learn to bring along a fan. I saw a bitty little thing that can fit in your pocket and runs on a battery. Think I'll buy one before it gets too hot."

"I used to carry one of those folding ones along with me. I'll look around the house and see if I still have it."

"Oh, you'll have it somewhere. You never throw anything away." Kit stood. "I'll go get some more chairs and bring the coffee carafe out here."

The other two dutifully followed her in, so she put them to work bringing the chairs in from the back deck and setting out a tray. By the time the others arrived, the wicker table had a cloth over it, the tray in place, and chairs around it.

"Oh, this looks just like a picture out of Martha Stewart," Harriet Spooner gushed as she sat down in the cedar rocker with peony-flowered cushions. "Everyone, I brought Beth Donnelly along with me. She's our new pastor's wife and she said she likes to quilt, though I know she wasn't too impressed with the WECARE meeting. She did meet Teza there after the meeting was over."

"Welcome." Kit motioned to a chair. "Glad you could join us."

Beth smiled. "Thank you."

"This is Sue Gunderson. Her quilt won Grand Champion at the county fair last year, and she's just like Kit. You two are so creative you put me to shame."

"Thanks, Harriet, but I've seen your yard." Kit picked up her clipboard so she could sit down. "Several others called to say they couldn't make it. If you'd all like to get some coffee and a piece of pound cake, we can begin right away so you can get back to all the things I know you have planned for today."

As the women helped themselves, Teza caught her eye. "Don't say any more about the fruit quilt," she whispered. "I want this meeting to concentrate on the other one."

"Well, look who's here," Kit whispered to Teza before she stood to welcome their newest guest.

"I'll be," Sue murmured and leaned back in the glider.

"Elaine, good of you to come."

"Thank you. I heard about this meeting at the Fourth of July celebration, and while I know I should have called . . ." She put out her hand and shook Kit's.

"No, not at all. Everyone is welcome." Kit motioned to the group. "I'll let everyone introduce themselves. Ladies, this is Elaine Giovanni, head of the women's auxiliary and our token woman on the hospital board."

Elaine stopped at the top of the steps.

"Your landscaping is just lovely. What do you do to get your roses to bloom so abundantly?"

"I took Harriet's advice" — she motioned to Harriet Spooner — "and sprinkled alfalfa clippings under them. That and lots of compost."

"It most certainly worked." Elaine took the remaining chair and set her briefcase on the floor beside it, then turned to the others.

When the introductions were finished, Kit nodded. "All right, ladies, I thought I'd tell you a bit about the background of our idea." She told them about the newspaper article, talking to Marcy at the hospital, and where the quilt idea came from. "So, while I know we can't earn enough for the mammogram unit, we can do a lot toward encouraging community support by kicking off a campaign. Any questions?"

"Are they sure that article was correct about the high wires? I thought the utility company put all those old fears to rest before they strung those." Sue fanned herself with a napkin.

"I brought that issue and others up at the hospital board meeting last week, but if you do your research, you'll find there are at least two sides on that issue. As far as I can see, the truth is that the lines can cause cancer." Elaine pulled a portfolio out of her briefcase. "If any of you want to read my findings, you are welcome to do that."

Harriet Spooner reached for the file. "Thanks, I'd like that."

"We also discussed the state of the current mammogram unit." Elaine flipped to some notes in her file folder. "There are sound financial reasons not to purchase a new one, things like Medicare cutting back on the amount they pay both for the mammogram and the doctor to read them, other insurances are following suit . . ."

"Well, if that don't beat all. What is our government coming to?" Harriet looked up from her reading. "If you ask me —"

"So what that really means to us is that we are on our own as far as the board is concerned, but then that is not unusual either. Through the years, the guild has picked up the slack on many needed projects, like the isolettes we just purchased for the neonatal unit," Elaine continued.

Harriet didn't seem to realize she'd been interrupted.

"Yes, the guild has done a lot for our hospital. We are grateful for the work they do." Sue poured herself another cup of coffee.

"That is well and good," Teza said, "but let's talk about the project at hand. Who knows what kind of good God is going to bring of this." Teza looked at Kit in time to catch a flash of disagreement. *Just you wait, my dear. God has some real surprises in store for you.*

"Thank you, Elaine, Teza. So, are we all in agreement that this is a project that is needed and that we'd like to do?" Kit reached down to the pile of pattern books at her feet while watching for nods. "Good. I marked some patterns I thought might be really lovely, and we're open for suggestions from all the group. I think once we've decided on a pattern and the colors, then I'll get an article in the paper so we can have a cutting day, opening it up for anyone who wants to take home blocks to stitch."

"Are we going to do this by hand or machine?" Sue asked.

Kit looked around the group again. "I think machine stitch the blocks and the top, then hand quilt it. We also have to decide on size, king or queen. What do all of you think?"

"I'd think king, then if someone had a

smaller bed, it could hang down like a bedspread." Elaine flipped pages in the book she'd picked up. "You do understand that the quilt would be more valuable if it is hand stitched?"

"Anyone else?"

The others shook their heads and continued searching for patterns.

As the books were passed around, the women discussed different designs. Sue brought some pieced blocks out of her basket as examples, too, and Teza shared one with a star motif.

"So we agree then on the Starburst pattern?" Kit finally asked, holding up the book to the correct page.

"I think it would be lovely, and in shades of burgundy to rose to cream with that touch of blue, my, I would want to buy it myself." Harriet stroked one of the squares, pointing to a dark royal blue in the pattern. "I don't know how I can commit to all the quilting, though. My Leslie's going to have her baby about the time we'd be ready to set up the quilting frame."

"No problem. I think getting the squares done will be the major part." Kit studied the design they'd agreed upon.

"Good, but I have another question."

Harriet shook her finger. "Who's going to head up this thing? You? Teza? You're both busier than a one-armed paper hanger."

"And who's going to pay for the supplies? We can't just piece this with leftovers. It has to be a work of art." Sue set her coffee cup back on the tray.

Kit looked around the group. "Any suggestions?"

"We could ask for donations," Beth offered. "I'd be willing to take charge of that part."

"Why, thank you, dear." Teza leaned forward and patted Beth's arm. "Good of you to volunteer."

"As far as the leader, Teza, you are the best quilter and designer in four counties," Harriet said.

"Or the entire state of Washington," Sue added.

Teza shook her head. "Come now. I . . ." *God, help me. How can I take on anything else right now?*

"You are." Kit spoke with the kind of conviction that set everyone to nodding. "But I was kind of hoping we could do this by committee."

Sue groaned and flopped back in her chair. "You know what they say about committees. That's what created the camel."

The others chuckled, glancing at one another and chuckling again.

"But think, if we each take responsibility for one part . . ." Beth added.

"Of course we can do that, but you still need someone in charge to oversee and make sure things are rolling along."

"Are you volunteering?" Harriet, sitting on the glider with Sue, gave her an elbow nudge.

"Nope. I'll take charge of getting all the supplies there the day we cut, but I don't want to head it up. Means I'd have to talk in front of a group, and I'd rather die than do that. Fact is, if I stood up there, I'd most likely keel right over." Sue looked down at the floor as if expecting to see herself there.

"I just cannot take on another new project before the farm is put to bed in the fall." Teza looked to Kit. "But you know I'll do whatever I can."

Kit squirmed in her chair. "Don't you all go looking at me. I . . ." She rolled her eyes and shook her head, at the same time chewing on the inside of her lip. Her sigh was one of resignation. *I was really hoping Teza would offer. She's the best.* "Just remember, if I oversee, you get to do all the work."

"Spoken like a true bird colonel," Elaine said under her breath.

A round of chuckles fluttered the leaves of the wisteria. A house finch flew to her nest at the opposite end of the porch. Missy whined at the screen door.

"Okay, if Sue is in charge of cutting day, who will be responsible to make sure all the squares are done in time? I'd thought we should have it ready by October, which seems far away now, but time will go mighty fast."

"Do we have to have it ready for October? I mean, I know that's breast cancer awareness month, but what if we kicked this drive off in February or late January? Isn't that more realistic?" Sue counted the months off on her fingers. "That gives us less than three months to finish it, and that doesn't leave any time to display the finished quilt and build up an interest."

Kit nodded. "You're right. Unless we did it for next October . . ."

"Why wait that long? I'll contact some of the other women's organizations in town and see what they can do to help us promote this." Elaine wrote herself a note on her calendar. "And I know the hospital guild will be excited about this too."

Kit nodded again. "So we are in agreement then on the pattern, and you'll trust Teza and me to do the designing and buying the fabric?"

"I'll be happy to help with that too." Elaine looked over her half glasses at Beth. "I'm sure Myrna would let me use my discount at her fabric store for this."

"And I'll make sure we get enough donations to pay you back," Beth added.

Teza rotated her shoulder. Reaching for the cherries must have aggravated that muscle even more. She caught Kit looking at her and shrugged. "Just a bit sore from picking cherries this morning. Thank you, Kit, for the delicious cake. That pound cake recipe is about perfect."

"Should be, I got it from you."

"And I got it from my mother who got it from her mother . . ."

"Don't you love family heirlooms like that?" Sue picked up her basket and got to her feet. "Here, I brought you a slip of my geranium that you so admired. This one's been in my family for generations too."

"That the one that blooms all winter long in your upstairs window?" Kit held out her hand with a smile.

"You want a slip too?" At Harriet's nod,

Sue said, "Come on over right now and I'll get you one. I rooted this one for Kit, but you can get that thing to grow just by putting a slip in water."

Teza and Kit watched the others make their laughing way down the walk, waving good-bye and stopping to admire a spectacular rose bloom on the way. "You did fine, dear, even though you kind of got railroaded there at the end."

"That's the problem with having a good idea — you usually get appointed to be the one to make it work." Kit let Missy out and began to clean up.

"I think, if you'd want, Elaine would gladly take over."

"Most likely. I get the feeling she likes to run things. But she didn't volunteer and I don't know her well enough to ask her. Do you?" Teza chuckled and gave a slight shrug.

"Now, we have to discuss your mammogram. I got a letter from the traveling van that they had to pull it out of service for a time. I think we should go on up to Seattle to Virginia Mason. That's about the best hospital in the area."

"What a waste of time and effort. There's a perfectly fine hospital in Olympia and another in Tacoma. I can't take an entire day off right now, and you know it. Besides, this is all a tempest in a teapot."

"Teza, Marcy said that's what she thinks you should do, and she would know. Surely it's better not to take a chance. I want you around to see my grandchildren, you know. They need an Aunt Teza, just like I did."

"Mercy sakes, a couple of more months won't make any difference. I feel fine."

Kit stared at her, arms crossed, one foot tapping.

"This is a preventive measure, you know. The doctor seems to think our machine here is all right."

More tapping. Kit's eyebrows drew closer together.

"Oh, all right. Make the stupid appointment for when it is convenient for you. Just make sure you give me two weeks' warning. They probably won't have an opening until September anyway."

"I know, and then the apples will be ready, but we'll be going before then. Mark my words, if I have to bribe the receptionist."

"You'll need a referral."

"I'll get the referral." Kit softened her tone, adding a touch of wheedle. "We could stop at Pacific Fabrics in Puyallup and look at their fabrics."

"Kit Cooper, you could nag a saint to death." Teza marched down the steps. "If I didn't love you so much, I could get real ticked off at your butting in, you know."

"I'll call and let you know as soon as I find out something. You want me to come out and pick cherries this afternoon?"

"Suit yourself." Teza ignored the butterflies sipping at the roses and the perfume that assailed her nose. *Pesky, interfering woman, she knows things like this should be left for winter when I have more time.*

FOURTEEN

"I think she's really mad at me."

Missy whimpered at Kit's feet.

"No, I'm not talking about you, girl, or even to you, but Teza is in a snit. And I don't know how to handle it, really. Ignore her? Apologize? Why, when I am doing it for her own good? Tough as she is, I know it's not the pain of the mammogram but purely that she'd rather spend her time doing other things."

Missy bumped against Kit, a more determined tone in her voice also.

"Okay, okay, I get the picture." Kit leaned over and stroked the dog, rubbing her ears the way Missy liked. Kit moved over to the chair and sat down, the easier to pay attention to the dog, and continued thinking about her aunt. Something bothered her, but she couldn't quite get hold of it. Teza looked tan, or at least what Washingtonians thought of as tan, from her work in the yard, her voice had sounded the same as always; was it that she'd gotten testy over the mammogram thing? That wasn't like Teza. Kit closed her eyes, the better to see her aunt. Light bulb! Had Teza lost weight?

The ringing phone drew her to her feet. Better get to drawing up a list of supplies for the quilt project and computing how much fabric to buy. One thing they hadn't done as a group was set up a timetable, but with a goal of a winter auction, that wouldn't be as difficult. *Ha, as if finishing the quilt by October wasn't stress enough.* She caught the phone just as the answering machine kicked in.

"Hello. Sorry, can you wait until that thing runs through?" When the line clicked clear, she heard Ryan's voice.

"Mom, why don't you learn how to turn that recording off?"

Why didn't you learn to clean your room? "Most likely because I don't know where the instruction book is. How are you?"

"Fine, and so is school. How come no one warned me summer could be hot over here?"

"You think all the wheat fields would have been a clue?"

"Mom, since when do I know zip about wheat fields?"

"Sorry for the hole in your education. What's up?" It wasn't like Ryan to call during the day, on a weekday.

"You talked to Dad lately?"

How do you define lately? Within the last three months, then yes. Within the last seven days, then no. She allowed a noncommittal "um" to fill in the gap. "Why?" Always safer to answer a question with a question.

"Because I had the weirdest call from him last night."

"Oh?" She stretched the simple word into a question.

"Is there something wrong between the two of you?"

The question she'd been dreading for several months now. "What makes you ask?" Kit took refuge in another question while she struggled to come up with a workable answer.

"I think he'd been drinking. He apologized for not being a better father and for letting us all down."

Oh, Mark, what is happening with you? "I see." *No I don't. What a lie. Good grief, I don't want to deal with stuff like this over the phone. And here, the morning had been going so well. Why, I haven't even cried once. Or felt like it — until now.*

"Ryan, I think your father is struggling with . . . with . . ." *Do I call it a midlife crisis? Or grief that he doesn't want to admit?*

Or, a thought beyond bearing, is there someone else in his life? Was that what he was referring to by the "letting us down"?

"Mom?"

"I'm here. Just trying to puzzle this out. Maybe you should call him back and just talk with him. Perhaps that would be best." *I don't want to be in the middle, not anymore. I've been there, done that, and I refuse to do it again.*

"I would, but he didn't give me his phone number. That's one of the reasons I called you."

Kit now understood what people meant when they said their hearts dropped to their shoes. *Gotcha,* an evil little voice snickered.

"Mother?"

"I always call his cell phone, since he's had to move around so much lately. Or you could send him an e-mail." She flipped through pages in her address book until she found the number. "You have the number?"

"Yeah, I just found it. Why do I get the feeling there is something going on here that you don't want me to know about?"

Funny you should ask. "All families go through a difficult period after a child dies, Ryan, and we're no exception. Give it time. Things will work out."

She could hear doubt in his silence. "So you're still planning on coming home between semesters?"

"Yes, I'll see you in a few weeks. I'm thinking of taking the train home unless I find someone to ride with."

"Good." After a bit more discussion, she hung up and leaned her head against the cabinet. If only she could pray. But why pray to a God who says he will be there for you, then snatches your daughter away? If Teza knew how far from faith she had drifted, she'd be on her knees night and day.

Kit poured herself another cup of cold coffee and popped it in the microwave. So much to do and so little will to do anything. She forced herself to put the dessert things in the dishwasher, wiped down the counters, and stared into the freezer to see what she should take out for dinner. It was about time to cook a big pot of something so she could eat leftovers and put a couple of baggies of the same in the freezer. Thinking along those lines, she took out hamburger and set it in the sink. Goulash sounded about as good as anything. If she hadn't promised Teza she would fix at least one meal a day, she'd most likely live on peanut butter and popcorn. Not combined, of course.

What had Mark said to cause Ryan such consternation? And, the big question, was his call liquor induced? Had all of this driven him to drink?

"Oh, Mark, come home where you are safe." *We're supposed to be holding each other up and drawing closer because of our adversity.* That's what the book she'd been reading said. What a crock. If that is what happened in real life, where was he? Or were they going to become a statistic? The book also said 80 percent of marriages dissolved after a son or daughter died or experienced a life-threatening illness.

"Not if I have anything to say about it!" She slammed her hand down on the counter, making Missy jump and look up, accusations wrinkling her already wrinkled face.

"Sorry, girl, but there must be something I can do. If I had an address, I'd send a card or a letter. I can do e-mail, that's for sure." She thought of the computer that got used for downloading sewing and craft things from the Internet. *But if he wanted to keep in contact, wouldn't he have been e-mailing me?*

So when did you check last?

To shut off the accusing voice, she climbed the stairs to the home office and turned on the computer. All the family knew how seldom she logged on, especially in the summer. Two or three times a week — max.

While she waited for the computer to boot up, she straightened papers, filing some of the mail and putting the bills in the drawer to be paid. Another one of those things that Mark used to do. At least he had electronic deposit with his paycheck, so she didn't have to worry about money.

Missy laid her chin on Kit's shoe and heaved a sigh.

"You're feeling left out too? Well, join the club." Kit sniffed back the tears that attacked without warning or provocation.

After logging on, she waited again, idly scanning the subject lines as the e-mail downloaded. A joke from someone, two spams, a message from Jennifer and none from Mark. She read the joke, a poor one that she deleted instantly, ditto for the spams, and called up Jennifer's note.

Her questions echoed Ryan's. What is going on with Dad? Are you all right? The job was going fine, but she missed the Northwest. Did Kit have any idea how hot and humid Texas could be?

"That's one reason we live here, Jen," Kit mumbled. "I hate humidity and melt in prolonged heat." She clicked the reply icon and told Jennifer the same as she had Ryan. "Talk to your father yourself." She mentioned the quilt project and deleted mention of Thomas.

She stared at the screen. *Wonder why I did that?* With a shrug she left it as is and added, "With love, Mom. P.S. I'll try to remember to log on more often."

"Okay, dog. I'm going outside to work in the garden for a bit. You can drool over the birds or stay inside, your choice." An ear-ringing bark was her answer.

On her way out the door, Kit snagged her clippers and gardening gloves from the shelf and stuck the green stretchy tape in her pocket. It had replaced worn-out pantyhose as plant ties sometime earlier.

She went down the flower beds deadheading the roses, checking for aphids, and pulling the few weeds that managed to sneak through the mulch. After fetching bamboo stakes from the gardening bench, she tied up the glads before they grew leggy enough to tip over and snipped dead blossoms off the late-blooming anemones and irises. Missy rolled over and wriggled around, scratching her back on the grass, her front feet flopping, back feet kicking the air. When she snorted and lay there, looking up at Kit as if saying, "Come on, get with the belly rubs," Kit laughed and complied. Sinking down on the grass, she rubbed Missy's belly, watching a hummingbird visit the Apple Pink penstemon, hovering and drinking from each tubular blossom. When her fingers slowed, Missy kicked her feet, rolled back right up, and crawled up into Kit's crossed legs.

"You silly girl, you're too big to be a lap dog." With both arms around the dog's neck, Kit rested her chin on Missy's head and watched the blackbirds ferrying food to their growing brood in the birdhouse on the top of a pole stuck in the dahlia bed. While she kept the bird feeders empty of seeds at that time of the year, every once in a while, a sparrow or house finch would light and check it out.

"How do you suppose he can bear living in hotels all the time when he enjoyed our yard as much as I do?" She shook her head. "I just don't get it."

A snore from the dog in her lap made her look down. Missy lay on her back, head tipped over Kit's thigh and two broad paws flopped on her chest. Perfect trust in picture form. A picture of herself climbing up into God's lap zapped through her mind.

"No!"

Missy jerked awake, scrambling to her feet, her head swiveling around to see what was wrong. She woofed, halfheartedly, in case there was something going on she didn't see.

"Don't mind me. I just got blindsided by a memory. God, I'm not doing that anymore. I told you that. I can't trust you anymore."

Can't or won't?

"And I'm tired of those voices too." Kit took the clippers and attacked a euonymus, whacking the straggling branches back as if they were poison ivy or oak.

"I'm not doing that anymore. I'm not, I'm not."

She stomped across the grass to the garage and brought out the orange construction-sized wheelbarrow, threw the rake in, and stomped back across the yard to clean up her mess.

That done, Kit headed for the lower level where the compost heaps awaited her. Throwing the trimmings in a pile that she'd chop by running over it with the lawn mower, she took the pitchfork stuck in the pile that needed turning and went at it as though she were attacking an invading army.

Dig . . . shove the fork deeper. "No more."

Lift . . . strain. "Mark, you're a jerk."

Dig. "No more."

Lift. "Who needs . . ."

Heave. *"You."*

She dug, lifted, and heaved until her shoulders ached, until sweat and tears ran down her face and chest. Kit was puffing so hard she could only mutter her diatribe. Gasping, she leaned on the pitchfork handle and stared at the now empty bin. Empty, just like her.

She stared at the three three-sided composting bins Mark had built especially for her. She could add boards to make them higher or dismantle the whole thing to move it to a different area if she so desired.

Kit wiped her face with her shirttail and, after sucking in as much air as her chest could hold, released it all and felt the last vestiges of anger disappear on the slight breeze. She stabbed the fork back into the top of the heap she'd turned. "*I* need you, that's who."

She wiped her eyes again and headed for the house.

The message light was blinking when she glanced at the phone. She punched the button and heard Teza.

"I thought you were coming out to pick cherries. I sure could use some help."

"Oh, drat and blast. How could I forget something like that so quickly?" Kit checked the time. Almost two. Amazing how time flew when you were having fun. She washed her hands, made a peanut butter and jam sandwich, called Missy in, and with sandwich and can of soda in hand, tucked her purse under her arm and headed for the car. She'd eat on the way.

Dusk fell too quickly as the clouds came up in the west, growing darker in spite of the sun.

"The rest of those cherries will just have to take their chances," Teza said with a head shake. "If they split, they split."

Kit set her bucket on the wheelbarrow. "There aren't many left at least." She stretched her hands above her head and twisted from her waist, trying to pull the kinks out of her shoulders. "Besides, since when are the weatherman or even black clouds necessarily on the nose with rain?"

"True." Teza grasped the handles of the wheelbarrow and with a grunt began pushing the load up to the barn.

"Here, let me do that." With a grin Kit shouldered her aunt out of the way and pushed the load onward.

Once the cherries were in the cooler, Kit rinsed her hands in the sink Mark had plumbed out there for just that purpose and wiped her hands on a towel. "How about coming over for dinner with me, and let's finish designing the cancer quilt? I've been playing with it in my mind, but I need to get it down on paper and have you look it over."

Teza made a moue. "I should do those cherries that are really ripe . . ." But then she shrugged. "They'll wait until morning. You want me to bring anything?"

"No thanks. Just your brain and experience."

"Well, 50 percent isn't bad." Teza reached up to pull the counter window down and flinched in the process. After throwing the bolts, she rubbed her shoulder.

"What's wrong?"

"Either I pulled a muscle the other day, or else all the cherry picking is getting to me."

"You're sure that's all?"
"Kit, I'll see you at your house."

Once home and cleaned up, Kit took strips of cooked chicken out of the freezer and thawed them in the microwave while she filled two bowls with mixed salad greens she'd picked that morning. By the time Teza arrived, the salads were ready and the muffins just out of the oven.

"Poppy seed dressing or roasted garlic?"

"Either." Teza bent down. "Yes, Missy, I see you. I just needed to put my things down before I could pet you." She took care of those obligations and sat in the chair that Kit indicated.

"I thought we'd eat out on the deck, but the wind came up too much. Iced tea or coffee?"

"Coffee would be fine."

When seated, Kit picked up her fork, then waited while Teza bowed her head. Saying grace was another of those things she'd put aside for quite a while . . . or forever.

"My, this is good." Teza broke open a muffin. "Cranberries?"

"I tossed a handful in. Thought it would go well with the chicken."

"It does. Interesting meeting this

morning, don't you think?"

"That's for sure. Never dreamed Elaine Giovanni would show up like that."

"I'm glad she came. Did you notice the look on her face when you introduced her?"

"No, why?" Kit stopped chewing.

"Your comment about 'token woman' on the hospital board?"

"Oh." Kit tightened her lower jaw in a flinch. "It just slipped out. I didn't mean anything by it."

"She covered well, but . . ."

"But I stuck my foot in my mouth and now I have to chew?"

"Something like that."

Kit groaned when the phone interrupted them but rose to answer it anyway. "What a dumb thing to do. Hello."

"Kit, this is Beth Donnelly."

"Well, hi, what a nice surprise. I'm sure glad you came today."

"Me, too. I was wondering, I mean I had an idea for the quilt and I . . ."

"Interesting. Teza is here and we are going to work on the designing tonight. You want to come over?"

"Really? I mean I wouldn't want to put you out on the spur of the moment or anything."

"No chance. Come as soon as you can."

Kit hung up and turned to smile at Teza. "Beth Donnelly is coming to help us."

"Good. I'm looking forward to getting to know her better."

An hour later the three of them were studying the picture of the quilt the group had chosen to use.

"My grandmother always said she chose colors by their meaning and what she wanted the quilt to say. She said blue is the color of truth and red is for life and passion."

"And since burgundy is a blued red, that will fit really well too." Teza sat back. "We'll use the cream when we have some pieces with patterns, or cream on cream. That'll make the design much richer, too. See, here along the edge of the star, we're going to have to fill in with triangles to straighten the edge."

"What if we put the triangles in a blue print and that first border in either a solid blue or blue on blue?"

Beth took her pencil and began drawing on her pad of paper. "We could do the corners like this." She drew two squares, one a nine patch and the other another star with cream fill-in.

"If we did the nine patch, we could do one border of blocks, say the same size as in the nine patch but only two blocks high."

The discussion continued until Teza sat back in her chair. "This will be a work of art, that is for sure."

"I love the colors. I can just picture it." Beth studied the drawing she'd made.

"You have a real talent for drawing, don't you?" Teza pointed to the pad.

Beth looked from the pad to Teza and then to Kit, puzzlement creasing her forehead. "Not really, I mean this is just triangles and straight lines."

"All in balance and proportion," Kit added.

"I never thought of myself as an artist. I just make quilts and things."

"Fabric artist perhaps?"

Beth sat as if caught in a children's statue game. Her lips parted on an exhale, her eyes widened, and the corners of her mouth tipped up just enough to brighten her eyes. "You really think so?"

Kit and Teza swapped glances of delight — and nodded in perfect sync.

"I . . . I guess I'll have to think about this . . . I mean, I'm not, uh, real talented, you know."

"Right." Kit rolled her eyes. "Let's get some iced tea. I was hoping to get pattern pieces cut out tonight, but it's getting late."

"Are you going to use the plastic template stuff?"

"I think so, that way the cutters can work faster."

The three made their way down the stairs.

"I love the way you have all your family pictures on this wall." Beth stopped halfway down. "You have a beautiful family. What are their names?"

Kit stopped, too, and pointed to each picture as she named them. "That's Jennifer, our eldest. She just started her career in public relations in Dallas. This is Ryan, the youngest. He's attending Wazoo, or rather Washington State University in Pullman."

"And this?" Beth pointed to the third picture.

"That's Amber, she's . . ." Kit felt her throat close.

"She's waiting for all of us in heaven." Teza's soft words pooled in the silence.

"Oh." Beth swallowed and looked to Kit. "I'm so sorry. How can you stand it, I mean you are so . . . so . . . ?"

I can't stand it, I just keep on going. Kit

sniffed and ignored the urge to weep.

"How long ago?"

"Two years."

"Does it get any easier?" Beth whispered.

Three steps below the younger woman, Kit looked into Beth's eyes and understood. "How long ago was it for you?"

"Seven months. Our little boy died before he was born." She sniffed and chewed on her bottom lip, pools of tears darkening her eyes.

Kit took her hand. "I think no matter how old they are, the hole is there — in our hearts."

"Does it ever heal?"

"I hope so, Beth, I sure hope so."

"I . . . better be going, uh, it's getting late and . . ."

"Iced tea won't take but a minute." Teza put an arm around Beth's shoulders.

"No, I . . . I'll . . . I have to go." Beth broke away, and snatching her purse off the coffee table, headed for the front door. "Th-thank you."

"She's running even worse than you." Teza dropped her hand on Kit's shoulder. "Poor child."

FIFTEEN

"George, have you been listening to a word I've been saying?"

"Of course. You are figuring ways to get money for the new mammogram unit, whether we on the board think that is the best thing for our hospital or not." He picked up the book he'd laid in his lap and went back to reading. Or at least to turning the pages.

"Whyever would it not? Don't you men understand how important this issue is? Just because you don't have breasts . . ."

George laid his book back down and looked at her over the tops of his half glasses. "Have you looked into how much money we lost in the last couple of years offering mammograms?"

"So money is more important than women's health?" She could feel her jaw tightening, along with the back of her neck. She rolled her head from side to side and consciously relaxed her mouth.

"That's not the point."

He'd assumed his doctor-lecturing-a-dim-patient demeanor, which always made her want to snap back. She controlled the urge and smiled instead. "Then tell me what is the point." *Oh, Doctor, god of us all.*

"If we don't keep within the budget, we won't have money to keep the doors open, and then no one will get help of any kind. We haven't invested heavily in other new diagnostic equipment for the same reason."

"No, we invested in a new entry, new carpets, new furniture . . . the list goes on."

"You know that Jefferson insisted on all that and put up a good portion of the finances. After all, it was his money, and an overhaul of the entire complex was long overdue."

"And went way over budget."

"I can't be held responsible for that." He rubbed a hand back over his thinning hair. "If you hadn't missed those meetings, you'd have understood all that."

"Oh, I understand all right." *I'm not stupid, you know.* "And I know that Medicare cut back on the amounts they pay for mammograms —"

"And for reading the results. David Ashley doesn't work for nothing either. Although the way things are going, we'll all be working for next to nothing pretty soon. We're being regulated to death, and between the government and the HMOs, we're not allowed to treat patients like they should be or like we think they should be."

"George, I know all that."

"But you think we're taking it out on this one area of the hospital. Talk to the other departments, and you'll hear the same thing."

"So I'd think you'd be glad to have some outside help."

"Fine, you get the machine. Who's going to pay to operate it and read the results, let alone maintain the beast?" He kept his place with one finger and waved the book at her. "You have to look at the whole picture."

"Then recommend we close down the entire department and send our women to Olympia or Tacoma or even Seattle. Half of our older ladies have no way to get that far, and the other half will be screaming bloody murder, which they are going to do anyway if more studies show that the power lines are causing a cancer cluster in our area."

"I wish it were that easy, but that's why we've chosen to partially subsidize the mobile mammogram unit."

"Which is broken again and unable to travel."

"How do you know that?"

"Heard two people discussing it somewhere." Elaine's jaw was beyond relaxing now. Why couldn't they just talk without falling into an argument?

"I still think if it were the men getting squeezed and . . ."

"Oh, give it a rest, Elaine. That claim is an old boat that won't float." He set his book on the round table beside his leather chair and stood. "I'm going to bed."

At the sound, Doodlebug raised his head from the pillow where he'd been sleeping on the corner of the couch and yawned. He watched George exit the room before deciding to stay where he was.

Oh sure, just walk out. As usual, nothing is resolved. Even the Bug knows better than to go with you. Elaine watched George's stiff shoulders and rigid back as he strode out the French doors that closed off the library. Going after him would be a waste of time. He'd disappear into the bathroom, emerge sometime later, and crawl into bed, falling instantly asleep, all without glancing at her, as if she weren't even there. He'd perfected the routine to the point she knew he could practically do it in his sleep.

She picked up her glass of Chardonnay from the side table and sipped, staring out to the deck overlooking the lighted pool and on to the evergreens lower on the hillside. There had to be a way around this. Money was usually the way. Who in town might want to donate appreciable sums of money? The county? What about the power company? The oncologists? Having state-of-the-art diagnostic equipment here would keep the treatments closer too. Jefferson City was just too remote to require everyone to run to Olympia or Tacoma for diagnosis and treatment. The money was out there. She would just have to find it.

She stood and crossed to her cherry wood filing cabinet, pulling out the drawers one at a time, looking for all the grant materials she'd gathered over the years. Perhaps all the money needn't be raised locally. Perhaps the mammogram unit was just the beginning of an entire breast cancer specialty for Jefferson City. *If you build it, they will come.* That famous line regarding a baseball field in the middle of a corn patch was surely applicable here. Or was the adage "if life gives you lemons, make lemonade" even better? The women of Jefferson City were certainly being given lemons.

She'd do it in spite of a hospital board that couldn't see beyond its balance sheet. Someone had to have a bigger dream, why not her?

"I'll get it." The next morning Elaine swung the front door open with a smile.

"Registered letter for Elaine Giovanni." The courier held out a clipboard. "Sign right there, Mrs. Giovanni." He looked down at the dog yapping at her feet. "Hey, Doodlebug, you sure are a good dog."

Doodlebug nearly turned himself inside out with wiggles, then barked again as if proving he was in charge.

Elaine signed the clipboard and handed it back. "Yes, he thinks he's a Great Dane and tough enough to take on Goliath up the street."

"I don't trust that dog at all. When he stands beside Mrs. Tungsten, he's up to her waist and just stares at me, like he's daring me to make a wrong move. You ever seen him lift just one lip? Makes me want to stay in the truck. But she is so nice."

"I know, but once you are in his house, that big harlequin body just rolls over and begs you to rub his belly. He's all show." She took the letter without glancing at the address.

"Well, I tell you, he's made a believer out of me and every mail carrier or meter reader on this route. We all give him a wide berth." The slender man with the ready smile turned to leave. "You take care now."

Bug barked once again as she swung the door closed and read the return address. "Who could this be from?"

Doodlebug put tiny paws up on her leg and whimpered, then yipped when she ignored him.

"Hush, Bug, I don't have time right now." She slit the envelope open with the pewter letter opener on the walnut entry table that had been in her family for four generations, one of the few pieces she really cared about. Most of her other antiques had been purchased at estate sales and on her travels. She set the opener back in the inlaid wood tray and, pulling out the letter, read as she made her way back to her office.

"Good grief, the old bat turned this over to a lawyer after all. The nerve of her. Now I'm going to have to gather all the correspondence from the power company and everything, and then send it all over to Frederick. Why we didn't buy her out years ago is beyond me." She glanced down at her whimpering dog. Doodlebug looked as if she'd been beating him, ears low, tail dragging on the floor, eyes imploring her forgiveness. She scooped him up as she sat down in the leather chair behind the desk. "It's not you, silly dog, it's Bumblehead and Bootsie next door. Why can't I just call dear hubby and dump this all in his lap? No, in this house *I* call the lawyer. *I* have to be the one to search out the papers." She pulled out the file drawer from the credenza behind the desk and withdrew a folder that contained everything that had transpired regarding the fire. Knowing the old broad from prior incidents, she'd been prepared, but still, it was the thought of the whole thing. Maybe if George had gone over there years ago and laid down the law . . .

"He'd most likely have gotten his head beaten in by those cretins." She rubbed the dog's ears with one hand, while flipping pages with the other. "Huh, Bug?"

Pushing the numbers on the phone with one French-manicured nail, she patted the dog now curled in her lap as she waited.

"Yes, hi, Darcy, is Frederick available? This is Elaine Giovanni. No? No, just have him call me. If not in the next hour, then after five. I have a couple of errands to run. Okay, thanks."

"One more delay." She stuck the file back in the drawer and shut it. *How many times has that woman sued us, or at least threatened to, over the years? You'd think her attorney would be sick and tired of it, but then he makes good money off her.* Shaking her head, she set to making a list: fabric store, grocery store, dry cleaners. She tapped the end of her pen on her chin. *One more thing . . . ah, post office.* Tucking Bug under her arm where he liked to ride, she headed for her sewing room to pick up the list she had tacked on the cork board. One of these days she needed to go to a real fabric store, like the warehouse in East Portland. She added Celine's Attic to her list. Perhaps she'd gotten more antique laces and doilies in. Some of Elaine's most sumptuous pillows had come from unique finds at Celine's.

The phone rang as she was about to go out the door. "I'll get it," she called to Juanita. Thinking it to be Frederick, she said, "Thanks for returning my call so quickly."

Silence. "Uh, Mother?"

"Oh, Ramsey, dearest, I'm sorry, I

thought it was Frederick. How are you?"

"Why would he be calling you?"

Elaine sighed. "Long story involving guess who?"

"Mrs. Smyth up to her old tricks?"

"Of course. This time she is accusing us of negligence because the power lines fell in her backyard and started a fire."

"So?"

"So she says our trees broke the lines in that awful windstorm we had this spring."

"And did they?"

"No, the electric company said the lines were old and the wind snapped them. But you know Mrs. Bumblehead."

A chuckle. "Mother . . ."

"I swear she and that dog look just alike, back and front."

"I don't know why you and Dad don't just sell that house and move somewhere else."

"Your father move? Think of whom you are talking about here."

"What are you and Dad doing this weekend?"

"Uh, nothing much that I know of. Why?"

"I thought I'd fly home Friday and stay until Tuesday, if that's all right."

"Of course it's all right. Since when do

you need permission to come home?"

"Well, since I want to bring someone with me."

"Oh." *A guy? A girl? What's that sound in his voice?*

"I hope you'll like her."

Love, that's what it is. "I . . . I'm sure we will. Have you known her long? Does she have a name?"

"A few months and yes. Her name is Jessica Freewater."

"And you have a break now?"

"I can take one. I'm between rotations. I go to surgery next, so Dad will be happy. I need to get going, just wanted to check with you."

They said their good-byes and Elaine hung up the phone. A girlfriend. While Ramsey had dated in high school and college, he had never cared for any woman deeply enough to want to bring her home. *You should be excited,* she scolded herself, *not looking at this encounter with trepidation. Surely he would choose someone who would make a good doctor's wife. Someone with the patience of a saint.*

She knew George dreamed of his son coming into practice with him, not necessarily as a surgeon, but not a family practitioner either. Specializing would add to the years before Ramsey could do that. Had they talked about such things, these two men of hers? Obviously not in her company.

"I'm leaving now," she called as she opened the door to the three-car garage. "Is there anything else you can think we need?"

"No, all is well," Juanita responded.

All is well, now wouldn't that be a switch. Elaine opened the door to her silver BMW. She glanced over at the SUV and decided to stick with the BMW. She could put the top down if the sun came out, which looked like a strong possibility. A ride with the wind blowing her hair might do away with the thoughts of Mrs. Bumblehead. She checked her watch. While she'd allowed plenty of time earlier, the phone call had eaten away at it. Now she needed to hurry to meet Kit and Teza down at Myrna's Fabric Hut so they could choose fabric for the cancer quilt. Surely nothing else would slow her down now.

SIXTEEN

"Eat worms, red worms skinny worms . . ."

Beth heard the tune and tried to burrow farther under the covers. She shuddered at the thought, but the tune sung in Garth's strong baritone made her giggle.

"Garth, go away."

He leaned closer to her ear, and his breath tickled the hair curling around it.

Why can't I ignore the itch? Finally she dashed at her hair and rolled over to sit up. "Not fair." Blinking failed to dispel the sleep from her eyes, eyes that felt raw, as if they never got enough rest. That could be because the last time she glanced at the clock she saw a red five and two other numbers on the clock radio face. Now it said nine. Garth must have gotten up not long after she finally fell asleep.

"You've had your run?" Her voice cracked from lack of water.

"And weights and breakfast and . . ."

She put up a hand to stop his litany.

"And I brought you coffee just the way you like it, vanilla cream and one teaspoon sugar, well stirred." He picked up the mug from the bedside and wafted it in front of her face.

Inhaling the heavenly fragrance brought her closer to fully awake.

"Isn't there a commandment against torturing your wife?" Beth scooted the pillows up behind her and pressed against them, reaching for the mug as soon as she was situated. While the fragrance could be compared to ambrosia, the first sip always brought a smile to her face. She closed her eyes again, this time in bliss.

Garth sat on the end of the bed, studying her through eyes that assessed rather than loved.

She took another swallow before resting the cup on her thigh. "All right, what is it?" *I know I'm not going to like what he has to say.* She tried to read him, but his intense concentration set up a barrier. "Garth."

"I made an appointment for us with Doctor Kaplan. He's a Christian psychiatrist, a former pastor who has gone into counseling. I've known him for some time and" — he shifted under her steadily deepening glare, the pace of his speech picking up — "and I'm hoping and praying he can help us."

"By *us* you really mean *me*."

"Honey, whatever is going on with you is mortally affecting us, and now it is beginning to affect my ministry as well. I can't concentrate on the things I need to do when I'm so worried about you."

So now I'm single-handedly destroying not only my own life but the whole church. She felt like digging her fingernails into her scalp and ripping her hair out. Instead, Beth put the mug to her lips and drank two swallows, nearly gagging on the offered bribe. *Get me in a good mood so you can drop a bombshell on me, that's what you've done.*

"You can go if you want, but I'm not."

"Beth, please. Something is eating you alive, and you won't let me help. I don't know what else to do. Your mother even called me at the office she is so worried about you."

"Everything will be fine when I get pregnant." She stared at the coffee mug in her lap.

He let the silence stretch, and she could feel his gaze boring into the top of her head. All she wanted was to go back to sleep. Tired. She was so terribly tired.

Beth set the mug on the nightstand. "Excuse me, I need to use the bathroom."

After flushing the toilet, she turned on the faucet and squeezed toothpaste onto the toothbrush, scrubbing her teeth savagely, as if she could scrub away the words she wanted to hurl like spears in his direction. *How dare he make an appointment without consulting me first.* She could hear the two men: "Yes, I need help for my little wife. She's got a touch of depression." She rinsed her mouth and watched the water circle and gurgle down the drain. *If only problems could be dealt with like spit: Just wash them down the drain.* After washing her face, she took the brush from the drawer, returned to the bedroom, and sat on the edge of the bed as far away from her husband as she could get. She meticulously pulled the tangles out of her naturally wavy hair, cut slightly longer than shoulder length. Her hair had been the envy of her friends growing up, and now she kept it long because Garth loved it this way.

Maybe I should get my hair cut so I don't have to spend so much time with it. Maybe I could just crawl back under the covers until . . .

She could feel Garth's gaze piercing her back.

"I think we should go."

He'd tempered his voice again, using the tone that said he was trying to be reasonable, so why couldn't she try to be agreeable.

"Please, it's only an hour, and if you don't like him, we won't go again."

No, you'll find someone else and then someone else, and they'll try to dig out my whole life, and then you'll know and you'll hate me forever. "Please, Garth, give me a little more time. I'm sure I can beat it with a bit more time."

He shook his head. "I don't think you can. I've watched you, prayed for you, and made excuses for you, and all I see is you getting worse and worse."

"I went to the WECARE meeting with Mrs. Spooner. And yesterday to the quilting group — twice. I even volunteered to collect money for the supplies. I really like those women." *I cook and clean and do laundry and . . .* She had to stop. Which of those things, those necessary parts of her life, had she been doing with any regularity lately? She ran her inner eye over the past week. Ever since the Fourth of July, other than going to Kit's house, all she could see was the bed or the sofa and her sleeping on one or the other.

"I know you're finally making an effort,

but I can't handle this anymore."

The defeat in his voice ripped at her heart. *YOU can't stand it? What about me? It's not like this is something I choose to do.* Beth had to stop again. *You did choose. Those years ago, you made the choice.* She surged to her feet, heading back for the bathroom. Garth caught her midway to her destination and wrapped his arms around her. He held her close while the tears spurted forth again like an artesian *oil* well, bathing everything in black, a harbinger of death, not life like a spring of water was meant to be.

"Beth, I'm getting afraid you will do something to injure yourself."

She shook her head, but the words she needed to say clogged her throat. She stepped back from his embrace, her knees so weak she wasn't sure if they would hold her up. "What time is the appointment?"

Please don't whistle. Sitting beside Garth in the car on the way to the appointment several hours later, Beth tried to ignore the stabbing headache behind her eyes. The shower hadn't helped clear her head. All she'd wanted was to go back to sleep. At least when she was sleeping, the pain went away, if the nightmares didn't sneak up and throttle her. She rubbed her forehead and tried to close off her ears.

"Headache?"

She nodded gingerly. Movement aggravated it, and the motion of the car added nausea to the mix.

"Be sure you tell him how often the headaches come. Perhaps there is a physical reason. That's why I wanted you to see a doctor."

"I don't have a doctor yet." Nor a dentist, nor a hairdresser, nor a friend, nor a — Actually what she knew she needed most was a friend, a nearby friend, not like Shawna, who lived so far away. But building friendships took time and . . . and she rubbed her head again, wishing she could just rub the thoughts away too. It was all her own fault.

"The doctor will see you now." The friendly woman behind the desk smiled as she motioned them toward the door. "Go right on in."

Garth rose and handed her the clipboard with the form he'd been filling out. "Thank you." He took Beth's hand and led her to the door.

She wanted to pull back, say she'd wait for him out there, run from the room, anything but go toward that huge, dark, heavy door.

It opened just as Garth put his hand on the knob, and a man stood in the entry.

"Garth, good to see you. This must be your lovely wife, Beth." The man shook Garth's hand and extended his to Beth. "I've heard such good things about you. I'm James Kaplan."

"Good to meet you." She forced the words past trembling lips.

"Please, sit down." He motioned to three chairs set somewhat in a circle. "Take your pick."

While the two men exchanged further small talk, Beth took the burgundy leather wing-back chair that looked safe enough to hide in. She glanced around the room. Books filled some shelves, teddy bears, trucks and dolls occupied others, and a ten-gallon aquarium with several bright orange swordtails sat on a table in one corner. The room was decorated in earth tones set off by an abstract painting ranging from darkest midnight to the palest sky blue, and by a cobalt blue bottle on the windowsill. The windows revealed a bird feeder hanging from the eaves and overlooked a small garden. A concrete bird bath sat amid the spiky leaves and golden trumpets of daylilies. Altogether a placid spot.

Dr. Kaplan himself would be lost in a crowd of medium: medium height, medium brown hair, medium face with no distinguishing features except the warmth of his eyes. They flashed with life and beckoned confidences. His voice was deep of timbre yet gentle, like the kiss of a mother healing an owie.

Beth wrapped herself in her arms and tried to disappear into the leather comforting her skin. How well did he and Garth know each other, and how often had they discussed his poor little wife who couldn't get over the death of her child? She stared out at a goldfinch flashing his bright feathers as he dipped and fluttered in the bath. A tiny rainbow played hide-and-seek with the droplets he threw so vigorously about. A silence and the feeling she'd been asked a question brought her abruptly back to the room.

She looked to Garth, who was staring at his shoe tops, hands clasped, elbows on his knees. No, not he. Then to the doctor, whose gaze rested quietly on hers. "I . . . I'm sorry. Did you ask me something?" She swallowed. "I was . . . was just watching your birds out there." Her voice trailed off.

"They are a pleasure, are they not?" The doctor turned to smile at their entertainment. He straightened again and nodded toward her. "I just asked if you would like to tell me about yourself, help me to know a bit more about you."

Beth glanced at Garth. Same position, same closed-off look, as if he'd drawn away from her, left her stranded to — She could feel her heart rate pick up, her breath come more quickly.

"I . . . I . . ." She shrugged, not an easy task due to the grip of her elbows by her hands. "What do you want to know?"

"Oh, perhaps something you like to do."

"I love to sew, to quilt, to keep a good home for Garth." She paused, hoping he would ask her something else. Her mind screamed around a track like stock cars in a dead heat. She waited, but this time she couldn't pull the silence in around herself and hide in the chair.

"Tell me something you don't like."

He caught her by surprise. "Why . . ." She thought to the evening with Mrs. Spooner. "I don't like gardening, squishy things." *I don't like feeling the way I do, I don't like being here, I don't like — no that's not strong enough — I hate who I've become.*

Had she thought loud enough for him to hear?

"Can you tell me when this sadness began?"

Did I say that or did he surmise that?

He reached across the space, a tissue in hand, making her realize that tears were sliding down her face.

"After the baby died."

"That must have been terrible for you."

All she could do was nod and blow her nose.

"And that was how long ago?"

Two lifetimes. She glanced at Garth, who nodded for her to continue. "About seven months."

"And has there been another pregnancy?"

She shook her head. "No." One of the smallest words in the English language and the most deadly. A killer of dreams and a slayer of hope.

"And you blame yourself?"

"Wouldn't you?" The words lashed out before she could cut them off.

"Most likely. We all have a tendency to do that. It's part of the grief cycle, but we can go beyond that when we are ready."

Maybe you do, but . . .

"Have you ever taken any mood elevators, a simple drug that is nonaddictive but can help you deal with things more realistically?"

She sent Garth an I-told-you-so look. "No, and I don't want to start that now or any time."

"What is it about medications that bothers you?"

Beth stood and started for the door, catching both men by surprise.

"Beth, wait." Garth started after her.

"It was just a suggestion, not an order." Dr. Kaplan stood too. "Please, sit back down. Let me finish."

His voice plucked at her heart like gentle fingers plucking a melody from finely strung guitar strings.

She returned to her seat, perched on the edge, ready to flee. Her heart pounded and she clenched her fingers in her lap, the thumb on top, kneading the other.

"Are you eating?"

She shrugged. "All right."

"No, she isn't." Garth caught the explosive tone in his voice and replaced it with concern. "She's lost so much weight her clothes hang on her."

"I see. And sleeping, how is that?"

"I have a lot of nightmares and then I'm tired all day. So tired."

"Are you getting any exercise?"

She shook her head, knowing now that if she weren't honest, Garth would tell on her. "I used to walk." *I have a baby stroller so that we, or rather Garth, can even run with it. To get our baby out in the fresh air.* Garth must have put it up in the garage, or perhaps he'd gotten rid of it like she'd asked.

"I suggest you take up walking again. You know we have a good community center here. A group of women walk the track every day. Someone new is always welcome."

"Um." An almost nod. Now if that wasn't a noncommittal response . . .

"Do you like to read?"

"Yes."

"I have a book here for parents who've lost a child. Perhaps reading it would be helpful for you, and then when we meet next week . . ."

"Next week?" She stared at Garth. "You said . . ." She sank back. *Just agree, that doesn't mean you have to show up.* After all, who knows what can happen in a week? "I'll see."

"We'll be here." Garth stood and held out his right hand. "Thank you, Doctor. I appreciate your fitting us in on such short notice."

Beth kept her hand by her side and nodded, until he held out the book and she had to reach for it. "Thank you."

God, sometimes I wish I were a drinking woman. She followed Garth into the elevator and stared up at the numbers as they ground down the four floors to the street.

SEVENTEEN

The calendar never lies.

"We can't get in to Virginia Mason Hospital until the middle of August," said Kit into the mouthpiece.

"That will be fine, dear." Teza sounded vague.

"No, that will not be fine, but unless there is a cancellation, we're stuck with it." Kit leaned back in her chair, staring at the calendar on the wall above her desk. *Four weeks, almost five. Here, I've been on the phone for an hour. Why do I feel such a sense of urgency and Teza doesn't at all? This makes no sense. After all, it's her body, not mine.*

"Remember we're meeting Elaine at Myrna's at 2:00."

"Good. She has a new shipment in, some lovely shaded patterns that will go well with the prints."

When they hung up, Kit stared at the calendar again. Ryan would be home in about a month. Maybe Mark would come home then, at least for a few days. They could go to the Sound for Labor Day weekend. Well, not if Mark couldn't handle the memories. That place was rife with them. Kit stared at the family picture she had tacked to the corkboard on the wall of the built-in desk. Mark with his three teenagers, all in their swimsuits, the sun so bright on the water it sparkled in the picture. What a day that had been. She put her feet up on the desk and crossed her ankles. They'd had endless fun water-skiing back when they still had the boat. Mark had coached each of the children as they learned to ski. How Amber had loved water-skiing or anything connected with the water for that matter.

She could hear them laughing.

"Dad, you can't do it. You're too old to learn on a banana ski." Jennifer played spotter sitting in the back of the sixteen-foot runabout.

"Too old!" Mark and Kit yelped at the same time, he on the dock, Kit driving the boat.

"Too old, too old." Ryan and Amber chanted from their seats on the dock.

"Give it up, Dad." Jennifer could hardly talk for laughing.

"Just because I've tried three times and

your mother nearly drowned me, I shall never give up."

"You could take a break and give one of us a chance," Ryan, always a mediator, suggested.

"Don't mention the *b* word while I'm preparing to attempt this feat." He raised his voice. "Hit it."

Kit gunned the engine. The boat groaned and took off, and Mark absorbed the shock to his arms. To everyone's surprise, he held his balance and was skiing.

"Dad's up," Jennifer yelled, taking her job as spotter seriously.

"For how long?"

"He's signaling faster."

"Is he nuts?" Kit looked back in time to see her husband cutting over the wake on the port side of the boat.

"He's got it, Mom." Jennifer yelled above the roar of the engine. "Go, Dad, go!"

Looking in the rearview mirror, Kit could see her eldest daughter waving her arms and screaming her delight. Hair in a ponytail, her trim figure was shown to advantage by the black tank suit worn to gray on the rear. Kit looked over both shoulders before beginning the curve that would bring them back to the dock. "Signal your father to let go when we go by so one of you kids can take a turn." She, too, had to shout to be heard above the sixty-five horsepower motor, water curling along the sides of the boat, the slap of the bow when they hit a wake. The wind tangled her hair, the sun burned her nose, even through the sunscreen she'd applied but most likely sweat off. Much to her surprise, she'd become the ski driver, thinking in the beginning that she'd be the perennial spotter. But she loved the power in the throttle, the blue of the water, and the joy of seeing her family have such fun learning and then perfecting their water-skiing.

Kit eased back on the gas as she passed the floating dock, then cut way back and circled around to idle just off the end. Mark had skied right into the shore and stepped off without getting dunked.

"Show off."

"Took me a bit but I made it. Who's next?"

"Let Ryan go first, he's the baby." Amber poked her little brother.

"I should go first. I'm the oldest." Jennifer reached for a ski vest.

"You can go. I don't mind waiting." Ryan took the ski from his father and carried it out to the end of the short pontoon dock. "You want to go from here or start in the water?"

"From the dock." Jennifer threw a rope to the dock, and Amber pulled them close enough for Jennifer to climb out.

Mark gave her the instruction, and typically, Jennifer started to argue with him until he threw up his hands and stepped back.

"Do what you want, then."

She made it up on the first try.

Leave it to Jennifer, Kit thought as she followed Amber's instructions to speed up. Towing Jennifer was far easier than Mark, just because she was lighter. But when she took one hand off the bar to wave at some guys in another boat, down she went.

Kit cut the motor and slowly circled back until the tow rope came within Jennifer's reach.

"She's not ready yet, Mom." Amber flapped her hand at her mother.

"I know. See, Jennifer, guys'll get you in trouble." She didn't need to look to know that Jennifer wore a scowl on a face made red by something other than the sun.

"Okay, hit it."

Three failed tries later, Jennifer signaled them to pick her up. "I'll take two skis any day. That stupid thing just won't go straight coming up out of the water. The dock was a cinch."

She grabbed a beach towel and wrapped it around her. "That water's awful cold yet."

"I can tell. Your lips are blue."

By the end of the day, they'd had their fill of skiing, eaten all the fried chicken, potato salad, and Wacky cake, drank two gallons of pink lemonade, bought two six packs of soda, and finished those off too.

Kit pulled her thoughts back, only to realize she had tears meandering down her cheeks. Even the good memories brought on the tears.

"No wonder Mark doesn't want to be here. Maybe he's just tired of my tears." *Or maybe he needs to cry too — and can't.* The small voice sounded wise beyond anything Kit could come up with.

She glanced at the clock and propelled herself upright. She needed to wash, change, and make it to Myrna's Fabric Hut in twenty minutes.

How could I have spent half an hour at the lake without leaving the house?

Tapping her fingers on the steering wheel, Elaine waited to turn left at the light on Main. When the green arrow showed, she pulled out, staying in the center turn lane. She was just about through the intersection when a car that had been signaling a right turn, coming from the opposite direction, pulled out and swung too wide, clipping her right rear panel. The crash sounded like a demolition derby.

She banged the wheel with the heel of her hand and yelled several imprecations that didn't suit her ladylike demeanor whatsoever. "Just what I need, another tie-up. Why does everything always happen to me? Minding my own business and now look." She pulled over to the side of the street and stepped from her car, billfold in hand with all of her information. Striding back to assess the damage, she kept herself from screaming at the other driver only through a monumental force of will. *Oh, great, an old geezer who most likely shouldn't even be driving anymore. Why didn't I take the SUV? It's got a bumper strong enough to stop a tank.*

"I . . . I'm so sorry." The old man limped from his car and stood looking myopically at the damage. "I guess I hit the gas too hard."

"I guess you did all right. Do you have your insurance information?" She motioned him to the sidewalk so they were no longer in the road. *With my luck, we'll get hit by a passing looky-loo.* She glanced around. Where was a cop when you needed one?

"Ah, yes, right here." He fumbled in his back pocket and finally pulled out a leather wallet that should have been retired and interred years earlier. With shaky fingers he sorted through various cards and finally pulled out both his driver's license and an insurance card, laying them on the right front fender of his car.

Elaine did the same and took out her notebook to write down what she needed. The man lived out in the country. Finally looking at him, she realized how shaky he was. "Are you all right? I mean, did you get hurt?"

"No, no, I had my seatbelt on. And this blasted palsy, been suffering from it for the last couple of years. Getting old sure ain't for sissies, like that man said. Uh . . . Who was he? Famous comedian, you know who I'm talking about. Oh, pshaw, well, it'll come to me."

Elaine looked up from her writing. "You mean George Burns?"

"Yeah, that's the one, the short guy."

The old man's hands shook so badly, she wondered how she'd ever read his writing. And why is he still driving with such a condition?

"If you need a witness, ma'am, I saw what happened." A young man dressed in running clothes stopped beside her.

"Thanks." She took his name and phone number just in case. Who knew what this old man would claim after he thought about it for a while?

"Oh, and I called it in. The dispatcher said a patrol car should be here fairly soon."

Soon must mean one thing to the police and another to me. She checked her watch. They'd been standing around here at least fifteen minutes already.

By the time the city police arrived, she was ready to chew someone's ear off.

"Hey, Mrs. Giovanni, didn't realize it was you who got hit." Officer Hendrickson had been in her Sunday-school class some years before. "How's Ramsey doing?" He pulled out his pad and flipped it open as he inspected the damage to her car.

"Good, he's coming home for a long weekend." Elaine swallowed her anger and faked a polite smile.

"Good, good. Anyone get hurt here?"

"No, at least that's the consensus right now."

The officer checked the damage to the old man's car. "Sir, can you tell me what happened?"

Elaine listened as the man gave a totally truthful account of the accident. At least he was accepting blame for what had happened. Her insurance company would be glad to hear that.

"You have anything to add?"

"Not really. I know I was in my lane and had the right of way." She handed him her insurance card so he could finish filling out the paperwork. "What a pain in the keister," she muttered.

The officer gave her a sympathetic glance and extended his notebook for her signature. "You both need to fill out accident forms within twenty-four hours. Get them at the station and notify your insurance agents immediately." After getting the man's signature, he flipped his notebook closed. "That'll be all, folks." He turned to the old man. "Unless you think you need to be seen at the emergency room?"

"No, no, I just need to get about my business." He climbed back in his car. "Oh, would you please look at that fender to make sure I can turn corners?"

Elaine returned to her car and checked the rearview mirror to see Officer Hendrickson pulling the crumpled fender out from the wheel. She ran her fingers through both sides of her hair and let it fall back in place. One more thing to add to her to-do list, take the car in for an estimate.

"I didn't need this now. Why me?" *With my luck, he'll decide he's injured, probably have a heart attack and sue me.*

She pulled into the parking lot beside Myrna's Fabric Hut and looked once more at the damage on her way past. *George will most likely think it was my fault. Like I was speeding or something.*

She straight-armed the door to the fabric store and entered as though she had a strong wind behind her.

"My, you look ready to rip someone apart." Myrna looked up from where she was cutting fabric.

"An old man just hit me and crumpled the entire back side panel. Took almost an hour by the time the policeman finally got there and did his bit. Old geezer shouldn't be driving anymore, shaking like he does. What's this world coming to anyway?"

"What was his name, the man who hit you?"

"Donaldson, out on Lower River Road. You know him?"

"Of course, his wife has been coming in here for years. You know her, Esther, makes those wonderful angels. Has Parkinson's now and can't sew any longer. He takes care of her. Swears he won't put her in a nursing home like everyone tells him he should."

Elaine groaned. "Oh no. She made that angel for me one year, the one I hang above the fireplace. Now he'll probably lose his license." She thought back to her brusqueness at the site. *If only I'd put two and two together.* She shook her head. "What a mess."

"So how can I help you today? Besides your order that's here, I got some new tapestries in. I think you might like some of them. Wild animal prints are getting more popular all the time." Myrna led the way back to the upholstery fabrics.

Elaine trailed her fingers over the velvets as they passed. She'd need more of those for the holiday projects.

"Here we are." Myrna pulled out one of the racked rolls so Elaine could see more of the print.

"Gorgeous. Give me two yards of that one and the same on this. Oh, and look at this one with the roosters. Amazing how popular chickens have become all of a sudden. While you cut those, I'll go look for trims."

"I've got some to complement these. That red for the roosters was real hard to match. I saw something done with both sides of that one." She flipped the rooster print to show how appealing the back side was too.

"Good idea. Why don't you just give me your entire roll of quarter-inch cording?"

"Figured you'd be wanting that again soon, so I ordered extra. There's some gold lamé that might work too."

By the time Elaine was writing the check, she had two large bags full on the counter.

"Now is there anything else I can get you?" Myrna asked.

"Yes, I'll take these out to the car, and then I'm meeting here with Kit Cooper and Teza Dennison. They're heading up that quilt project to purchase a new mammogram unit for the hospital." She checked her watch. "Good thing they are running a bit late too."

"I heard about that. Was wishing I had time to take part in it." Myrna left her cash register to help Elaine carry out the sacks.

"We sure have been hit with a lot of breast cancer in this town. Every time I turn around I hear of someone else." She stopped to look at the damaged quarter panel. "What a shame. Accidents happen so quickly."

"I know. George is going to have a fit." *But I plan to do something about the cancer problem. I wonder what it would take to rally all the women in this county, or if that is even possible?*

"There're Kit and Teza now." Myrna waved as the two cars drove into the parking lot.

"Afternoon, Myrna." Teza hugged the store owner. "I suppose you've already heard that we're shopping for a special quilt." She smiled at Elaine. "I saw some of your pillows over at the hospital gift shop. My, but you do beautiful work."

"Thank you." Elaine gestured toward the bags in the backseat. "Myrna has some lovely new fabrics. I'm sure we'll be able to find what we need here."

The women made their way back into the store and ambled down the aisle to the calico section, all of them stroking bolts of fabric as they went, stopping to comment on something that caught their eye.

"What colors do you have in mind?"

Myrna snagged a shopping cart and brought it with her.

Kit turned from pulling out a bolt of fabric with a deep burgundy background. "From this to mauve, then several shades of royal blue, with creams."

"The pattern is a variation of the starburst." Elaine stopped at the cream section. "King size."

"Sounds lovely. Why don't we pull all the bolts that look like possibilities and then lay them out on the cutting table. I've installed a true color light above that table so we can really see the colors."

"What a good idea. I have one of those in my workroom now." Teza reached up to pull down a blue bolt and flinched before she could catch herself.

"Here, let me take that." Kit took the one bolt down and another near it. "That shoulder getting worse?"

"No, but you know how long it takes for pulled muscles to heal. I put Ben-Gay on it at night and that helps."

"Let's take some of those watercolor prints to the table too. They go really well in a quilt." Myrna pointed to another row of fabrics.

By the time they finished pulling bolts they had twenty on the wide cutting table, all separated according to basic color.

"How many colors do you need?" Myrna looked to Elaine.

"Kit has the design. I'm just one of the worker bees on this project."

"Oh." Myrna turned to Kit. "Sorry."

Kit laid her notebook open on the table and unfolded Beth's drawing, then turned the page to her list of supplies and fabrics. "We figured ten to twelve with six of the red family, three of the blue, and three creams. But that's why we're all here, to make those kinds of decisions."

"Okay. Then let's do the reds first." Myrna stacked the other bolts off to the side. They laid out ten ranging from light mauve to deep burgundy.

"Take this one away, too orange." Elaine pulled out one bolt and folded the end over before setting it back in the cart.

They debated, put two of the watercolor bolts in with the others, moved them around, pulled out two more.

"This starts with creams in the middle, right?" Myrna studied the drawing again.

"Unless we start dark and go toward the light." Teza laid one of the cream bolts at the dark end.

"No." Both Elaine and Kit spoke at the same time, half smiling at each other.

"I like the way you planned it here, with the light in the center, going toward the dark. Seems richer that way."

They finally settled on seven in the red tone. After stacking them up, they laid out the blue. Only two bolts worked, since some had too much yellow or green and others red.

"True royal blue isn't easy to come by." Teza laid another bolt in between the two they had and took it away again. "I like that solid one and this one with the small white flower in it."

"We could use the solid one for the backing too." Elaine fingered the folded edge of the bolt. "There's plenty here for that."

"I thought we'd back it in the dark burgundy." Kit tapped the bolt on the bottom of the stack. "The blue is just for accent."

"Hmm." Teza studied both bolts. "I don't want to be the tiebreaker. Myrna, what do you think?"

"Either one will be beautiful." She studied the fabrics. "What about the cream while we think on that."

With only three creams that looked good together, that was easy.

Kit looked toward her aunt and saw that eyebrow rise. Did she want to chew on shoe leather again? Not really, but the picture in her mind said a burgundy backing. The eyebrow inched upward. Kit sighed.

"You're right. The lighter blue will look lovely, and our stitching will show up well on it too." *Teza, you don't play fair, not at all. One would think you'd back your niece, your only niece for that matter.*

"Good." Myrna flipped one of the cream bolts over a couple of times so the fabric lay flat for cutting. "How much of this one do you need?"

Kit numbered each of the bolts according to where it would fit in the design and laid out the list of required yardage. "I've added extra in case someone loses or ruins their square. The worst thing would be to run out of something after all the cutting."

"Well, if that's the last decision, I need to run." Elaine glanced at her watch. "Amazing how time can rip by in a fabric store."

"Thanks for your help." Kit reminded herself to warm up the smile and tone. "We'll be cutting next Wednesday."

"You already put the article in the paper?"

"No, Harriet did. It will run on Friday."

"Good. I'll see you then. Oh, who's going to wash all this?"

"I will, no big deal. They can iron it at the cutting."

"Thanks, Myrna. And you'll do the discount?"

Myrna nodded. "I planned on it anyway."

By the time they finished cutting fabric and batting, bagged it all, and Myrna figured the discount, most of another hour had passed. Teza looked around for her fruit prints while Kit chatted with Myrna.

"This is going to be a beauty," Myrna said more than once. "I love seeing a quilt go from idea to finished product, and this one is going to do a lot of good. You mark my words, this quilt is destined to be a real blessing, most likely more than any of us know."

"I hope so."

"I don't just hope so, I know so." Myrna patted the bags. "This is a God project. The blessings will be there."

Kit stifled a sigh and pasted on a pleasant smile. Another one like Teza. Sometimes she felt ganged up on from every side.

EIGHTEEN

"I don't want to go back there again."

"Come on, Beth, what was so terrible about it?" Garth pushed the coffee cup on the kitchen table to the side and leaned forward.

Beth forced herself to sit quietly. After all, this was just Garth across the table, and they were in their own home. Nothing to be afraid of here. *Afraid. Where had that word come from?* She tried to think, but the darkness seemed to seethe around her ankles like octopus arms, the sucking cups clinging to her, dragging her down.

"What are you afraid of?"

Now you sound like the doctor. "There must be some other way."

"Some other way to what?" He smoothed his hair back with both hands, as if needing something for his hands to do.

"To . . . to help me."

"You do agree that you need help?"

Beth stared down at her hands clenched in her lap, one thumb wearing the skin off the other. "I . . . I guess so. If . . . If I could just have a baby, everything would be all right. I know it would. So why won't God give us a baby?" *You know why. It's all your fault. You killed one, and God took the other. Why should he trust you with any more?* Beth squeezed her eyes shut and tangled her fingers in her hair, pulling, moaning to block out the voices in her head.

"Beth! Beth! What are you doing?" Garth came around the table and grabbed her hands. "Stop, Bethy, honey. What is happening to you?"

She watched as if from the other side of a wide chasm, seeing herself writhing in the chair, long mahogany hairs floating to the floor, seeing the tears run down both their faces, feeling the despair that oozed up out of the cavern and enveloped her in blackness.

When she awoke some time later, she was lying in bed, Garth stretched out beside her, sound asleep. She lifted her hands to find them wrapped in towels with duct tape bracelets holding them in place. *What . . . what have I done?* Her scalp burned and itched. She wanted to scratch it, but that was impossible with the boxing gloves on. *Think, what happened?* She remembered sitting at the table, remembered the frantic feeling — from what? What had they been talking about? *Think, Beth, think.* But nothing would come, other than a blackness that, like a black paintbrush, painted over any thoughts that made sense.

Sleeping was far easier than thinking.

When she woke again to a raging thirst and an imperative need for the bathroom, Garth was gone and her hands were still covered and taped. She swung her feet to the side of the bed and stood. A wave of dizziness almost sat her down again. But she had to go too bad to wait.

"Garth! Garth!" The croak went no farther than the bedroom door. No way could she get her slacks down with the mitts on. She staggered to the door and out into the hall. "Garth!" She screamed his name. Nothing. Where had he gone? With the pressure mounting she tore at the duct tape with her teeth, catching the edge on her right wrist and peeling the tape off bit by bit. She shook off the towel and headed for the bathroom and relief. Her anger burned bright and quick. Whatever possessed him to bind her hands like that and then just leave her? What could she possibly have done to deserve such treatment?

She stormed down the hall, through the kitchen and out the back door, sure he must be working in the garden. But only the flowers and the birds with a butterfly or two filled their backyard. Next door the children were laughing and teasing, with the sound of an adult voice nearby. In the yard on the other side of theirs, the neighbor boy played with his dog, someone else laughing at their antics. All the world had children but her. She massaged her scalp with her fingertips and stared at the hairs that came out with her hands when she stopped. "Good grief, am I losing my hair now too?"

"No, not until you pulled it out."

She jerked around to stare over her shoulder. She clapped a hand to her heart, felt it race under her palm. What he'd said penetrated, sending her heart tripping even faster. Her breath caught in her throat. "What do you mean?"

He sat down on the step beside her. "You don't remember?"

"I remember waking up with towels taped to my hands and having to go to the bathroom so bad I nearly wet my pants, and you were nowhere around to help me. Whatever got into you?"

"Into *me?*" He took a breath and lowered

his voice. "Beth, you were screaming and pulling your hair out."

"Don't be ridiculous!" *Garth, what are you doing? Trying to make me insane? Or am I insane?* "I remember we were sitting at the table talking, and the next thing I remember is waking up in bed and my hands were in mitts, but you were sound asleep beside me, and before I could say anything, I fell back asleep. And then you were gone."

"I covered your hands so you wouldn't hurt yourself."

Beth kept shaking her head as he continued.

"You tore at your hair and then you fainted, fell right off the chair. I carried you to bed and was going to call the doctor, but you seemed to be just sleeping, so I waited. You slept for a couple of hours. I knew you were exhausted, so I covered your hands and took a nap too. Dr. Kaplan said that a mild tranquilizer might help, so I went down and he gave me some samples. I thought I'd be back before you woke up."

"You're not making this up, are you?" She knew the answer by the look on his face. One thing about Garth, he never told a lie. Not even a polite one. She covered her face with her hands, ashamed to look at him. "Garth, I'm so sorry. I'm so ashamed."

"Ashamed for what?" He put his arm around her, but she pulled away.

"The way I acted."

"I think you are real close to a nervous breakdown, and Dr. Kaplan agrees with me. He'd like you to call him. He'll see you anytime. I think he'd even make a house call if we asked him."

Beth could tell Garth was trying to keep this light, as if they were discussing nothing more important than what to have for dinner. She clasped her arms around her legs and laid her cheek on her knees. Nervous breakdown. They put people in mental hospitals for nervous breakdowns.

"I'll take the pills, okay? Did he say what the side effects might be?"

"Sorry, I didn't ask, but they're probably on the package." Garth rose and returned in a minute or so with a glass of water and a capsule, taking the steps down to the lawn so he could hand them to her, all the while watching her as if afraid she might go off again.

She put the pill on her tongue and chugged down half the water, then held the glass in both hands, resting it on her knees. *I never dreamed I'd be taking pills for my sanity. Good old anti-pill Beth, look what you've come to.* When he sat down beside her, she laid her head on his shoulder. "Did we have lunch?"

"Nope, you didn't have breakfast either, other than a cup of coffee. You feel up to José's?"

"I'd rather stay home."

"Fine. I'll go get tacos or something. You have a preference?"

"No. Whatever you decide." She clasped her arms around her legs again.

"You sure you'll be all right here alone?" He laid a hand on her shoulder, and she laid her cheek against it. She nodded. He bent down and whispered in her ear. "I'm glad you took that pill."

I hope I will be. "It's not Prozac, is it?"

"No. But I don't remember the name. You can look on the box. It's in the bathroom."

"Umm."

After Garth left, Beth moved over to the padded lounger and set the back at half reclining. A mew from bushes beside the patio made her sit upright again. "Hey, kitty, is that you?" While the half-grown cat had seemed to establish this yard as his territory, he still hadn't let Beth pick him up. She watched the rhododendrons, and sure enough, there he came, sneaking out from the safety of the bushes. He sat on the edge of the concrete patio and began to clean himself.

"You look more like a cat now than a roughneck stray."

He stopped licking his front paw and looked over at her as if waiting to see what she would do next. When she neither moved nor spoke, he went back to his grooming.

"You've sure been cleaning up the food."

Lick, scrub ear, lick, wipe eyebrows, lick, back to side of face. He changed paws and started on the other side of his mottled coat. With dusk coming on, he faded into the shadows without changing his position.

"I wish, if you really are going to be our cat, that you would let us help you. And I don't mean just feed you." *Anyone who came by here would think I truly am batty, talking to myself.* She let herself sink into the cushions, her eyes drifting shut. Even clasping her hands over her middle became too much like work, so they fell by her sides.

At a sudden weight on the cushion by her knees, her eyes jerked open just in time to meet the gaze of the questing cat. She smiled and closed her eyes again. She felt him turn around and settle into a circle, the heat of him warming her knee. When he began to purr, she marveled at the depth of it for such a small cat, the sound sinking her ever deeper into peace. If only she could stay like this, neither awake nor sleeping. No nightmares, no pointed looks from Garth, no one yelling in her mind. Perhaps the pills weren't so bad after all.

Beth thought about the other evening working with Kit and Teza. Such nice people. *I wish I'd stayed for iced tea. Perhaps the cancer quilt will help me make new friends.*

The purring vibrated against her knee. The kitten trusted her enough to sleep beside her. Perhaps she could trust Dr. Kaplan. Or Kit. Kit had lost a child too. *But will she hate me if I tell her my secret?*

NINETEEN

"Have I forgotten anything?"

Missy followed at her ankles as Kit returned from one more trip to the car.

"I know you don't like to be left alone so much, but this is really important."

Kit bent down and rubbed Missy's ears. "Now it's your job to take care of the house, you know."

A sigh answered her admonishment, a sigh that only a put-upon basset could state so emphatically. Missy lay down, her chin on the floor, since her front feet didn't extend far enough to cushion her jaw. Her gaze followed Kit from kitchen to sewing room to retrieving her purse on the entry table to checking to make sure the back door was locked.

"You be good now." The soulful gaze from the dog on the floor followed her out the door.

"Worse than a toddler, that's what she is." Kit tossed her purse on the passenger seat and gave herself one more moment to check her inventory before heading to the Senior Center.

She'd washed all the fabric, but it needed to be ironed before it could be cut, so her haul included an ironing board. The Senior Center had another, and Teza was bringing a third.

Kit waved at her neighbor and took a sip from the silver-and-black stainless steel coffee mug with a top to keep the contents hot for a long time. Ah, modern conveniences did make life easier at times. On the other hand, she didn't used to drink so much coffee. Her full cup was always getting cold. She hated to think how many gallons of cold coffee she had poured down the drain.

She honked and waved at Thomas riding his bike on the sidewalk. *Time to invite him back for a Missy tussle.*

Unloading her things at the center, Kit stacked as much as possible on the luggage cart. At least she hadn't had to drag her sewing machine along too.

Inside, she glanced around the room, assessing how to set up most efficiently.

"Good article we had," one of the women said, waving the clipping. "Did you write it?"

"No, that was Harriet's job. There was another one in the *Shopper's Weekly,* too."

Several women gathered round to help set up.

"I brought a full carton of gallon Ziploc bags and the diagram for piecing each square." Sue held up the box.

"What if we get someone who can't sew well?"

"Anyone can sew a quarter-inch seam."

"Don't count on it. That's why we make up some extra bags." Kit set the enlarged diagram she'd drawn on a thirty-inch pad of paper up on the easel. The pieces were numbered in sew order, which to sew to which. "Just like the handout you have, right?"

"Sure. I sewed several to make sure this was the easiest way." Sue laid out her completed squares, done in leftover bits and pieces to use as examples. "I'm going to turn these into potholders when we're done." She flipped the diagram sheets to show a ten-inch square in a heavy outline. "After they've pressed them, they lay their finished pieces on this to make sure they've sewn it all to scale."

"I'm impressed. Good thinking. You really think we'll get someone showing up who can't sew? After all, the articles read 'all quilters.' "

"Better safe than sorry."

As the women talked they set out patterns, quilting squares, rotary cutters and cutting mats.

"Those who aren't experienced with these things" — Kit held up a rotary cutter — "we'll set to pressing fabric and filling the plastic bags."

"Sorry, I'm late." Teza breezed in and set down her carry-all with quilting supplies. "Here." She handed Kit a plastic bowl. "I brought apricots for a snack."

As more women filed in, the tables gradually filled, and the noise level rose in proportion.

At Kit's insistence, Teza stood at the front of the room, and when the chattering continued, she clapped her hands to get their attention.

"Welcome, welcome, ladies." She waited before continuing, then spread her arms wide and embraced them all. "As my mother always said, 'many hands make light work', and with all of you willing to participate, why, we'll have this quilt finished in no time. As you know, we have chosen to make this quilt" — she pointed to the large colored-in picture of the finished quilt — "to earn money for a new mammogram unit for the hospital. We need to give Kit Cooper credit for the idea." She pointed to Kit and everyone clapped. "But all of us will now have a part in making that dream come true. The quilt will fit a king-sized bed, so we won't bother to count all the stitches it will take." At their ripple of laughter, she smiled back. "At this point, since I see some new faces here, I'd like everyone to stand and introduce yourself. I'll go first since I'm already standing. I'm Teza Dennison, and I've been quilting longer than some of you have years. I have no idea how many quilts I've made or helped with." She pointed to Kit, who stood as commanded.

"I'm Kit Cooper, and while I haven't been quilting as long as Aunt Teza, she taught me, so I learned from a master."

At Teza's nod Beth stood. "I'm Beth Donnelly, and I'm new in town. My husband is Pastor Garth Donnelly of the Jefferson City Community Church. I've been quilting for five years or so, but this is my first time on a community project like this." She sat down and smiled back at Aunt Teza.

The woman next to her, as dark as Beth was fair, stood and flashed a smile around the room. "I'm Elsie May Sojourner, no relation to the famous one, and I learned quilting at my grand-mammy's knee, where if you didn't do it right, you kep' redoin' it until you did. I wore out more than one piece in the learnin'." Her rich voice matched the twinkle in her dark eyes.

"Welcome, Elsie May. Haven't seen you for a long time."

"Well, I had to go on down home and take care of my mother. She died a month or so ago from breast cancer." Her voice cracked in the telling. "That's why I want to do anythin' I can to help fight this vicious disease. My mama didn't deserve to die so young."

"Uh, Elsie May, I'm so sorry to hear that." Teza nodded to the next woman.

"I'm new in town too. My name is Dawn Engels, and I have one question. I can sew my square on the machine, can't I? My hand stitching is for the birds."

"That's right, machine stitching for the piecing and hand quilting when we have it all together." Teza smiled at the newcomer. "Welcome to Jefferson City." She smiled at the woman at the end of the table. "Mrs. Giovanni?"

Elaine stood and smiled around the room. "I'm Elaine Giovanni and I've been sewing since I was old enough to hold a needle but unable to thread it. I haven't done many quilts. Pillows are my specialty.

I'm hoping we can get more than just this group working to raise money for the mammogram unit. Ladies, we need better medical care in this town, and I believe it is up to us to let our needs and demands be known."

Applause ricocheted around the room as she sat back down.

Two more stood before Teza continued. "I thank you all for coming, and now we'll let Kit lay out the plan for the day."

Kit stood beside the easel and flipped to the diagram. "I'm going to walk you through the piecing as a refresher, and then we'll all split up to work on whatever section you'd like, probably trading off so the cutters don't get sore muscles. If you brought your own equipment, make sure you have your name on it."

Within a few minutes three people were standing at the ironing boards, and others had lined up to pick up the sturdy plastic patterns for the pieces they would cut.

Teza made her way to Beth's side. "Hi, Beth. I'm so glad you joined us the other night. How have you been?"

"Fine. I even managed to get my sewing machine set up." Beth's smile wore trembles of hope.

Teza looked into her soul and saw sorrow. "Good for you. I would be lost without mine. Beth, I was wondering . . . After the blocks are done, would you like to be one of the hand-quilters on this masterpiece? We might be doing that here, but I have a feeling the quilting frame will be set up at Kit's. You saw her nice big living room, and it isn't being used for much right now."

Beth gripped Teza's hand as though she'd caught a lifeline. "Oh yes, oh yes, I would love to. I mean you haven't seen my work yet or anything but . . ."

"You'll do wonderfully, I can tell." The urge to take the young woman in her arms made Teza give her a slight pat on the shoulder. "You take care now, you hear?"

"Yes, of course." Beth nodded and loosed her hand.

Like an animal retreating into its den, Teza thought. *Something is definitely wrong here, but there is nothing I can do at this point. Oh, wait, there is.* "Do you and your husband like apricots?"

"Of course."

"Perhaps you'd like to come out to my place and pick some. They are just coming on."

"You have an orchard?"

"Oh my, yes. Come and see."

"I'll ask him."

"Good." Teza pointed to Harriet Spooner standing at Beth's side. "I think she wants to talk with you."

"Thank you."

Those eyes, dear Lord, what is it this child needs?

Teza continued on around the room, stopping to talk with each woman, most of whom she knew to varying degrees.

"Hi, Teza." Elaine looked up from where she was cutting deep burgundy triangles, her rolling blade sharp against the heavy plastic ruler.

"Good to see you again. Thanks for helping choose the fabrics."

"You're welcome. Anything to get us a new mammogram unit." She made another cut. "Have you thought of marketing possibilities yet?"

"No, not really. That is more in Kit's line. You should talk to her."

"Oh, I will. I've been thinking how this group, the guild, and anyone else we can rope in could all work together. We can make big things happen that way."

"I'm sure. I stopped by the guild booth at the Fourth of July. Your pillows are true works of art."

"Thank you. I do love to make them." Elaine stared down at her hands. "Must be that Puritan ethic, got to keep one's hands busy." She moved her plastic quilting square. "Isn't there an old saw about empty hands being the devil's workshop?"

"Something like that." Teza looked up when she heard Kit call her name. "Excuse me."

"Hobnobbing with the hoi polloi, I see." Kit stopped in her rush to make sure someone else had the supplies she needed.

"I think we should ask Elaine if she'd like to be one of the hand-quilters."

"Elaine Giovanni?" Kit's right eyebrow flirted with her bangs.

"I think she needs us."

"Like another hole in the head." Kit paused. "You're serious, aren't you?"

"Very much so."

"If you want to, go for it, be my guest, whatever."

Some chose to work right on through lunch, while others broke to eat with the usual senior crowd. Through the afternoon, helpers came and went as they had time. By four o'clock, the last of the Ziplocs was sealed and distributed. Each woman signed her name, address, and phone number on the checkout sheet.

"Now remember," Kit repeated again, "these have to be returned to me by August second. We want to hang this for display as close to the first of October as possible."

If she heard "no problem" once, she heard it fifty times. Some women took one or two squares and others ten, but all promised to have them completed within the allotted time.

"The sooner the better." Kit's response came automatically.

"Are you sure you really want me to help hand quilt?" Beth stopped beside Teza at the table.

"Of course, my dear. And I do hope to see you out at Bit of Heaven Farm. Just go out Old River Road. You can't miss it on the left."

"Thank you."

Teza watched as Beth left the room, her plastic bags clutched in one hand. She glanced down to see that Beth had taken five and promised to take others if someone got in trouble with meeting the deadline.

"Thank you all for your help." Kit turned from loading her ironing board into the van while the others also packed up their things.

"You are most welcome. It will indeed be a beautiful quilt." Sue kneaded her back. "I need to learn to cut sitting down."

"Or raise the tables."

"That's what I did at home. Followed that extension woman's advice and made my machines, tables, chairs, and everything ergonomically correct for me. Cut back on my chiropractor calls fifty percent."

"Really?" Kit pulled the rear van door down and slammed it shut.

"You should have Mark raise your sewing table up tall as you are."

"Good idea, I'll suggest that." *If and when he ever comes home.*

TWENTY

"Can Missy come out and play?"

Kit looked down at the dog dancing at her feet, then out to the boy. "Do you think she wants to?"

Missy yipped, but before she could get her front feet up on the screen door, Kit opened it and out she went. Her deep bark played counterpoint to Thomas's little-boy giggle. When she charged him, he fell back on the grass and threw his arms around her neck, both of them rolling and making all the noises small boys and dogs are supposed to make.

Kit watched for a few moments then headed back to her sewing room. The ringing phone stopped her. She snagged the phone as she went by. "Hello."

"Kit, this is Beth Donnelly. Sorry to bother you but . . ."

"No bother at all. How are your squares coming?"

"That's my problem. I guess something happened to my sewing machine in the move. It isn't working right at all, so I had to take it in to the repair shop."

"To Barnaby?"

"Yes, he said he can have it back to me in a week, but that doesn't give me any time to sew them."

"I have an extra machine here. Why don't you come on over, and we can have a sewing party, you and me?" Kit glanced out the door where dog and boy were mashing the grass.

"Really?"

"Of course. Half an hour?"

"I'll be there as soon as I can. Thanks."

Kit hung up and continued to the stairs. Something puzzled her about Beth's voice, but she couldn't quite put her finger on it. Up in the sewing room she cleared away the red, white, and blue pieces that would be a quilt for Ryan — his Christmas present — so Beth could use that machine. She'd done one for Jennifer's first Christmas away from home, and now she should have all kinds of time to make Ryan's — *should* being the operative word. She glanced up to a framed cross-stitch piece she kept at the top of her cork and peg board: "Thou Shalt Not Should Upon Thyself." She'd bordered it with red hearts and a twining vine. So many shoulds. She should go help Aunt Teza. She should make more of an effort to help Mark. While she had no idea how to help him, she knew she should be doing something. She should go out and mow the grass. She should go back to church, but why? All she did was cry through the service, which made everyone around her uncomfortable, and then they didn't know what to say — so to make it all easier for everyone, she stayed home.

Besides, why should I praise you when you let me down?

In everything, praise ye the Lord.

"That's not fair. I memorized Bible verses when I was a kid, and now you bring them back to me. I don't want them, can't you tell?"

Her eyes filled and she sniffed back the tears. Far as she could tell, God didn't play fair at all.

I will never leave you nor forsake you.

"See, that's what I mean." She finished sewing the first two pieces of each block, as if stringing one bead after another. Now to cut them apart and press the seams flat. She stood and took her long string of pieces to the ironing board, where she had a cutting mat, rotary cutter set up, and the iron ready to steam.

"Mrs. C?"

She turned to smile at Thomas. "What can I do for you?"

"Can I take Missy for a walk?"

"Sure you can, but don't be gone too long."

"Down to the park?"

"Okay, but don't let her off the leash. And I never tie her up anywhere either."

"Okay." He leaned against the doorjamb. "What are you doing?"

"Sewing pieces of fabric together for a quilt."

"Who's the quilt for?" Hands in his shorts pockets, he ambled across the room to study the ironing board and all its paraphernalia.

"We're going to auction it off to make money for a new machine for the hospital. Are you hungry or thirsty?"

"You got any Popsicles?"

"No, but I have cookies." She reminded herself to add Popsicles to the grocery list.

"Okay."

Back down in the kitchen, she held out the cookie jar. "Peanut butter all right?"

Thomas nodded and helped himself to two. "Thank you." He started for the door, then turned to look at her. "You coming?"

Well, I wasn't planning on cookies right now but I guess so. "Okay." So much for sewing pieces together. She followed him out to the deck, where she took one Adirondack chair and he the other. Missy flopped on her side, one long ear covering her eye.

"When is your boy coming home?"

"Another couple of weeks."

"Does he like school?"

"Sounds like it. He won't get much of a summer vacation this year."

"Your dad coming home too?"

"My dad? Oh, you mean my husband?"

"Uh huh. What's his name?"

"Mark Cooper. Our son's name is Ryan."

"My middle name is Mark."

"Are you named after your dad?"

"Nope. So when is he coming home?"

I wish I knew. Why do you have to ask so many questions? "You ready for another cookie?"

He nodded. "I'll get it."

The screen door banged behind him as he returned and handed her one. "What kind of cookies did Amber like?"

"Chocolate chip. Jennifer . . ."

"That's your biggest girl."

That's my only girl now, at least the only one I can still talk with. "Yes, she liked peanut butter best, and Ryan loves Oreos."

"My sister likes Oreos best too."

Ah, something about your family. "What's her name?"

"Lindsey."

"How old is she?"

"Fifteen. She likes to watch soaps. Ugh."

"Ugh is right. Well, I better get back to work."

"I could help you." He fingered a frayed edge on his shorts.

"Ah, okay. I thought you wanted to take Missy for a walk."

"She's too tired." He nodded at the softly snoring dog, who hadn't moved from her original position.

What can I have him do? "Sure, come on and help me." *Where's his mother? Did she die? But wouldn't he have told me when we were talking about Amber?*

"You ever pitted apricots?"

"What are apricots?"

"Sort of like peaches but smaller." Pleased with her idea she led the way back into the house. "You can pit them, and I'll cut them up."

She pulled the produce drawer clear out of the refrigerator and set it on the table. "These are apricots."

"Can I eat one?"

"Yup." She took out another bowlfull. "You get those two big plastic bowls out from under there" — she pointed to a cabinet door — "while I get the knives. You like it?"

He shrugged. "Okay."

Once they had the supplies set up on the picnic table, she demonstrated how to hold the apricot with one hand and slice it in half. "The pits go in this bowl and the fruit in that one." She watched him as, tongue between his teeth, he did exactly as she had shown him, except for the pit that went thumping onto the desk. "Wheeoo."

"You might want to point them into the bowl. If Missy finds them, she chews on them and might crack her teeth."

"Oh. Are apricot pits harder than bones?"

"I don't know."

"Well, bones don't crack her teeth."

"True, but if she cracked an apricot pit, the inside seed might not be good for her."

"Is it poison?"

"I don't know."

"If a new apricot plant comes from the seed, how can it be poison?" All the while he plied her with questions, he continued slicing apricots, as if he'd been doing so for years.

"You know, you learn fast how to do

things. Are you sure you are only seven?"

"I'll be eight in October."

"Oh, that explains it." She kept the smile inside.

" 'Splains what?"

"How come you learn so fast."

He shrugged. "I'm smart, too." No hint of bragging, just a fact.

"How do you know that?"

"My dad says so."

Ah, good for your dad. "You think if I invited your family for dinner one night, he would come?"

"If he got home from work in time."

"How about Friday?"

"We can ask him."

"Good, I'll call him tonight."

Thomas frowned. "Maybe I better tell him to call you."

"Okay." She held her dripping hands over the edge of the bowl. Cutting up apricots was not a job for one who wanted to keep her hands clean.

"Thanks for all your help." She would put all the apricots in plastic bags in the freezer for now, then bake a pie when Ryan came home, but turn most of them into jam when she had more time during the winter.

"What time is it?"

She checked her watch. "Almost one."

"I better go home."

"Are you late?"

"Not much." He picked up the bowl of pits. "In the trash?"

"No, over in the compost heap. The middle one of those three wooden bins down the bank there." She pointed to the wooden structures.

"What's compost?"

"New soil for the garden."

"And you make it?" His eyes grew round. "I didn't know anyone could make dirt."

"You just dump the pits down there, and I'll explain how it works some other time." She watched him trot dutifully down the slope, Missy right beside him. She picked up the full bowls of golden fruit and, stacking one in the empty crisper drawer, took them into the kitchen. While this wasn't what she had planned on for the moment, at least the apricots were ready to bag.

Thomas stuck his head in the back door. "I washed my hands at the hose. Did you know Missy likes to drink out of the hose? Bye."

"Thanks for helping me," she repeated.

"Welcome." His voice came from beyond the deck.

She went to the door and watched as he carefully made Missy stay inside the yard and then locked the gate behind him.

"I think he's an old man in a boy's body."

The doorbell rang as she poured the last of the fruit into gallon-size freezer bags and sealed them. "Coming." Wiping her hands on a dishtowel, she opened the front door. "Come on in, Beth. I have to put these apricots in the freezer, so you go on up. I cleared off the Singer for you."

"Do you need some help?"

"No thanks. I'll bring up iced tea, too." Kit motioned her guest toward the stairs and continued on her way to the kitchen.

She could hear the machine already purring away when she mounted the stairs, taking two glasses of tea along with sugar and sweetener on a tray. "You picked that up fast."

"It's just like my machine, only a bit older. My mother gave me hers when she bought a new one. When it wouldn't run, I about panicked." Beth laid her hands in her lap. "Not knowing where to go for anything in town can be so frustrating."

"I really admire people like you who can move to a new town and settle right in. I've lived in this house ever since Mark and I married."

"Did you grow up here too?"

"Yes, never have done much seeing the world." Kit held out the tray. "I wasn't sure what, if any, you used for sweetener."

Beth took the glass and waved away the sugar. "Hard to believe there really are people who've lived in one house all their life."

"Other than college, I'd never lived in more than one house before either." Kit sipped her tea and set it on a coaster on a cabinet beside her machine. "The iron is on. If you need anything, I'm sure it's here." She moved the ironing board so Beth could use it more easily too and began cutting her pieces apart and pressing the seams flat. As she finished each one, she set it on the growing stack at the end of the ironing board.

Two hours later, they'd sewn, pressed, and chatted more like longtime friends than just acquaintances when Beth asked, "Kit, how do you deal with missing Amber?"

"I don't." Kit stopped. "No, I'd better rephrase that. I just keep putting one foot in front of the other and go on. Keeping on keeping on, I guess."

"Do you get angry sometimes?"

"Oh yeah." *More than I could tell you.*

"I don't know which would be worse. Never knowing your baby or having her taken from you older."

"I don't either, but I suspect the gaping wound is always there." Kit stopped stitching and turned to look at her young friend.

Beth used a corner of a growing quilt block to wipe her eyes. "I want a baby so bad."

The despair in those words brought Kit up out of her chair and across the short space separating them. She knelt in front of Beth and took her shaking hands. "Ah, my dear, when you are ready, there'll be a baby. You're young yet."

"I'm so afraid there won't be." She raised tear-washed eyes to look Kit in the face. "I . . . I think sometimes I am losing my mind. Garth is making me see a psychiatrist."

"For depression?"

"How did you know?"

"Someone once suggested I do the same."

"So did you?"

"No, but I haven't closed the door on the idea yet. I don't see anything wrong with getting help. Grief takes a real toll." Kit sniffed and dug in her pocket for a tissue. Finding none, she stood and grabbed the box sitting on the shelf and held it out for Beth, too. "No sense drowning these pieces before they get to their right place."

Beth dabbed her eyes and smiled in spite of her sniffing. "Sometimes I'm so afraid I'm going to cry forever."

"I know. A friend of mine wrote me and said that God keeps our tears in a bottle." *Where did that come from? I hadn't thought of that since I put the card away.*

"Really? Where did she read that?"

"Not sure. In the Psalms somewhere."

"Thanks."

"You are most welcome."

They both returned to their sewing with only the machines murmuring for a gentle time — until the phone rang close to four. Kit thought about letting the machine pick it up but dug under some fabric for the phone in her sewing room and answered it.

"Hello, this is Virginia Mason Hospital in Seattle calling. We have a cancellation for tomorrow at ten if you could bring Mrs. Dennison up then."

"Oh my. Let me call her and call you right back. Wait a minute, how long will you be there? I might have to go out to her place to ask her."

"I'm here until five."

"Good, don't give it to someone else. I'm sure we can get there." She hung up and turned to Beth. "That was the hospital in Seattle. I've got to find Teza." She dialed Teza's number. The phone rang until the machine picked it up. "Teza, if you're anywhere near, pick up the phone."

When nothing happened, Kit left a brief message and, grabbing her purse, headed out the door. "Make yourself at home. I'll be back in a few minutes."

TWENTY-ONE

"I wish I spent more time in here." Elaine looked around her workroom, enjoying the rich colors and designs of tapestries and velvets, velours and silk brocades flowing from tubes in a corner bin, draped over quilt stands, or folded in stacks. Her sewing machines, both an industrial and a top-of-the-line Viking, serger and embroidery machine all sat ready with true lighting and banks of glorious threads and trims. Shelves with doors, drawers, and pullout baskets lined one entire wall. Her cutting table had collapsible additions on all four sides so she could lay out fabrics and projects of nearly any dimension. Doodlebug's basket sat near a sunny window, his favorite place other than her lap. Bookshelves surrounded the windows above, beneath, and even between them.

Someone had told her this was a sewer's dream room. She believed that easily, having dreamed of something like this long before it came into being.

When George told her to do whatever

she wanted, his only stipulation had been that she get top-of-the-line tools, which she'd done. A screen saver on the computer in the corner changed embroidery designs continually.

She picked up her bags of quilt pieces and sat down at her regular machine next to the ironing board that pulled down from the wall. One of the perks of sewing quilt blocks was the freewheeling flow of ideas that went on in her head at the same time. She checked to make sure her digital tape recorder was at the ready so she could record them and began threading her machine, humming under her breath. After pinning the pattern to the cork board above her machine, she took pieces one and two from the Ziplocs to begin her sewing chain.

Her mind roamed back to Ramsey's visit. Short though it was and uptight as she'd been beforehand about meeting the young woman he was bringing home, still things went well as far as she could tell. George took the weekend off and didn't even go in for rounds, an unprecedented act of self-restraint for him.

"Mother, Father, I'd like you to meet Jessica Freewater." Ramsey, too, had obviously been feeling the pressure, but why, she didn't know. After all, what did he expect? That they would be rude and insufferable? Surely he knew their good manners would never allow that.

"I'm pleased to meet you." Jessica's voice had been pleasing and her handshake warm. She flashed Ramsey a look that told his mother the two were more than just acquaintances or a date for the weekend. "You have no idea how I've been looking forward to meeting you and yet scared to death at the same time." Her cheeks flared from pink to red, but her smile and light laugh said she didn't take herself too seriously.

Where did Ramsey find this treasure? She had shoulder-length light brown hair with the kiss of auburn highlights, a heart-shaped face and green eyes that sparkled like a marquis-cut emerald in the sun. She stood nearly as tall as Ramsey, who at five ten had always wished for more height. The two were a perfect foil for each other, he with his father's formerly dark hair and flashing Italian eyes, and she so fair and sparkling.

Her son, who easily could have become an internationally known soccer player, had followed both his own and his father's dreams into medicine. He appeared to be doing everything right, even down to looking for a wife in the same profession.

Juanita liked her too. *And already I'm dreaming of finally having a daughter in my life.*

Elaine turned her chair to the ironing board to clip and press.

Jessica had surely charmed George with her questions of a practice in a small town like Jefferson City.

"You don't get to specialize as much as in a city like, say, Tacoma or Seattle, but we don't have the pressures either," George answered.

Elaine tried to think back to when he hadn't had so much pressure. "At least not until you end up in charge like I did," George added. Both Ramsey and Jessica chuckled at that, and George nodded to her.

"So, you think there is room here for another oncologist, especially relating to women's issues?" Jessica asked.

Elaine looked from Ramsey to Jessica and on to George. She had yet to tell him of her dream for a cancer center. Could this young woman possibly be a piece in the puzzle?

"I don't see why not," Elaine answered with a slight smile.

She let her mind wander the corridors of her dream, only keeping superficial track of the animated conversation regarding night duty and cases that called for extra study or research, whether the patient lived and thrived or withered and died.

One of these days she'd take Ramsey aside and confide her vision, but not yet. Not until she'd begun to figure out the funding.

Elaine turned to Jessica. "Are you aware of the high incidence of cancer in our area, especially breast cancer?"

"No, no one's mentioned that." Like lasers, her green eyes focused on Elaine. "What kind of studies are being done?"

"One entails the electrical transmission lines that run from the dam to Olympia and the surrounding area." She glanced up to see George give a slight shake of his head. Why did he not want them discussing this? She raised an eyebrow his way, and he shook his head again, a barely perceptible movement that she'd learned to read long ago.

She acquiesced and reached for the silver coffeepot at her side. "Would anyone like more coffee before Juanita brings the dessert? It's your favorite, Ramsey. I got apricots from Teza, and we made pie." On that she wasn't stretching the truth. Her apricot pies were renowned, and baking them herself had become a point of pride.

"I told you my mother would have something special for us. Nothing like hospital food to make you appreciate real home cooking."

The only awkward moment occurred when Jessica mentioned she would like to work on the Mercy Ship for a year or two, and Ramsey agreed with her. The thought of her son putting himself in danger made Elaine's stomach clench. Who knew what all they might contact in those third-world countries.

"I believe that is what God is calling me to do." Jessica had said it with such a lovely smile that Elaine swallowed a comment and knew George was biting his tongue also. It wasn't as though they didn't go to church. Of course they did, but Ramsey was their only son.

After the young people left, George had scraped his hands over his balding head. "So are we going to have a Christian fanatic in our family?"

"Now, who knows if this is really the woman for him." But Elaine knew she was. She'd recognized the look of love in her son's eyes. "We didn't raise him that way. I mean we took him to church and taught him morals and ethics and the proper way to behave without going overboard."

"We shall see." George didn't lose the worry crease between his eyebrows until he buried himself in a Dean Koontz novel he'd been reading.

Juanita appeared in the doorway, interrupting Elaine's thoughts. "You want lunch?"

"Is it that time already?" Elaine checked her chain of growing blocks. "Give me half an hour, okay? I should be done with this by then."

"There are phone calls too."

"Anything critical?" At Juanita's head shake, Elaine added, "I can do them later. *Gracias.*"

She finished ironing the last seam and stacked the blocks one on top of another. She'd deliver them tomorrow on her way to the hospital guild meeting. One more thing off her mind. She'd done her part.

Juanita appeared in the doorway again, this time with a vase of cream rose buds, their petals peach on the inside. "These came for you."

Elaine stood so she could inhale the fragrance of the very long-stemmed beauties. "Aren't they gorgeous. Whoever . . ." She reached for the card on the plastic three-pronged stick.

"He love you very much."

"What makes you think that? You know who sent them?" While she watched Juanita shake her head, Elaine slit the envelope open and pulled out the card. In small precise letters, George had written, *Please do not go through with the face-lift. There can be irreparable complications. Love George.*

She stared at the rose buds a moment before looking back at Juanita and handing her the card.

"I told you so."

"Don't you know it's not polite to say that?"

Juanita widened her dark eyes. "So fire me."

Elaine took back the card and read it again. With a sigh she tucked it back in the envelope.

"So?"

"So I don't do the surgery. At least not right now." She half closed her eyes and stared at her friend. "You didn't tell him, did you?"

Juanita shook her head. "No, but I thought about it."

"I wonder . . . ?" Elaine shrugged one

shoulder with her head slightly to the side.

"I bring food out now."

After lunch on the deck, where she watched an eagle rise on the thermals over the fir-covered hills between her and Mount Rainier, she felt ready to attack the grant proposal she wanted in rough form before tomorrow's meeting. There was matching money out there or even straight-out grants if one did her research properly and wrote a dynamite proposal.

She'd done her research all right — in books, online, magazines, telephone — and even pulled out all the stops on this one. Back in the office she retrieved her files from the drawer in the credenza behind the desk and spread them out on the cherry surface. Now, how to put her dream into words, words that would convey both need and scope.

She followed a form outline she'd used before and began typing. Screen after screen filled with information as she continued writing, compiling information from all her sources into one document.

"You like iced tea?" Juanita set a tray down on the only space of wood showing on the desk.

"Yes, thank you." Elaine leaned back in her chair and blinked to clear eyes and mind. "What time is it?"

"Almost five. Barbecuing chicken for dinner. Doctor say he be here about six."

Elaine glanced at the desk calendar where she and George both wrote their schedules. No meetings tonight. If there were no emergencies, they would have a quiet evening — wasn't that a novel idea?

"Don't be snippy," she reminded herself. She'd known what she was getting into by marrying a doctor. At least she'd been warned by another woman who'd been married to a doctor who'd been married to the hospital.

And now her son was following in his father's footsteps, only marrying a woman who walked the same track. More power to them, but how Jessica was going to manage it all was beyond her.

"You've already got them married, and there has not been one word of upcoming nuptials."

Doodlebug put his paws up on her knee, so she leaned over and scooped him up. "Where you been all afternoon, Bug? Sleeping in the sun?" She sorted her work into the proper folders and returned all the files to the cabinet. With the desk back to its normal neatness, she left the room, the dog under her arm.

"We have time for a swim before dinner, what do you think?" Doodlebug kissed her chin with a lightning tongue, his tail beating a tattoo against her rib cage.

Never a big lover of being in the water, nonetheless, Elaine did her mile of laps every day she could get in the pool without freezing on the way out from the house or back into it. With the heated water, she could swim all year round if only she could talk George into building a cover for the pool. Between swimming and walking the treadmill, she never had to worry about dieting, a fact that made some of her friends resent her trim figure. She set the dog down on the chaise lounge, along with her cover-up with a pocket for her recorder. Half a mile of laps later, she got out, picked up the recorder, and reminded herself to order a bolt of cream brocade she'd seen in one of her magazines, along with two cards each of the three trims. Back in the pool for more laps, pictures floated through her mind of the various pillows she could make from the new fabric alone or combined with some she already had in stock.

She'd just finished her mile and was drying off when George strolled out on the deck one level above the pool, wineglass in hand.

"I poured yours, too, since Juanita said you were out here. You coming up, or shall I bring it down?"

"We'll come up. Come on, Bug." Doodlebug raced up the cedar steps ahead of her, rushing over to jump up on George's lap as he leaned back against the cushion of his deck seat, feet crossed at the ankles.

"You look mighty comfy."

"And I plan to stay that way. I told them to call the service. That's what we have doctors on call for." He handed her the glass of Chardonnay from the table beside him.

Okay, George, dear, what's come over you? Elaine sipped from her wineglass, watching her husband over the rim. She toweled her hair again and shook her head, finger combing her hair back into place. "Thank you for the roses, they're gorgeous. Regarding the face-lift, I won't."

"Good."

"How did you . . . ?"

"Hear about it? Doctors talk to each other, you know."

"Oh." *So much for that patient confidentiality.*

"You're beautiful the way you are. Why take a chance?"

Elaine nearly dropped her wineglass. *You really do notice me. Amazing.* "Hard day?"

"Umm." George didn't open his eyes. "Lost a woman on the table. All of a sudden her heart just quit. No warning, no response. I hate things like that."

"Sorry, dear." *But that goes to prove you are not God, no matter how hard you try.* "Must have been her time to go."

If looks could kill, George's might have withered her to a stalk. "George, you know you always do your very best, so why blame yourself?"

"I should have seen it coming." He rocked Doodlebug's head from side to side, the dog making ferocious noises and loving every minute of the tussle. "Sometimes I think I should get into another line of work. Something that isn't life or death every time I turn around."

"Like maybe painting houses or some such?" She knew how much he hated painting. Years earlier, before they could afford to hire painters, he'd made his point perfectly clear.

"Right. Maybe it's time to retire, let the younger men take over."

"Like Ramsey?"

He nodded. "And Jessica." He let go of the dog and turned to look at her. "He called today to ask what we thought of her."

"And what did you tell him?"

"What could I say? We hate her looks, disagree with her politics? I said she is beautiful and will be a credit to our profession, and if she wants to join him in our practice, there is most assuredly a place for her here in Jefferson City."

"Did he mention the Mercy Ship?" When George didn't answer immediately, she turned to study him more closely. "There is something you are not telling me."

"He said he wanted to go too, said he would have chances to do more surgeries there than anywhere else other than war. And they've talked of going to Bosnia or some such place too. I don't like it any better than you do, but he has to live his own life." He drained his glass and raised his hands. "So there you have it." He shrugged and let his hands fall. "He said he'd call you tonight if he had a break, but he's on duty. I'm going for a swim. Tell Juanita I'll man the barbecue when I get out."

Elaine sat in the encroaching shade and

contemplated her wineglass. If only she could solve the problems not only of the world but of her family as easily as bubbles rose to the surface of champagne. No way was this a good time to present her ideas to her husband. As if there really were any good time. Besides, perhaps it was better to present her plans to the guild first. She'd know more by tomorrow night, that was certain, and sometimes handing a man a *fait accompli* was better practice anyway.

TWENTY-TWO

The calendar never lies.

"If we're going to have this finished, quilted, and everything by October one, we really need to get moving."

Kit looked over at the woman who just walked in the door. Somehow, in spite of the gray, windblown day, she had not a hair out of place. "Thank you for the reminder."

"Sorry." Elaine took a seat. "But it just hit me how little time we have. Sometimes you wonder where it goes."

"True, and how to hang on to some of it a bit longer." Teza smiled at each of those gathered around the table. "Now you all received a special invitation to be part of this group that assembles and quilts this project. All of the blocks are in now" — she glanced for confirmation at Kit, who nodded — "so we can lay it out today and begin stitching the blocks together. We have three machines here for that part. I thought while we are laying it out, we can listen to the reports of the various committees and get an idea how things are coming together — pun intended."

A chuckle rippled over the group like leaves dancing before a brisk wind.

"You think we can get it up on the stretcher today?" Elsie Mae asked.

"Depends on if we want to stay until midnight or thereabouts." Sue reached for a bag full of squares, nodding for the others to do the same. "If we get them stacked according to colors, laying it out will be easier."

"Some of these aren't pressed well enough."

"I brought the ironing board. We can set it up over there." Kit nodded to the wall where the outlets were free and set one of the machines on the table to get it opened and ready.

"I'll press." Beth pushed back her chair and headed for the ironing board.

"How was your trip to Seattle?" Sue asked as they emptied the plastic bags and started dividing the piles.

"We had a great time at Pacific Fabrics in Puyallup. I found several more fruit prints for that other quilt I told you about." Teza set aside a couple of blocks that weren't pressed enough.

"I know, and a mammogram is a

mammogram is a mammogram." Sue nudged Elsie Mae. "You notice that wasn't the thing Teza remembers."

"Or chooses to think about."

"It wasn't bad, a different machine than we have and not so smashing. Of course it only takes me half as long as the rest of you." She rolled her eyes at Kit. "Then they did a chest x-ray, I donated some blood, and we left."

"And after getting up at four so we could beat the Seattle traffic and getting home about four, she cooked apricot jam until I don't know when and bottled it." Kit snipped threads off some of the blocks before she put them in the correct pile. "My aunt, the wonder woman."

"Do I detect a slight bit of annoyance there?" Sue put some saccharin in her smile to Kit.

"Of course. I was so tired when I got home, I took a nap and still went to bed early."

"But you drove, dear. I catnapped partway both up and back."

Kit's snort told what she thought of that comment.

"So now I've done my duty, and certain persons who shall remain nameless can quit yammering at me." Everyone else chuckled at Kit's shrug and innocent face.

Until next year when we have to start all over again. Kit smiled at her aunt.

After a brief silence, Teza motioned to Elaine. "Why don't you start off with your report?"

"Good, I will." Elaine set her briefcase on the table and removed several file folders. "I contacted the places in town large enough for this event, but it really comes down to the community building at the fairgrounds or the high-school gym."

"You think we'll have that many people?"

"I have a feeling this is going to get bigger than any of us ever dreamed. Every nonprofit in town is excited to be part of it, especially those with women on their boards. I heard someone even talking about sponsoring a 10K walk/run where participants get sponsors to pay so much a mile or however they want. Andy Stephanopolis out at the country club wants to have a golf tournament in conjunction with the auction, all the proceeds going to the drive. You know his first wife died of breast cancer?"

"Maybe that's why interest is so high here. Too many lives have already been devastated by cancer of one kind or another." Sue laid another block on a stack. "I talked with a reporter at the paper, and she said she'd like to do a series called *A Community Fights Back.*"

Elaine looked to Kit with an I-told-you-so expression. "The hospital guild is solidly with us, and they've all been calling everyone they know to ask for items to donate to the auction. So now do we want a silent auction or an auctioneer?" But before anyone could answer, she passed out sheets of paper and went on. "This is the list of things we must make immediate decisions on. As you see, I've narrowed down the date to two possibilities to avoid schedule conflicts with other events. Both of the buildings I mentioned will be available then, but we need to reserve the facility now. So that is the next item. Date, place, and a title. Everyone wanted to know what we are calling this so they could begin working on it right away."

"Whew." Teza laughed and widened her eyes. "Do any of the rest of you feel like a tornado just blew through here?"

Elaine chuckled along with the rest of them. "I thought I was going to have to convince people to help, but it was like everyone was waiting for something like this to come along." She shrugged. "Amazing."

"God's timing." Teza nodded and smiled at the same time. "And yes, that is always amazing."

"Well, I don't know about that but . . ." Elaine ruffled her papers. "Can we go ahead and vote on these three things. Perhaps a show of hands will do?"

"Hands," several said at the same time.

"Good." Elaine held up a calendar. "We have a choice of the last two weekends in February unless we want to delay until April and the weekend after Easter. The only advantage to that would be the golf tournament. The weather might be more cooperative by then."

"Does everything need to be on the same weekend?"

"No, not necessarily, but if we get some big-name golfers in here, they might have deep pockets to bid on the quilt and all the other items."

"Maybe they'd even donate something." Sue laid her pieces down and leaned forward, elbows on the table.

"Yeah, like a round with Tiger Woods." Beth set her iron down.

"I doubt he'd come to something this small." Kit shook her head.

"For sure he won't if he's not asked." Beth brought another stack of pressed blocks over to the table. "I'd contact him. I'm done gathering donations for the quilt supplies, so that wouldn't be any trouble."

"You would?" Sue sat back and fanned her reddening face. "For someone so quiet, you are full of surprises. Whew, 'bout time to turn on the air conditioning."

"Just a hot flash, my dear." Teza smiled and patted her arm as Sue groaned.

"Can Andy pull something like that together so quickly?" Kit took another stack to be pressed over to Beth.

"He'd like April better, but you know February can be such a beautiful month here."

"And it can snow," Elsie Mae reminded them.

"So I'm sensing we might back up to April?"

"I'm in favor. I move we choose April." Elsie Mae smacked her hand on the table.

"Anyone else? Hands in favor." Elaine nodded. "Good, that's that then. Now, the place. Here's my opinion. We can decorate out at the fairgrounds and not have to work around school affairs so that would lessen the pressure that weekend."

"Decorate?" Kit looked up from the threads she was clipping off some of the squares.

"Sure, we'll make it a gala event this town won't forget," Elaine continued. "When I talked with Rod at The Steak House, he suggested we choose a theme and invite area hotels and restaurants to have a cook-off or a tasting where each displays their foods and people pick and choose and vote for the best. He said there's not been an event like that in our area, and it's about time. They call it *The Taste of Portland* down there. He thought places from Tacoma and Olympia might want to participate."

Kit leaned back in her chair. "And here I thought making a quilt was the major undertaking."

"It is. The quilt will be the symbol of all we are doing. The final results will show what people can accomplish when they work together." Elaine could hardly stand still from the excitement.

"So we all agree on the fairgrounds?" Elsie Mae set a pile of sorted pieces in the middle of the table. "Let's push these tables together so we can lay out the pieces."

"The community center — hands?"

Again it was unanimous.

"So we will have the event on April 29 at the fairgrounds. Good thing there's plenty of parking there too. Now, for a title."

"Save a breast, it may be your own." Sue shrugged when her suggestion drew laughter. "Well, it might."

"True."

"Do we want the words *breast* and *cancer* in the title?"

"Or *mammogram unit?* That's what our goal is."

Ideas started popping.

"Stitch in Time Festival."

"Festival of the Quilt."

"Quilt Fest."

"Doesn't it need to mention more than the quilt?" Beth's forehead wrinkled with her thoughts.

"How about Support a Breast?" Groans.

"To be specific: Jefferson Memorial Hospital Charity Auction." More groans.

"Naming things is really difficult." Teza propped her chin on one hand. "I'm not good at it."

"Me either." Sue shook her head, then whispered to Teza, " 'Buy a Boob Squeezer.' No? I'm no good at this either. I'm going back to the blocks." She laid out some more of the quilt squares. "I know, 'The Block Buster.' "

"Let's table this for now and come back to it later, okay?" Elaine laid down the pen she'd used to take notes and glanced down the list. "Someone, somewhere will come up with something."

"That's something we can pray about." Teza looked up from sorting blocks.

Elaine put her files and organizer back in her briefcase. "I'll go get sandwiches at the deli. Turkey all right for everyone?" She glanced around the room. "Okay, any other drinks than the coffee and tea here?"

With no takers, she waved off their offers of money and headed out the door. "Yes!" She thumped on the steering wheel of her newly returned BMW. "If we can get national coverage, so much the better for the cancer center. *The little town that could.* Maybe we can even get those power lines moved. Easier than moving a town."

She picked up her phone and dialed the deli to place her order. All because a couple of women decided to do something about a community problem. The PR possibilities were endless.

When she returned with her flat box of sandwiches and set them on the table, the women left off their jobs and came to eat.

"Here," said Teza, handing her five dollars.

"No, this is my treat. You were all

working so hard, I figured this was the least I could do."

"And you've been doing nothing?" Teza raised an eyebrow.

Elaine smiled back and turned to answer a question from someone else. When all were served, she sat down next to Beth.

"So how are you enjoying Jefferson City now?"

"Better. Getting to know the women here with the quilting has helped a lot."

"I know I'd never have made it as a pastor's wife. Have to be nice to everyone, even though you'd as soon walk away." Elaine unwrapped her sandwich. "And most churches expect you to do twice as much as anyone else."

"Or they're afraid the new pastor's wife is going to come in and take over." Sue pulled open her bag of chips. "That's what happened at our church."

"Who did the choosing here?" Beth looked around. "I mean, from all those other women at the cutting day, why us?"

"I prayed about it and felt led to ask each of you." Teza smiled around. "I guess God feels we all have special talents or something to contribute. And with six, even with all our other obligations, we should be able to have four working at a time."

"So when will we get together to put this up on the frame, and will that be here?" Elaine took out her calendar.

"Would Monday be all right for everyone?" Kit glanced around to catch their nods. "And I have a largely unused-at-the-moment living room where we can leave it set up. As far as I'm concerned, anyone can come at any time and quilt when you have time. I thought maybe twice a week for the entire group."

"That would be only fourteen sessions until it would need to be done." Elaine counted the weeks out in her organizer. "Will that be enough?"

"I doubt it, but that depends on how long we can work at a time. We can discuss that later." Sue folded up her napkin and papers. "We better get back to work and quit gabbing. I'll take one machine." She picked up a stack of blocks that now were in sewing order.

"I'll cut the border squares then, if you want to do the nine-patch pieces." Kit looked to Teza.

"That leaves you and me on the other machines," Elaine said to Elsie Mae. "You can switch off with any of us from pressing, you know, Beth."

"I know. Kit, did you get the quilt back stitched together?"

"Yes, and pressed too. It's folded in that plastic tote over there."

The stitchers kept Beth busy as she clipped threads and pressed seams. As soon as they had one stack stitched, they handed the long strip to her and picked up another stack.

"Make sure you keep the numbers pinned in place." Teza stood and stretched. "I've numbered the strips according to where they go in the finished pattern."

"Oh, I forgot that." Sue stopped sewing and took two numbers over to Beth's backup stacks. "Here, these go on those."

"Do you know which is which?"

"No, of course not. Teza?" Sue stood with a strip in each hand. "Help!"

Teza studied the blocks, checked against her master, and put the numbers on the right ones. "See, no problem."

"See the dummy who got so busy sewing and talking she forgot to do it right."

"Happens to the best of us. Praise the Lord we caught it now when it was easy to take care of."

Elaine kept her face from betraying what she was feeling by concentrating on her sewing. *Praise the Lord, eh? How come such a good, nice, and talented woman had to go overboard on the religious side? Shame. Would Jessica be like that? I mean, after all, I go to church but I keep it in the right place, that's all. Proportion, that's what is important.* She glanced around the room. She hadn't heard Beth talk like that, and she was a pastor's wife. You'd expect it more from her.

She switched her thoughts back to the PR for the Jefferson City Gala. They still needed a good caption, one that would say what they were doing and say it with class. Why was everyone so leery of using the words *breast cancer?* She carried her final strip over to Beth at the ironing board.

"You want to switch places?"

"Sure." Beth picked up a folded strip. "This really is going to be beautiful, isn't it? I love the colors."

"*Rich* is a word I would use. But I've never hand quilted anything this huge before." Elaine set the iron to pressing the seams in the string she brought over. "Have you?"

Beth shook her head. "But then the two quilts I did, I quilted all by myself."

"How big were they?"

"One was for my single bed and the

other a baby quilt." She cleared her throat. "But then I've done lots of little projects. I'm working on a wall hanging now for my mother for Christmas."

"I see. I do like making my pillows. I did several crazy quilt tops in velvets with all the different kinds of embroidery stitches. The woman who bought them called them 'breathtaking.' Can you believe that?"

"Yes, I can. I have a feeling you create a lot of breathtaking pieces."

Elaine watched as Beth took over the idle sewing machine. What a nice thing for her to say.

By the time they shut down for the day, there were only a few more strips to be sewn to the quilt body before it could be assembled.

"So we'll meet at my house on Monday?"

"I can in the morning," Sue said, "but I have to baby-sit in the afternoon."

"I have meetings that day." Elaine closed her organizer. "But I'll clear Tuesday and Thursday each week for the quilting."

"It'll be easier to set up tables at your house, then we can clip it right on the frame without folding and moving again." Teza and Beth folded the finished portion of the quilt top.

"Fine with me. You all have my number. Let me know if Monday is a problem. Otherwise we'll meet Tuesday as planned."

They gathered up all their supplies and, with loaded luggage carriers, headed for the cars.

"What a day." Elaine slammed the trunk on her BMW. "Are the rest of you as tired as I am?"

"Glad someone mentioned that, thought it was just me." Sue stretched her neck from one side to the other. "And now I have to go home and fix dinner. I'll let Kelly choose. She always asks for hot dogs."

"Thanks, everyone." Kit climbed into her van.

No matter how gray it is, I'm getting in the pool and the hot tub when I get home. With a nice glass of wine. I earned it. Elaine honked the horn as she drove out of the parking lot. *I wonder how many thousand stitches go into a quilt like this? And all by hand.* She held out her left hand and looked at her squared-off acrylic nails. *Can I quilt with fingernails like this? Do I even want to do this? Whyever did she choose me?*

TWENTY-THREE

"Do you have time to take me back to Seattle?"

"Of course, why?" *The cancer is back, no other reason they would want to see her immediately like this.*

"Just said they needed to run more tests."

"When?"

"Tomorrow morning, soon as we can get there."

Kit wished she were out at her aunt's house right now so she could see Teza's face. The phone was far too impersonal. "Do you want me to come out?"

"Not unless you want to pick beans. I hate to let them get too big, and rain is forecast for tomorrow."

"How many rows do you have?"

"Three. I have a woman coming for forty pounds at five. And the cucumbers need picking too."

Kit checked the clock. Three-thirty. If she could find some helpers, they could do it. "Have you asked Vinnie to help?"

"No, I just got off the phone with the

doctor's office. I can drive myself up there, you know, I just thought . . ."

"Don't go there, Teza. You know I will drive and spend the night at your house whenever you need me. The real question is, how are you?"

"Me? I'm fine, why? There's no sense worrying about this. God knows what is going on, and he's in charge." Teza paused as if waiting for Kit to respond before continuing. "So why would you need to stay at my house?"

"I figured you would say that." *But do you mind if I panic some? You're my only older relative, and I want you around for a good long while. A hundred years or at least the rest of my lifetime.*

"I'll be out picking, so don't worry if I don't answer the phone."

Kit hung up long enough to flip her church directory open and begin calling. Within five minutes she had four pickers and was headed out the door.

"Garth, honey." Beth draped her arms around her husband's neck as he sat in the deck chair.

He tilted his head back, the better to see her. "What?" He sniffed. "Mmm, you smell nice."

"I know you have a meeting later this evening, but I wondered if we could go out to Teza Dennison's farm right now and pick peaches."

"Pick peaches? Now?"

"What's wrong with now? I have dinner in the oven, and there's still plenty of light, if we hurry." She smoothed the hair back over his ears. "I'll make you a peach pie."

"I'm on my way." He turned and rose in one smooth motion. The cat leaped from the deck corner and hid under the rhododendrons again.

"You think that animal is ever going to trust us?"

Beth locked her arm through his. "He'll have to if he keeps eating like he has. He'll soon be too fat to move."

Once in the car, Garth kept turning his head to look at her on the way out of town.

"What's wrong?" she finally asked.

"Nothing, but I can't believe the change in you. Those pills must be really working."

If you only knew. "Maybe because I get a good night's sleep with no nightmares, I have some energy again. They say sleep deprivation can cause a person to do strange things."

"Well, whatever it is . . ." He patted her

knee. "I'm sure glad to see my girl is back." He propped one elbow on the open window frame. "Did I tell you Dr. Kaplan called to see how we are?"

"No." A sheet of clear ice dropped into place between them.

"He wants to see you alone this time." Garth glanced her way. "Will you go?"

Her hands clenched in automatic response, the upper thumb rubbing the skin off the other.

"Beth?"

"Turn left here. That's her farm sign."

"How did you know about this?"

"Teza is a member of the group I've been quilting with. We're making the quilt for the mammogram unit. She invited us to come out."

"Sure is a beautiful place. I always dreamed of having a farmhouse like that one." He pointed to the gray two-story house with white trim and a white wraparound porch.

"Maybe someday. You park over there." Beth pointed to the area beyond the fruit stand.

"Hey, maybe she sells the peaches already picked."

"You need to earn your pie, Reverend. Come on." Beth waved at Teza as she got out of the car. "We don't have much time, but do you still have peaches to pick?"

"Most certainly do. Come on over and help yourselves to buckets. I'll be right with you." Teza returned to helping the customer in front of her.

"See, she has baskets of peaches right there where we can pay our money and start eating." Garth took the metal handle of one of the gallon-size white buckets. "You expect me to fill one of these?"

Beth nodded.

"I might damage my lily white pastoral fingers, have pity. Or even mercy."

"Fingers that don't mind digging up worms certainly can't be queasy at picking luscious peaches." She took his arm and pulled him toward the peach trees.

"Hey, don't I get to climb the trees? When I was a kid, that was the best part of picking fruit."

"No, I try to make it easier for pickers now." Teza caught up with them. "Most of our trees you can reach from the ground. I have ladders over there for the highest branches, but you're tall enough you'll have no trouble."

"Teza, this is my husband, Garth, the Hungry. Garth, meet my friend, Teza Dennison."

Garth put out his hand. "I'm glad to meet you. What a beautiful place you have here."

"Thank you. Help yourselves." As another car drove in, she excused herself and headed back to the shop.

"She's nice." Garth picked a golden peach with a red blush and rubbed off the fuzz on his jeans before taking a bite. "Not quite ripe, but still better than any at the store."

"That's because they haven't been subjected to a cooler. Takes the flavor away."

They filled their buckets and walked back to the barn.

"Sorry I had to desert you," Teza said with a wide smile.

"Well, if the other stuff is as good as your peaches, you'll see us out here often." Garth nodded toward a basket of plums. "We'll take those, too."

"Tree ripened has a lot going for it." Teza picked up two plums and handed one each to Garth and Beth.

"I'll take that basket of really ripe peaches. I promised Garth a peach pie."

"Good. Here's a copy of my favorite peach pie recipe." Teza handed Beth a printed index card. "Guaranteed to make a husband sing for joy." She tucked a one-page calendar in too. "Just so you have an idea when things get ripe here. Looks like almost no late peaches this year, too cold for the bees, but the gravenstien apples come on late this month. Best for pies and applesauce in my estimation."

"You take care of all of this?"

Teza nodded. "Since my husband died five years ago, but I have good equipment and a neighbor who helps when I need him."

"And she is a master quilter too." Beth pointed to a set of pieced place mats. "How do you find time for it all?"

"You can't garden after dark or in the winter, so then I sew."

Beth glanced at her watch. "Oh, okay, we better hurry, or the dinner will be burned. Thanks, Teza."

"Thank you and come again."

That evening after Garth left for his meeting, Beth peeled and sliced the ripe peaches, then added sugar, cinnamon, flour, and some lemon juice. Keeping out enough for one pie, she froze the rest. Alone in the quiet house, her thoughts returned to Garth's request that she see the psychiatrist by herself this week. She didn't want to go as a couple, so why should she want to go by herself?

The voices arguing in her head made her hands shake again. *You have to admit the pills he gave you did help. If you agree to take the prescription, perhaps everything will be all right, and you won't have to keep going to see him. I don't need anything. As a good Christian, shouldn't I be able to handle a little sadness by myself? What good Christian would kill an unborn baby?* The last was said with the sneer.

The trick to handling all of this was just to never be alone where the voices could take over. *Keep so busy I can't hear them.* She rolled out the pie dough, arranged it in the pie tin, and added the pie filling she had ready. After fluting the crust with her fingers, she cut slashes in the pie top and sprinkled a bit of sugar over the crust. She glanced at the clock as she put the pie in the oven. Eight-thirty. It should be out and cooling before Garth got home with the ice cream he'd promised to pick up.

After cleaning up the kitchen and leaving a cut-glass bowl of peaches on the kitchen table, she headed back to her sewing room, where the quilt she'd been piecing now waited on the hoop for her to quilt it.

Sometime later, smelling smoke, she returned to the kitchen to see smoke seeping from the oven door. "Must be done, it ran all over the oven." She turned on the fan over the stove and opened the window and sliding glass door. Opening the oven, she shook her head. Juice all over the oven all right, but the crust not brown enough to be done. She retrieved the salt shaker and tossed some over the oven spill to keep the smoke down. She wanted a baked pie, not a smoked one. Her eyes burned as she flapped a dishcloth to send the smoke outside.

Surely the smoke alarm should have gone off. She returned to the hall to check that, only to find no winking red eye. Dead batteries.

"If it's not one thing, it's another." And here she'd hoped to have a couple of hours to work on her quilt.

By dark all the fruit and vegetables were picked, everyone had taken some home, and the two refrigerators in the store were full too.

"You take those home, and I'll take the last up to the house. Vinnie said she'd watch the store tomorrow." Teza arched her back before rubbing her shoulder.

"That still bothering you?"

"Umm, somewhat."

"Did you mention that to the doctor?"

"Kit, I haven't been to the doctor, and why would I complain about something so simple as a pulled muscle?"

"Well, you've been tired lately too."

"How do you know that?"

Teza's question betrayed her. "Just a suspicion. You've had dark circles under your eyes for another thing. And you've lost weight."

"Oh, pshaw. I always have dark circles, part of my makeup. Your mother always had dark circles too, and you would if you didn't cover them with that stick stuff you use. Some things are just genetic. Now, get on home with those apricots if you want to pit them tonight. They're pretty ripe."

Kit set the last bucket of apricots in the rear of her minivan and slammed the hatch. "I'll pick you up at seven."

She got in the car and lowered her window. "How about if I call the prayer chain?"

"Not until we know anything for certain." Teza waved her off.

Kit drove out the driveway, her emotions bouncing between resignation and rage.

Teza is right. There is no sense worrying until we know more. God, you can't do this! Please, please, you took my mother and my daughter. My husband is alive, but only you and he know where. Of course those at his office did too, but she refused to lower herself to ask them, to admit she didn't know. *Now, please leave me Aunt Teza.* The mind war raged, leaving her drained to the point of utter exhaustion. When she got home, she rearranged the refrigerator and shoved the fruit inside. Maybe Thomas would like to come help her pit and chop them after she got back from Seattle.

One by one she called the quilting group to tell them assembling the quilt would have to wait until Thursday. Gently she cut off their questions, only saying Teza needed more tests. But when she crawled into bed, sleep skipped out the window. Surely this is something Mark would want to know about. She got up again, went in her sewing room to boot up the computer, then went down to the kitchen to make a cup of chamomile tea. Chamomile was known to aid in sleep.

She typed in his address, *Aunt Teza* on the subject line, and began:

Dear Mark,

Due to your wishes, I have not tried to contact you and been content with waiting for you to call. But I believe you would want to know about this, since Teza is one of your favorite people. We went to Seattle last Friday for her mammogram. Long story, but the one here is prehistoric. They called today and said they want to see her for further tests tomorrow. Now, you know as well as I do that they only do that if they see something bad. She has had a soreness in her shoulder for the last week or so, and I think she's been more tired than usual. She blames all the fruit picking, jam making and such, but I don't feel good about this.

Other than that, I miss you like another piece of me is gone. I do hope you are planning to come home while Ryan is here. I know Jennifer won't be able to come then, but at least she is happy with her job and her apartment.

Missy and I have a new friend. His name is Thomas and he is seven. He is hoping Ryan will play ball with him. He doesn't know yet that I'm a pretty fair pitcher, but I might get out the pitch back and warm up. Come home and play with us.

I love you always,
Kit

She reread the message, made a couple of changes, and sent it off.

Her new messages included one from Jennifer extolling the joys of her new job and bewailing the housing costs. She'd been to see the Rangers play but wished she could have seen the Mariners instead. She'd missed out on their last series in Arlington.

Kit answered the message but didn't include her concern about Teza. Time enough to tell after they had more information.

She sent that message and shut down the computer without checking E-Bay or some of the other sites she enjoyed. While her tea had grown cold, she finished it anyway and trundled back to bed. The bed seemed to be an acre on nights like this more than others. She cuddled Mark's pillow, hoping for a faint whiff of him, but fabric softener was all she smelled. Fabric softener and sadness.

God, I am all alone. It's not fair. This isn't the way it should be. When things get hard, husbands and wives are to hold each other up. That's what we vowed, "in sickness and in health" — we didn't say whose. She flipped over on her back. *And here I am talking to you when I promised myself never to do that again.* Tears leaked down her temples and into her ears. *Why can't I just hate him for leaving me? Yeah, I know, I promised to love and cherish, but how do I do that when I have no idea where he is or who he is with? That old "no news is good news" is a real weak saying, really weak.* She rolled over and reached into the drawer on the nightstand for a tissue. After wiping her eyes, she blew her nose. When sleep finally came, the alarm didn't allow it to hang around long enough to do a whole lot of good.

TWENTY-FOUR

On the drive to Seattle, Teza directed the conversation to her new quilt pattern, gardening, the cancer quilt, her flowers, anything but the coming tests.

At one point Kit turned to her. "Did you by any chance put in an overnight bag?"

"No."

"But what if they decide to keep you there longer?"

"I think they would have mentioned that possibility, don't you?"

"I don't know. It just entered my mind."

The predicted rain drizzled on them all the way north. The entire Northwest seemed to be weeping. Teza took out her crocheting. She always had a stocking hat in progress, sometimes for infants at the hospital, other times for older children. This one was soft pink baby yarn.

"At least this time we know where we are going," Kit said as she turned into the parking lot closest to the oncology department. Once she found a parking place, she got out and reached into the back for her canvas bag containing a novel, the latest *Quilting* magazine, a bottle of water, a tiny nativity scene to cross stitch, and cotton yarn to crochet a dishcloth. Long days in hospital waiting rooms passed more swiftly with plenty to do; she'd learned that the hard way. What she didn't have along were Amber's schoolbooks, snacks, and an inflatable pillow for Amber to sleep on. They'd usually brought a fleece throw, too.

How she hated hospital waiting rooms.

After they trundled Teza off, Kit spent some time in the gift shop looking at the card rack and bought several. She browsed through the books, searching for something for Annie Nelson. She'd not called or been over to see what she could do, or bring something for dinner, or just visit. Guilt again. *It's not like you've had a family or even a husband to take care of, you know.* That voice again, so richly accusing. How many hammer blows would it take to silence the thing?

Back in the waiting room she found a corner chair where she could set up her space. Bottled water on the side table, a lamp to stitch by. Which to start first? She'd done bits and pieces of most of her bag of tricks when Teza returned at three-thirty and said the doctor wanted to see them now. Kit gathered up her projects, repacked her bag, and joined Teza on the march to the House of Horrors.

Doctor Pagnielli, as he introduced himself, motioned for them to sit, and he leaned against the front of his cherry wood desk. He crossed his arms over his chest and looked from Kit to Teza. "I'm sorry to be the bearer of bad news, but the cancer has returned and appears to have metastasized to the right lung." He walked to the wall of x-ray and CAT scan films and switched on the light. "Actually, there is only a very small tumor in the breast, but the lymph nodes appear to be involved, and this dark spot in the lung is of concern." He pointed out each area, his voice soft with the sibilant *s*'s typical of an immigrant from the Middle East. "While some of the test results are not yet available, I believe we need to treat this immediately and aggressively. How long has it been since your first mastectomy?"

"Six years, almost."

Kit had watched Teza sitting straight and yet relaxed while she felt herself knotting up like yarn after a kitten had played with it. "Please, would you define immediate and aggressive?" Her voice was firm, as if she were discussing the merits of homemade jam versus store bought.

"Yes, of course. My recommendation is radical mastectomy, including the lymph nodes, chemotherapy to shrink the tumor in the lung, and attack any other sites we are not yet aware of. Radiation would start as soon as possible on the lung also. I believe we need a full-body MRI to see if there is any other involvement that might benefit from radiology or surgery."

"But why the mastectomy instead of a lumpectomy?" Teza asked.

"To forestall any future involvement."

"So you are saying the cancer has spread to her entire body?" Kit had to clear her throat twice to get the words out.

"No, I'm saying we want to know as much as possible about what we are dealing with."

"And if I choose to not do anything?"

"Teza!"

"No, dear, let me ask my questions." Her voice was steady, firm.

"Then it will spread and you will die." The doctor switched off the lights behind the pictures of doom and returned to his desk perch.

"How long?"

"I can't say for certain. Possibly six months to a year."

"And if I choose alternate treatments?"

He shrugged. "I do not know."

"Could the treatments be administered at our hospital in Jefferson City?"

"I can look into that." He made a note to himself on a clipboard. "Was your first mastectomy done there?"

"Yes."

"Did you do a program of chemotherapy?"

"No. They felt the original tumor was encapsulated, and chemo was not needed."

"Radiation?"

"No."

"And you've had six-month and then yearly mammograms?"

"Yes."

"And self-examinations?"

"Yes."

"We will do everything we can. There are new protocols now, and we will tailor the treatment to be most effective for your body."

Teza rose. "I will let you know what I decide."

"What?" Kit couldn't believe her ears.

"I see." The doctor stroked his chin with thumb and forefinger.

"I want to know all my options, and I will pray for wisdom in what to do."

"The longer you wait, the farther it will spread."

"I understand that, but surely a few more days or a week will not make a significant difference." One would have thought she was the Queen of England dispensing whatever it was the Queen of England dispensed. Kit alternately wanted to stuff a rag in her aunt's mouth and fall pleading into her arms.

"If you would be so kind as to lay out your plan of action and fax it to my home office, then I will call you on Monday to set up a time when we can confer." Teza extended her hand. "Thank you for your concern. I know I am not following what you would call 'normal protocol,' but this is my body, you see, and I have to live with it. Come, dear." She reached down for Kit's hand. "Let us be on our way."

"Are you out of your everloving mind?" Kit hissed as soon as they entered an elevator by themselves.

"Can we wait until I get some food in me before we begin this discussion?"

"Fine, do you want to eat here or someplace else?"

"I thought the restaurant at the Double Tree Inn at South Center. Unless the traffic is so bad that we should eat near here and then head south."

Kit checked her watch. Nearing five. "Let's give it a try. At least it's not a Friday evening."

The one good thing about Seattle traffic was that trying not to hit or be hit by someone left no time to discuss the pros and cons of the treatment offered and Kit's all-out horror at her aunt's attitude. Mandatory concentration on driving required all the mental energy Kit had.

"That sure was good pie last night." Garth looked up from reading his Bible, coffee cup beside his elbow on Tuesday morning. "Just think, two peach pies in three days. Some kind of record."

"Thank you." Beth stretched both arms above her head, pulling at the kinks in her shoulders. A jaw-cracking yawn cut her stretch short as she clapped a hand over her mouth. " 'Scuse me."

"You're excused."

Beth glanced over to where the pie sat under a clear plastic cover. "Looks to me like someone's been in the pie since last night."

"That darn cat got into the house after all, did he?"

"Amazing how adept he is, put the plate in the dishwasher even."

"Good thing we picked extra peaches, huh?"

"We?" She arched a brow and tried to give him a stern look.

"Well, they weren't ripe enough to eat, so I did put some in the bucket. I could always go out and buy more."

"Pick some more?"

He wrapped an arm around her hips and pulled her in close to him. "You heard me."

Beth laid her arm across his shoulders and her cheek against the top of his head, breathing in his good man scent. "You already been for your run and everything?"

"Yup."

She tucked her hair back behind her ear. "Any more of that coffee left?"

"Just the dregs. You want a sip of mine?"

"No, I'll make more. You want breakfast?" She crossed to the coffeepot and removed the filter, tossing it into the coffee can Garth kept under the sink to be added to his compost, a project he'd started after talking with Harriet. At least the meeting she'd attended with Mrs. Spooner made her more aware of what kitchen scraps could be used. "God wastes nothing and neither should we." That must be a Spoonerism, since if the woman said it once that evening, she said it ten times. "Funny that you are into gardening, and I'm the one who went to the composting seminar."

"What's that you said?"

"Nothing important." Beth looked out the window to see the cat sitting on the shelf under the sill, looking in. "One of these days you're going to be tame enough to come inside and be part of the family."

The cat jumped down and stalked over to his dish.

"Well, if the way to a man's heart is through his stomach, why would it be any different for a male cat?" She left off fixing coffee, retrieved the box of dry cat food from the pantry shelf, and stepped outside to pour some in the cat dish. "There now, can I go back to my coffee?"

The cat watched her, still poised to leap and run, until she stepped back inside the house. Then he edged forward and crouched down to eat, still facing her with the dish between them.

"Oh, ye of little faith, poor kitty." She

thought about what she'd just seen and said. No matter how sweetly she talked, how much food she gave him, he still didn't trust her.

Am I like that? Not trusting God because I've been hurt? She shook off the image. *It's not God I don't trust, it's me, my own fault. He can't trust me.*

She returned to making her coffee. "Did I ask you if you'd eaten breakfast?"

"No, but yes." Garth closed his Bible and notebook and stood. "I ate a breakfast bar earlier."

"That's all you want?"

"For now. I need to get going. Don't forget your appointment today with Dr. Kaplan."

Oh, I didn't forget, I just don't want to go. She kept her gaze on the coffeepot as if mesmerized by the dripping brown liquid.

Garth crossed the room and put his hands on her upper arms. "Please, Beth, if you can't do this for you, do this for us. My whole world seems brighter because you've been feeling better."

You think mine hasn't? You think I like sinking into that black mire that oozes up and wraps itself around my feet to pull me down? She knew if she looked down right now, she would see it, shiny bubbles popping on the top of the viscous mass, writhing around her ankles.

"Yes, I'll go." Her whispered agreement was all he needed.

"Good. You want to come by the church afterward, and I'll take you to lunch?"

"We'll see." She kept herself rigid, not allowing her spine to lean back against his warmth and strength.

He waited, obviously hoping for more from her before he dropped a kiss on the back of her head and stepped back. "You won't be sorry."

I already am sorry. I'm sorry I got up, I'm sorry I agreed, I'm sorry that I will never live long enough to say enough I'm sorrys. Her shoulders curved inward to protect her heart that looked to never heal.

"And here I started out the morning really well and now look at me." She glared at the face in the bathroom mirror. She'd just stepped out of the shower and removed the frilly pink shower cap, shaking her hair loose down her still damp back. "Manipulated is what I feel, and I'm just going to tell him so." While she wasn't sure if by *him* she meant the doctor or her husband, even anger felt better than the blackness hiding either under the bed or behind the closet door.

She hung on to that anger through making the bed, straightening the towels, even scrubbing her teeth. She stomped down the stairs, after not allowing herself to enter the sewing room, because she'd never be able to stay mad if she started sewing, poured another cup of coffee, ate a piece of naked toast, and headed for the car. She gave about two seconds to the thought of walking, since it was such a nice day, but deep-sixed that idea. If she walked that far, she'd never be able to stay mad. Staying mad was a problem. Succumbing to the blackness took no effort at all.

"You can go right on in," the receptionist said with a smile, one that Beth barely returned.

"Thank you." The words forced themselves from between her tightly clamped lips. Yes, it was the doctor she was mad at, for now. Garth would hear about it later.

"Ah, Mrs. Donnelly, how are you today?"

"Fine."

His right eyebrow twitched, but he toned down his smile and reached to shake her hand.

No matter what her desire, she could not

be rude enough not to shake hands. His warm clasp when he covered her hand with his other and the gentle smile he gave her were almost her undoing.

She could feel her lower lip begin to quiver and the tears stinging the backs of her eyes. Blast the man, why couldn't he be the ogre she made him out to be?

She took her hand back and strode over to the wing-back chair, perching on the edge and strangling her small purse on her knees. Tell him. Let him have it!

"So how has your week been? Did the prescription I ordered for you help?"

"I felt better as soon as I got some sleep for a change." She sucked in a deep breath. "I must tell you that I am here only because my husband forced me to come."

"Forced you?"

"Would you prefer blackmailed me?"

"Not really, I'd prefer you came because you believed I could help you."

Her snort told him what she thought of that idea. "I'd rather just take pills if I must and not come here."

"Ah, but you see, I have you there. I am the one who dispenses the pills."

"Then I'll quit taking them, too." *And go back to where you were?* The voice seemed to be sitting on her right shoulder. She waited a moment for the one on her left to chime in.

"Garth called me, frantic because he said you were injuring yourself." The words fell like a leaf to the surface of a pond, but even light as the leaf lay, ripples spread in circles across the silent face of the water.

"I . . . I don't remember that." She could see again the hair lying on her pillow and more brushed out the next time she combed her hair. Her scalp had ached for several days.

"But do you now believe it happened?"

She nodded, her hair falling forward to provide a veil on the sides of her face. "Garth never lies."

"I see." He waited, sitting back in his chair as if he had all the time in the world.

A tear dripped down on her ravaging thumb.

He handed her the tissue box. "Beth, what are you angry at?"

She shook her head. *Me, it's myself that did it all.* The words careened around her mind like a hard-driven racquet ball against the walls of the court.

"What are you afraid of?"

Funny, that's what someone else asked too. But I know my fear — *Garth will find out, and that will be the end of our marriage.* "That I will never have a baby to hold and love." She whispered and shook her head, her hair veil swaying from side to side. She tried to bury herself in the arms of the chair.

"I see."

What do you see? I've told you so little.

"You know that anything you say here will never go beyond the walls of this room without your permission? This is a safe place, Beth. Whatever has gone on in your life can be brought out here, talked about and forgiven. The medication I gave you is only a stopgap to help you sleep and be able to assess things more realistically."

He stopped and waited again. She could feel his gaze, gentle on the top of her head. The fish tank gurgled in the corner, and the birds sang on the feeders in the courtyard.

But tears are silent drops of pain.

"I . . . I can't." Her whisper carried the years of guilt, of horror, of despair.

She blew her nose and wiped her eyes, clenching the tissue in her fist. *Thirsty, I'm so thirsty.*

"Tell me about your childhood. Where did you live, who are the members of your family?"

"Uh . . ." She fought to bring her mind back to the present question. "My mom and dad and my brother and sister and I lived in Cottonwood, Arizona, until I was about ten, when we moved to Phoenix."

"Did you like Phoenix?"

She halfway shrugged. "It was all right, after a while at least. But my mom went to work too, and I hated to come home to an empty house."

"Is your brother older or younger?"

"Three years younger. He played baseball every chance he got, so he spent a lot of time at the ball fields."

"What about your sister?"

"She thought she knew best for everything."

"And you, what did you like to do?"

"Oh, read and sew, watch TV. I usually got straight A's. I learned to cook after that so Mom wouldn't have to when she got home. My sister was always off somewhere. I loved music, so they got me a piano."

"You took lessons?"

"Some, but I picked out a lot on my own." She wiped her nose again. "I play a lot by ear."

"What do you like to do now?"

"Read, sew, decorate our house . . . We don't have a piano so . . . so I play at the guitar sometimes. I usually like to entertain but . . ." *But I can't invite people over now. I don't know anyone and I just don't have the energy.*

"This move was hard on you."

"I had to leave my baby behind."

"The one that died prematurely?"

"Yes." *And the other one, too, but I left that one a long time ago.*

"Depression isn't unusual after losing a baby."

"But I should just get over it and get on with my life, right?" The venom in her voice shocked even her.

"I didn't say that."

"No, but you . . ."

"But I what?"

"Nothing."

"Have you kept a journal?"

"No, I started a baby book but . . ." She shook her head again, then tucked the right side of her hair behind her ear. "I didn't have any more to add, so I put it away."

"I suggest you start a journal for yourself this time and just write down whatever comes to you. You might be amazed at what you learn. Will you do that?"

"I'll see."

"Does that mean you'll think about it or

you're just brushing me off?"

She could feel a smile tug gently at the corner of her mouth. "I'll think about it."

"Good." He pulled out the side drawer of his desk and laid his prescription pad on it. After writing on it, he passed it over to her. "I'd like you to continue taking these for the next week, one half an hour or so before bedtime, as you've been doing. And then come back so we can talk some more. If you will."

Beth stared at the birds outside. "All right." She took the paper and stood. "Thank you." *I guess.*

"I have something else for you." He handed her a card from a little basket on his desk. Business card size, it looked rather innocuous.

Beth glanced from the printing on it to his face.

"It's a verse I use to get me through things that seem beyond my ability. 'I can do all things through Christ who strengthens me.' "

She started to shake her head but put the card in her pocket. If he only knew what she had to get through.

TWENTY-FIVE

Who would be calling this early? Elaine reached for the phone. "Hello."

"Good morning, Elaine. I needed to reach you before I went into court."

"Good morning to you, too. I have a feeling this is not good news." Since when did attorneys call early or late without it being bad news?

"This is more in the way of a pain in the neck . . ."

"Ah, delightful Mrs. Smyth."

"You got it. As you know, she went ahead with her threat and filed a case. Her regular lawyer turned it down, but she found someone else who is pursuing this like it was his ticket to the big time."

"And your advice?" *Why do I get the feeling I'm not going to like this?*

"I'd say settle and get her off your back but . . ."

Elaine didn't hear the *but*. "Settle? No way! That woman won't be satisfied until she owns our house, George's practice, and our retirement."

"Elaine, calm down." His chuckle broke through her diatribe. "I know what she is after, and people like her keep many lawyers in business."

"Along with cluttering up our court system."

"That too, but here's what I propose we do. Her insurance covered the damages, and yours declined that, right?"

"Yes. They think she's full of hot air, too. I've thought of buying her out, but that place would need some major work to make it saleable, and she'd charge me an arm and both legs."

"Might not be a bad idea, considering the stress she adds to your life, but that's not what I was going to say. I'm suggesting either mediation or binding arbitration. Either way, she has to accept the ruling. I'm sure they will see right through her verbosity and cantankerousness. Or there is always Judge Judy. She loves stuff like this. You talk it over with George and get back to me."

Elaine hung up the phone still chuckling. *Wait until George and Ramsey hear this one.*

She looked down at the little dog on her lap. "Maybe I should just sic you after that mangy beast of hers. Think you could take a chunk out of Bootsie?" She cuddled Bug to her chest and kissed his soft ears, crooning love to him at the same time.

Doodlebug kissed her ear and closed his big eyes in bliss. This was the way a morning was supposed to be spent. After all, what was more important in life's scheme of things than cuddling the dog? Keeping him from slipping off her lap with one hand, she pulled out the file drawer and retrieved her work on the grant proposal and her outline for the dream. She checked her watch. An hour and a half until the board meeting, then the regular meeting following the lunch. Getting the guild board behind her would be the first step.

"Sorry, Bug, but you need to go get in your bed." She set him on the floor and tried to ignore the sorrow in his eyes, the look of abused dog he assumed at will, tail dragging, ears down. She'd swear he was going to cry big tears at any second.

"Good dog."

He slunk up in his new bed with the arched half cover and lined with half of his favorite soft blanket. Turning around once, he gave her another soulful look, this one accompanied by a deep and heart-wrenchingly sad sigh.

"Doodlebug, you are the biggest ham

I've ever seen." She shook her head and started reading, making notes on a clip-board as she went along. She knew one reason she'd managed to obtain so many grants over the years. She made sure all the details were covered. Research and details; money was out there if one knew how to go find it.

Finding the money in Jefferson City would be the job of those in the guild. They knew who had deep pockets and could figure out how to convince those folks to part with some of their largess.

Winston Henry Jefferson IV was at the top of her list. If she could convince him that her dream was his dream . . . hmm. She flipped through her Rolodex, stopped at his business card, read it, thought a moment, and dialed.

"Hello, this is Elaine Giovanni and I'd like to speak to Mr. Jefferson please."

"I'll see if he's available."

You bet your sweet Marianne he is. There were advantages sometimes in being the wife of the head of surgery. While she didn't call in her markers very often, when she did they were effective.

"Good morning, Elaine. How are you?"

"Good, good. I have a favor to ask if you don't mind."

"Ask away and I'll do what I can."

She could picture him leaning back in his cordovan leather chair, his feet up on the walnut desk that had belonged to his great-grandfather, like most of the other lovely antiques in his office and home.

"Are you available for lunch tomorrow, or another day this week? I have some ideas that I think you might be interested in."

"Tomorrow would be fine if we could make it at one."

"Good, how about Joseph's?"

"My favorite. I'll see you then."

I knew it was your favorite. You've said so often enough. "Thank you."

She hung up and wrote herself a note in her organizer. George was after her to use a Palm Pilot or handheld PC, but she held out on that. She quickly typed an outline for the board meeting, ran off ten copies, and put them in a file folder that joined the file folders already in her briefcase.

"Ladies, can we come to order?" She waited in the conference room, looking around the board table at the hospital. "And please have your reports ready. We need to deal with plenty of business today."

The chatter settled down, along with the shuffling of paper.

"Good. I call the August meeting of the Jefferson City Hospital Guild board meeting to order. Will you please read the minutes of the last meeting?" She nodded to the secretary.

One by one she ticked down the items on her outline. Treasurer's report, committee reports, and old business, in which they wrapped up details related to the isolettes and the festival booth. When she announced new business, a hand went up.

"I think we need to discuss all that's already happened for the quilt event. I know that officially we aren't even a part of it yet, but there is plenty of excitement going around."

Elaine paused for a moment. "To remain within Robert's Rules of Order, I believe we need a motion first, signifying our intent."

The first woman who spoke rolled her eyes. "Okay, Madame Parliamentarian, I move that The Jefferson City Hospital Guild take an active part in the movement to purchase a new mammogram unit for the hospital, er, The Jefferson Memorial Hospital."

"I second it."

"All in favor." Elaine paused for a moment. "All in favor, say aye." A murmur rippled through the room. "The ayes have it."

"Now can we discuss it?" Silver-haired Sandy Stenerson looked Nordic enough to be a Viking queen. "Good. Let's each compile a list of anyone we think might be willing to donate. I know there will be more at the meeting later. And I volunteer to chair this part."

"Good. Thank you. Ladies, please pass your lists to Sandy. Make sure you have contact names and phone numbers, along with a good description of the donation."

"And tell them if they give us a picture of themselves and their donation, we will use it in the promotional material," Sandy added.

Elaine gave them all the particulars the quilt group had decided as to dates, place, and other activities. "Andy will take care of the golf tournament, Rhonda Pettinger will head up the 10K run/walk, but all of us can help by running or walking it ourselves and obtaining sponsors or sponsor someone else. Since we have until April, the possibilities are endless."

"You mentioned a cook-off?"

"Either that or offer an area where chefs,

restaurants, and such can showcase their specialties."

"Or both? A cook-off in the afternoon and the showcase that night? I mean, if we're going to do this, we might as well go all the way." At their nods, another woman continued. "I think we should ask Mary and Peter Mangini to head that up. Since he retired, he's been a bit at loose ends, and a project like this would be perfect."

"You mean both the cook-off and the showcase?"

"No, the showcase. He knows every chef from Portland to BC and east to the Mississippi. Well, maybe not all of them but . . ."

"The other thing, if we get official sponsors for each event, they would pay for the out-of-pocket expenses."

Elaine glanced at her watch. "I have one other thing that I'd like to bring up before we adjourn. While it's not something we can do immediately . . ."

The group settled back down and all looked toward her.

"You know that old saw, when life hands you lemons, make lemonade?" Nods greeted her comment. "Well, I believe that's what we need to do here in Jefferson City." She paused, watching their faces, most of which looked confused. "I'm speaking of the high incidence of cancer in our area, specifically breast cancer."

"But is it proven we have a higher rate of cancer, or is it really the fault of late detection due to that dinosaur of a mammogram unit?"

"No, the rate is indeed higher here. Many experts think it's caused by the high-voltage transmission lines."

"Are there any statistics for before the power lines went in? That's only been in the last twenty years."

"Good question. I didn't search back that far, but I'm sure someone has if we can just find the source."

"Let me look into that." The woman on her right wrote herself a note.

Ah, good, they are buying into this. Elaine pulled another paper out of her stack. "I believe our lemonade should come in the form of a specialized cancer center here in Jefferson City." Another pause, this one pregnant by anyone's standards. "We can start out with breast cancer, and perhaps leave that as our focus, but the field for women's medicine is wide open for expansion. We have a good hospital, and we can attract specialists and become a satellite med school with oncology as our focus. We live in a beautiful region conducive to healing and could possibly encourage alternate forms of treatment so that everyone who came here would have the benefit of cutting-edge research regarding cancer treatment."

Comments from the group bombarded her.

"Lady, when you start to dreaming, you sure do go for the top."

"And here I thought a new mammogram unit was most likely beyond possible."

"You wouldn't be mentioning this dream of yours if you hadn't done some more homework."

"True." Elaine smiled and nodded at the same time. "I've started proposals for grants to help with the mammogram unit."

Elaine checked her watch and banged the gavel. "Ladies, time to adjourn so we are not late for lunch. We can continue the discussion into the general meeting." *Where I hope we'll be getting lots more ideas and volunteers.*

A hand went up at the end of the table. "What if the quilters don't want our help?"

"Oh, we're already helping; this will just make it official. I know Kit Cooper well enough to know she'll be overjoyed. When she introduced the quilt idea, she said she hoped the women of Jefferson City would work together to make this happen. And that's exactly what we are talking about."

Elaine gathered her papers together, making sure things were in order for the afternoon meeting, and followed the others out of the room. As usual, lunch would be in the meeting room at Miss Mary's Tea House, one street over and one block down. Elaine used her cell phone and, after checking for the number in her address file, dialed Kit's number. The answering machine picked up. She left a message and followed the others over to lunch.

By the time the meeting ended, they had committees in place, and the women left sparkling with enthusiasm.

Elaine tried Kit again and hung up when the answering machine clicked on.

On her way home she swung by the dry cleaners to pick up George's shirts and stopped at the antique store to check out the latest needlework and linens she'd heard about. Antique lace, doilies, and trims were all things she incorporated into her pillows, so she was constantly on the prowl to add to her stash.

"I picked these up with you in mind." Celine brought some pieces out of the back room and laid them on the counter. "I don't put them out until I've shown you."

"Thank you." *Since I buy enough to keep you in business, I should hope so.* Elaine flipped through a cutwork tablecloth and napkin set. She could cut around the stains if she couldn't remove them. She also looked through some tablecloths from the fifties, a stack of doilies, and odds and ends of lace.

"I found you another hatpin, too." Celine laid a hatpin trimmed in jets, the black beads catching the light. "Exquisite, isn't it?"

Knowing that if she showed her pleasure, the piece would double in price, Elaine searched for a flaw to comment on. Finding none, she agreed and turned back to the linens.

"I'll take these then."

"What about the hatpin?"

"Oh, that's right. You said you wanted $25?" She named a price half of the original offer.

"No, I said it was $49.50."

Elaine cupped her elbow in the opposite hand and tapped a forefinger on her chin.

"Will you take $35, since I am buying all these?"

"Elaine Giovanni, you will be the end of me yet. How can I stay in business and furnish you with all these lovely assets to your pillows when every time I show you something, you haggle about the price?"

Elaine shrugged, her eyes crinkling at the corners. "You know you love it just as much as I do, and in the end, we both come out with a good deal." She handed over her credit card and waited while Celine rang up the sale and packaged the goods, making sure to double-wrap the hatpin. "Call me when you have more."

"I will."

"I'm especially looking for more cutwork, so if you see any . . ."

"Have you gone on the Internet?"

"Not really. You having much luck there?"

Celine waggled her hand in the universal win some, lose some sign.

"As I said, if you find any, let me know." Elaine left the shop and, after placing her purchases in the trunk, drove on home.

Doodlebug met her at the door, yapping his pleasure at her return or scolding her for being gone so long, she wasn't sure which.

"Easy, Bug, let me put these things down and then . . ." She turned at the fast clicking of his nails on the tile just in time to see the end of his tail going out the door. "Doodlebug, get back in here this instant!" She dropped her briefcase and packages on the chair by the entry table and headed back out the door.

Ferocious growling and snorting doubled her pace. "Doodlebug!" She paused on the brick steps just long enough to glance to the right and see Doodlebug snapping and snarling at Bootsie, who had come to deposit his daily offering on their side lawn. Bootsie lunged at Doodlebug, but he leaped sideways and grabbed a chunk of Bootsie's jowl in the process. The bulldog set up a howl as though he'd been mortally wounded and headed for home, but not before Elaine could see blood staining the dog's white coat.

"Bug, get over here." Sure that Doodlebug had been injured, Elaine ran to where the little dog was kicking grass with his hind feet and barking the bigger dog away.

Elaine snatched him up and checked for injuries. "Doodlebug, what have you done?"

"Grrrrrrrr." The growl continued as Bug warned off his long-gone adversary.

"We're in trouble for sure now."

TWENTY-SIX

"I no more feel like having the quilters here than running a marathon."

Missy followed Kit from the living room to the kitchen, to the bathroom to freshen up, to the garage to dump in a load of laundry, to the kitchen for a cup of coffee, and back to the living room to dust.

"Dog, just go lie down."

Missy's tail drooped.

"I'm sorry, girl. Taking my bad mood out on you isn't going to help a bit." Kit bent down to rub the long catkin-soft ears and stroke down the dog's back. "Okay, now I have to get back to getting ready whether I want to or not. Feel like laying bets with me that Teza will call and say she is just too busy to come? Then I shall be in a real uproar, you just watch."

The phone rang.

"See, I told you." Kit headed back to the kitchen and picked up the receiver. "Hello." Just in time she kept herself from saying, "Teza."

"Hi, Kit, this is Sue. I'm running a bit

behind schedule, but I'll be there as soon as I can. Anything more I can bring?"

"Any marking pencils?"

"Sure. And I baked a peach upside-down cake for dessert."

"Sounds wonderful. See you when you get here."

Kit hung up in time to hear a knock on the front door and then the soft glide of it opening. "Come on in."

"We are," Beth answered.

"I brought sliced cucumber salad." Teza walked into the kitchen.

"Well, it's a good thing we didn't bet." Kit glanced down to see Missy dancing around the guests, tail whipping enough to cause bruises on shins and calves.

"Who bet?" Teza opened the refrigerator door and set her salad on a shelf. "Aren't you eating at all? Look at this empty fridge."

"Of course I'm eating." Kit wasn't about to say that popcorn had become a staple. "I just cleaned it out last night." She tried to assess Teza's state without looking too obvious. She knew there were dark circles under her own eyes that even cover stick couldn't hide. Not sleeping did that to you. "I made apricot nectar for today."

"How did you do that?" Beth handed

her a covered dish. "Chicken salad for sandwiches."

"Put the apricots through the blender."

"Skin and all?"

"Yup. Added lemon juice to keep it from turning brown. I've canned it like this in the past, but this time I put the extra in the freezer in ice-cube trays. Then I can bag those and use them in whatever size batch I need."

"How clever." Beth set a grocery sack on the counter. At Kit's questioning look, she smiled. "Bread. I was hoping you had lettuce. Ours bolted."

"I do, all washed even. This is working out wonderfully well. You want to help me move those tables in from the garage? Three eight-foot ones should be adequate."

The doorbell rang as the two went out the door to the garage.

"I'll get that," Teza called.

"How was the trip to Seattle?" Beth took the side at one end of the folding table, Kit at the other.

"Bad. There's a spot on her lung and most likely in the lymph nodes." They wrestled the table up the two steps and through the kitchen door, half dragging it into the living room. "Hi, Elsie Mae. Make yourself at home, please." They propped the table on its side against the coffee table.

"We'll put this up." Teza took one end and nodded to Elsie Mae to help her. Kit and Beth headed back to the garage.

"Oh, Kit, I've been praying it wasn't so."

Yeah, goes to show how much good prayer does. But she kept the mutter to herself. No sense hurting Beth's feelings.

"So what are they going to do?" The two of them hoisted the next table.

"Nothing."

"Nothing?" Beth dropped her end of the table, then picked it up again. "Sorry."

"Teza has asked for a week to research alternative methods of treatment to see if she wants to do anything at all." Kit choked on the last words.

"Oh, Kit. I'll put her on our prayer chain at church. Garth could come see her."

"Don't say anything, please."

"But have the elders from your church anointed her with oil and prayed for her healing?"

What kind of kooks do we have here? "Ah no. Our church has a prayer chain, but she asked me not to post it yet."

"I see."

Nothing more was said as they set up the

third and final table, but Kit could tell there was plenty going on behind Beth's lovely eyes.

"Hi, Elaine, welcome," Kit said over her shoulder on her way to the kitchen. "Sue said she was coming but she'd be a bit late." Kit returned from the kitchen with a damp cloth to wipe down the tables. "All the quilt things are there in those plastic tubs. We need to mark all the quilting lines first."

Elsie Mae lifted the quilt top from the bin. "We need to press this again."

"Of course. Beth, would you please show her the way to the sewing room? The ironing board is all set up."

"Sure." The two went up the stairs while the others moved the tables together and laid out rulers, templates, and marking pencils.

"So, Teza, what did they say at the hospital?" Elaine pushed one of the bins under the tables.

"The cancer has returned."

"How bad?"

"In my lung, the breast, and lymph." Teza gestured to the right side of her body.

"So they'll do a mastectomy?"

"I haven't decided."

Elaine looked to Kit, who did the classic

shrug with raised hands. "Let me get this straight. The cancer has metastasized, they wanted to do an immediate mastectomy, a radical I assume, and you haven't decided yet?"

"No need to yell."

"I'm not yelling." Elaine toned her voice down and looked to Kit, who shrugged again, head tipped slightly to the side. Elaine sucked in a deep breath and started again. "What is there to decide?"

Kit looked up to see Beth paused on the stairs, one hand on the rail, the other fingering the locket at her throat.

"Sorry I'm late." Sue came through the doorway as she spoke. "Uh oh?" She looked to each woman in the room, now frozen as if in a tableau. "Did I interrupt something?"

Kit forced a smile to welcome her friend. "No, we're just discussing Teza's options here."

"Options?" Sue crossed her arms over her chest. "Okay, Teza, dear, what's going on?"

"I really don't think this is the proper place and time to . . ."

"Teza, this is Sue you're talking to. You might as well be my aunt as Kit's, since I've known you from when Kit and I were in kindergarten." She glanced at Kit. "Or was it nursery in church?"

"Either, both, call it forever." Kit tucked her smile back inside. Leave it to Sue to get right to the point.

"Right. So you just tell me what's going on. This is the right time and the right place."

"Yay, Sue." Beth pumped a closed fist. "You tell her."

Teza raised both hands, palm out. "I've asked for a week, that's all. I want to explore the options and pray about this. After all, it is *my* body." She snapped out the last words. "Remember, I've been through this before."

"But you haven't had all of us before." Beth's gentle voice cut through the friction like oil through water and settled the chop.

"To gang up on me, you mean?"

"If that is what it takes." Sue headed for the kitchen to set her cake on the counter. "Surely the coffee must be ready."

"Oh, I'm sorry. I forgot." Kit hurried into the other room. "Thank you, dear friend."

"You are most welcome." Sue wrapped her arms around Kit and hugged her close. "We won't let her go."

"I know, but sometimes we have no control, no matter how much we care." Kit blinked. There would be no crying today.

"I know how well we know." Sue brushed her eyes with the back of her hand. "Times like this I sure am grateful God knows what he is doing. Just wish he'd clue me in."

Kit kept her doubts to herself. She and Sue had had many such discussions in the two years since Amber died, and they'd finally agreed to disagree. Or rather, Sue ignored Kit's doubts and went on as if they were nonexistent. More than once she'd just shrugged and said, "You'll come around. God isn't going to let you go." And kept on praying.

Kit measured the coffee into the basket and poured the water into the coffee maker. "There, that'll be ready in a couple of minutes. I have iced tea in the fridge, and I can make hot tea if anyone wants."

"Some days like today, you wonder where the summer went. I'll ask if anyone wants hot tea." Sue left and Kit got down the coffee mugs, a couple of tall glasses, and the sugar bowl with sweetener packets on the side. She retrieved her tin full of various kinds of tea bags and set that by the mugs. The coffee maker beeped.

Elsie Mae came down the stairs as Kit

stepped to the door to announce the coffee was ready. "I love your sewing room. What a peaceful place."

"Thank you. Other than the backyard, that's my favorite room. Coffee's ready, ladies. Come help yourself."

Elsie Mae spread the quilt top over the tables. "Now, isn't that just lovely?"

"No one drinks or eats near our baby," Elaine announced as they returned to the living room. "I think we should put our names on our cups so we remember which is which."

"That's why I set out the bunny mugs. Just remember which is yours. Mine's easy." Kit held up a white mug with a ceramic bunny climbing over the lip.

"Wherever did you get such a delightful collection?" Beth asked.

"Every one who knows Kit gave her bunny mugs until she cried uncle." Sue pointed to hers. "I brought this one back from California one year."

"Okay, I figured since we are all old hands at this, we would mark only a few dots on each side of the diamonds, using quarter inch from the seam. That should save us some time. Then I have a number of templates for the borders, and we need to decide which we want."

"I'd think we should stay with geometrics like interlocking diamonds or squares or such." Beth set her mug down on a coaster on the coffee table. She withdrew a pencil and notebook from her bag. "Like this." She drew several examples.

"Or angled lines." Kit drew lines in the air so Beth could see what she meant.

"Or squares within squares, going from large down to small."

"So many choices," Elaine said. "If you do that, you could use diamonds or triangles, too."

"Okay, we need to vote. Beth, can you show us your designs there?"

Beth held up her paper and pointed to a running zigzag. "I think this one in lines half an inch apart."

"How about that one for the upper and mirror it with a lower, then stitch a small cancer ribbon in the center." Teza drew with her fingertip on the page, and Beth finished the design.

"I like that." Elaine leaned over Beth's shoulder. "You want to come and draw designs for me sometime? You're good."

"Thanks." Beth held up the pattern. "I'll draw the cancer ribbon and we can cut a template for that. As for the others, if we mark the high point and low point and then keep the lines half or quarter . . ."

"Half." Elsie Mae held up her twelve-inch square. "I think we need to draw a line between high and low points so the zigs and zags will all match." Like the others, she used her finger for an air drawing.

"Someone has to figure out how many zigs and zags." Beth left her drawing.

"Not me." Elaine shook her head. "I hate math of any kind."

"Nor me." Sue picked up a marking pencil and a short see-through ruler. "I'll start marking the diamonds in the star."

"Teza, you're it." Kit handed her aunt a pad and pencil. "I'll measure to be exact."

"Make sure you leave room for the nine-patch blocks in the corners."

They marked up until lunch, ate, and went back to marking. Sue had to leave about two. By three, they were ready to layer the quilt. They spread the lining on the table, right side down, and laid the batting over that carefully to make sure there were no wrinkles. When that met everyone's approval, they laid the quilt top in place, checking so that it was perfectly centered. Then, after pinning it in strategic places, they began basting from the center out, lines running diagonally to the corners and in a cross right at the center.

"I'm sorry," Elaine said about four. "I need to get going. Can we just leave this here?"

"That's the plan." Kit straightened her creaking back. "I can work on it some more tonight, perhaps finish the basting . . ."

"And then we can get it on the frame." Teza nodded to the canvas-clad lengths of wood bundled along the back of the sofa.

"I can't come back until Friday." Elaine pulled the thread through her needle and let the tail hang. "But I've never put a quilt up on a frame before. I just used a hoop."

"I have." Elsie Mae took another basting stitch. "And I can come tomorrow for a while in the morning."

I have a feeling, Kit thought later after she'd shown the rest of them out and returned to her living room, *a feeling that I'm going to be living with this for what will seem like a long time . . . A very long time.*

TWENTY-SEVEN

"Please, Teza, for God's sake . . ." At the frown on her aunt's face, Kit rephrased her plea. "Maybe for my sake then, if you won't do it for yours."

Teza sat in a beam of sunlight, but even the gold outline did nothing to soften the steel in her jaw.

"Kit, you are not listening to me. I didn't say I absolutely wouldn't accept treatment. I said I want to explore all the options."

"But the longer you wait . . ."

"Remember, the doctor agreed that a week would not make much difference one way or the other."

"When he said it needs to be treated aggressively, he didn't mean by eating tofu or something. He meant surgery, radiation, and chemo — *now!* Teza, you are all the family I have left . . ."

"Now, Kit dear, that just isn't true. You have Mark, Jennifer, and Ryan."

"Right!" Kit stomped halfway across the room and swung around to face her aunt. "Mark is God knows where, and only God knows when, or even if, he will ever come home. Jennifer is building her own life in Dallas, Texas, which is nowhere near Jefferson City the last time I looked at a map. Ryan is clear across the state and will only be home off and on for visits because he is building his own life too. So what do you mean, I —"

"What do you mean," Teza interrupted gently, "that only God knows when or if Mark will come home?"

"I wasn't going to tell you that."

"Tell me now."

"I don't know where he is."

"You have no way of getting ahold of him?"

"E-mail. Or in an emergency I could call his office and they would contact him. I refuse to do that."

"What about his cell phone?"

"He lets it go to voice mail and calls me back." *But I never go that route.*

"He never answers?"

The shock on her face made Kit shrug. "He said he needed a break, couldn't deal with all that had gone on, couldn't stand the memories at home or here in Jefferson City — so, he ran."

"When did this come about?"

"Six, seven months ago." Kit mentally

counted off the months. "Actually eight. He left right after the first of the year."

"And you never told me."

"I never told anyone. I figured give him a couple of months and he'd be okay, come home again, and we could work on getting back to normal. Whatever in the world normal is."

"I see." Teza looked up from twisting her wedding ring on her finger. "But if you had told me, I would have been praying with you."

"Yeah, that's something else you don't quite understand. I gave up in the praying department. If God didn't heal Amber, why would he care about this? After all, it's only a marriage."

"If he numbers the sparrows, is not your marriage of more concern?"

"Wasn't Amber of even more concern?" Rage exploded like a geyser as hot as Old Faithful's steam. "If he cared so much, where was he when I needed him?"

"Right beside you and under you, all around and in your heart. He did as you asked. He healed Amber, just not in the way you wanted."

Like the geyser that shoots and retreats, Kit drew back within herself, mopped her eyes, and swallowed more tears. "Whatever."

"Oh, my dear, I pray you will finally let it all go and let the healing come in. He wants to help you, but you won't let him."

Here I am trying to comfort or rather encourage you, and you are doing the opposite. Not that this is much comfort, but then what is? "I want Amber back."

"The way she was?"

"No, of course not. Who in their right mind would wish that on anyone, let alone one they love."

"She's waiting there for us all. What a rejoicing that will be. And I believe she is watching out for you here and now. I don't believe heaven is some far distant place, or the Bible wouldn't have talked about that man who looked down and saw his brothers making the same mistakes he did — the one who asked God to send them someone from the dead to warn them."

"I want to believe that she is close by, but oh, what I would give for that phone to ring and hear her 'hi, Mom,' one more time."

"One more time would still never be enough."

Kit's shoulders sagged. Too much, all too much. "So what do you want me to do?"

"I want you to help me research alternative treatments. We can contact the Cancer Society and see what they suggest. I plan on going to a bookstore to check out the titles."

"I can do that with Amazon.com or Barnes and Noble's Web site. Online can be faster."

"Okay, let's make a list so we don't overlap. It's not that I don't plan on following the doctor's orders, you know. It's just that I want to do what's best. I mean losing another breast is no big deal, just that after that I won't have any more to give away."

Including lungs and innards and bones and . . . Oh, Lord, please. Kit swallowed her plea. *Haven't I lost enough?*

Come unto me, you who are heavy laden, and I will give you rest.

You're not playing fair again.

Whatever it takes, my dear Kit, whatever it takes.

Now, that was no Bible verse she'd ever heard.

"What is it, dear?"

Kit shook her head. Surely she was just going bonkers with it all. Voices in her head, on her shoulder, or wherever.

They sat and wrote two lists, one for

each of them, and finished up just as the doorbell rang.

"You have a customer."

"I know." Teza rose and headed for the door. "You want some more apricots?"

"No thanks, unless you need help."

"I think I'll sell all the rest."

Kit followed Teza out the door, hugged her, and after quick good-byes, got in her van. Too much, things were getting to be too much, and there was nothing she could do about it. About the time you thought you had life under control, something would broadside you and send you spinning back into panic mode.

Life changes in an instant. Oh, to be back in the times of bliss when a major problem was a ten-dollar error or even a hundred-dollar error in the checkbook, or getting caught by a fender bender in the grocery parking lot. Or someone came home late.

Ah, those were the days.

In her own driveway, she leaned her forehead on her crossed hands at the top of the steering wheel. "Okay, God, so do I take a chance on you again? Do I pray and trust you to take care of Teza, to take care of Mark, as if I could do anything about him right now, my two children, this quilt project, those others with cancer in this town, my marriage — if you can call this strange limbo I'm in a marriage — so what next? What do I do?"

She waited, wishing for a skywriter, or perhaps the rhododendron by the garage to burst into flames, or an angel to appear. Evidence that God did indeed hear her and, even more importantly, that he cared. And that he could be trusted.

A knock on the car door snapped her out of wherever she'd been. She looked out to see Thomas standing there, concern wrinkling his forehead, nearly hidden under his Mariners cap.

She smiled. At least she hoped that's what it looked like and opened the door.

"You okay?"

"I guess, how about you?"

"I thought maybe you was crying."

"Nope. Just thinking."

"Missy was crying when I knocked on the door. When you didn't come, I was going home, but then I saw you drive in. I thought Missy might want to play."

"I'm sure she does." Kit grabbed her purse and keys and got out. "Where've you been lately?"

"We went to visit my aunt in Tacoma."

"Did you have fun?"

He shrugged, both hands buried in the

pockets of his baggy jeans. "My dad said we might go to a baseball game, but we didn't."

Kit unlocked the front door and stood back so Missy and Thomas could greet each other. They followed her inside and directly through the house to the back door.

"Can we go out?" Thomas leaned over for an enthusiastic doggy kiss.

"Of course." Kit picked up the mail that had been scattered by Missy's broad dancing feet.

An envelope with Mark's handwriting caught her attention. She checked the postage cancellation. Salt Lake City. When had he gone there? Or, better question, how long had he been there? Or, even better, was he still there?

She slit the envelope open with a fingernail and pulled out a card. "Thinking of you" was the caption arched over a bouquet of roses. Inside he'd written, "Busy as ever but I saw this card and thought of you. Please understand, Kit . . ."

She lowered the card and stared at the wall. *How can I understand anything from you? That you would just walk out and not let me know where you are or what's happening with you. Mark, you do not make sense.* She returned to reading the card.

"Please understand that it is not you I am running from, but, oh, I guess I cannot even explain it to myself. I am trying to find the time to come home for a visit when Ryan is there, but don't count on it. Thanks for the e-mails. Mark."

"Not 'love Mark' or 'as ever Mark' or 'yours Mark.' " She glared in the hall mirror and started to crumple the card, but stopped. He had thought about her. He was not filing for divorce or shacking up with someone. Well, at least not that she knew. He could be and this was just a cover.

She wandered into the kitchen to hear Missy's woofs of delight and Thomas's giggles, sounds of home and happiness, all the things Mark was missing.

Sometimes the rage at what he'd done burned hot and fierce. Other times she just questioned without ever receiving answers. Which was best? Was she growing indifferent? Should she just divorce him and get on with her life? Was that what he wanted? Was that what she wanted?

"No, and a thousand times no. I do not want a divorce. I signed on for the long haul, and one of us better believe in our wedding vows. For richer, for poorer, been through both of those, in sickness and in health, been there, too, but where does desertion come in?

"Ah, Amber, if you can see all this, it must just be breaking your heart." At that, the tears gushed, and she headed for the bathroom to drown a washcloth.

When she could talk without sniffing again, she fetched Popsicles out of the freezer, puppy treats out of the pantry, and ambled outside to the deck.

"Hey, you two rollers, treats."

"Thanks." Thomas sat down on the cedar steps beside her, and Missy caught her tossed treat to lie down to munch it.

"You missing Amber?"

"What makes you think that?" She nibbled on the yellow ice stick.

"Your eyes are red and . . ." He made signs to show puffed up.

"Sometimes I just start to cry."

"Oh. Where's your dad?"

"My husband, Mark?"

He nodded.

"Away on business."

"He sure stays gone a long time."

She almost asked, "Where's your mother?" but kept her question to herself. Thomas would tell her when he was ready.

"My dad goes on business trips. He went to Alaska one time."

"Really?"

"Uh-huh. He likes baseball, too."

"I've been thinking. I used to pitch for the kids. I could get out the pitchback, and we could give you some batting practice."

"Old ladies pitch baseball?"

Out of the mouths of babes. She licked the last of the ice off the stick. "Well, if you think I'm too old . . ."

"Guess we could try."

Kit thought about the work waiting for her. "I got a deal for you. We play ball for half an hour, and then you help me weed the garden."

"I don't know what weeds are."

"I'll show you." She looked sideways at him. "You on?"

"I guess. I don't got my mitt, though."

"You don't need one. You'll hold the bat. I'll get the pitchback down and we can set it up, then I need to warm up a bit." *Oh, crumb, how long since I pitched? Four years? When did Ryan get beyond me? How long since Amber played softball?*

"You sure?"

"Yup." She stood and turned to the garage. "The pitchback is hanging up in the rafters, so I need the stepladder. Good thing I didn't put it in the garage sale."

"You pitch pretty good for a lady." Half an hour had worn them both out. Kit was sure her arm and shoulder would be screaming at her in the morning, if they waited that long.

Missy had retrieved most of the balls and lined them up on the steps. She lay on her belly in the grass, both back legs stretched straight back.

"Thanks. Now to the weeding. I'll get the trowels."

"Can I have something to drink?"

"Like water?" She pointed to the fountain Mark had installed when the kids were little to keep them from running in and out all the time.

"Sure. Does that work?"

"I think so." She got up, stifled a groan — pitching used leg muscles, too — and crossed to turn the handle. Nothing.

"Oh well, come on in. I think there is some lemonade in the fridge." One more thing that Mark wasn't here to fix. "Maybe it got turned off last winter so it wouldn't freeze and just never got turned back on." Or was it the winter before? Time passing, again that sense of a freight train bearing down on her. Or maybe she'd already been run over and just didn't know it yet.

TWENTY-EIGHT

"Bootsie did not almost bleed to death. You tell me if you think Doodlebug could grab that fat bulldog by the throat. He couldn't get near the neck, let alone tear the jugular. There was blood on the dog's face, maybe a bite on the ear or cheek. One chomp and he'd have killed Doodlebug." Elaine propped the receiver on her shoulder. "No, Frederick, I didn't see the whole thing, but then neither did she. She was coming out the door when I got out there. Bootsie was crying loud enough to wake the dead. That's what brought her outside. Besides, that dog was in our yard, and we, including our dog, have a right to defend our yard."

"I hear you, Elaine, but I also have to let you know what is happening. She, Mrs. Smyth-with-a-Y, alleges that your "vicious dog," I am using her words, attacked her "precious Bootsie" without provocation."

"He was doing his business in *our yard* for heaven's sake!"

"Take it easy. I'm on your side, remember?"

Elaine raked her hair back with quivering fingers. *The absolute nerve of that woman.* And here all these years she'd done no more than ask politely if they would keep Bootsie home. "I swear that woman will drive me to desperate measures." She didn't mention the *kill* word, but she had thought it plenty of times. No, she didn't really want to kill anyone, just get even. But how, short of dumping a truckload of manure on their front yard, did one get even for years of scooping dog poop out of the yard? "I think it is malicious intent."

"What is?"

"She trained Bootsie to poop in our yard. I know she did. She most likely gave him treats every time he unloaded before coming home."

"Elaine." Frederick was laughing now.

"So did we complain, file a legal complaint? No, we cleaned it up — a lot of it, mind you — in the interest of keeping peace in the neighborhood. Well, from now on, we will throw all of it back in her yard, and if it accidentally hits the house, so be it. And if you want to continue as our attorney, I would suggest you quiet that boisterous laughter immediately if not before." She felt the edge of her mouth twitch but crushed the incipient smile with firm resolve. "So, revered lawyer, what do you suggest we do over this latest altercation? Other than burn them out, that is. Or buy them out is my suggestion, but George has always put the kibosh on that. But then perhaps we should make him do the poop-scoop detail for a few weeks and see what he thinks then."

"In scrubs no less." Frederick went off on another fit of laughter.

The thought of George in green scrubs, even to mask in place, out in the yard with scooper shovel and the rake she had bought specifically for this terribly unpleasant job made her smile and then chuckle. "Stop it, stop laughing, or I shall report you to whatever august body polices the rank and file of attorneys."

"No one polices attorneys. We litigate that away."

"Frederick, you are now laughing at your own jokes. There should be a law against that, too."

"Oh, I'm sure there is, somewhere on the books in some obscure little town." He took a deep breath and his voice returned to normal.

"I can just see this, the case of *Chihuahua v. English Bull Dog.* No judge in his or her right mind would take that one on."

"So what are we going to do?"

"Offer to pay the vet bills."

"Vet bills, for a little scratch like that? I swear I'm taking this to one of those TV judges."

"Yeah, it's about dumb enough to do that with, but this all comes back to the fire. Mrs. Smyth is out to get you over the power lines accident."

"But the insurance paid for the entire thing. What in heaven's name is she suing for?"

"Pain and suffering, of course."

"There was no pain, only inconvenience. And that woman would suffer over a hang-nail."

"Especially if you caused it." He answered someone else. "I gotta go. Thanks for the good laugh, and now you know what is happening. I'll keep you in the loop."

"Thanks, I guess. If you can figure out some way to put a lid on that woman, I would gladly double your already astronomical fees."

"I'm a miracle worker at times, dear Elaine, but I am not God."

She hung up, chuckling along with him. Doodlebug leaped up into her lap as soon as she sat down and, after a quick chin kiss, turned around twice and lay down with a sigh.

"You know, you're the cause of this latest fracas. But you sure put that stupid Bootsie on the run." She lifted his chin and looked in his eyes. "You know what, though? He could have eaten you with one gulp. Don't you go doing that again. You hear me?"

He blinked once and yawned, pink tongue with one brown spot on the tip curling and uncurling. Laying his head back on her thigh, he sighed again.

If only life were so easy. How in the world do I get even with that fool next door? Something that will shut her down for good, or make her move out. There must be a way before something terrible happens.

Elaine spent the next hour on the phone before getting ready to meet Winston Henry Jefferson IV for lunch. While she showered, she thought about her presentation. What was the best way to get him to think her dream was his, that he came up with the idea of a major cancer center in Jefferson City first?

She was still mulling the ideas over as she drove to the restaurant.

She arrived at the restaurant ten minutes early and asked to be shown to their table. Long before, she'd learned the efficacy of being the first to arrive for any business presentation to establish her territory. She took the side of the booth facing the door so she could see him enter, pulled a small wrapped package out of her briefcase, and set it in the middle of the table. She thanked the waiter for bringing water and set the menus in place. Glancing around the room, she smiled at two women she knew, took a sip of water, and thought again about how to introduce her subject.

Winston Henry Jefferson IV entered the front door wearing his politician's smile and firm stride. The maître d' showed him back to the table and left him with a smile.

"Hello, Elaine, so good to see you." He took her hand in a courtly manner, so reminiscent of an earlier time that she was sure she heard his heels click. "I hope I'm not late."

"No, not at all." She indicated the seat with one hand. "Sit and make yourself comfortable. I thought you might enjoy a booth more than the chairs." In fact, she had asked the maître d' as to her guest's preference. Anything to make him as comfortable as possible.

"Oh, I do. You must be a mind reader." Winston took his seat, unbuttoning his natural linen sports coat as he sat. "Nice day, isn't it?"

She nodded and pushed the package toward him. "I thought of you when I saw this."

"How nice of you." He unwrapped the silver box and held up a clear paperweight with a saying embossed in gold: *You can if you think you can.* "So very true." His wide smile showed perfect orthodontic work. "Thank you." He set the paperweight down on the table and leaned back, hands clasped on the table in front of him. "Have you decided yet what you will have?"

Elaine nodded. "I always have the chicken Caesar salad. Best I've had anywhere."

"That sounds good. Think I'll do the same." He set his menu off to the side, squaring the corner up with that of the table.

The waiter stopped at their table, and they gave their orders. Winston ordered a glass of wine, but Elaine declined, knowing that she needed the clearest head possible to put her plan into action.

Over the salad they talked about their families, hospital gossip, and the ubiquitous weather. When the waiter took their plates and refilled her iced tea, she leaned forward.

"Winston, you've done such an excellent job on the refurbishing of our hospital that I wondered if you've thought of other avenues to make Jefferson Memorial of more service for our community."

"You didn't invite me to lunch to talk about the mammogram unit, did you?"

"No. We've already discussed that, and while I understand your position, I and the other women of the town will take care of that. I've been thinking of something more far reaching than one machine."

"Really. And what might that be?"

Here we go. She took another sip of her iced tea, keeping her gaze locked on his all the while. "Have you ever thought what an ideal place Jefferson City might be for a cancer center? Done right, I believe it could put our town on the map. We've been getting a lot of bad press regarding the transmission lines, so why not turn that to our advantage?"

"So why not?" He sat up straight and leaned slightly forward. "What do you have in mind?"

"A bigger hospital, oncology specialists, cooperation with alternative treatments, a place where one could come for total healing. We could be a teaching hospital. Perhaps one of the universities would have a satellite here. Bring new blood into town that would revitalize our entire area. We live in one of the most beautiful places on earth, and everyone knows that natural beauty helps restore peace and wholeness. We could call it the Angela Jefferson Women's Oncology Center, in honor of your mother, who did so much for this hospital in her lifetime."

His eyes had brightened and he nodded repeatedly. "Perhaps if we'd had something like this here back then, she might still be alive today."

"Perhaps so. Saving lives is what our hospital is all about."

"That and improving the quality of life." He took his glasses off and polished them with the table napkin. "A major cancer center, eh? My word, Elaine Giovanni, you do dream big. Have you mentioned this to George yet?"

She shook her head. "I thought as head of the board and benefactor, you would be the place to start." She could tell by the cock of his head her words had pleased him.

"Something like this would take major doing, a lifetime perhaps."

"But a worthy lifetime. What a difference it could make in people's lives, far beyond our scope to dream."

"And it would be a solid investment also. State-of-the-art diagnostic equipment, the latest in medications, what about even a research wing? Perhaps a pharmaceutical involvement. We could offer stock as an investment opportunity. What if our scientists came up with a viable cure?"

"You would be carrying on a family tradition." She gave him her warmest smile. "I have some information I've been collecting if you would like it. Other places have undertaken similar ventures. I thought to look into that eye clinic in Chehalis. They're the Nordstrom of corneal transplants, first-class service all the way, make their patients feel like royalty, really a class act."

"We could be like that."

The faraway look in his eyes gave her a secret smile. No doubt about it, he had caught the dream. Now to see what he would make of it.

She sat back and crossed her ankles, sipping her iced tea and dreaming dreams of her own. How to get even with Mrs. Bootsie.

TWENTY-NINE

"You would not believe what is going on at my house." Elaine dumped her bag on a chair.

Teza looked up from tightening one of the corner clamps on the quilting frame. "No, what?"

"Well, I have a little fawn-and-white Chihuahua named Doodlebug, you know, a little dog." Elaine held her hands for both height and length, neither large. "Our neighbor — she makes it her lifetime aim to keep friction going — has a fat, white English bulldog named Bootsie that looks amazingly like Mrs. Smyth-with-a-Y and insists on messing in our yard. The dog, not the woman."

Chuckles set the others to sharing glances.

"Anyway, Monday my dog charged out the door as I was coming in, chased said dog out of our yard and, in the altercation, bit him. Drew blood. So now this charming candidate for the least-liked woman in the world, or at least the county, is suing me. And it's not the first time . . ." Elaine waved her hands in the air. "I'm not telling you this story to create laughter, so could you just listen without howling."

Kit and Teza glanced at each other and broke out again. Beth held her stomach, and Elsie Mae leaned against the wall, wiping her eyes.

"D-Doodlebug is how big?" Beth tried to keep a straight face.

Elaine showed the size again.

"And the neighbor dog, what's its name?"

"Bootsie."

"Bootsie. I see." She nodded, eyes wide. "And Bootsie is how big?"

Elaine held her hand about two feet off the floor. "Like that." And spread her hands about a bit more than a foot apart. "And that wide."

"And the bitty Doodlebug . . ."

"He thinks he's a Rottweiler."

"Uh-huh. Chased B-Bootsie out of your yard, even drew blood. Did your neighbor see all this?"

"No, but she and everyone else within three blocks heard it. Bootsie screamed like he'd been maimed and then charged home. Of course leaving his mess behind." Elaine made digging motions with her fingers. "And Doodlebug stood there, digging grass clippings and kicking them behind. You know how dogs do. Big studly dog." Her eyebrows headed for her hairline. "Doing his best imitation of a big dog's bark and or growl. Bootsie could have eaten him with one gulp."

"You could take this on a comedy show. You know, funniest home movies, that kind of thing." Elsie Mae sank down on the sofa, wiping her eyes. "I can just see it all. And I s'pose you were yellin' at the other dog and callin' to Doodlebug. And she was screaming. Good thing you weren't turned in for disturbing the peace."

"There's no peace where that woman is concerned. None." A chopping motion followed the words.

"So what are you going to do?" Kit shook her head. "What a mess."

"Yeah, right. Big mess, big stinky mess, that's what he's been leaving in our yard for the last ten years."

Beth looked around at the others. "What can she do?"

"Put up a fence? It wouldn't have to be high to keep a fat dog like that from jumping over."

"Restrictions from the homeowners association. No fences beyond the front corners of the houses. We thought to do that, even filed a special petition."

"She actually filed a suit against you?"

Elaine nodded. "She's an ambulance-chasing-attorney's dream. Her regular attorney wouldn't even take this one. He doesn't have to bother. He's gotten rich on all her other cases." Elaine dug her sewing kit out of her bag. "Well, since you already have the frame set up, we might as well get to this. If you think of any solutions, let me know."

"Well, the Bible says heap burning coals of kindness on your enemy's head." Teza threaded her needle.

"I'd heap burning coals all right, but the law might get upset."

"No, of kindness." Beth pulled a chair over to the frame.

"We have always tried to be good neighbors. Back in the early days we invited them for barbecue, included them in the neighborhood gatherings, sent over Christmas presents, you know, all the friendly stuff." Elaine shook her head and kept on shaking it. "Not anymore. But getting even sounds like a wonderful idea. I'm just not sure how — yet."

"So it isn't just Bootsie." Kit sat down,

threaded needle in hand. "By the way, Sue can't make it today."

Elaine watched as Kit tied a knot in the end of her thread. "That's different. Can you show me how?"

Kit demonstrated wrapping the thread around the needle and pulling it all through. "Makes a strong, but nearly invisible, knot."

"Hmm." Elaine made it on the second attempt. "Thanks."

"Now, if only Bootsie" — Kit bit back a giggle — "were so easy."

"On a different subject, Beth, how are things at your house?"

"I have a stray cat that is beginning to come around. We've been feeding him for weeks, but he's still easily spooked." Beth kept her eyes on her needle. *And I nearly fell apart again this morning. I thought the pills and this quilting were really helping, but getting out of bed was more than I could manage.*

"You've seemed happier lately," Kit said.

"Have I? Good. Being with all of you helps."

"I've missed out on something." Elaine stopped stitching. "What's happened?"

The silence stretched until Kit said, after getting a nod from Beth, "Beth lost a baby a few months before coming here."

"Oh, you sweet thing. I lost my first one too. That's so hard to take." Elaine reached over and gave Beth a hug. "Any time you need to talk, why, I've got a ready ear."

"Thank you. Thank you to all of you."

"How's that hubby of yours taking it?"

"H-He thinks I should be over it by now. After all, the baby never lived . . ."

"And this is the pro-life man? Of course that baby lived, inside of you right where it belonged."

"I know, but I mean . . ."

"We know what you mean, dearie." Elsie Mae reached across the quilt and patted Beth's hand. "No wonder your eyes have been so sad, haunted almost."

Oh, if you only knew. If I could tell you, maybe . . . But Beth pasted a smile on lips that wanted to quiver and turned to Teza. "What kind of fruit do you have out at your farm now?"

"A few apricots left on the trees, peaches are in full swing, cucumbers and beans in the garden, beets and carrots are ready too." Teza stopped. "Oh, and corn. I almost forgot that. Kit, I tucked a couple of cobs in your refrigerator for dinner."

"She grows the sweetest corn you'll find anywhere." Kit turned when Missy whimpered. "Coming, girl." She got up to let the dog out but stopped. "And she never picks it until you get there. Best corn in the world."

"You and Garth can come on out again and see for yourself. I really enjoyed meeting him."

"You could visit our church sometime. Garth is starting a new series of Bible studies about living in faith." *Which would be helpful if his wife could do that.* "They were really popular at our other church."

"We could come visit, couldn't we?" Teza looked to Kit.

"Sure, where?"

"Beth's church?" Teza raised an eyebrow.

"I guess. Elsie Mae, how many children do you have?"

"Four. Two boys and two girls. One is married, so I have a grandbaby too. Best thing that ever happened. Like they say, if I'd known how much fun grandbabies were, I'd have had them first."

When they broke for lunch, Kit set out the food they'd brought and refilled the coffee maker. "Come and eat."

"How about if we say grace first?" Teza asked.

"Ah, fine. Go ahead." Kit set down the plates and bowed her head.

"Father, we thank you for the day, for our time together, for the women you will bless through our making this quilt, and for the food you have provided for us. In Jesus' precious name, amen."

"Thank you, that was right nice." Elsie Mae patted Teza shoulder. "Is this the sore one?"

Teza nodded, so Elsie Mae began rubbing the shoulder.

"Ah, that feels so good. Thank you." Teza leaned her head over to the other side to give more space to the seeking hands.

When they returned to their stitching, Elsie Mae asked Teza, "Forgive me for being forward, but why are you hesitating about the treatment?"

Kit held her breath and just kept on stitching. In and out, rock the needle in, pull the thread taut and in again, all the while being careful that the layers did not slip.

The silence, other than pulling thread, wore an intensity, as if every ear strove to hear beyond the words. To hear the heart within.

Teza cleared her throat. "I've been through this before" — the silence grew heavy, pushing them down into the quilt — "and it came back." Teza straightened and stretched, but instead of returning to the basting, she stared out the window.

Kit fought the constriction in her throat. *Teza, please. God, please. Someone help.*

"What are you afraid of, darlin'?" The words shimmering like dust motes in a sunbeam, the rasp of thread through cotton screaming in pain. The fragrance of lavender embroidered on shifting air currents that carried it in and through and on.

Teza sighed, a sound dredged from the far recesses of her heart, and, gathering all the forgotten pains that lingered there, released them to float with the lavender like incense before the throne of God. "I didn't know I was afraid. Am afraid. I think — I thought I was being wise and waiting for God to tell me what to do. Using my mind to make good decisions. That may still be right, but you asked, what am I afraid of." She crossed her arms and rubbed her elbows as if she were cold. "I'm not afraid of dying, for then I shall be with my Lord."

Kit drew a tissue from her pocket and turned away to blow her nose.

"I don't want to leave the ones I love,

but that is not fear. When I look back on the time before, I came so close to breaking, my faith, I mean. I never want to turn my back on my Jesus, for then I cannot see him, and if he is not there, then I am lost." She dug in her pocket but came up empty.

Kit took her a tissue and pressed it into her hands.

Lost, dear Teza? And if you fear being lost, what about me? I've railed at him and shoved him away, raged and cried and yet . . .

"But he said, 'I will never leave you nor forsake you,' " Elsie Mae whispered.

"I know. That's what I've hung on to all my life. I believe, Lord, help thou my unbelief." Teza blew her nose. "So to really answer your question, I guess I am afraid of the pain, for that is what closes my inner eyes and tears me apart."

"But there are ways to help with the pain. Have you heard of Healing Touch?"

"No, only his."

"Well, this is from him. People, especially nurses like me, are being trained in how to help cancer patients deal with the pain, especially breast cancer pain. You and I will go through this together . . ."

"So I will not be alone?"

"Not that you ever are."

"I know, but sometimes I felt so alone. When you wander in that land of drugs and pain and your mind isn't working right and your body is not functioning like it should, you try to hang on to God's hand, but your grasp slips and . . ."

"And he hangs on to you."

And me? Has he been hanging on to me all this time, and I thought I'd run far enough he couldn't catch me? Kit heard a whisper, or was it only in her head? *See, I told you so. I promised, and I never go back on my word. I forgive you.* Kit pushed the needle through to the edge of the fabric and pulled the thread through its eye so only a tail hung free. But have *I forgiven you? No, yes, who am I to forgive you?* Tears streaming so she was nearly blinded, she headed for the back deck. The sun had broken through the clouds sometime during the afternoon and now glittered in the droplets left from the shower. She sank down into the Adirondack chair and put her feet up on the matching foot bench.

Forgiveness. To forgive is to forget, is it not? How do I forget? You say as far as the east is from the west is how far you put my sin away. You remember it no more. I cannot do that. Do I want to do that? How should I know? The thought of . . . this is too big for me. And here I am out here by myself when I should be in there with Teza. She tried to get up, but the weight pressing her down was too heavy.

Lord, I am tired of fighting. I give up. Kit blew her nose again and laid her hands in her lap. Missy whined at the door. A humming-bird roared by her, clicking his way to the feeder, darting after the jeweled adversary who dared to impinge on his territory. *Am I like that hummingbird, carrying on when I could be sitting at the feeder, sipping and sharing with enough for each of us? And without fail, you would refill the feeder? Not forgetting like I sometimes do.* Lassitude stole over her, as if all her energy drained out her feet and slipped through the cracks in the deck, never to be seen again. Since she had not the strength to keep them open, her eyelids closed and she drifted on a stream of love.

She opened her eyes to see Teza sitting in the other chair, not sure how much time had passed.

"Where are the others?"

"Gone home."

"Sorry I left."

"That's all right."

"Are you — I mean did you . . . ?" *Did you what, you're not making much sense.* Kit took a deep breath. And stopped. She inhaled another. *Is this what freedom feels like?*

She looked over to see Teza sleeping in the other chair. Her hand lay open in her lap, slightly cupped, innocent as a child's hand waiting to be filled. What had really happened here? Had she imagined it all? Or what? Kit breathed in again, a breath that seemed to pop open little pockets, letting the breath go into dark places that hadn't felt the breath of life for too long a time.

THIRTY

The calendar never lies.

Time is up, Teza. Today the week is over.

Oh sure, that's a great way to greet someone. But then maybe that's why she called me to come out, to tell me what she decided. Kit glanced down at the file folders she'd been filling with information. One thing for sure, there were no guarantees with anything. And while breast cancer treatments had experienced some progress since her mother died, there'd been more advancements in automobile engines. She'd read that in an editorial in some big newspaper. What an indictment!

She wheeled the van into Teza's yard and parked by the arbor leading to the house. Gathering up her research, she stepped out and paused to enjoy the red blossoms of Paul Scarlet roses rioting over the arbor.

"Out here."

Kit turned and looked toward the garden at Teza's call. "What are you picking now?"

"Cucumbers. I have someone coming for fifty pounds any minute. You want to help?"

"Why am I not surprised?" Kit knew she was muttering, but she also knew it would do no good. Obviously cucumbers came before cancer. She made her way to the cucumber rows and grabbed a white plastic bucket.

"You want the gherkin-size picked too?"

"No, leave them for later. I don't have time for gherkins, and no one has requested them. I'll sort the big ones out for relish."

Kit had just filled her bucket when she heard a car drive in.

"Perfect timing." Teza tossed the last cuke from her row into the bucket and stood to wave to her customer. "Be there in a minute." She smiled at Kit. "If she doesn't want all of these, you can take the rest."

"I'm not doing pickles this year."

"Why not?"

"I have plenty left. With no one but me at home, we don't go through so many."

"Okay, then I'll make them up for the stand. I never can have too many pickles to sell."

Kit sighed. There was no stopping her,

so why try? "You want me to pick more?"

"No, you go on up and pour the iced tea. I made biscuits this morning, so I thought we could have those. You haven't had lunch, have you?"

"Is it lunchtime already?"

"Past." They lugged the five-gallon buckets over to the stand, and Kit helped weigh them.

"No, don't sort them. I'll take them all," the customer said. "I use the big ones for relish." They set the boxes of cucumbers in her trunk and waved her off.

"Well, that's good. Neither one of us has to worry about pickles tonight." Teza dusted off her hands and linked her arm through Kit's. "Let's go for that iced tea. I'm thirsty as a dog in the desert."

Kit headed for the bathroom to wash her hands while Teza took over the kitchen sink.

"You want your biscuits warmed?" Teza called.

"Of course. Biscuits should always be warm." Kit dried her hands on the guest towel and made a face at the one in the mirror. She'd left her files out in the car. "Be right back."

When she returned, the glasses were

filled, and Teza was putting the biscuits in a cloth-lined basket.

After they sat down at the table, Teza drank some of her tea, then they both buttered and jammed their biscuits.

"I put lavender blossoms in the dough. What do you think?"

"I think they are delicious. What a novel thought."

"I read about using herbs in cooking and baking, made 'em with dill before, fennel was too strong, caraway is good, and parsley doesn't give much flavor. I bet rosemary would be good, and I'm going to try that purple sage growing out in the herb garden too."

Here we are talking about herbed biscuits, and the important stuff is just lying there. She eyed her files. *Like a rattlesnake.*

"Teza, what have you decided?"

"About what?" Teza rolled her eyes. "Oh, that. I'll have the treatments at the hospital, do all I can with diet and supplements, pray mightily and ask others to do the same, and keep on reading up on other things to do. Thanks to Elsie Mae, I'm over the fear for now. I believe relaxation and picturing myself well will be the hardest. I hate sitting still for a minute, as you well know."

Kit felt like a punctured tire. All the arguments she'd put together, all the time spent looking for information, and here Teza had it all worked out.

"What brought you to this kind of decision?"

"I prayed and asked God what he thought and if he would make it clear to me. Near as I can figure, he said to cover all the bases."

"I'm sure that must be scriptural." Kit's eyebrow refused to stay in line. She blinked the tears of relief back and hid her grin behind the glass of iced tea.

Teza stared into Kit's eyes. "And I'm counting on you, too, for the praying part, and don't go giving me that song and dance about not believing any longer. You and I both know that is a bunch of hooey, so you can just quit running the other way and turn back so God can help you with your own healing. There now, I've said my piece, and you know I'm right."

Kit choked on her biscuit and felt as if her lungs were going to explode with the coughing. When she finally got her breath back, she took a swallow of tea and leaned against the back of the chair.

"You all right now?"

"I will be."

"Now, I read up on Healing Touch, and I think we need to learn a lot more about this. I'm looking forward to talking with Elsie Mae again. Wish I had known about that program my first time through this. Maybe the cancer wouldn't have returned."

"Maybe." Kit took another bite of biscuit. "These sure are good."

"Thanks. You know something that frustrates me?" Teza gestured to the stack of information Kit had brought. "They don't agree. You can read three different experts and studies and get three totally conflicting conclusions." She wagged her head from side to side. "So I intend to read all the scriptures on healing so I know more what God has to say. I seem to have forgotten a few, but the one that comes to mind the most is 'if two or three agree on anything in my name, it will be done for them.' Now there are two of us, and I'm hoping Beth will be a third, most likely Elsie Mae, and if anyone else wants to join in, so be it."

The desire to run out the door and keep on running until she got home and could lock herself in her own house forced Kit to her feet. But instead of running, she brought the pitcher of iced tea back to the table. *God, this isn't fair. You know I can't do this. If Teza's health depends on my prayer power, you might as well take her home now.* She sank back in her chair. No way could she tell Teza she wouldn't do this. No way, and yet — what if her lingering doubts negated whatever power their prayers had? Did her doubt cause God to refuse to heal Amber?

No, I believed back then. You let me down. You said to pray believing and I did, but you didn't do your part. The rage she'd thought gone since Friday flamed up again. *God, you expect too much!*

"My dear, what is it?" Teza laid a hand on Kit's arm. Her gentle voice broke the dam, and Kit laid her head on the table and bawled.

When the storm passed and the hiccups were all that remained, Teza handed her a cool wet washcloth.

"Now, I want you to go lie down in the hammock and I'll bring some cucumber slices for your eyes."

Kit held the washcloth in place. "Cucumber slices?"

"I read they are good for taking out the red and the puffiness. And if they don't work on your eyes, we can always eat them."

A chuckle caught in Kit's throat and turned to a snort. "Teza, you come up with the darndest things — lavender biscuits and cucumber poultices. And the frustrating thing is — they work." Kit rose and headed for the hammock.

Half an hour later she could attest to her aunt's apothecary procedures. Her eyes felt 100 percent better. Hooray for cucumbers. And the peace she'd felt on Friday returned too.

"Just leave that stuff here and I'll get it read." Teza gestured to the stack of file folders. "In the meantime, I have a little book here I'd like you to read." She held it up so the title was visible. *The Healing Light* by Agnes Sanford. She makes a lot of sense, much more so than most of those medical people. Promise me you will read this, starting tonight."

"Teza, I . . ."

"Please."

Kit took the book. "Oh, all right. It's not like I have nothing else to do tonight."

"You can finish the squares this afternoon. You don't have to do pickles."

"Unless, of course, I want to go out and pick some cucumbers just for pleasure."

"Right." Teza reached out and patted her cheek. "See you at the meeting."

Kit started down the steps and stopped. "When is your doctor's appointment?"

"I told them I'm not going back up to Seattle. They will have to send all the information down here and work through Dr. Harrison. I like her and I trust her."

"Do you want me along when you discuss protocols?"

"Yes, of course."

"So be it." Kit waved with the book in her hand. Now not only would she have to pray, she'd be returning to the war zone.

Her arguments and tears continued all the way back home and into her garage. Same hospital, same medical complex, a repeat from all the time she and Amber spent at radiology, overnight on the oncology floor for treatments, out-patient chemotherapy, doctor appointments, blood work. She banged on the steering wheel. "You're asking too much. I cannot do this!"

I am with you always.

"No, you're not."

Trust me.

"I'm trying!" She laid her head on her arms crossed on the steering wheel and gave in to the tears. Tears that only flowed seconds and stopped on their own, leaving her feeling washed clean instead of drained, peaceful instead of destroyed. Was it a miracle or . . . ?

After walking into the house and washing her face again, she checked the answering machine. Sure enough, a flashing light. Perhaps Teza had changed her mind about the prayer thing. She pushed the button to hear: "Hi, this is Beth. Please check your front porch. I brought you something, but you weren't home. Thank you for Saturday."

Kit erased the message and went to the front door. A gaily wrapped box held a miniature pink rose in a large cup. The note said, "A teacup rose for one who shares love with her roses and tea. Love, Beth."

A spicy fragrance wafted by as Kit lifted the box to smell the blossoms. "What a nice thing to do." She took the box inside and lifted out the mug. A Baggie in the bottom of the box held a crunchy puppy treat. The card read, "For Missy, who also loves a lot." Kit gave Missy her treat and centered the rose-bush on the dining room table for the moment. "You'll need more light than this, but for now, I can enjoy you more this way."

She wiped her eyes and blew her nose.

Where were those cucumbers when she needed them?

Every time she passed by she glared at the little book sitting so innocently on the table. She sewed, she weeded, she made dinner, she ate dinner, she washed up, she tried to watch television, she talked on the phone. The book could as easily have been screaming *read me* for all the frustration it caused her.

"I know a promise is a promise but . . ." But nothing. At nine o'clock she snatched up the book, climbed the stairs to her bedroom, brushed her teeth, got into her nightgown, and climbed into bed. It wasn't even dark yet.

She turned out the light at eleven because her eyes were so gritty from all the crying earlier in the day that she could no longer see. She finished the book by noon the next day, having started reading again after she fed the animals and herself, when the birds broke into their morning arias. She lay on the glider on the front porch watching Mr. and Mrs. House Finch feed their brood in their annual nest above one of the porch posts. According to Sanford, healing prayer was so simple. As was the faith that God would answer.

"You know I don't like 'no.' So now I'll

admit you answered, only it was no to my way and yes to yours." She chewed on the inside of her cheek. "God, you know how I miss her. And now you're asking me to trust you with Aunt Teza. If you take her, who will I have left?" Tears leaked again.

Me.

The mother finch flew past on her way to feed the kids. Father finches fed the kids too.

Would God her Father do any less?

THIRTY-ONE

"I know this is rude, Teza, but what did you decide?"

"Thanks, Beth, I've been wanting to ask but was afraid to." Sue spoke to Beth but stared at Teza, as did the others. The four women had just pulled their green, fiberglass high-backed chairs up to the quilting frame.

"Why, I decided that I'll go for treatment like the doctor recommended and count on God and Elsie Mae to help me handle the pain and heal more quickly. Teza wiggled her thimble down on her finger. "I'm still learning about other alternate programs, but reading Agnes Sanford's book, *The Healing Light*, helped me realize I can fight back in very simple ways. I made Kit read it too. Applies to more than just cancer, of course."

"I read that years ago," Sue said. "Forgot all about it, but I'm sure it's still on my bookshelf."

"Can I borrow it?" Beth asked.

"Sure, I better write myself a note." Sue

dug in her bag for paper and a pen.

"Agnes Sanford says to relax and picture God's healing light flowing all through me, to see it burn up the tumor, or eat it up, or however I see best. I made myself do just what she said. She takes the reader step by step to help her relax. I felt so warm and peaceful when I did it. When I called Elsie Mae and told her about it, she said we'd do more of the same."

This is my perpetual-motion aunt talking about relaxing? Kit kept her amazed thoughts to herself. She continued stitching without looking at Sue, who could read her thoughts far too easily. At this moment, giggles would not be polite.

"So when do you see the doctor?"

"I'm going back to Dr. Harrison here on Thursday, and she'll lay out the program."

"Good. I am so relieved." Sue and Kit tried to hide their smiles of relief.

"Me, too." Beth took a threaded needle out of her kit. "Garth said to tell you those peaches were about the best he's ever had. I baked two peach pies, and he ate most of both of them."

"Good thing he's just a growing boy." Sue began stitching in one of the diamonds.

"He's going to be a really big boy if he

keeps that up." Teza's comment made the others chuckle.

"You all got a lot done since I was here last."

"I know. Four of us worked Friday, then Beth came over Saturday and Teza on Sunday. My backyard and garden need major work, but you know how addicting quilts are. Just like having a jigsaw puzzle set up. Every time you go by you say you'll just put in a couple of pieces."

"And it's an hour later before you look at the clock. Good thing the phone rings sometimes."

"Speak of the angels . . ." Kit pushed her chair back so she could go answer the phone. *I should get a portable phone for just such times as this.*

"That was Elaine," Kit announced on the way back. "She can't come today. Something came up."

"Like Bootsie?" When they all laughed, Sue laid down her needle.

"I can tell that missing a session means missing out on more than stitching. Fill me in." By the time they finished the story, she was laughing as hard as the rest of them. "I know that Mrs. Smyth-with-a-Y. My husband did some repair work for her. He said never again. Nothing pleases her. She put a stop payment on his check because he didn't do something that he says she never asked him to do." Sue shook her head. "I suppose this is gossip and I better shut my mouth."

"Poor woman." Teza sighed. "To be so unhappy."

"Sad, huh?" Sue looked to Beth. "Pastor Garth sure preached a great sermon Sunday. I heard good comments from several people."

"Thanks, he needs to hear things like that."

"Hit me right between the eyes." Sue touched her forehead in the appropriate place.

"What did he talk about?" Teza asked.

"Trust, that's what. I realized I have a real issue with that. I can remember the girls saying 'Mom, you just don't trust us.' Now, why would any true-blue mother trust her teenagers? I mean, I did but I didn't. I guess it was more not trusting anything or anyone around them. Trust is earned, that part I do understand."

"And easily killed." Kit spoke in the direction of her stitching fingers.

"You oughta come with me next week, Kit. Might be different going to a new church, a good thing."

"Maybe I will." Kit caught the look that flashed between Teza and Sue. *Ganging up on me, that's what you're doing.* "How's the taming of the kitty coming, Beth?"

"If I lie on the lounger and close my eyes, he'll jump up and curl tight against my knees, but if he senses I'm awake, he leaves. Silly cat. One of these days he'll let me pet him. He just doesn't know it yet."

"Cats are perverse creatures, not easy-going like most dogs." Kit glanced over at Missy, stretched out on her side with one long ear flopped over her eye, snoring in a spot of sunshine.

"Like Bootsie?" Beth giggled as she shook her head. "I think of that, a real David-and-Goliath kind of thing, and I just have to laugh."

"So, Teza, what's happening on the farm?" Sue asked.

"I brought corn on the cob for lunch, and there's some in there for all of you to take home for dinner. Made twenty quarts of hamburger pickles yesterday. Hardly get them on the shelves and people buy them. Maybe I should go into the pickle and jam business."

"In your spare time." Kit shook her head. "Here you are, seventy years old with cancer, and you can still work rings around the rest of us."

Teza ignored her niece. "I am going to start the fruit quilt. I decided since it's appliqué, it will be a good thing to take the blocks along for stitching during treatments and tests, keep my mind off the procedures. Give me something to look forward to." She pushed the needle through the layers with the leather thimble on her middle finger.

"It sounds beautiful. I'd love to help you with it, if you want an extra set of hands." Beth pulled the new thread through her needle and returned to her stitching. "Did anyone count how many diamonds we have in this thing?"

Kit shook her head. "Didn't have the heart. I could put some music on if you'd like." She glanced around, but no one took her up on her offer.

"Where is Mark working now?" Sue asked. "Been so long since I've seen him, I almost forget what he looks like."

"Ah." *Come on brain, kick in gear. Make something up! Do something!* "Near Salt Lake City."

Sue looked up from stitching. "What? Did I say something wrong?"

"Ah, no, not at all." *Liar. You knew that*

one of these days someone was going to ask. You should have been prepared.

"Okay, my friend. Out with it." Sue stabbed her needle into the fabric and cupped her hands on the frame.

Kit sucked in a deep breath. *Tell her. Get it out in the open where you can deal with it.* "Mark took an extended leave of absence." *That's one way of describing it.* "He . . . he felt he couldn't deal with all the memories here and needed some time off." The confession trailed to a whisper.

"When?"

"January."

"All this time, and you didn't tell me anything about it?"

Kit ducked her head. "I know but . . ."

"Don't feel bad, she didn't tell me either." Teza stood and stretched. "I think we need a coffee break here. I'll go put it on."

"Oh, Kit, I'm so sorry." Beth reached out and stroked Kit's hand.

"I . . . I thought that I should keep his secret for him. That if I just hung on, pretty soon he'd realize what he'd done and come home. I never dreamed it would be this long."

"Have you heard from him?"

"Oh yes. Not every day but . . ." *Not*

often, hardly ever, that's closer to the truth, so really the truth is somewhere in the middle.

"Do Ryan and Jennifer know?" Sue returned to the conversation.

"Sort of." *I sound like the wimp of all wimps.*

"Sort of! So you've been bearing this alone all this time, on top of the grieving for Amber." Sue took a deep breath to slow and lower her voice. "Good, now that that's out, how can we help you?"

Kit shrugged. "I don't know how to help myself. I just keep busy and try to act as if nothing is wrong. I've been hearing from him more often lately, though. I think that is a good sign."

"Good sign, my foot. He deserves to be horsewhipped. Walking off and leaving you all alone like this. Where is his head?" Sue's eyes glinted fire, and she stabbed the needle through the layers so hard, she yelped.

"Don't bleed on the quilt!" Kit snapped back.

"I won't!" Sue sucked her finger. "Teza's right. I need a cup of coffee." Finger in her mouth, Sue pushed back her chair and stomped off to the kitchen. "You still keep Band-Aids in the cabinet?"

"Yes."

"You've had so much to bear." Beth knelt beside Kit's chair.

"Yeah . . . well, we all have. That's just the way life is. Sometimes it plain stinks."

THIRTY-TWO

The calendar never lies.

"Honey, I need you to come bail me out!"

Bail you out? "Where are you?"

"Jail."

Beth stared at the calendar on the wall by the phone. August 21. Sure enough, this had been the day of the demonstration at the abortion clinic. Garth hadn't reminded her this morning because he knew how adamantly she was against his taking part in such things, let alone leading them. She'd made her opinion known several years earlier, not that it had done any good.

Now, what she'd always feared had come true. Her husband, the abortion fighting preacher, had been arrested.

"What do I have to do?"

"Bring the checkbook down so I can post bail."

Beth sat down in the chair, her knees no longer strong enough to hold her up. "Where?"

"City hall, around on the north side. There's parking right out there. You'll see a sign that says Police Station Detention Center. The officer on the desk will tell you what to do."

"Garth, I . . ."

"Beth, just get down here." His tone snapped at her out of the receiver.

"Yes, sir!" Beth let her annoyance ring through the words before slamming the receiver back in the cradle. The nerve of him, yelling at her like that. It wasn't as if she had to bail someone out of jail every day of the week. *How should I know what to do? Serves you right. You can just sit there and . . .* She clapped her palms to her cheeks. "How can I even think such things?" *How can I go down there by myself? Do we have enough money to get him out?* "Please, Lord, I don't want to do this." While her mind teemed with questions and pleas, she combed her hair, saw a stain on her blouse, changed into a T-shirt under a denim jumper, applied lipstick, and locked the door behind her. She reached for her purse to get out her car keys, only to find no purse on her shoulder.

"Oh, Lord, how can I be so stupid? Garth will kill me, and I don't blame him one bit." If only they had put a key under a rock or something. If only she hadn't been in such a hurry. If only they knew the neighbors well enough to have asked one of them to keep a key.

"Why did I even answer the phone? If I had been over at Kit's quilting, I wouldn't be in this fix." She sat down on the front porch step. "Now that is one of the more stupid things I've said in a long time." She rubbed her temples with her fingertips. "Come on, Beth, think."

Are there any windows open? Not trusting her memory, she walked around the house, checking all the windows. Those open were on the second floor. Big help.

"So, dummy, what are your choices?" *Run away from home.* Can't do that without car keys, although that had been something she'd thought about lately. *Sit here and bawl.* That was so close to happening she had to keep blinking to thwart the tears. *Ask the neighbors for help.* What could they do, jimmy the locks? Why was it that in the movies they could open any door within ten seconds with a credit card? She'd tried it once, no luck. *Sit here and bawl.* Closer to becoming a reality every second.

Bash in a window. No, that would make Garth really mad. However, sitting in jail longer than necessary would most likely make him madder. *Good thinking. Ha, serves him right. No, it doesn't you wimp. At least he is standing for what he believes in while you hide under the covers.* She surged to her feet, picked up one of the bricks that sat on an angled edge lining the front walk, and stomped back up the steps. The first time she tapped the glass only a ping sounded.

"Here goes nothing." She stared at the lower left-hand pane. This house would be so easy to burgle with twelve panes in the front door like this. She smacked the lower left one a good one, and glass shattered into the shirred lace curtain and down to the floor. Taking a hint from a police show she'd seen one time, she removed each shard of glass still stuck in the frame and laid it carefully off to the side. When cleared, she reached in, pushed the curtain aside, and felt for the doorknob. At least she hadn't set the deadbolt. Of course, that was impossible without the keys. With the door now opened, she tried to sidestep the glass on the floor, thought about sweeping up the mess, grabbed her purse with the car keys off the counter, and headed back out the door. At least she could turn the deadbolt now.

Here I am worrying about the deadbolt when Garth is sitting in a jail cell waiting for me. By now he must be thinking I've gone bonkers or something and won't ever show up.

At least the car started. That would have been one thing too much. She checked her watch. Over an hour since Garth had called.

Don't go speeding. All I need is a speeding ticket right now. The officer would ask, "What's your hurry?" and I'd say, "I'm on my way to the station to bail my husband, a political activist, out of jail." By the time she parked in the parking lot, her hands were so sweaty they slipped on the steering wheel, her heart was doing cartwheels, and her feet wore size twenty concrete boots. She sucked in a deep breath, locked the car door with the keys so she couldn't leave them inside, and started for the door, ten miles away. Never had a parking lot been so huge, nor a street so wide, nor three steps so high. Since the building must have been built at the turn of the century — the last one — the hall needed paint, the floor new covering, and at least they could put in bigger light bulbs. The officer behind the beat-up metal desk appeared about as old as his surroundings, and if he was happy about anything at all, he didn't notify his face.

"Help you, miss?"

"Uh, yes, my husband is here. He, uh, needs bail."

"Name." The man set his fingers on the keyboard in front of him. The phone rang. " 'Scuse me." He answered the phone, typed some information into the computer. "That'll be officer Kennedy. I'll put you through to him." He clicked a button on the phone, laid the receiver back in the cradle, and looked up to Beth.

"Name?"

"My name?"

"No, your husband's."

"Reverend Garth Donnelly."

"Ah, that pastor that got hauled in with the picketers." His condescending tone told her exactly what he thought of such goings-on. "Shame it got violent."

"Violent! Is Garth hurt?"

"I can't tell you anything about that. Take a seat over there, and someone will come for you."

Beth sat down on a wooden bench and leaned back against the wall, closing her eyes so she wouldn't have to look at the older man sitting at the other end of the bench. *Turned violent? What could have hap-*

pened? Garth had been involved in other protests, and she knew he always made sure everything was legal. After all, demonstrating for what you believed in was an American right.

Her thumb had about created a scab on the back of the other by the time a woman came to get her. Her name tag said Officer Benson, and her face looked slightly familiar.

"Hi, Mrs. Donnelly, you can come with me now."

Beth stood. "Do I know you?" How inane did that sound? "Please, I'm sorry . . ."

"No, you don't know me, but I've seen you at church. I'm always in such a rush I don't stick around to meet people, even the new pastor and his wife. Sure sorry to be meeting you like this."

Not half as sorry as I am. "Ah, can you tell me anything? The officer out there said something about violence. Is Garth injured?"

"No, he was lucky. Some idiot threw a rock through the window, and several people got cut by flying glass."

Beth thought of the pile of glass at home. That ought to make Garth even happier.

Officer Benson slowed her pace and

leaned closer to whisper in Beth's ear. "If you could talk him out of doing things like this, it would be good. The judge here in town is going to have fits three sides from Sunday over this. And since Pastor Garth is one of the organizers, it won't go well for him."

Beth groaned. *Please, God, help us.*

"They're just lucky no one in the clinic was injured." She opened a door and motioned Beth to go through.

Two hundred fifty dollars later, Garth started the engine and backed out of the parking space without a word. He checked both directions and pulled onto the street, accelerating, eyes straight ahead.

Beth kept sneaking glances at him. Was he angry? Of course he was. Angry at her? Angry at himself? At someone else? Trying to act as if this were an everyday occurrence? Most likely all of the above. She leaned her head against the headrest and closed her eyes. If he wanted her to ask the questions, he'd be waiting a long, long time. Right now an "I'm sorry" or "thank you" would go a long way. Instead he kept on driving. She knew Garth well enough to recognize his silence. He'd talk when he wouldn't explode.

When they turned into the driveway, she decided she'd better prepare him. "Garth, I had to break a window in the front door because I locked the keys in the house."

"Wonderful." The sarcasm grated on the one nerve she had left. He stopped the car and turned off the ignition before turning to her. "But that's the least of our worries."

"What do you mean?"

"I mean this could go to court."

"Who threw the rock?"

"How did you know about that?" Garth asked.

"Officer Benson. Did you know she's a member of our church?"

"Yes. Several people on the police force are members."

"So who threw the rock?"

He shook his head. "I have no idea. All our people knew how important it was to keep the peace. I know they are all innocent. This makes no sense at all."

Beth looked down to her feet, almost expecting to see the muck sucking at her shoes.

"What if it was someone who wanted you to get in trouble?"

Garth stared at her. "Like framed?"

"Yes."

Garth stared out the windshield. "Well,

I'll be . . ." He turned to look at her. "You could be right."

"Are you hungry?" She knew the question to be inane, but she didn't want to hear what Garth was going to say next. Court meant lawyers, and lawyers meant money and time, large sums of each. Neither of which they had. Publicity for the cause was good, notoriety was not.

"Sure." He looked out where the western sky was pinking after a desultory sunset. "You want to go out?"

"No." *Not when we're going to have to come up with who knows how much money. Not that we can squeeze much more out of our budget anyway.* She opened her car door and got out. Now he would see the glass mess. If she'd known how long she was going to be sitting at the jail, just waiting, she would have swept up the glass before she left.

When the broken glass crunched under their soles, Garth clenched his jaw and shook his head, not looking at her as she scurried to get the broom and dust pan.

That night after a dinner of grilled-cheese sandwiches and tomato soup, she left Garth working in his study and returned to her quilt hoop. When the phone rang a bit later, she kept on stitching, knowing that Garth would pick it up in the study.

"For you," he said, poking his head out the door.

"Oh. Who is it?"

"Shawna. She sounds even more hyper than normal."

"Garth." She playfully smacked him on the shoulder and went back into their bedroom to pick up the phone. At least he was talking again.

"So what's up?" she asked after the greetings.

"You'll never guess."

"Just tell me. I'm not into guessing games tonight."

"Are you sitting down?"

"On the bed."

"I'm pregnant."

Beth swallowed and forced her voice to sound natural. "How wonderful. Shawna, I am so happy for you. When is the baby due?" *Put some life into your voice or she's going to be hurt.*

"Well, I waited three months before telling anyone this time. Just couldn't go through having to tell them again we'd lost the baby."

"I know." She and Shawna had held each

other up through hard times in the conception field. Then, when she and Garth made it through the danger time with their baby, they all rejoiced. Until he died.

"This time the doctor says we are out of the woods, and I'm about done with the all-day sickness, so I just had to tell you."

"So you're due in January?"

"Right on. Late January. Oh, Beth, I can't wait."

Beth could hear the tears in her friend's voice and forced back the ones in her own. "I really am so happy for you. Garth and I will be praying for you and the baby. You take it easy now, you hear? Do exactly what the doctor tells you."

"Yes, Mother Beth. Oh, I wish you were here. It's so hard when your best friend is light-years away."

"Tell me about it."

"So now that I've told you my news, what is happening there?"

"Well, I just bailed Garth out of jail." *If I keep the news on other stuff, maybe I won't have to tell her about the depression.*

"Jail? What did he do, rob a bank to give money to the poor?"

"No, he is not Robin Hood, no matter what he thinks. He was picketing an abortion clinic, and some idiot threw a rock through a window. A couple of people were injured by flying glass, so it was deemed a riot and they all got tossed in jail."

"And you had to go bail him out?"

"Right."

"Aw, Beth, I bet you were upset."

"That's putting it mildly." *And I still am. I am embarrassed, angry, and resentful about the money going to pay bail rather than bills.*

"What are you going to do for money?"

"I don't know. Maybe I'll have to get a job." Beth twisted a lock of hair around her finger.

"But Garth doesn't want you working outside your home."

"I know, but perhaps that option went the way of the abortion clinic."

"Maybe your church will help pay for it."

"I don't know."

She did know the next night when Garth came home from a meeting with the elders and deacons. She didn't need to ask. One look at the thunder cloud on Garth's face, and she knew the answer.

"They unilaterally reprimanded me for meddling in things not becoming a pastor of the Jefferson City Community Church. As if sticking up for the rights of the unborn was not the duty of every Christian walking this earth. They don't tolerate murder in the streets, but murder in the clinic is permissible."

"Most likely they feel that way because it is legal."

"So is drinking, but we don't encourage it."

Don't bark at me. This isn't my fault.

"They knew when they hired me that I am an antiabortion activist. I did nothing to hide that, and I thought they agreed with me."

"They most likely do in a more reserved way."

"Yeah, as long as it costs them nothing. They don't want to get involved. Christians in name only. Say the right words but no money to back up the mouth."

Beth watched her husband wear a path in the carpet. What would he say if or when he found out that his wife had done exactly what he was fighting so persistently and with such dedication?

"So what are we going to do for money to pay bills and buy groceries?"

"I don't know, but I'm sure God does." He stopped and stared out the window. "Guess we better hope our garden produces real well."

Or I get a job. Perhaps I should hang out my shingle as a seamstress. That is one thing I do extremely well. How would I go about advertising? Or maybe my husband is going to have to stuff his pride in his pocket and let his wife get a real job. I didn't train and work as a dental assistant for nothing. Besides, it's not like I have a baby to care for.

THIRTY-THREE

The calendar never lies.

Kit stared at the calendar. Teza's first radiation treatment and Ryan coming home, both on the same day — the day after tomorrow. No word yet from Mark as to his plans. *Lord, I wonder how long I'll be able to stand this.*

But at least they were e-mailing fairly regularly.

She thought back to the evening before. She'd been looking for more information for Aunt Teza when an instant message beeped onto the screen. It was Mark, the first time he'd done such a thing, the closest thing to a telephone conversation they'd had in a while. She'd replied immediately.

"Hey, how are you?" She clicked "send" and watched the red letters appear in the box.

"Good. How's Teza?"

"Ready to start treatment."

"Had there been any doubt?"

Had there ever. "She wanted to research all her options."

"Options?"

"You know, like diet, supplements, treatments in Mexico, all kinds of stuff."

"So what is she going to do?"

"Everything. All that she can manage."

"How bad is it?"

How I wish I knew. "Radiation and chemo are never easy."

"Sorry, I know that. Why did she wait so long?"

"No symptoms. At least that's what she says."

"Tell her I love her."

"You tell her. She's online frequently." She typed in Teza's e-mail address. She waited awhile until another blue line appeared.

"You mentioned something before about getting a job. Anything there?"

Why? Do you want me to get a job? "No, I've not had time to follow up on that." *Do I need to think about supporting myself?*

"Well, I need to go. I've got work to do. Take care of yourself."

"You too. Love, me." She waited for a response but none came. No chance to ask the questions that multiplied like a virus. She signed off the Internet, her enthusiasm for research gone with the blink of a cursor. She propped her chin on her hands and stared at the picture of Mark pinned to the bulletin board. He and Ryan, fishing poles and two small trout dangling on a line between them. There hadn't been enough for dinner for the three of them, so she'd fried them for Ryan's breakfast the next day.

They looked so much alike, same roundish faces, brown hair with a lick of curl. Mark's had receded noticeably, but with their hats on that hadn't shown. But they both had cleft chins, a male Cooper trait. They flashed goofy grins over the fish, all for her benefit she knew. She'd often told friends how the Coopers were the only people who had a salmon that had grown a full twelve inches or more after going in the freezer.

A knock at the door the next morning made her dust her hands on her apron to answer it.

"Whatchya doing?"

"Hey, Thomas, how are you?" She held open the screen door. "Come on in."

"What are you baking?" He eyed the flour-whitened counter.

"Cherry pie. Ryan is coming home tomorrow." She went back to rolling the bottom crust. The filling sat in a bowl all ready for two pies. "These are the cherries I got from Aunt Teza."

"Oh. You think Ryan will play ball?"

"I'm sure he will." She picked up the rolled dough and laid it carefully in the glass pie pan, then began rolling the next.

"Can Missy come out and play?"

"She's in the garage. You can let her out."

"Was she bad?"

"No, I just forgot to let her in after she followed me out to the washing machine." She laid the next crust in the pan and poured the filling into both.

"Ryan likes cherry pie?"

"That's his favorite kind."

"What kind did Amber like best?" Thomas perched on a kitchen chair.

"Apple, like her father, but cherry was her second favorite. Do you like cherry pie?"

He shrugged, his shoulders coming up to his ears. "Never had none."

"Oh. Your mother doesn't bake pies?"

He shook his head. "Can I give Missy a treat?"

"Sure, you know where they are."

I guess I need to remember that not every-one bakes pies anymore, or most other things for that matter. Missy's toenails skittered on the floor as she greeted Thomas with whines and whimpers, a sharp bark answering his command to speak. As they whooshed out the back door, Kit dabbed water around the edge of one lower crust, laid the upper in place and, using thumbs and forefingers, crimped the edge. She cut five slashes in the upper crust and followed the same pattern with the second pie. All the while she rolled and crimped and slashed and put them in the oven, she thought of Thomas's family. He never mentioned his mother, his father worked long hours, and his sister would rather watch television than do anything else.

She glanced out the window to see boy and dog playing with the ball and running, falling and exploding with giggles and barks.

After putting fresh sheets on Ryan's bed, she'd set out the pitchback and play ball too. She'd not been home for much batting practice lately.

Up in his room, she stripped the bed, put on new sheets, and dusted the desk, bookshelves and anything else that needed it. His trophies took extra time as she buffed each one — baseball, basketball, and speech — quite a variety and the symbols of many dedicated hours. Ryan had been good at whatever he undertook, always striving to do his best, or at least keep up with his older sisters. While Jennifer excelled in her studies and was a natural musician, Amber and Ryan were superb athletes plus brains.

She dusted the picture of his basketball team, senior year, second in state in the Single A division. Ryan made the all-stars as a guard. She gazed at him in his uniform, holding the basketball on his hip. He'd dedicated his triumph to his sister Amber, who he said encouraged him and challenged him to always go the extra mile.

She brushed the tears from her cheeks, glanced around the room to make sure all was ready for him, and picking up the laundry, she took it down to the washing machine.

She checked on her pies and had just closed the oven when the phone rang.

"Hi, this is your pain-in-the-neck aunt. My first radiology appointment is tomorrow at 9:30. Could you please drive me, just in case? Oh, and that will be my time five days a week."

"Of course. How did the mapping go?"

"I'm indelibly marked."

"When's the first chemo?"

"I go in Saturday morning. This first one is an overnighter."

"Boy, all at once."

"Yes, and I see the nutritionist on Tuesday. Ryan is coming tomorrow night?"

"Late afternoon. I forget when his last final is. Summer school can be different than the rest of the year. I've got two cherry pies in the oven, and Thomas is outside with Missy."

"Good. I'll see you about nine o'clock then?"

"Right." Kit hung the phone up and took down the calendar to write TR in Monday through Friday at 9:00. TR, Teza's Radiology. That meant for these first weeks, she'd be late for the quilting. "Oh well. They can all come in and start without us."

She wandered into the living room where the quilting frame dominated the room as it had many winters in the past. She glanced at the recliner. If Teza wasn't feeling well, she could take a snooze right there and still feel a part of the group.

She sniffed. Yep, the cherry juice was boiling over. The pies must be about done. At least this time she'd been smart enough to put tinfoil in the bottom of the oven.

With the pies cooling on the rack on the counter, she took out of the jar several chocolate-chip cookies that she'd baked just that morning, along with a puppy treat for Missy, and headed on outside. Perhaps one of the quilters would be by later.

"Treats!" She held them up as she called. Both child and dog ran to the deck and dropped panting on the bottom step.

"You look a bit warm." She handed Thomas his cookies and tossed the bone for Missy to catch. "You been having fun?"

"Umm." Thomas nibbled his treat. "You had fun too?"

"Yes, I did. Ryan's room is ready for him, the pies are done, and I thought we could get out the pitchback. Did you bring your mitt?"

"O'course." The look he gave her made her smile. He nodded to the Adirondack chair where he'd left his mitt.

"Dad took me to see the Tacoma Mariners play." He took a bite of his treat. "They won, four to three."

"Good game, eh?"

"My dad caught a foul ball. He gave it to me and I got it signed."

"How wonderful, Thomas. We used to love going to Cheney Stadium to watch the Mariners play."

"Still like the Major league Mariners better."

If Mark were here, maybe we could get tickets, and we'd take Thomas with us too. "You want more cookies?"

"Nope, let's play ball."

"Right you are." She pulled down the bill of his hat purely for the pained look he gave her. Laughing, they dragged the pitchback out onto the lawn and retrieved the bucket of balls, bat, and her mitt from the garage. After throwing awhile to warm up her arm, she called, "Batter up," and waited for Thomas to get himself set. He planted his feet just as she'd shown him, lifted the bat over his shoulder, and leveled out his top elbow, pointing it right down the pitching line.

"Very good. You remembered everything."

"And I gotta keep my eye on the ball."

"Right on."

Her first pitch bounced on the plate.

"Good eye. Don't you go chasing any bad pitches."

Pitch two was even with his helmet.

"Too high."

"Yeah, I know. Got to get the range here." Her next pitch came straight in, level with his waistband.

He swung but only caught the top of it.

"Foul ball."

"Who's that playing baseball in my backyard?"

At the sound of the voice, Missy leaped to her feet, her deep bark heralding the arrival of a friend.

"Ryan!" Kit dropped the ball back in the bucket and ran to throw her arms around her son. "How did you get here so early?" She hugged him, leaned back to look in his face, and hugged him again. "Oh, I can't believe you are really home."

"So this must be Thomas." Keeping one arm around his mother's waist, he stretched out his right hand. "I hear you are quite a ball player."

Thomas shook hands, then dropped to his knees beside Missy. She woofed until Ryan knelt down and rubbed her back and ears. "Good dog, how you been anyway?"

"I play with her so she don't get fat."

"Looks like you been doing a good job. And you're keeping Mom here in shape too. Whata guy."

"That's not me. Mrs. C is not fat."

"Thank you, Thomas. What a nice thing to say."

He shrugged. "It's true. And you pitch good for a lady."

"She pitches good, period. She and Dad taught me all I know about baseball. And it looks to me like she's got you standing just right too."

"You want something to drink? Are you hungry?"

"Drink will be fine if you have lemonade. You like lemonade, Thomas?"

"She always has lemonade and Popsicles. Cookies today."

"Same old Mom."

"She ain't old."

" 'Scuse me." Ryan looked to his mother. "You've got quite a champion here."

"I know. You two sit over there by the table, and I'll bring out the pitcher and glasses. I don't suppose either of you would like chocolate-chip cookies too?"

The guys nodded, and Missy woofed and wagged her tail.

"Not you, silly dog. Thomas, you want to come get her a puppy treat, too?"

With the snacks on the table, Kit sat down with her boys. "Now answer my question. How did you get here so early?"

"Rob took his final last night, so we left early this morning. Came over White Pass. Those high mountain lakes were just crying for a fishing line."

"Oh, I'm sure."

After he'd drained one glass and started on the next, Ryan looked at Thomas. "How about if Mom pitches, I catch, and you bat?"

"Yeah!" Thomas's eyes shone as if he'd been offered a trip to the World Series.

At dinner that night, mother and son ate on the deck, catching up on their news. When a silence fell, Ryan leaned back and clasped his hands over his belly.

"Dad won't be coming home this time, Mom."

"How do you know?"

"He called and told me."

But he was too chicken to call and tell me? What is with that man? She took another drink of her iced tea to hide the quiver in her lips.

"Do you think he'll ever come home?"

The question hung on the still air.

"I don't know," Kit said softly. "I just don't know."

THIRTY-FOUR

"Dear Lord, I confess and give you my fears. I know you are God of everything, Creator, Sustainer. You are bigger than radiation and wiser than the doctors. And I know you are holding me in the palm of your mighty hand . . ." Teza paused and laid a hand on her heart that had a tendency today to double-time. "Please don't let me climb out. Father, I don't want to go through all this again, I don't." A tear plopped on her hand. "I don't."

She returned to reading Psalm 91. Snakes and young lions could surely be read treatments, machines, and doctors. "No harm shall befall me. And yet chemotherapy does just that — harms any fast-growing cells, like stomach lining, hair. If only it would kill only the cancer cells and not the others." The memory of nausea and vomiting knocked on the door of her mind, but she refused to open it. "I'm in the shadow of the Most High, and nothing can touch me here." She read the entire psalm again, putting "I" in all possible places. "The angels will bear me up so my foot does not dash against a stone. Lord, I surely need some bearing up about now."

The urge to flee to her garden and hide in the corn rows brought her halfway to her feet, but she forced herself to sit back down. She leaned against the wicker chair and watched the robin digging in the lawn for the morning worm. When Mrs. Robin had three wiggling worms in her beak, she flew off to feed her children.

"You provide, Lord. You always have, and I know you always will." Teza turned to her prayer list and brought each name on it before her Lord, spending extra time on Mark's name. "Father, he needs to be here where he can receive all the love we have to give him, not off by himself, like an old sick dog going off somewhere to die. Is he going to church, reading your Word, praying? Father, I seriously doubt it. I get the feeling he's just licking his wounds, and they aren't healing." The thought of a scab on a sore came to her mind. "Yes, he's building scabs when the wound is festering underneath, and he doesn't even know it. Oh, my poor boy." Images from the years since he and Kit married floated through her mind, him building shelves for her sewing room, Kit's sewing room, a wagon for the children, flower boxes and planters, all of them together on picnics, birthdays, Christmas. Through the years he'd become the closest thing to a son as she'd ever had. And now she ached for him.

Mr. Robin hopped about on the lawn, his beak wide as he heralded the joy of a new day. His mate returned to search for more worms.

Teza closed her Bible and sat to watch until he found his worms and the two flew off. Then she rose and walked back into the house. On the way she stuck her finger in a pink-and-white fuchsia basket to see if it needed water. It did. One more thing to get done before she left.

Vinnie was coming to man the farm. She'd pick corn to order and knew where folks should go for U-pick. She and Kit would return to her house for quilting. One of the girls would bring her home if need be, but she could nap there too. And Ryan was home. Ah, it had been a long time since Spring break. All those years of the children running in and out of her house like they did their own, their bikes parked beneath the mountain ash trees. Since their own grandparents had lived in Seattle, Teza and Karl stood in for them, attending all the recitals and ball games, speech contests, and 4-H events. After Deliah died of breast cancer, Kenneth had remarried and moved to St. Louis where he was closer to his new wife's grandchildren than his own.

Teza continued pondering the changes life brought as she fixed herself a soft-boiled egg and toast. Maybe it was time she talked with Mark. Interfering, that's what he'd think, but hey, aunts could sometimes get by with more than wives or mothers.

After eating, she watered all the pots and hanging baskets that graced the porch and its nooks and crannies. She set up the cash register for Vinnie and gathered what she needed to work on one of the blocks for the new fruit quilt. The pan in a quilted carrier held a still-warm peach cobbler for lunch.

"Hey, Vinnie, thanks for taking over," Kit called and waved when she got out of her car.

"No problem. You take good care of her now." Wearing faded overalls and a red shirt, Vinnie looked every inch the farmer as she greeted the first customer of the day.

"I think she would help you more often

just because she loves your customers," Kit said as she opened the rear door of the van. "That and her tractor."

"I know, but I don't want to be a burden." Teza set her carrier on the floor. "You think some of the quilters would like peaches?"

"I'm sure they would, and they can come out and buy them. We don't want to be late."

"I know." Teza climbed in the van and buckled her seat belt while Kit did the same.

"Oh, that cobbler smells heavenly. Ryan has already said he hoped you would bake one while he's home."

"I'll make one just for him. Is he glad to be home?"

"We played ball with Thomas for an hour, and then I worked on the quilt while he caught me up on all his news. My little boy grew up while he was away."

"That's the way it is supposed to be."

"I know" — Kit flashed her a sort of smile — "but he's still my baby and will be as long as he lives."

"He's been grown up for a long time. All three of them matured so quickly when Amber was diagnosed with cancer. I've seen other families fall apart, but those three stood by and for one another. You raised them well, Kit. I'm proud of you, always have been."

"Now you're going to make me blubber." Kit sniffed, this smile a bit watery.

"I know. Going through this again is real hard on you."

"The first time I went back to the hospital, I thought my insides were falling out, and I couldn't keep them together. But I've visited people there enough that it's not so bad now."

"Have you been back to radiology?"

"Sure, mammograms are right down the hall. I might go see Marcy, if she's free, while I wait for you. Maybe get a cup of coffee."

"Good. Did you bring something to work on while you wait? Because if you didn't, I brought two blocks for my fruit quilt, one for each of us."

"Did you use freezer paper?"

"Of course. Do you want the pear or the cherries?" The two shared a smile and climbed out of the van. Together they traversed the halls to the radiology waiting room, and Kit took a seat while Teza stepped to the window to tell them she had arrived.

"It will be just a few minutes, Mrs. Dennison. Have a seat." The receptionist, who looked barely out of high school, smiled and motioned toward the maroon, padded chairs.

"Looks like a different place, doesn't it?" Teza indicated the fresh paint, carpet, and furnishings. A fifty-gallon saltwater fish tank bubbled in a divider in the middle of the room, so all the patients could see the colorful Moorish Idols, damsels, and trigger fish. Anemones and shrimp moved gracefully on the bottom and along the rock formation dotted with live coral. "Now that must have cost a pretty penny. And so necessary too."

Kit glanced at her aunt. "You have to admit it is beautiful and, maybe to some people, very calming."

"Are you saying I'm uptight?"

Kit raised her eyebrows and tilted her head slightly. "Let's appliqué." They'd just taken out their separate Baggies with hoops, ten-inch squares of fabric, and various colored bits already folded over the fruit-and-leaf-shaped freezer paper. Embroidery floss and needle and thread completed the kits.

"Hard time getting to sleep last night?" Kit held up her bag.

"I figured I'd sleep on the table." Teza handed Kit a small, pointed scissors. "I did get in a couple of hours though. How about you?"

"Like a baby."

"Good."

"A cranky, colicky baby."

Teza chuckled "Sorry. I thought perhaps you and Ryan sat up half the night talking."

"No, he crashed by the time I quilted one diamond. Said he hadn't slept much for the last week."

"Mrs. Dennison?" a young woman announced in the open doorway.

Kit squeezed her aunt's hand. "I'll pray for you."

Teza smiled. "Then all this is worth it."

When they returned to Kit's house, all the other women were chattering and quilting away until Kit and Teza stepped through the door. Silence greeted them for only a moment, but the intensity of it felt like a wall. Then Beth leaped to her feet and came to stand in front of Teza.

"Are you hurting? Hungry? Exhausted . . . ?" She reached for Teza's hand. "Can we hug you?"

"Of course, I'm not blown glass that's

going to shatter. Let me get a drink of water, and while I lie in that recliner for a bit, you can tell me all that has gone on."

A collective sigh greeted her announcement.

"I'll get the water. You want ice in it?"

"Please."

"That good-looking son of yours let us in, not that the door was locked or anything." Elaine waggled her eyebrows. "What's the term they use now for hunks?"

"I heard some girls giggling and throwing flirty looks at a couple of boys and calling them 'hotties.' " Sue rolled her eyes.

" 'Hotties'?" Elsie Mae put a hand over her mouth to stop a sound more like a snort than a chuckle.

"But that's most likely passé by now."

"Or a long time ago. Not that we ever used language even remotely like that." Kit set her and Teza's bags by the closet door and met Beth returning from the kitchen, tall glass of ice water in hand. Beth fussed around Teza until she was sure everything was comfortable and returned to her chair.

"So what did we miss out on?" Kit sat down and smiled her thanks at Beth, whom she was sure had been the one to leave a threaded needle in her place. When Beth nodded, Kit smiled again. "What a nice person you are."

"You wouldn't have thought so the other day."

"What happened?"

"I had to go down to the Detention Center — they no longer call it a jail — to bail my husband out after the protest at the abortion clinic."

"You mean the one that turned violent? I saw it on the news." Elaine looked up from her stitching.

"Yes, but none of the protesters threw the rock. We're sure of it. Garth always gives strict instructions to do nothing to impede traffic or to be rude, crude, or destructive in any way."

"What if someone wanted them to get in trouble?" Sue asked.

"But who? We are within our rights as citizens to protest publicly. Garth had the permit, and everything was done legally and in order."

"So you had to bail your husband out?"

Beth shuddered. "It was awful . . . a really terrible day. I had to break a window in our door, since I'd left the keys on the counter and . . ."

"So Garth had broken windows all over the place."

"He was really upset."

"I told my kids if they ever get caught for drinking or bad driving and they get hauled in, I wasn't coming to bail them out." Sue's sigh of disgust could be heard clear to the other room. "They could just stay there."

"But what if it were your husband?" Beth tucked her hair behind one ear.

"I'd like to say same rules apply, but I'm not stupid. Thank God I never had to live up to my threat."

"Wait a minute. Let's go back to the rock thrower." Elaine waved her hand for attention. "Now, who would get the most out of the situation if violence started?"

Shrugs and confused looks were her only answer.

"Not Garth, that's for sure. Nor me. And our church board is really unhappy," Beth volunteered.

"No, but if those hot-headed, crazy prolifers get a bad rap . . ." Elaine motioned outward with her hands.

"The abortion clinic comes out smellin' like a rose. *Their* rights are being trampled on by those narrow-minded, legalistic Christians who think they know what's good for everybody," added Elsie Mae.

"You sing it, sister." Sue smacked her palm to her forehead. "Why couldn't I figure that out without someone drawing me a picture?"

"You really think this was planned?" Beth looked from one to another of those around the quilting frame.

"Most likely no way to prove it, but I'd bet my . . ."

"Bootsie on it?" Kit raised both eyebrows and tucked her chin.

"I was going to say BMW, but I'd rather bet Bootsie anytime."

"Surely if the police started questioning, someone might have noticed something."

"There will be no investigation," Elsie Mae said with a heavy sigh. "They have what they want. There'll be fines and rhetoric, the judge will yell at, no, rather, severely admonish Garth and his people, the abortion clinic owners will go on television piously touting the rights of women to choose, and it will be all over until the next time."

"And with my husband's dedication to the cause, there'll be a next time."

"What kept you from being there too?" Sue asked.

Beth stared down at her frozen fingers.

When Beth didn't answer, Kit intervened. "Someone has to stay home to go bail the protesters out."

"Uh oh, sorry." Sue grimaced and looked to Kit for help.

"Excuse me." Beth pushed her chair back and headed down the hall to the bathroom.

"That child has a mountain of hurts she is carrying around inside her," Elsie Mae said, taking two more stitches. " 'Less she gets help, she's goin' to crumble down into little bitty pieces. Dear Lord, give us the best way to help her."

"Amen to that." Sue looked over to Kit. "And we thought all we were doing was sewing a quilt."

"So what's happening with the Bootsie saga?" Kit asked after lunch while they were settling back at the quilting frame. Teza took Sue's place, since she had to go home to take care of Kelly.

"He hasn't done his business in my yard for the last couple of days. Maybe Doodlebug ran him off for good."

"Now, wouldn't that be something. Maybe you'll have peace at your house after all."

"Oh, Bumblehead will follow through on the suit, if I know her."

"Maybe not." Teza wore a thoughtful expression. "Remember the heaping coals we talked about?"

"Believe me, Teza, I've tried kindness and it didn't work. Now I'm going to figure a way to get even."

"I see. I'll pray you don't get hurt in the trying."

"Don't worry about me. I'm pretty resilient." Elaine got to her feet and picked up her bag. "And on that note, I need to get going. Quilting tomorrow?"

"You know the door is always open for anyone who has a few spare minutes, or hours. Teza has her radiation Monday through Fridays at 9:30, so we'll always be back as soon as possible."

"How long is Ryan staying home?"

"About a week is all. He found a job in Pullman and starts a few weeks before his classes begin." Kit stood and walked Elaine to the door, then followed her outside when Elaine beckoned.

Elaine lowered her voice to a whisper. "When does Teza have her first chemotherapy?"

"She goes in Saturday morning. Be there at least a night, probably until Sunday afternoon or evening. Why?"

"Well, her hair is going to fall out immediately, right?"

"Well, within a few days it starts, I guess."

"I think we should give her a hat party."

"A hat party — what a marvelous idea."

"I thought perhaps we could each make her a different kind. I have a pattern for a turban that will look smashing on her."

Kit squinted her eyes to think back to her patterns. "I think I have a denim one that I could put a sunflower on for working around the fruit shed."

"Good. I wanted to check with you first, but tonight I'll call the others. Maybe we could all have them ready by next Wednesday or so. Don't you think she would feel up to it by then?"

"I sure hope so. She didn't have chemo last time, just the mastectomy, so I don't know how her body will respond."

"I'm putting my hope with that Healing Touch program of Elsie Mae's. I want her to do a presentation to the hospital board and the guild also. If there is anything we can do to alleviate some of the suffering, we do need to do it." She set off down the steps with a wave over her shoulder.

Kit watched her go. *Hard to believe that's*

the snobby Mrs. Giovanni I met a long time ago. Still thinking about the difference in the Elaine she thought she knew and the one who'd become part of the quilting group, she went back into the house to the quilting frame. Now if she could only figure out what all was bothering Beth.

THIRTY-FIVE

The calendar never lies.

"I'm sorry, honey."

"I know. Other women get babies, I get my period. My mother says I should be grateful I'm so regular. Somehow I find it a bit difficult to praise God for this." Beth sat on the edge of the bed, her head in her hands and her hair veiling her face.

Garth tucked her hair behind her ear and kissed the shell of translucent skin. "Beth, you do know that I love you, baby or not. I didn't marry you because you might bear children."

"Yeah, well, good thing." She looked longingly at the rumpled bed. To crawl back under the covers and sink into sleep. Forget the day, the period, the despair that shadowed her mind.

Instead she stood and headed for the shower. She had an appointment with Dr. Kaplan, and then she'd join the group for quilting. Like Kit said, "If you keep busy enough, the grief is easier to bear."

So are you going to tell him what's really

wrong? Not in this lifetime. But how can he help you if you aren't honest? He can't help anyway. No one can. It's just something I have to live with.

The argument pounded in her head like the water pounded her body. At least she could turn the water off.

Beth stopped her car in front of the Rainier Building where Dr. Kaplan had his office and stared at the corner of a concrete wall covered by creeping fig. The stems and leaves traced an intricate pattern of light and shadow. Behind that wall was the courtyard where birds fed at the feeders and splashed in the bath, and day lilies raised golden trumpets to the sun and harbored bees and humming-birds. Such peace in so small a space.

Except for the doctor and his penetrating questions. Four weeks she'd been coming now and she knew she was better, but was it the pills or . . .

"Lord, I don't want to go see him any longer." *Not that I ever wanted to, but Garth feels so strongly about it. Of course he isn't the one coming, just me.* She took in a deep breath, held it, and slowly let it all out. Dr. Kaplan had taught her that. As she exhaled, her shoulders relaxed and her neck lost its stiffness.

When Garth had continued his sermon series on trust on Sunday, trust and obedience had been the themes. She remembered the song from Sunday school when she was little. "Trust and obey for there's no other way to be happy in Jesus, but to trust and obey."

Well, what if you'd disobeyed? Sure, it sounded so easy. Confess your sins. He would forgive your sins and cleanse you from all unrighteousness. First John 1:9, the Christian's bar of soap. *So how many times have I confessed this? A hundred, a thousand?*

Beth glanced at the clock and opened her car door. Would today be the day? She fingered the letter she carried in her purse — a letter written to that baby that never had a chance to live because she had taken that chance away from him or her. She thought back to the middle of the night when she'd written the letter. "Dear baby in heaven, I'm so sorry I was so selfish that all I could think of was me and what would happen to me. They said I'd forget after a time, that you were nothing more than a cluster of cells, not a real baby yet. They lied . . ." But Beth knew "I'm sorry" would never be enough.

If I give him the letter, then Dr. Kaplan will understand. Will he hate me too? Or will he say I have to tell Garth so he can hate me?

The urge to get back in the car and go to Kit's — where she could lose herself in the quilting, laugh at jokes, enjoy the conversation — made her pause. She glanced back at the car, then at the front door to the building. Smoked glass. Like her life, murky and dim.

Trust. All right, Garth, I'm trusting. Each time I walk through this door, I'm trusting. A picture of her cat at home flashed through her mind. Trust took time to build. Just this morning . . .

"Hi, Kitty. Boy do we need a name for you." He mewed, looking up at her with wide green eyes. "You look so much better, although a bath might still help." She leaned over and emptied the rest of the can of kitty tuna in his dish. Instead of waiting for her to leave as he used to, he'd bellied right up to the plate and, crouching on all fours, began to eat. She paused, then trailed gentle fingers over his back. His back arched under her hand, so she stroked him again. "Would you look at that? I can finally pet you." The desire to pick him up needled her, but she resisted, just stroking him from head to tail again. He'd trusted her at least that much.

Trust. She left the car, entered the building, forcing herself to walk down the hall and open the office door. Her heart felt ready to leap out of her chest.

"So how has your week been?" They were sitting in their assigned seats, Beth hugging the wing-back chair, Dr. Kaplan across from her, relaxed and open.

"I've been working on the cancer quilt."

"Cancer quilt?"

"It's a community project to buy a mammogram unit for the hospital."

"What a great idea!"

"We're quilting it one diamond at a time."

"You really enjoy quilting, don't you?"

Beth nodded. "At least with sewing, you can look at it and say that it's finished. It doesn't have to be redone again in the morning."

"True. How is Garth?"

"Okay. Oh, you mean about his arrest at the abortion clinic?"

"Yes. The newspaper made it sound like there had been a riot."

"One stone is hardly a riot."

"But he's been arraigned?"

"Yes." Her thumb attacked the other.

"When is the hearing?"

"This morning." She couldn't look at him. She knew what he was going to ask. Staring at the birdbath, she waited.

And waited. Keeping her head down, she angled just enough to peek at him from under her lashes.

"I told him I would never go to court with him!" The words burst forth like a newly opened fire hydrant. "He knows I want no part of his political activism. I told him."

"Did he ask you to go?"

"No, but I had to go down and bail him out of jail."

"I see."

No, you don't. How can you when you don't know the whole story?

"So, do you feel like you should be there with him?"

The words dragged out of her. "A good wife would be."

"So, because you refuse to take part in his pro-life activities, you are not a good wife?"

Beth shrugged and looked back out at the birds, her arms now clenched around herself.

Dr. Kaplan reached down beside his chair, picked up a fluffy white bear with a red ribbon around his neck, and handed him to Beth. "Here, sometimes hugging a bear helps."

She clutched the toy, stroking his wonderfully soft fur with one hand.

"Can we back up a bit?"

Her shrug barely raised her shoulders.

"How did you feel when you went to the jail?"

"Scared. Angry. I almost didn't go."

"Why did you go?"

"Because there was no one else."

"He could have called an attorney or a member of the church."

"I guess."

"Do you always do what you think is right?"

"Mostly." She hugged the bear tighter.

"And you thought bailing Garth out was right?"

"He told me to bring the checkbook and come down there, so I did."

"Did you tell him how you felt?"

"I . . . I don't remember."

"Do you tell Garth anything that you think about?"

Oh, please, don't ask me any more questions. She drew back into the chair, wishing she could melt right into it.

"Not that I'm thinking of starting a business." *Not that I had an abortion.*

"Why?"

"Why what?"

"Why do you want to start a business?"

"We need the money. Garth thought the church would help pay his legal costs, but I don't think they will. The elders are not happy about this."

"I see." Dr. Kaplan matched up his fingertips and rested his chin on the pointers. "So why haven't you told Garth about your business idea?"

"I just thought I could make some extra money for when we need it. Lawyers are expensive."

"Garth doesn't want you working?"

"He says it is the man's job to take care of his family. And that we must trust God to take care of our needs."

"And you agree?"

Again that infinitesimal shrug. Her stranglehold increased on the bear. "Garth is the head of our home." She knew she sounded like a parrot and that she was copping out.

Tell him. I can't. Tell him. She buried her face in the bear's ear.

When she looked up again, he asked.

"How is your journal coming?"

"Fits and starts."

"Something I've found that helps in the grieving process is writing a letter to God, telling him how you feel. You might want to write one to your son too."

Beth jerked and clamped the bear tighter. *Oh, you mean my baby who died.* She swallowed and asked. "Do you think it could help?"

"I've seen it do so. Would you be willing to try?"

She sighed. And nodded, half a nod as if only half of her could agree.

"If you need me, you know you only have to call. I am here for you, and if I'm not here, my service will find me and I will return your call."

"Okay. I mean, thank you."

The letter in her purse burned her fingertips as she left the office.

She looked the other way as she drove past the courthouse on her way to Kit's house. Glancing in the rearview mirror, she saw only puffy eyes and a red nose. No way could she go in looking like this. But if she went home and Garth was there, he'd want to talk with her. He'd ask her what was wrong, and she'd have to say nothing, and they'd both know that was a lie. One look at her face screamed that.

So instead she stopped at a service station and went in the rest room to put cold water on her face and fix her makeup. Thank God for cold compresses, concealer, and powder.

When she walked in the door at Kit's, the group was rerolling the fabric so they could continue quilting. "It's gorgeous." Beth stopped a ways away so she could see as much of the quilt as possible. The flowing shades of burgundy and mauve outlined by cream looked both regal and warm. "I never realized how gorgeous it would be. The blue is a perfect accent."

Teza stopped beside her and gave her a quick hug. "It is beautiful, isn't it?"

Beth wished she could lean into Teza's strong arms and just float for a while. Or maybe she needed cuddling the way she'd cuddled that bear, if her tears didn't drown him. She looked up at Teza, into eyes so full of love that her own brimmed over, instantly, as though flipping a light switch.

"You've had a hard morning?" The whisper was gentle as a dandelion kiss.

Beth nodded. "I . . ." She took a breath of courage. "I'm seeing a counselor."

"Good."

That one word permanently joined a friendship that was already basted together.

"I know some Christians feel we should be able to let God handle all our problems. We can, but sometimes we need help. Wise counselors are a real gift from God."

"Thank you." Beth sneaked an arm around Teza's waist and hugged her back.

When Beth took a seat, Elsie Mae leaned across the table. "I saw that good-looking husband of yours going into the courthouse. Must be the hearing was today."

Beth nodded.

"You tell him there's lots of us praying for him."

"Thank you." *You don't know how glad I am to be here instead of there.*

After a silence stretched for a bit, broken only by the hiss of thread through fabric, Teza announced, "When we're done here today, if any of you want to come out and pick cucumbers, I'll give you a real deal."

"Maybe we should have a pickle party," Elsie Mae suggested.

"You mean you really make pickles?" Elaine looked around at the others, who all nodded. "I've never made a pickle in my life. I thought they came in jars."

"I don't suppose you make jam or jelly

either." Elsie Mae looked over her glasses to see Elaine shaking her head. "Well, but you do quilt with even stitches and your pillows are gorgeous. What about it?" She looked to each of the others. "Is she forgiven?"

"Deprived is more like it." Teza smiled at their looks of shock.

"Well, at least that's better than depraved." Elaine rolled the tip of her tongue in one cheek. "I think we're due for a coffee break. My rear is so tired from all this sitting every day that I've ordered a new one."

"Good luck. When you find the catalogue to order from, let me know." Elsie Mae stood and stretched her arms over her head. "It's my shoulders that get stiff. I must sit hunched over or something."

As they poured their beverages in the kitchen, Elsie Mae leaned her head from side to side, trying to pull the tension out of her neck. "There must have been a cat fight going on right under my bedroom window last night. I didn't sleep a wink."

"They were most likely doing something other than fighting, but the caterwauling of two cats mating is enough to wake the dead." Sue poured herself some iced tea.

"Or keep the whole neighborhood

awake. Why do they always choose my yard? I don't even have a cat."

"Let your dog loose."

"Oh, sure, and have him come back all bloody and get an infection." Elsie Mae set the pitcher back on the counter. "I'd need a dog the size of a Mack truck."

"I don't know, remember my Chihuahua chased that English bulldog out of our yard the other day. Even drew blood."

Sue nodded. "Heart size is more important than bark size."

"You'd think people would keep their cats indoors. I saw another hit on the road." Beth shuddered and leaned against the doorjamb. "Just breaks my heart." *And makes me cry like about anything else does.*

Kit set a plate of gingersnap cookies on the table. "Had to beat Ryan off these, so you better enjoy them."

"Where is he, off seeing his girlfriends?"

"No, he took Thomas down to play ball at the park. The two of them really hit it off."

"Sounds like he is as nice as he is good looking." Elaine filled a glass with ice cubes from the refrigerator door and added iced tea. "Cats fighting, hmm? Interesting."

"If I can ever get that stray cat on my

deck into the house, I'll never let him out." She turned to Elaine. "You know we haven't even chosen a name for our cat yet."

"Doesn't sound like he's quite yours. Maybe when he gets tamer something will come to you."

"Maybe." *Seems it takes me a long time to work anything out.*

But as they filed out of the kitchen and sat back down at the quilting frame, Beth's thoughts returned to her counseling session. Would she ever be brave enough to tell Dr. Kaplan everything?

THIRTY-SIX

As Elaine left the quilters she could feel an idea swirling around, gaining strength at each turn like a tornado as its fingers head toward earth. She drove slowly toward home, waiting for her idea to touch down. How could she get dogs barking or cats fighting under Mrs. Bootsie's window? It would drive her nuts. Even nuttier than she already was. A teenager gyrated along the crosswalk, keeping time to the music only he could hear through his earphones.

"That's it!" She slammed her hand on the steering wheel. "Vigilante on the move." Keeping her inner chuckle under control, she swung by the local electronics store, chatted with a young man who had given her good advice on earlier purchases, and left the store with two sacks of merchandise and instructions. Once home she took her tools out of their boxes, followed the clerk's diagrams, and, within a short period of time, was ready for the next step.

She drove out of town to the Jefferson County Humane Society.

"I'm here to look for a dog," she told the woman at the desk. "I'm not sure what I want, but I know I'll know when I see it."

"That's fine, take your time." The woman led the way into the aisle between pens containing dogs of every color, size, and breed. "Call me when you want to take one out of the pen."

"Thank you, I will." Elaine steeled herself against the pleading eyes and wagging tails that begged her to take them home. When she found a pony-sized dog with a bark to match, she took a small recorder out of her purse, turned it on, and held the microphone closer to the pen. She continued on down the line, recording dogs barking. When she had fifteen minutes of tape, she made her way toward the door.

"If I had a country place I'd take all of you home with me. But thanks for your help."

Back home Elaine fiddled with her gadgets until they were working the way the young man had said they would, then called Mrs. Smyth. The phone rang and rang with no answer.

She slipped her sandals on and, with palm-sized speaker in hand, crossed to the side of her neighbor's house. She could hear Bootsie barking, confirming no one was home. Under the master bedroom window, she planted her device on the trunk of a gnarly juniper. She checked the drive to find no one coming and hurried back across the yards to her own front door, snickering all the while.

"Just wait, Doodlebug, tonight we get even."

She did her laps in the pool, sucking in a mouth of water on a giggle when she heard her neighbor's cranky car drive into the garage. She stopped swimming to cough, and when she could breathe easily, commenced her strokes. Tonight would be the night.

Should I tell George? The thought made her smile, inside this time. *No, George wouldn't appreciate the brilliance of this plan.* But it would be so much more fun to share with someone. And Doodlebug, smart as he was, wouldn't understand.

That evening George nodded and smiled at her recital of the quilting meeting, but she would have bet his year's salary he didn't really hear her. After nearly thirty years of marriage, she knew the look that said he was either planning a difficult surgery or solving a problem at the hospital, but she let it go for now. Half an hour after he went up to bed, she tiptoed up to find the lights off and the snoring on.

She went back down to the deck and pulled her new toy out of the bag by her chair. She watched the Smyth house until she saw all the lights go out. Good thing they were the early-to-bed kind of people, like George. She waited another half hour and flipped the switch.

A dog barking convention convened in the backyard next door. She raised and lowered the volume, playing the control knob like a virtuoso. She managed to keep her glee to a whisper. "It works, it works." Doodlebug leaped from her lap to the deck, adding his warning to the din.

Lights came on. Someone leaned out the window and screamed, "Shut those dogs up!"

Elaine upped the volume.

In a few moments the light came on in Mrs. Smyth's kitchen. A mighty scream rent the air. "Fire!"

Elaine shut off the tape. Was their house on fire? She saw no smoke. Surely there was no fire.

Within minutes a fire truck roared up to the house next door.

Mr. Smyth met them on the front step, his voice carrying like a megaphone of old. "It's out now, though, thank God. Some barking dogs woke us up, or the house would have burned down around our ears."

Elaine leaned back in the chair and stared up at the stars. Doodlebug leaped up in her lap.

"Bug, I can't win. And this was such a wickedly delightful plan. What do I have to do to get even?"

"She wouldn't even let me stay with her." Kit threw her bag down in the recliner.

"I'm assuming you mean Teza." Sue looked up from threading her needle.

"Who else? Stubborn old Norwegian, sometimes I . . ."

"Takes one to know one." Sue's grin made Kit want to shake her.

"You could show some sympathy for crying out loud." Kit looked to each of the other quilters. "Like I told you, I planned on spending the day to make it easier for her, and she told me to go home and quilt where I'd be doing someone some good."

"Leave it to Teza. Yes!" Beth pumped air with her fist. "My hero. And besides, we're here to help you."

"So I guess you'd better just sit down here with the rest of us and put your fingers to work." Sue rolled her eyes at the others. "Some people will go to any means to get out of work."

"Did everyone get coffee and . . ."

"And I brought lunch." Elaine nodded toward the kitchen. "I put the things in the fridge, if that's all right with you."

"Hey, didn't I hear about a fire out your way last night?" Sue looked toward Elaine.

"How'd you hear already?"

"Doug is on the volunteer fire crew. They got called out about ten. Seems some barking dogs woke the people in time to prevent any real damage."

"It was next door, and you don't know the half of it." Elaine huffed a breath and told them her wonderful scheme. "Why can I never get even? It's just not fair."

Beth tried to hide a giggle and failed. She deepened her voice to announcer quality. "And thus goes the continuing saga of Elaine versus Bootsie. Tune in tomorrow for the next installment of *Life in Jefferson City*."

"You're too young to know about old radio shows." Sue elbowed her neighbor.

"Not when your husband is addicted to *The Shadow* and other old stuff. Besides, you can hear some of those old programs on Public Radio. I love them."

"Well, do any of you have any suggestions?" Elaine looked around the group.

Kit caught her eye. "Teza and Beth gave you good suggestions the other day." *Is this really me saying such a thing?*

"Thanks. Like I'm about to do the kill-her-with-kindness thing. She'd be too dense to figure it out anyway. I like the burning coals angle of it, though."

Beth groaned. "I think that's God's part of it."

"Oh, just my luck."

"Hey, I've got a problem I could use some help on," Beth said.

"Hope they do better for you than for me."

"Mine's easier. Well, you all know about Garth and the court, and I've been thinking how I can help out, so I came up with starting a seamstress kind of business. I really do love to sew and . . ."

"That's a good idea," Kit broke in. "While there are a lot of women who sew in this town, there is no real seamstress business as such. You should do well. Get some business cards made up off your computer and printer. I found some really pretty card stock down at the office supply, and you can use a template from your word processing program, easy as pie."

"I'd need a name before I could even do the business card bit."

"How about Sewing by Beth?"

"Or, 'You Rip, I Fix.' "

"Fit and Sew."

"Or Sew and Fit."

"Stitch in Time."

"Time to Stitch."

The titles came from all of them. Beth stopped stitching and reached down in her bag for a notebook. "Stop, I have to write them all down." She did and looked at the list. "I like Sewing by Beth best."

"Good, then you make your cards and hand them out to everyone you know," Elaine offered. "In fact, you give them two, one for them to keep and one for them to give away. Then you post them at like the cleaners, the grocery stores on their bulletin boards, places where foot traffic is high."

"But, well — I haven't mentioned this to my husband yet. I thought I'd just bring in a bit of money on the side, to help out, you know."

"I'd tell him, dearie, right up front." Elsie Mae leaned forward to make a point. "You shouldn't never try to keep secrets from your man. It'll just turn and bite you on the butt."

"Elsie Mae." Kit covered her surprise by rolling her lips together.

"Th-thank you, I think."

Elaine studied the stricken look that quickly changed back to a smile on the younger woman's face. *Something is going on here. I wonder what it is she's hiding. He's really a gorgeous man too. Shame he's in trouble with the police. I bet he is too proud to have his wife working.*

"Are you going to specialize in anything? Like alterations, home decor, wedding dresses?" Kit asked.

"Wedding dresses?" Beth's voice squeaked. "I . . . I hadn't thought that far. All those beads and lace, oh no, I couldn't do something like that."

"So, alterations?"

Beth nodded.

"Hard to fit people?"

She winced. "I guess, but I've never done such a thing."

"Then no."

With each comment Beth melted closer to the back of her chair. "I . . . I just thought to be a Proverbs 31 wife." At Elaine's blank look, Beth continued. "You know, she sells things, dresses her family and all the servants or slaves, however you want to interpret it."

"I guess you don't have to worry about the slave part anyway." Elaine leaned across the corner of the quilt frame and patted Beth's cold hand. "Don't mind me. I just love promoting these kinds of things, and the more we know about your business, in fact, the more *you* know about your business, the more we can help you."

"That's for sure," Kit added with a nod. "You never know what one of us will hear and be able to pass on to you."

"So do you think you can bring in your business cards this week? Bring me a bunch, and I will hand them out at the hospital guild meeting next month. Several ladies there are always looking for people to hem slacks and skirts, that kind of thing. What are you going to charge?"

Beth flopped back, arms falling at her sides. "I have no idea."

"Call that cleaner downtown who advertises alterations. Tell them you need something done, like hem a skirt or put in a zipper and ask what they charge." Sue tied a knot in her thread. "Then I'd check the Olympia or Tacoma paper, and if there are ads for sewing, do the same thing."

"You are all so smart. Thank you."

"Not smart, wise. Comes with age,

hopefully." Elsie Mae snipped her thread off. "Least ways, I been prayin' for wisdom a long time, and God says he'll give it to all those who ask." She raised her eyes to look heavenward. "And, Lord, I do need plenty. A bucketful would be just fine."

Beth giggled and took up her stitching again.

"Now since Teza isn't here . . ."

"I know, we can talk about her."

"No, we can talk about the hat party." Elaine dug in the bag at her feet. "I brought some hat patterns I had at home in case some of you didn't have any. I'm making this turban, one in a dressy fabric, one in real casual. I've made others like it for cancer patients."

Beth reached for one with a turned up brim. "This looks like fun."

"I'm doing one similar to that out of denim." Kit pointed to one of the hats on the pattern cover. "I made one before, and it turned out really nice. You know what?"

"Oh, oh, light bulb time. I saw it go off." Sue touched her forehead.

"What if we all brought hats, and when she opens hers, we can all put them on. You know, make her feel — well, I don't know. Maybe it isn't such a good idea."

"Yes, it is. She'll know we're all pulling

for her." Elsie Mae nodded. "I've got such a great crocheted hat. I'll see if I can get one done. If it were winter, I'd already have some in stock."

"She'll be needing winter hats too."

"You crochet hats?" Beth looked from Elsie Mae to around the group. "You all do so many different things. What an amazingly talented group." Beth glanced at her watch. "Oh, my, I better get going. Garth should be done with his sermon by now, and then we're going up to the lake for a picnic. I'll see you all on Monday, unless you come to our church. We'd love to have you." She smiled directly at Kit.

Kit shrugged. "We'll see how things go."

"Bring your business cards."

"I'll have them by Wednesday." Beth's voice floated back through the open front door.

"Such a sweet child." Elsie Mae stood and stretched. "These old bones need to move around."

"I'm sure she would appreciate knowing you think of her as a child when she is trying so hard to be the kind of wife her husband needs." Kit eyed the recliner. "Wonder how Teza is faring."

"From the look in her eyes at times, I think that *child* has a dark secret that is tearing her up inside." Sue rubbed her forehead. "I'm going to have to sit straighter or wear one of those braces that holds your shoulders back." She leaned her head toward one shoulder and then the other. "Think I'll go out in the backyard to stretch a bit. Anyone want anything from the kitchen?"

Later, when they were gathering their things to leave, Kit looked back at the quilt. "You really think we are going to get this done by the end of September? We sure have a long way to go."

"Maybe we should have a couple of all-nighters. Would your husband mind if the ladies came over and sat up all night laughing and quilting?" Elaine stopped on the front steps and looked back to Kit.

Kit shook her head. "No, he wouldn't mind." *Not even if he were here.*

THIRTY-SEVEN

"Do you mind, Garth, if I go over to Kit's for a couple of hours?"

"No, not at all. I'm going to work in the garden, and then we can go out for pizza or something." He touched her cheek with a gentle finger. "I'm just so glad to see you up and about and interested in something."

"Umm. I don't know how we're going to finish this quilt unless all of us put in every hour we can find. See you later." Beth reached up to give him a quick kiss. "Oh, and by the way, two different people stopped me today to say how excellent your sermon was. Just thought you should know."

"Thank you."

She waved as she picked up her bag and headed out the door to the garage. The sun had yet to win the daily battle with the gray cloud cover, but brief patches of golden light showed that the skirmish was turning. Beth opened the window on the passenger side so the fresh air could come in without tangling her hair. Her thoughts turned to the business venture. A patchwork sign to hang in their front window might look nice, if Garth didn't mind. After she told him, of course. But really, what was wrong with having a home business?

Beth parked in front of Kit's and waved when she saw her out working in her front roses. "I thought I'd come quilt for a while. You don't have to come in, you know."

Kit snipped off a few more dead blossoms. "No, about time I went in. Can I cut you some to take home?"

"I would love that. Thank you."

"Good, go get yourself that flat basket up on the porch, and I'll start cutting."

Beth sniffed each blossom as Kit handed it to her. "Now, when you get home, you snip off the ends underwater, and then they'll keep a lot longer. Some say put an aspirin in the bottom of the vase. That helps longevity too."

"Why cut underwater?"

"The stem is very porous and as soon as I cut it, a bubble of air blocks any more water absorption. So if you cut it again underwater, the stem sucks up water and will keep doing so."

"I always wondered why they said to do

that." Beth held the basket end with all the blossoms up to her face. "Ah, the fragrance. The petals feel so soft and caressing, as if they were made to be felt and not just smelled."

"True." Kit stripped off her garden gloves and put them in her garden apron pocket.

"How's Teza doing?"

"I talked to the nurse first thing this morning. Teza's been vomiting but seemed in good spirits, tired, of course. They said we could come get her about five. She should be over most of it by then."

Beth stopped at the top of the steps and turned to look back toward Mount Rainier, which had just pushed aside the cloud cover and reigned supreme. "So beautiful. I never dreamed I'd be living so near the base of a mountain like this. It's the first thing I look for in the morning and the last at night."

"I know. I'm like that too."

I will lift my eyes unto the hills; from whence cometh my help?

Stop that! You aren't playing fair again. Besides, I know the rest of the verse, and my help does not come from the hills. But if you recall, it did not come from you either.

You got through it, didn't you? I carried you

when you weren't even aware.

Kit shook her head. Such preposterous thoughts. *As if God really was there, is here.* She shook her head slightly again.

"Are you all right?" Beth leaned forward.

"Oh, I will be." Kit leaned against a porch post. "Do you ever get the feeling God is trying to tell you something you don't want to hear?"

Beth laughed, the tinkling notes teasing the slender purple fuchsia blossoms dangling over her head. "All the time."

"Strange, when I begged and pleaded for his help, he seemed silent and aloof, and now that I don't want anything to do with him, he won't leave me alone."

"You don't want anything to do with him?" Beth put her basket on the wicker table and took one of the chairs.

"Not especially, although that is changing now too. Sometimes it is just too much and I give up."

"Pardon me for being nosey, but does this have something to do with Amber?"

"Yes."

"I know. I felt that way after our baby died. I thought sure God was punishing me for something."

A pause while Kit sat down in the glider. The creak of the hardware as she moved it with her foot sounded friendly, as if joining in on the conversation. "Strange, I wonder why mothers think that? I've spoken with other women who thought that too. Janey, Sue's daughter, is a nurse. She once told me that babies who die in utero have something wrong with them, and this was nature's way of dealing with such a situation. She said to think about how that baby goes right back home to heaven without having to live all these hard years on earth."

"I like that thought. My son would have been ten months old now. Seeing other mothers with babies has been so difficult. And now my best friend is pregnant, and I could hardly congratulate her." Beth wadded her skirt up in her fist. "What a creep I am."

"No, not a creep. I understand how you feel. For us, weddings are the pits. We won't get to see Amber married, enjoy her children. You just feel ripped off at times."

Beth took Kit's hand. "Ripped off is right. You know I'm working with Dr. Kaplan. He suggested I write a letter to my unborn son and tell him how I feel, how I felt, what I dreamed for him, that now will never be."

"Interesting. The one I'd write to is God

and really tell him what I think."

"So what's wrong with that? I heard Garth say one day, 'God has broad shoulders. If he is indeed God, he can take what we dish out.' " Beth leaned forward. "Perhaps one to Amber, too."

"Thanks, Beth. I'll think about it." Kit stood and picked up the basket. "We better get these roses in water . . ."

"And to the quilt." Beth stood. "Thank you. You are so easy to talk with."

"And you. How about lemonade, iced tea, or iced coffee?"

"Lemonade and a needle and thread to go."

"Someone's been sitting in my chair." Elaine set her bag on the floor on Monday morning.

"It wasn't me, that's for sure." Teza leaned back in the recliner. "I'll tell you, my own bed felt so good last night."

"I thought you were going to stay here."

"I was, but when I grumbled about how bad I wanted my own bed, Ryan came out and stayed with me. Not that he had anything to do other than sleep. I went to bed and never heard another thing until the robins were singing so loud I had to get up."

"You feel up to quilting?"

"Better than lying around." Teza leaned over. "I nearly finished this square before the medicine reacted." She held out the square with three red cherries and their leaves appliquéd in place, the stems embroidered along with a highlight in white on each cherry. "Three for the trinity, and now I need to find a verse that applies."

"It's going to be beautiful." Elaine handed it back.

"If you see any fruit fabric, pick me up a yard or so, would you, please? I'd like the blocks to be as many different patterns as possible."

"I most certainly will. Say, Teza, you don't have any old Hardunger do you? Or bits and pieces? I saw a piece worked on a pillow along with ribbon embroidery and some beadwork. Incredibly beautiful."

"I might have some pieces I've done or started and not gone on with. I'll see."

"I thought of asking at the Sons of Norway lodges in Tacoma and Olympia."

"That might be a good resource. Have you ever done Hardunger?"

Elaine shook her head. "No, I don't have the patience."

"All you have to do is count threads and

stitches in fours and fives on even weave fabric."

"No, you don't get those little wrapped bars and open patterns with just counting threads in fours and fives. Besides, it is tone on tone and, therefore, harder to see." Elaine looked over her shoulder at the quilt frame. "I better get to work. I can see I am behind some of the others."

"That's why someone was sitting in your chair." Kit handed Elaine a cup of coffee. "Helping you catch up."

"Is Sue coming?"

"Not today. She's taking Kelly school shopping, and if I know her, she'll see the prices, have a fit, go to Myrna's, buy the fabric, and spend the next three days sewing for Kelly. Elsie Mae can take her place." Kit rolled her shoulders first forward, then back. "Teza, how you feeling?"

"Like I should be out at the farm picking cucumbers. And I'm sure the beans are ready for the last picking."

"Now, you know Ryan is doing just that. He and Vinnie will do fine."

"I know, but I miss being out there." Teza pushed the recliner upright and came over to take a chair by the quilting frame. "At least if I'm working on this, I'm accomplishing something."

Ah, dear Teza, you don't have to work all the time. Kit wished she could tie her aunt in the chair and force her to rest.

"Actually when you're lying back in the recliner, you're accomplishing something far more important." Elaine took her thimble out of her sewing kit and smiled at Teza as she put it on.

"Like what?"

"Like letting your body heal. George says most people don't realize how much energy healing takes. Building new cells is hard work, and so you tire easily. The more you fight it, the longer it takes to become well again."

"Interesting you should say that," Teza said. "A nurse yesterday told me much the same about taking pain medications when needed. She said fighting pain uses energy, too, and then it slows down the healing. This morning I was reading, and the verse 'come unto me all you who are heavy laden, and I will give you rest' just leaped out at me. I imagine God was trying to tell me something, and then this discussion comes up. Isn't God amazing."

"You know, I found something really interesting in the research I was reading for Teza last night," Kit said. "Studies are showing that women who have had an abortion are anywhere from 50 to 100 percent more likely to develop breast cancer later in life. Something to do with differentiated and undifferentiated cells." Kit glanced up in time to see Beth surge to her feet, her chair falling backward. "Beth, what . . . ?"

"I have to go." Beth grabbed her bag and headed for the door.

"Sorry I'm late." Just coming in through the door, Elsie Mae blocked her way.

"I have to go." Beth tried sidestepping, but Elsie Mae dropped her bag and grabbed Beth by the shoulders. "Whoa now, child. You can't leave all upset like this."

"I have to go!" Beth tried wrenching away but instead collapsed sobbing into the older woman's comforting arms.

"Easy, baby, you come to the right place, here next to my heart." Elsie Mae looked over Beth's shoulder, question marks flickering across her face.

Elaine and Kit looked at each other and thought the same thing at the same moment. *Abortion?* Elaine mouthed. Kit nodded. *The other times Beth ran. Did we bring up this subject then?* The memory wasn't clear. *You poor child. Dear God, how do we help her?*

Elsie Mae walked the sobbing young woman over to the sofa and sat down, arm still around Beth's shoulders.

"I . . . I . . . I'm so sorry. I didn't know." Tears and sobs broke Beth's words into near unintelligible gibberish.

"And all these years you've carried this?" Elsie Mae stroked Beth's hair and laid her cheek against the wavy mass.

Kit brought a box of tissue from the bathroom and set it on the coffee table where Beth could reach it. She glanced up at Teza to see her eyes closed and lips moving in prayer. *Good, Teza, you pray, I wish I could. Ask and it shall be given you. But it wasn't then, so why would it be now?*

So ask now.

I can't. Kit laid a hand on Beth's shoulder and sat down in the easy chair. *What to say?*

"How old were you, darlin'?" Elsie Mae asked as she handed Beth a tissue.

"S-Sixteen. My b-boyfriend said I had to, and he p-paid for it. They said it wasn't even a baby yet, that I was doing what was best for me and . . . and him. I was so stupid! I never told anyone. They said to just forget it. I never dated again — until Garth." She mopped her eyes and blew her nose.

"Does Garth know?" Kit hated to ask the question.

Beth shook her head. Her hair now curly from the moisture, clinging to her cheeks. "No one ever knew. I thought about it once in a while, but then I'd stuff it back down and pretend it didn't happen. Until my baby died, and now I can't get pregnant. I know God is punishing me, and if I tell Garth, he will hate me." She clasped her arms around her knees and laid her cheek on her skirt. "Now I know so much more, and God forgive me, I murdered my baby."

"God does forgive. Did you ask him to?" Elsie Mae rested a hand on Beth's curved back.

"Yes. Oh, how many times I have begged him to forgive me."

"If we confess our sins, God is gracious to forgive us our sins and to cleanse us from all unrighteousness. Do you believe that?" Teza spoke so gently the words floated like dandelion down, kissing a brow here and a cheek there.

Beth nodded and used the tissue on her eyes again.

"Then you are forgiven. But you have to forgive yourself, too. Think on the Lord's prayer. 'Forgive us as we have forgiven others.' That includes ourselves."

"See, darlin', God don't want you carryin' this around anymore. You got to let it go, and when Satan starts to tell you how bad you are and God doesn't forgive you, you throw those scriptures right back in his face."

"But what if I never have a baby again?"

"That's possible, but maybe you had to let this go first. Give it to God . . ."

"You could write him a letter." Kit caught Beth's gaze and smiled.

"So I'm forgiven, just like that?" Beth sighed.

"That's why Jesus died, so we can be forgiven." Teza dug a tissue out of her pocket and blew her nose. "No matter what, so we can say, 'Lord Jesus Christ, have mercy on me.' And he does."

"Beth, darlin', have you told Garth?"

Beth shook her head. "He'll hate me."

"I surely do hope not, but I think you need to tell him."

"Now?"

"Good a time as any. We'll be prayin' for you."

"Do you all hate me?" Beth looked from face to face, to see all of them shaking their heads. "Really?"

"Uh, Beth, the only one who's been

hating you is you." Elaine waved her scissors. "But I sure could do something to those so-called counselors who feed frightened young girls such a lie."

Beth pushed herself to her feet. "If I can get a drink of water and wash my face, I'll go on home and tell Garth."

"Use the washcloth on the towel rack." Kit stood. "I think we all need a break now."

"Do you want me to drive you home?" Elaine asked. "Perhaps you shouldn't be driving in the state you're in."

"Thanks. But unless he throws me out, I should be okay."

"You think he would?" Elaine looked to Kit and Teza.

Kit shook her head. "I certainly hope not."

The rest of them stood on the porch watching as Beth walked toward the car. She waved once she was inside and started the engine to drive off.

"Let's just sit down here and pray for those children." Elsie Mae motioned to the wicker chairs. When they were seated with heads bowed, Elsie Mae began. "Heavenly Father, we bring Beth before you, a hurting, broken child who needs you to keep her close now as she does one of the hardest things, confess to her husband."

"Be with Garth, too, dear Father, open his heart to hear her and love her with your love and compassion." Teza paused. "Thank you for sending your son to die that we might live in forgiveness and grace."

Kit kept her eyes closed, but she could feel Elaine stirring beside her. *She doesn't want to be here any more than I do, does she? Beth, gentle Beth. Oh, such secrets we hide and suffer from.* At the amen, she opened her eyes and blinked, not realizing until then that tears had been leaking down her cheeks.

"You think the depression she's been under was from this?"

"Most likely." Teza leaned back against the seat. "Do you mind if I stay out here a bit?"

Kit looked at the dark circles under her aunt's eyes and the pale skin of her face. "Would you like to rest on a bed, or perhaps on the lounger on the back deck?"

"No, here where I can see the mountain is fine."

"Oh, God." Beth felt her heart thudding as if she'd been running. Garth's car sat in the driveway. She stopped, set the brake and got out, her hands shaking so she could hardly hold her keys. She reached back in the car for her purse, slammed the door, and forced her feet to move her forward. *God, please help me. Father, I cannot do this.* She opened the door from the garage to the house and stepped into the kitchen.

Garth turned from the counter. "Beth, you're home early."

"I have t-to tell you something. You better sit down." She pointed to the chair.

"What's wrong? Honey, you're scaring me." He sat on the chair, his gaze not leaving hers.

She clamped her fingers over the back of the chair in front of her. "I had an abortion when I was sixteen, and, Garth, I am so sorry." *Please come take me in your arms. Garth, don't look at me that way!*

But Garth just sat there, staring. Accusing. Then he got up and left the room.

THIRTY-EIGHT

"I can't believe you would do such a thing."

Beth stood in the arch to the living room and stared at her husband. His clothes from the day before were rumpled, his face unshaven, his hair in pillow-tossed spikes. But his eyes — Beth knew they would haunt her. Desolate, dark, as though anger had come and gone, leaving ashes in its wake. *But, Lord, I have to hang on to you. I am forgiven — you said so. Please, speak to Garth, heal his wounded heart.*

"Me, either." But that was then and now is now. "Can I fix you breakfast?" *You didn't eat dinner, and nothing around here shows you've even snacked.*

He shook his head. "Think I'll go for a run."

"Did you sleep?"

He halfway shrugged. "I was searching." He nodded toward his Bible. "God says I have to forgive you, but right now, Beth, I can't. You lived a lie all these years. Do I even know who you are?"

She almost said, "I'm no different," but

she couldn't. For she was different. Inside, she knew freedom, for the first time in twelve years. It bubbled up like a clear mountain stream from under a storm-hewn rock. Water, life-giving water. The living water that washed her clean.

Garth had not started the coffee maker, had not had a glass of juice, nor eaten one of the cinnamon rolls she'd made the day before. She got out the filter, measured the grounds, and poured in the water. With each action, a prayer for Garth rose with the fragrance. She wiped down the counters, set his place at the table, and warmed a cinnamon roll in the microwave. When the coffee maker beeped, she took her roll and coffee mug outside on the back deck.

Dew coated the chairs and lounger. The cushions had been left out overnight. The cat jumped up on the deck and walked over to the dish, his tail straight in the air. He sniffed it, sat down, and looked at her as if to say, "Come on, get with the program. I'm hungry."

"You before me, right?"

A mew answered her question. The cat yawned, barbed pink tongue curling between white teeth.

When she poured the kibbles into his dish, he crouched down, tail wrapped around his body as he crunched away. Beth flipped the cushion over on the lounger and moved her plate and mug from the round glass-topped table to the low one where a pot of bronze and gold marigolds bloomed. Another one of the little things Garth did to show his love, put pots of flowers where she could enjoy them. Could he . . . ? Would he . . . ? She sat down and swung her legs up on the lounger. When she tried to think what she would do if Garth couldn't forgive her, the thoughts wouldn't come, only *peace I leave with you, my peace I give you.* Peace, such a precious gift. She sipped her coffee and nibbled the edge of her roll. When the cat finished his meal, he strolled over, leaped up on the lounger and, sitting by her knees, began his morning ablutions. Lick the paw, scrub the face and ears. Lick the chest, go to the other paw for the other side of face and ears.

Slowly, afraid if she moved too fast, she reached out a finger and rubbed his head. When he stood and arched his back, she obliged and stroked his back. A purr rumbled in his throat and burst into full-blown kitty contentment. With two white front paws he kneaded her thigh, then hopped up in her lap to curl up and continued purring, his motor causing her and the entire lounger to vibrate.

Trust. She'd finally earned his trust.

Garth, freshly showered and shaved, poked his head out the door. "I have a meeting at church, but I'd appreciate it if you were here when I returned. Should be back in an hour or so."

"Okay."

"The cat's in your lap."

"I know." Beth smiled at her husband. "Pretty amazing, huh?"

Beth stayed where she was, praying and listening. Praying for the right words to say to him, listening for what God had to say to her. His love songs flowed liquid joy like the *Song Sparrow*'s aria. One song pleased her ears. The other watered her heart so long dry and near parched to death.

Her eyes closed and she slept.

"Beth." Garth touched her shoulder. "I'm home."

"Oh, Garth, I had the most wonderful dream." She paused. "At least I think it was a dream."

"What?"

"I felt like I was being rocked in mighty arms, stronger than anything I've ever known, but so gentle, even more gentle than my mother's. I looked down to see a baby in my arms, a newborn so red of face but sleeping with long eyelashes on round cheeks. A fuzz of red crowned her perfect little head, two tiny fists, one by a cheek, the other under the dimpled chin. 'And is she mine?' I asked. A deep voice rumbled in my ear, 'No, mine, but safe from further harm.' I dared to ask, 'My first?' My heart was about to leap out of my chest." Beth put her hand to her ear. "Like I heard him through his chest, he said, 'That one, I love with an eternal love, like I love you.' 'And will you trust me again?' I asked. I felt a rumble in his mighty chest, and suddenly I was back in the lounger. And the cat was purring. And, Garth, it was so real."

"I'm glad. Beth, I think I need you to tell me the whole story."

"Are you sure?"

"I'm sure." He rubbed his forehead. When she finished, he leaned back in the chair he'd moved to during her telling and closed his eyes. "I have to believe you had no idea what you were really doing . . ."

"Garth, I can remember the terror. I was frightened out of my mind. I think of all the 'I should haves', and I go crazy."

"Like you have been lately?"

"Yes. But no longer. I know Jesus forgave me. I believe it now."

"As do I. I fought and wrestled with the Lord all night. I know how Jacob felt, and I know I must forgive you or be in direct opposition to God myself, where I really don't want to be. I want to be in his perfect will. But I tell you, I've never struggled with anything so hard in my entire life."

"I love you, Garth Donnelly."

"And I you. No more secrets, okay?"

"Right." A thought hit her so hard she blinked. "Uh, there is one more thing."

Garth stopped in his reaching for her and sat back in his chair. "What?"

"I, uh, I've been talking with the quilters about starting a sewing business so that I could help with the money coming in. It may not be much, but you know how I love to sew, and, well, who knows if it will do anything or not. Do you mind?"

"When were you planning on telling me about it?" He crossed his arms over his chest.

"When I knew more about what I had to do."

"Beth, I don't mind if you start a business like this, but no more secrets. If either of us has an idea, we talk it over, up front not later."

"Yes, I promise."

"You're sure there's nothing else?" When she shook her head, he stood and reached for her hand. "Good. Let's see if we can do some serious damage to those cinnamon rolls."

"Anybody heard from Beth?" Teza asked.

Sue and Kit shook their heads. "No news is good news? If she needed something, she would call, right?"

"Or else she's in such deep depression she can't call." Sue laid out her needle case and sat down to begin threading. "How are you doing, Teza?"

"Fair to middling. I'd be home working, but Kit there said I was needed more here today."

"Knock, knock." Elsie Mae pushed open the door with a canvas-covered cooler swinging from one arm and her bag on the other. "I brought lunch."

"Do you need refrigerator space?"

"No, this will stay cold that long. I'll just set it in the kitchen."

"I could have helped you, you know, if you'd waited only a moment more." Elaine breezed in behind Elsie Mae. "Anyone heard from our child bride?"

"If she doesn't show up pretty soon, I'm calling over there to check." Kit set a plate of cookies on the coffee table. "Coffee's ready if anyone wants some. Tea's in the fridge."

"How come you two are back already? Or didn't you have radiation?" Elaine directed her question toward Teza.

"I have an earlier time now. We go at eight instead of nine-thirty."

"That gives you even less time at home in the morning."

"I know. Thank God for Ryan and Vinnie. They've been selling peaches like crazy, and the Gravenstien apples are especially good this year. I have a box out in the kitchen for you to all help yourselves."

About the time they all got sat down, Beth burst in the door. "Sorry I'm late, I overslept." She stopped and looked around the group. "What's wrong, is my dress inside out or something? My makeup smeared?"

"We're just makin' sure you are still in one piece, darlin'. You know you left here in a real hurry."

"Well, all through Monday night when Garth never came to bed or spoke to me or anything, I wasn't sure what was going to happen, but Tuesday morning we talked it out, and he said he forgives me." She sagged against a chair. "What a relief."

"You notice anything different about her?" Elaine asked.

"I do." Teza held out a hand for Beth to take. "She was pretty before, but now she is radiantly beautiful."

"That's for sure." Sue patted Beth's arm. "She's wearing the look of love."

Beth's cheeks turned a bright pink. "Is it that obvious?"

"Well, I wasn't talking about that kind of love, but we'll take whatever kind we can get."

When the laughter receded, Beth fanned her face. "Teach me to come late." She took out her needles, already threaded, then clasped her hands on the quilt frame. "I just want to thank all of you for being the kind of friends who . . . who . . ." She took in a deep breath and started again, her voice cracking. "Who knew how to be there to help me through this. Whoever dreamed that working on a quilt would change my whole life?"

"Perhaps we should quit thinking of this as the cancer quilt and call it the healing quilt instead." Sue smiled at Beth across the frame. "Who knows what else will happen?"

"I know something that will happen." Elaine stuck her needle in the quilt. "Ladies, on three. One, two, three." All but Teza reached down in their bags, pulled out a hat, and put it on. "Teza Dennison, in honor of your presence, we call this the hat day, and all of these fine creations are for you, so that while you may go hairless for a time, you will never go hatless."

"Oh . . . I don't know what to say." One by one, each woman stood, took off her hat, and placed it on Teza's head. A denim with sunflower from Kit, wild floral from Sue, blue and white gingham from Beth, red-and-white crocheted cap from Elsie Mae, and two turbans from Elaine, one in black silk with beads, bangles, and a feather, the other in red with white trim. "The black is for things like the gala, when you need to be dressed up."

Teza took her hats to the hall mirror and tried them all on again. "What a wonderful idea. I thought I'd go buy a wig but maybe not. These are" — she held her palms against her cheeks — "just too much. Thank you all."

"You are most welcome." Elaine sat back down from giving Teza a hug and turned to Beth. "Hats are something you could sew. Let the oncology department know so they could send their clients to you. You could have some on display and take orders." She stopped. "You did tell your husband about the business idea."

Beth nodded. "And he thought it would be a good thing. This would make it even better."

"If you'd like to put them on consignment at the hospital gift shop, I'm sure that could be arranged too."

"Thank you." Beth reached down in her bag and brought up business cards. "Garth helped me with these last night." She passed them both directions. "And everyone take two at least." She tipped her head in Elaine's direction. "She said to do it that way, remember?"

Needles flew for a time as they teased Sue about sewing a full wardrobe for Kelly, discussed plans for Labor Day, talked about the progress on all the other programs for earning money for the mammogram unit and other news about town.

When they'd finished lunch, Beth stood in front of Kit's family picture wall and, to Kit, asked, "When will Mark be home again?"

Kit felt as though she'd been jabbed with an ice pick, the pain slicing straight to her heart. "I . . . I don't know."

"What does he do?"

"He's a computer consultant for a firm out of Tacoma." Kit looked to Sue for help, but she half shrugged, half shook her head. No help there. And Teza looked about done in.

"Shame you can't travel with him." Beth followed the others over to the waiting frame.

Kit looked up in time to catch a laser gaze from Elaine. *Please, ignore her.*

"Your husband did some consulting for the hospital a couple of years ago, didn't he?" Elaine glanced up from her stitching.

Kit nodded.

"Shame he can't get more work locally."

"It is. Mark is so good at what he does, but then he's good at fixing or building most anything." Teza smiled at Kit. "He built the most perfect window boxes. I planted annuals in them and sold them as fast as we could put them out."

"I have two. Change the plants each year. I love them, hanging on the railing around my deck." Sue blinked and squinted to thread the needle. "I think they're making the eyes even smaller on these things."

"I could use some planter boxes like that." Elaine looked back to Kit. "You think he would build me some?"

Kit took a deep breath. "If I had any idea when Mark was coming home, I'd tell him, but I don't. He's been gone since January, and I really don't even know exactly where he is."

"Sad man on the run from God?"

"Well put, Elsie Mae. Most likely from God and all the things here he said he could no longer handle."

"Like grieving for Amber?" Beth spoke softly.

"And all the memories here. You can't really get away from them, but then I don't want to."

"You mean to say he left you all by yourself to grieve alone?" Elaine's question was rhetorical. "And you want him to come back?"

Kit nodded.

"I say send him packing. Ship him his things, and if and when he grows up, he can ask to begin all over again." Elaine glared at her needle rocking in the quilt layers to form another stitch. "The nerve of him. So many of them do that to us, leave us alone to take care of all the stuff that comes along. It's just not fair. Why do you . . . *we* put up with it?"

"You, too?" Elsie Mae raised an eyebrow.

"No. I mean, I — We were talking about Mark." Elaine let her hands fall in her lap. "Well, George has never left home. He's just married to the hospital."

"And would you throw him out?" Elsie Mae raised an eyebrow.

"The thought has crossed my mind at times."

"Mine, too, but then I think, give him time to come to his senses or work through the grief or whatever he needs." Kit sighed. "My marriage vows said for better or worse, in sickness and in health. We've had some of each . . ."

"But you had them together — up until now?" Elsie Mae nodded, the small kind of nod that encouraged Kit to dig deeper into her thoughts, memories where she so often feared to venture.

"Pretty much. I mean he was gone when Ryan broke his arm and through some of Amber's treatments, but he can't handle needles and . . ."

"And they call us the weaker sex." Elaine threw herself back in her chair, arms dangling, eyes glaring at the ceiling. A chuckle that leaped the spaces between them made it around the frame.

"So," Elsie Mae continued, "does Mark know about Teza?"

"Yes, we e-mail and he calls sometimes. He talks with Ryan and Jennifer. He sent me flowers with a card."

"And you know there's no one else in his life?" Elaine leaned on one elbow and stroked her chin between thumb and forefinger.

Kit closed her eyes against the ice pick again. "I hope not."

"But it has crossed your mind."

"Hasn't it yours when George is late coming home and leaves again on an emergency and . . ." Kit banked the fire before it flared beyond control. *Why is she pushing me like this?*

"And yes, I've thought of that. But in a town this small, I'd have to be awfully dumb not to find out about it. And if he did have an affair, he'd be in the divorce court faster than he could don surgical scrubs."

"Maybe I needed some breathing room too. How could I help Mark when I was bleeding all over the place?" *The tears that erupted for no reason or at any reason. Sleepless nights. Anger that would flare at some of the stupidest things.* "It's been two years now, and while I've adjusted somewhat, I . . ." Kit grabbed for a tissue and blew her nose.

"You need the other half of yourself holding you up." Elsie Mae stood and came around behind Kit. "Lord in heaven, Kit here is hurting so bad."

"That's part of it!" She hunched her shoulders forward as if to get away from the calming hands. "Why do I want to pray to a God who took my daughter? He could have healed her, but he didn't. I've been asking why for two years now, and it still makes no sense whatsoever."

Beth knelt on the floor and put her arms around Kit's waist. "You've helped us, now let us help you."

"I never thought my life would be like this, ripped up, torn apart. And yet, no matter how far or fast I try to run away, I know God is there. But sometimes I hate him for what he didn't do. What kind of a Christian am I to hate God?"

"Funny who he brought to this group." Elsie Mae looked to each of the women as she thought out loud. "Beth who couldn't forgive herself, and here's you who can't forgive God. And if I'm reading her right, Elaine can't forgive folks around her."

"Why should I forgive her, she's the one who's done all the rotten things?" Elaine glared at Elsie Mae as though she was dropping stitches as she sewed.

"The letters," Beth whispered. "Please write the letters. I know it helps."

"Lord Jesus Christ, have mercy on us all." Teza laid her hands on Beth's shoulder, and Sue, from the other side, laid hers on Elaine so that all of them were connected. "Heavenly Father, you know what we need, and we praise you for answering our heart cries. We thank you that you can heal us, that you never let us go, that you love us beyond time and measure. For your son's sake, have mercy on us all, O gracious Lord. Amen."

Several of them murmured amens and, wiping eyes, they sat back down at the quilt frame.

I give up again, Lord. I can't fight anymore. Tonight I will write those letters so that I can tell Beth I did it. Right now, please get me through this. Kit glanced up to see Elaine watching her. *So you got prayed for too. Won't hurt, you know.* Instead of saying what she thought or running off to hide, which sounded like an extremely good idea, she nodded slightly and returned to the rhythm of rocking the needle in, pulling it and the thread through, rocking again, stitch by tiny stitch. No matter what was going on with the stitchers, the quilt had to be finished.

THIRTY-NINE

Bleary-eyed from the tears of the night before, Kit fumbled with the coffee maker. On a morning like this, instant coffee would be helpful. It just might wake her up enough to make real coffee.

"Are you all right, Mom?" Ryan padded into the kitchen, Missy dancing along with him. Since he'd been home, the basset had taken to sleeping in his room. He scratched his chest and yawned, stretching his arms above his head.

"I will be. Coffee by IV would help."

"You look like heck."

"Thank you so very much. Just what I needed to hear." She braced herself on the counter, wishing the water would hurry and drip through the grounds she'd finally managed to get into the filter.

"You want me to take Aunt Teza to her treatment? I'll be out there anyway."

"Come to think of it, I thought you were going to stay out there last night."

"I was, but since we ended up going to the late movie, I didn't want to wake her coming in." When Kit glanced at him, he held up a hand. "Don't worry, I called her and told her I'd see her this morning."

"Sorry." From day one she'd drummed into her children's heads the importance of calling to let people know of any change of plans. Good to know something took. Now if she'd only accomplished as much with their father. He'd not even responded to her last two e-mails, but then who was counting? Other than she?

The machine beeped, and Kit grabbed the pot to fill two mugs. Drips from the filter sizzled on the hot plate.

"Bit of a rush, eh?" Ryan grinned at her over the lip of his mug, while inhaling the steam. "Sure beats campus coffee. This year I'm buying a coffee maker for my room."

"There's an older one out in the garage you're welcome to take. It's smaller than this one."

"Thanks. Since when did you start drinking so much coffee?"

Since I spent half the nights crying and needed something to get me going in the morning. Otherwise the thought of staying in bed might have became a reality.

"Mom?"

"Hmm?" She turned to him.

"Where did you go?"
"What?"
"Just now. You checked out. Where did you go?"
"Slow reflexes." *Liar. Too bad, I'm not going to tell him things like that. He'll worry and that's not necessary.* "Are you serious about taking Teza to her appointment? Wouldn't she rather you were out in her garden?"
"I can do both. You could go back to bed for a while."
"I look that bad, huh?" The coffee was beginning to revive her. Kit ambled over to the sliding glass door and looked out over the backyard where dew glistened in the pearlized light. The sun had yet to come over the trees and set the diamonds on fire. Missy's tracks through the dew-bent grass broadcast exactly where she'd been, and her yip announced that it was time to feed the dog. Kit heard Ryan pouring dry food into the dog dish. She opened the door, and a meadowlark welcomed the sun from the lower backyard. A dog barked two yards over, and Missy darted outside to listen better. She turned back when Ryan opened the screen door to set her dish on the deck.
"Think after I bring Aunt Teza back

here, I'll go get Thomas. He and Missy can play out at the farm."

"He's a good worker. He can help you too."

"Really?"

"He pitted apricots with me, pulled weeds, planted radish and lettuce seeds. He likes gardening."

"He likes being with you. Shame about his mother." Ryan plunked two pieces of bread in the toaster.

"What about her?"

"She left them a couple of years ago. They don't hear from her very often."

"How did you find that out?"

"I asked."

"I didn't think it was my place to ask."

Ryan retrieved the milk carton from the fridge and poured it on his cereal. "Guy talk, Mom. No matter how good a ballplayer you are, you ain't a guy."

"Gee, thanks for telling me." She lifted the toast out, buttered it, and took half of one slice.

"Hey, that's mine."

"Not anymore." Coffee mug and toast in hand, Kit headed back upstairs. Back to bed. No, she was too wide awake now. How could she best use the gift of a couple of extra hours? She stuck the last bite of toast in her mouth, set her cup down on the table by the rocker and picked up her Bible along with the tablet she'd written the letter on the night before. Once ensconced in the wing-back rocker, she laid the Bible in her lap and began to read the letter.

Dear God,

This seems so foolish, since you already know what all has happened, and yet I promised, so here goes. Remember all those times I begged and pleaded and cried to you to heal Amber? I claimed every promise you wrote in your book, I did everything I could, and yet you let her die. I am so angry at you for that, I can't even think straight half the time. I want to scream at you and hit you and throw things. You let me down when you promised you'd be there for me always. God! How I hate you! I tried to run away, I shut you out, I quit going to church because it just hurts too much. My heart has such a hole in it that I don't think it will ever heal. Why, God, why? You don't need Amber like I do. And no, I don't want her here to suffer but to be all well again. I want to see her graduate from college. I want to hug her and laugh with her. I want to go out to lunch and talk on the phone with her. Father, her laugh is so infectious. I love her so, and she's not here. I can't stand this. And Mark is gone, and you haven't fixed that either. Where are you now when I need you? I want to wake up in the morning to find this has all been a bad dream and I can go on with my life, the life I used to have, BC — before cancer. You know how much I hate that disease? It's not fair. Amber did nothing wrong to have had that. She didn't smoke or drink or do drugs. She was a good kid, becoming a wonderful woman. And you don't need her like I do.

As she had the night before, Kit wiped away her tears. The page wore tear dots, and some words were crossed out because she'd scribbled over them so much.

I want to hate you, but you know I really don't. I feel like a little girl screaming 'I hate you' at her mother, but somehow knowing what she needs the most is to be wrapped safe in her mother's arms. Thank you for not grabbing me up and shaking me like I know you could. David cried and ranted and raved at you too, and you still loved him. But how can I believe you love me when I hurt so bad I can't make sense of things? I told you once that I'd helped my children live, and if necessary I'd help them die, but I didn't mean it. Did you hurt like this when your son died? How could you let him die like that? I couldn't let my daughter die that others might be saved. I couldn't. But you did. And when he hung on the cross, you could have taken him right to heaven. But you didn't. God, how mighty are your ways. I don't understand. But thank you.

Ah, my dear daughter, Kit, I love you, I love you, I love you . . .

Kit remembered exactly how she'd written the words she heard and felt and knew so clearly. Words that lighted the room and her heart and poured out her pen. *I love you* filled the rest of the page.

She leaned back against the cushion of the rocker, letting the tears flow unheeded and hearing the words again. *I love you.* Feeling them as one feels the thunderous music of a mighty organ, absorbing it through the soles of the feet, the palms of the hand, the face, ears, and mostly the heart. The beating heart where we connect with God and the mind where we live with and in him. She laid a hand on her chest, feeling the steady beat of her heart beneath her palm. With every atom of her being, she knew he was there and she in his.

Kit tore the pages from the pad and folded them to tuck them in her Bible for now. One day soon she would write a letter to Amber. When she could see straight again. She wiped her eyes with a tissue and let her Bible fall open on her lap, her gaze stopping at an underlined verse. "Come onto me all you who are heavy laden and I will give you rest." She flipped to another page. "For God so loved the world . . ." As she'd learned in a Bible study years earlier, she put her name in and read it aloud. "For God so loved me, Kit Cooper, that he gave his only begotten son that when I believe in him, I have eternal life."

"So do I have to give you my daughter?" she asked.

You already have.

"And now I need to leave her there. Father, I have such a hard time giving you something and then leaving it there. I take it back and try to do it again. You know, this gets really tiresome."

"Come unto me all you who are heavy laden . . ."

"I hear you. And you will give me rest. I come and you give." She sat awhile longer, feeling the same peace she'd felt the night before. It blanketed the room so she felt it on her skin and inhaled it when she breathed. It caressed her eyelids and made them heavy, her hands so they lay in her lap, palm up, fingers slightly cupped so they too could be filled with peace.

When she awoke, the numbers on the clock read 8:00. "I never sleep in the chair." She flew into the shower, catching herself singing an old spiritual, "my Lord, what a mornin', my Lord what a mornin', my Lord what a mornin', gonna shout and sing all day."

"Ryan leaves today." Teza clasped her hands in her lap. She'd just finished another session of radiation and with each one felt more nauseous and weary.

"I know. I've certainly enjoyed having him home."

"Not that he's been there much. He took over out at my place, for which I am eternally grateful." Teza scratched her head under her hat of many flowers. They'd cut short what hair she had left to make it easier for her to care for it.

And how will we manage to do it all without

him? Kit kept her thoughts to herself, knowing that Teza didn't need any more to worry about. As his mom, she'd wanted to take Ryan back to school herself, but between the farm and the quilt, she decided not to volunteer. He'd found a ride with a lovely young woman. Kit doubted he'd miss his mother.

"Are you sure you want to quilt or would you rather —"

"Quilting helps keep my mind off feeling crummy."

"Okay." When they arrived at the house, Ryan had his bags packed and was waiting on the front porch.

"So soon?" Kit sat down on the glider. "You got that load out of the dryer?"

"Yes, Mother. And I washed my face and brushed my teeth, too. You want to check?"

"Just doing my job." She set the glider in motion with one foot. "Thanks for all your help with the picnic yesterday. It went well, I think."

"Thomas's father appreciated it the most. You'd think we'd given him a new car or something just because Thomas has been welcome at our house. He's such a neat kid. He told me he was going to come by after school this afternoon so you and

Missy wouldn't be lonely."

"Good. Adam is such a nice man. I was thinking he might like to meet . . ."

"Mother, no matchmaking allowed."

"Why not?" Teza chimed in. "Your mother's done a good job matchmaking through the years. Bringing people together is a time-honored vocation. Beats the personal ads in the newspapers and e-mail, that's for sure."

"Sorry. If she's so good at it, how come she never found anyone for you?"

"I told her to keep her mitts off my love life or lack thereof. I had a husband. He was a good man, and I don't want to break in another. Takes too much time and effort to get 'em trained right."

"Aunt Teza!" Ryan's shocked face made both women smile. He looked to the car stopping at the street. "My ride's here. You two behave yourselves now." He leaned over to hug Teza. "See you at Christmas."

Kit stood and watched him whisper something in Teza's ear that made her smile. What a charmer he could be. When he hugged her, she fought the lump in her throat.

"Dad will be coming home."

"How do you know?"

"I asked him, just no idea when."

"Thanks. I love you." She blinked back the tears. Good-byes had become increasingly harder since Amber died. Life changed in an instant, and she knew she had no control over it. "God bless and keep you."

"Why would he stop now?"

"I know." *Oh, how well I know. But trusting him with the ones I love is still hard, not that I have too many options. I mean, like can I take care of you? Ha.* She kissed his cheek and watched him grab his bags and head down the walk. *Please, God, send lots of guardian angels to watch over him.* Another car pulled up right behind the red convertible driven by a girl with long blond hair. The quilters were arriving.

September passed one stitch at a time, and each day the quilt came closer to completion. Teza finished her radiation treatments, had another chemo session, and prepared for her surgery on October second. In their spare time, she and Kit put the farm to bed for the winter, picking the last of the apples and packing them in boxes to be sold along with the pumpkins and squash. Come October, school children would arrive in busloads to choose and buy their pumpkins, but this year Vinnie, not Teza, would dress as the scarecrow.

Thomas and Kelly went to the same school and cemented their friendship that started on the Fourth of July. Kit sewed his Halloween costume early, a huge M&M from blue felt, his choice. His sister promised to paint his face to match.

Beth got into the hat-making business and began to take orders from other places as people heard about her cancer hats. She could hardly keep them in stock at the hospital gift shop.

Elaine had all her minions busy on the Spring Gala, which included the quilt auction. She'd even scheduled a regional television personality to be the mistress of ceremonies and to entertain that night. April promised to be both exciting and beyond busy in Jefferson City.

Mark and Kit e-mailed regularly and talked on the phone at least once a week. But Kit never pressed him for a return date, and he never volunteered.

"Today, September thirtieth, we put the binding on." Kit stared at the quilt nearly completed. "All those stitches, hard to imagine we got it done on time."

"Just look at our fingers and all the calluses, and you'll know we did it." Sue raised her hands so the others did the same.

"We're going to quilt along the binding, too, after we sew it on, aren't we?" Elaine studied the royal blue bias strips. "I hate mitering corners on both sides of the quilt. One side is bad enough. I don't even do that on my pillows."

"We don't have to miter both sides. The top can be flat." Elsie Mae measured one side of the quilt and then the other. "Came out real square, didn't it?"

"However, mitering the corners is the kind of finish a fifty thousand dollar quilt deserves." Elaine folded the bias strip in place to see how it looked.

"Fifty thousand dollars! Wherever did you get such an idea?"

"You have to set goals, and since this is for such a worthy cause, we need to set our goal high enough to be worthwhile."

"And here I thought fifteen thousand was stretching it." Like the others, Kit looked at Elaine as if she'd just sprouted daisies through her perfectly coifed hair.

"Whatever. Let's get on with binding it." Teza sat down in the corner chair. "Kit, you start pinning it right about here, and we'll run it around to make sure none of the binding seams hit on a corner." They did as she said, shifted to move one seam, and laid the right side of the binding to the top of the quilt, cut edges even. "Usually I sew this with the machine, but since Kit already basted and trimmed the edges, we'll just stitch it in place by hand." Once the binding was pinned, they each took up their place and stitched a half-inch seam.

"Where's this masterpiece goin' to hang?"

"First, you mean?" Elaine looked up from checking to make sure she was stitching clear through all four layers. "In the entry to the hospital, then in the lobby of the First Independent Bank, then the Rainier Building. As you come in the door, it'll be the first thing you'll see . . ." She closed her eyes to remember better. "Then Pacific Bank, that's . . ." She counted on her fingers. "Four. The Steak House in February is five, then back to First Independent in March. I'm just hoping they all like it so much they bid each other up. Oh, I forgot. It will be out at the Golf Club in April until the Gala."

"Did you have to twist their arms or something?"

"No, as a matter of fact, I had to turn

two places down. Their security wasn't good enough."

"Security for a quilt?" Teza stopped stitching and smoothed her hand over the surface. "Quilts are supposed to comfort, to keep people warm on a winter night. Hanging on a big wall with lights shining on it just doesn't seem proper."

"You can bet that whoever buys it will use it for advertising purposes. That's how it should be, if we can get the money we need from it." Since she was sitting next to Teza, Elaine clipped off her thread too, since both sections were now finished.

Elsie Mae looked over at Teza, who was sitting with her eyes closed. "How about if I give you a Healing Touch treatment while we wait for the binding to be finished?"

"Oh, that sounds heavenly. You make me feel guilty with the good care you give me."

"Well, I thought this might help prepare you for your surgery. The more relaxed you are, the easier it will be on everyone."

"Once in a while I feel myself getting a bit anxious, so I just picture myself in God's mighty arms where nothing can touch me, and it goes right away."

"That's what makes you such a good client." Elsie Mae pushed her chair back and stretched as she stood. The two walked back to Mark's office where Elsie Mae kept her massage table set up.

"I'm wishing for one of those treatments myself. Any reason why one would have to have cancer to be helped by it?" Sue pushed her needle through all the layers.

"None that I can see." Beth took up where Elaine left off. "By the way, I have something for each of you. In that box by the door." She nodded to a cardboard moving box across the room. "They're all different. You'll have to pick and choose."

"What?" Kit and Elaine looked at each other with matching raised eyebrows.

"I love surprises." Elaine stood and brought the box over to set on the coffee table. "Oh, look at these." She drew out a stuffed pumpkin with alternating sections of white dotted orange and orange with white stripes. The stems and leaves were made of green felt with yarn or embroidery thread tied in the indentations. "They are adorable." She took them all out and arranged them on the table so everyone could see.

"Beth, what a neat thing to do." Kit sorted through and chose one with harvest leaves and plain rust panels.

"I made them in different sizes and had

so much fun. Harriet Spooner came over and helped me stuff them. She is such a dear."

Kit studied the pumpkins. "Did you make any of these for sale?"

"I have some I could sell."

"Good. I want to buy three to mail to Jennifer to help decorate her apartment, one of each size." Kit rubbed her chin. "And if you want to put them on consignment, I'm sure Teza would love them at the farm shop."

"Between hats and pumpkins I could sew around the clock, every day of the week."

"And what does Garth say about all this sewing?" Elaine looked up from trying to make a choice.

"He can't get over it. Like me, he's totally amazed."

"By the way, what happened with his court appearance?"

"Everyone's amazed that this judge threw the case out. Said the fine was sufficient, ordered Garth to pay for the window repair, and reminded everyone this is a free country with freedom of speech, and protests come under that provision. He warned about watching out for troublemakers, though."

"Well, I'll be." Elaine shook her head. "Old Farnsworth came through."

"You know him?"

"Of course. He and I served on the planning board together. He upholds the rights of citizens, be they on either side of the law."

"Even the unborn?"

"Looks that way, doesn't it?"

"That's it, the last stitch." Kit clipped her thread and put her scissors back in the case.

"We did it." Beth spoke in a tone of awe.

Kit and Sue took two corners and held it up for everyone to see. "We made it by October first. Can you believe it?"

"And no all-nighters. What a shame."

"So we all need to be at the hospital on Monday morning to have our picture taken with the quilt as it is hung on the wall." Elaine stuck her needle back in her case and zipped it closed.

"Sorry, I'll be in surgery by then." Teza leaned back in the recliner. "Sure is a pretty piece."

"What about Sunday?"

"You can get a photographer there on a Sunday?"

"You bet I can. I'll call all of you with

the time, most likely around two or so."

Sue and Kit matched the corners and folded the quilt, starburst to the inside. "I have a zipped plastic bag that I'll put it in."

"Hey, now you can have your living room back." Beth took hold of one of the clamps. "Shall we take this down?" At Kit's nod, she and Elsie Mae did just that, strapping the frame pieces in a bundle with bungee cords.

"See you all on Sunday, then." Elaine gathered her things together. "And thanks for inviting me to be part of this." She went around the room and hugged each of them on her way out the door.

"You better go over that quilt and make sure there are no pins left in it. Looked to me like all the threads were cut close, but it needs checking."

"Yes, ma'am," Kit needled her aunt.

"I'll be praying for you," Elsie Mae said, hugging Teza gently. "We're goin' to beat this thing. Cancer, get yourself on out of here."

After the photo sessions and interviews for print, radio, and the local television station at the hospital on Sunday afternoon, Kit took Teza back to the farm at her insistence.

"I want to sleep in my house tonight, in my own bed, and I'll be ready on time. I won't eat after six, and I won't drink anything after midnight. I'm planning on a light dinner, and no, I don't want to come to your house to eat."

"Okay." Kit leaned her arms on the steering wheel. "I'll see you at six tomorrow morning."

"And you are not to spend the night worrying. This old breast isn't good for anything more anyway."

"I'm worry free."

"Did you hear from Mark?" Teza asked when she climbed into the van the next morning.

"No, did you?"

"I thought I would. We can leave my suitcase in the car, since I won't need anything out of it the first day anyway."

"Fine. I'll bring it in whenever you want." *Father God, I don't want to do this.*

Once at the hospital, a nurse whisked Teza away with the promise that Kit could see her again before surgery. "You can wait for her in room 215."

Kit made her way up the stairs and down the hall, wishing now she'd accepted Sue's offer to stay with her. *God, please, I'm counting on you to pull Teza through this.* She checked the numbers and entered a room with two empty beds right across from the nurses' station.

After a bit the same young woman wheeled Teza into the room, gowned and finished with the pre-op. "You might want to get up into bed because they'll be along with your shot fairly soon. Then you'll be really relaxed."

"I'm about as relaxed as I can get right now." But Teza did as told and listened while given instructions on how to work the bed. So with the bed raised and a pillow plumped behind her head, she pointed to her bag. "Will you please get my Bible out? I marked some places for you to read while you're waiting for me. And I brought a couple of quilt blocks for you to work on."

"Like I didn't bring my own things?"

"Just in case." Teza held her Bible between both hands. "I don't know what I would do without his Word to comfort me. You have no idea how glad my old heart is that you have come back to him."

"Me, too." Kit sat on the edge of the bed. "Forgiveness is a big thing."

"Yes, it is." A male voice drew their attention to the doorway.

"Mark!" Kit slid off the bed and flew into his welcoming arms.

"Well, it's about time." Teza held out her arms. "My land, how I've missed you."

Keeping Kit tucked against his side, Mark bent over and hugged Teza. "I'm so glad I made it in time. I thought to be home last night but got fogged in." He kissed her cheek.

Kit hesitated. "Are you here for a while?"

Mark's repentant gaze went directly to Kit's heart. "If you'll let me."

Thank you, Lord, thank you, thank you. Kit closed her eyes to hold the tears back. He came home, Mark came home. "No wonder Sue wasn't supposed to be here. God knew you would be."

"I'm here to give you your shot," the nurse interrupted. "Roll over, dearie." Within minutes, they had Teza transferred to a gurney and ready to trundle down the hall.

"I love you." Kit kissed her cheek.

"I know and I you." Teza laid a hand on Kit's cheek. "You're the daughter I never had, so that makes you the daughter of my heart. See you soon." She pointed to the Bible on the bed. "Read what I marked. God says it better than I can. Okay, boys, let's get this show on the road." She waved as she was wheeled from the room.

Mark clutched Kit's hand in his and looked her full in the face. "Can you forgive me?"

"Yes."

"Will you?"

"I already have, thanks to some heavy duty interference from our Father."

"I don't know how you'll ever trust me again."

"Teza always says 'trust is forgiveness in walking shoes. The two always go together.' "

"Yes. Makes good sense."

"Makes a good picture. Ah, my dear, I have so much to tell you."

"How about over breakfast? I'm starved."

"Leave it to a man to think of the important things." Kit picked up Teza's Bible and put it into her bag. "Wait until we tell the kids that you are home. They'll be dancing in the streets."

"In walking shoes." They strolled down the hall hand in hand, chuckles drifting over their shoulders like children playing in the comfort of Grandma's old quilt.

EPILOGUE

"I can't believe it is really here." Beth tucked her hand under Teza's elbow.

"Only God's grace brought this whole shebang together." Teza patted Beth's hand. "Brought the whole town together."

"I know." Beth pointed to a couple walking in the door. "Mark made it home again just in time."

"In more ways than one." The two shared a conspiratorial grin.

"All right you two, what's going on here?" Kit let go of her husband's arm long enough to give them each a hug.

"You three ladies look like the belles of the ball, far as I can see." Mark glanced around the decorated hall, the revolving mirrored ball above them flashing shards of light in all directions. Restaurants from the surrounding area had food pavilions at one end of the hall, their decorations exceeded only by the quality of their food. Tables with pink cloths invited guests to bring their samples and sit to enjoy them. Musicians played from the raised platform, everyone donating their services for the evening. At the other end of the long building, chairs were set up theater style for the auction, with the quilt serving as the backdrop for the program.

"Come on, let's go look at all the items for auction." Garth joined the group, carrying a plate of handmade truffles from the The Chocolatier. "Here, I brought enough for everyone."

"Why, Garth, we thought you were going to eat them all." Teza shook her head, the jewel-studded turban she wore throwing back the glitter from the ball overhead.

"I would if they were chocolate-covered cherries like the ones you made." He held the plate out for the rest to help themselves.

"You just want to ogle that Chevy, I know." Beth put her other hand through the bend of his elbow.

"My dad had one like that. The stories he could tell, why . . . if I won the bid on that baby, he would turn green and purple with envy."

"I'd rather have the Caribbean cruise." Kit closed her eyes in bliss at the smooth chocolate. "But chocolate like this takes a close second."

"Leave it to a woman." Mark locked his free arm with Teza's.

"Yes, a woman in menopause like your wife is entitled to all the chocolate she needs." Teza tugged on her two escorts. "Let's make sure we get in the front row. All the women who worked on that quilt are to be honored, and I don't want to have to walk too far in these shoes."

The group made their way forward, greeting others and teasing Garth as he used his suitcoat sleeve to rub a spot off the front fender of the 1957 Chevy Impala.

Volunteers in black tuxes handed out programs and ushered guests to seats.

The band ended their set with a flourish and announced that the auction would be starting in fifteen minutes. Folks were invited to finish up their voting for the food entries.

"There you all are." Elaine stopped at their row. "Isn't this the best crowd? Who'd have dreamed we'd have this kind of attendance?" She glanced at Teza. "I know, you and so many others have been praying, and we should give God the glory." She winked at Kit. "See, I've been listening."

"Never doubted it for a minute." Kit pointed at a seat on the other side of Mark. "We saved you a place."

"Maybe later. I want to make sure everything goes smoothly backstage." Elaine nodded toward the eight-foot thermometer off to the side. "Can you believe how much has already been earned for our mammogram unit?" Red paint filled in the bulb and registered at thirty-five degrees. Ninety-eight point six meant the $90,000 needed for the unit was theirs.

"The grant you earned helped with that."

"I know, but I'm amazed it came through so quickly. Usually those things can take a year or more."

Someone called her name, and Elaine fluttered a hand at them as she hurried off.

"Things sure changed a lot while I was gone." Mark laid an arm across the back of Kit's chair and leaned closer so she could hear above the buzz of conversation and bursts of laughter.

Kit nodded. And even though he'd been home for almost six months, minus three short business trips, he still didn't realize how much he'd missed.

His homecoming had been her most important Christmas present, and while they were still working out some problems, the Bible study they were involved in at Garth's church was helping.

"Ladies and gentlemen . . ."

The drums rolled, and a spotlight hit the man at the microphone.

"Welcome to the Spring Gala, Jefferson City's own community bash. Tonight you have the opportunity to bid on dream vacations, services, entertainment, a hot rod to call up the days of your youth, and our *pièce de résistance* . . ." The spotlight moved to the quilt that glowed like jewels in the brightness.

"The Healing Quilt! Sewn and quilted by citizens of Jefferson City who cared enough to dream enough to bring a state-of-the-art mammogram unit to our hospital. Right now I'd like all the women who worked on this quilt to come forward so we can give them the hand they so richly deserve. Come on, ladies, right over there, stand in the spotlight."

A spotlight made a circle on the floor, which was quickly filled with the women who'd helped. As he called their names, each of them raised her hand, and the applause kept on rolling.

Kit felt an arm come around her waist and smiled at Beth, who stood between her and Teza.

"We did it," she mouthed, and Kit nodded. In spite of all the illnesses and treatments and family emergencies, they'd finished the day before the October first deadline. Just as Elaine had promised, the quilt had hung first at the hospital right as folks came in the front doors, then several banks, a restaurant, the country club, and the medical center. It had been featured on television, radio, in newspapers, and even several magazines. The quilt had done its job long before it came here for the auction.

They filed back to their seats, half-blinded by the spotlight but laughing all the way.

"Now I know what a star feels like. I can't see a thing." Teza took her seat.

Kit watched her carefully to make sure she didn't get too tired. When she'd mentioned taking it easy, however, Teza shook her head.

"I can always sleep tomorrow. Tonight is a victory, and I wouldn't miss it for all the tea in China."

"Oh, oh, the wonder boy." Mark crossed his arms over his chest as Winston Henry Jefferson IV strode across the stage. "How come he can still look young enough to be carded at restaurants, while the rest of us . . ." He smoothed a hand over his ever-extending forehead.

"Genetics." Kit knew that her husband and Winston had competed for the captainship of various teams through much of their growing-up years. Rumor had it that Winston's father had bought good will for his son by treating the teams to pizza and ice cream or even a night or two at the movies. She'd been a couple of years behind them in school, but that didn't matter much in a town their size. She returned her attention to the stage where Winston had been talking about the inception of this event.

". . . We see the purchase of this state-of-the-art diagnostic tool as the first step in our plans and dreams to build the Angela Jefferson Women's Oncology Center right here in Jefferson City. And we hope you good folks open your pocketbooks tonight to create a brighter future for our community. Thank you, and have a marvelous time."

Teza leaned forward around Mark to give Kit a rolled-eye look, along with a slight shake of her head.

"Winnie is at it again."

Kit hid a chuckle behind her hand. Teza often told tales of boyhood pranks of the group Mark and Winnie hung out with, stories that made Mark invoke the old "Do as I say, not as I did" proverb with his children.

Kit applauded along with everyone else as Winston left the stage, mostly because she was glad he hadn't been more long-winded.

The auctioneer stepped up to the podium. "And now, what we've all been waiting for . . . who is going to take home this stunning quilt? Am I bid a thousand?" He went into his auctioneer patter and the price kept climbing. Two thousand, twenty-five, twenty-five hundred, three thousand.

"Come on now, folks, we've just begun here."

"Five thousand." A voice from the back brought a smile to the auctioneer's face. "Now that's what I like to hear. Give me ten."

Kit locked her folded hands under her chin. "Keep it going, dear God, keep it going."

The bids climbed to twenty thousand, and another of the bidders dropped out.

"This is going for a good cause now. Do I hear twenty-five?"

Kit twisted to see who it was still bidding from the back.

"You better sit still or we may end up buying a quilt." Mark spoke without moving his head.

"No, we don't have a card."

"Neither does that man up there, but they are catching his bids."

"Oh, who is he?"

"Got me, but he's sure helping the bid along."

"That's right, twenty-five, twenty-five, come on give me twenty-six."

"Thirty-five thousand dollars."

Who bid that? Kit kept herself still by steel will.

"Do I hear thirty-six? That's thirty-five to the man with the silver hair in the back. Anyone? Thirty-six."

"Too rich for my blood."

"Going, going, anyone else? Gone! For thirty-five thousand dollars. What is your name, sir?"

The applause started as the gavel fell, and as one, the women stood and turned to honor the man who bought the quilt.

If only I could whistle like Amber used to. Kit clapped until her hands were hot.

"Thirty-five thousand dollars." Teza leaned back against her chair as they sat down again. "Who'd a dreamed it."

"Winston bid for quite a while." Beth leaned toward Kit. "I think he liked it hanging in the lobby at the hospital like it did."

"I know. Would have been nice to keep it in the community."

They settled back to enjoy the remainder of the auction, groaning along with Garth when the car bid started higher than he'd dreamed of paying for it.

"So much for making my dad jealous. But then jealousy isn't good for him anyway."

"Don't tell me you were coveting that there automobile?" The man in front of them spoke over his shoulder.

Garth tapped one of his elders on the back. "Not at all, Wayne. Just dreaming."

The auctioneer moved the bidding right along, and the woman painting in the red thermometer kept busy. The closer the red line drew to ninety-eight degrees, the faster the bids flew.

When the gavel fell for the final time, Kit leaned back against Mark's arm and fanned herself with the program.

"I feel like I've been running a race or something."

"Me, too." Beth propped her elbows on her knees. "But you realize, hardly anyone has left."

"Pretty amazing." Mark stood and stretched. "I'll be right back."

Kit watched him as he left, thinking he was going to the men's room, but when he went up to the cashier, she gave Teza a questioning look.

"Did you see him bid on anything?"

Teza shook her head. "Although I sure thought about bidding on the house painters, but I'd have them paint the barn instead."

"Housecleaning for six months would have been my choice." Kit trapped a yawn with her hand. "Or that Caribbean cruise, like we mentioned. I didn't see who got that. Did any of you?"

"I was afraid to move in case I bought something I couldn't afford." Garth glanced over to where the new owner was talking with the dealer who'd donated the Chevy.

"Cars that are paid for are a real mercy." Beth tapped his arm.

"I know, but dreams don't cost a dime."

"True." She smiled at Kit as she caught the yawn. "How come we're yawning and Teza isn't?"

"Too tired to yawn."

"Then we better get you home." Kit picked up her purse and stood, glancing around for Mark.

"Sorry it took so long." Mark held up a Caribbean travel brochure. "Do you think we can fit this in our schedule?"

"Elaine, dear, I was really proud of you tonight." George kissed her cheek, then put his arms around her as they stood looking out the window toward the mountain. Lights twinkled in the blackness of both the sky and the land. "That has to be the coup of your career."

"Thank you." Elaine leaned her forehead against his shoulder. "You're not on call tonight, are you?"

"No. And I won't be much anymore, only extreme emergencies. I've decided to let the younger men do that. There's got to be some kind of privilege with age, don't you think?"

"I think age has only made you sexier." She popped out the first of the studs in his shirt and reached up to kiss his chin.

The next morning she stood at the window watching the sun come up behind Mount Rainier. With Doodlebug on one arm and a cup of coffee in the other hand, she thought back to what she called *the quilt months.* "You know what, Bug? After everything I've done and seen and heard these last months" — she sucked on her bottom lip — "I'm beginning to think there is more to life after all."

The brilliant orange disk broke free from the mountain. "And I don't want to miss out."

Dear Readers,
Back in 1986 when our daughter Marie died of cancer at age twenty-one, I had no idea what terrible, heart breaking grief is like. Yes, my father had died as well as other relatives, but they were older and, in the natural scheme of things, they would die before I did. But not my daughter. God had healed her once, and I felt sure he would do so again. He did, but not in the way I wanted. When someone asked me if I would write our story, I said only when God is adamant that the time is right. I asked him years ago whether, since I am hard of hearing to that still small voice, would he please say things three times so that I get the message. When the time came for this story to be told, he bombarded me with signals. Three, and then three, and then three again.

However, the story you just read, *The Healing Quilt*, is not the story I started out to write. It grew. My story is only a small piece of the stories of these four women who strive, like you and I do, to understand and live out forgiveness. Kit, who struggles with anger and grief over the death of her daughter, is not me but parts of me. Beth cannot forgive herself — haven't we all been there? Teza trusts God but still fears — ah, who can say that is not herself? And Elaine seeks to get even and sees no need to forgive, and yet is confronted by love anyway. Ring a bell?

These many years after 1986 I still cry at times. I miss Marie, but I remember more of the good times than the bad, and I'm thankful the pain of the memories is gone — most of the time. I know with everything that I am, that God loves me, forgives me, and extends the grace I do not understand but rejoice in daily to heal me and, through the sharing of my stories, helps bring healing and hope to others.

I hope and pray that you enjoyed this story, laughed some, cried some, and allowed God's love and mercy to flood your very being. I need to go blow my nose and wipe my eyes now.

Love

Lauraine

Resource List

The Compassionate Friends, Inc.
P.O. Box 3696
Oak Brook, IL 60522-3696
(877) 969-0010 (toll free)
http://www.compassionatefriends.org

The mission of Compassionate Friends is "to assist families in the positive resolution of grief following the death of a child." They provide suggested reading, online resources, and newsletters.

American Cancer Society
National Home Office
1599 Clifton Road NE
Atlanta, GA 30329
(800) 227-2345
http://www.cancer.org

The Society provides information on cancer, community programs, and research.

Y-Me National Breast Cancer Organization
212 West Van Buren Street, Suite 500

Chicago, IL 60607-3908
(800) 221-2141 (English)
(800) 986-9505 (Spanish)
http://www.y-me.org

Y-Me provides breast cancer information and support. Their hotline is staffed by trained peer counselors who are breast cancer survivors.

Bosom Buddies of Hawaii
The Queen's Medical Center
Pain Management Services
1301 Punchbowl Street
Honolulu, HI 96813
(808) 585-LIFE
http://www.bosombuddies.org

Bosom Buddies is in partnership with Healing Touch, toll free (877) 823-4088. Bosom Buddies provides therapy to ease the discomfort of breast cancer treatments.

In addition to the Web sites listed above, extensive resources can be found online, including the following:
http://www.breastcancersite.com.